---- ★ ----

"A bloke was murdered on the beach down there a week ago. Skewered through like a bloody kebab atop a sea turtle. I call the turtle a spirit because it's sacred to some of the clans, symbolizes one of their ancestral beings from the Dreamtime." His face was comical, but the intelligence behind his piercing gray eyes was indisputable.

She shivered. He made the macabre sound matter-of-fact. As if dead bodies were all in a day's work.

"You're serious? You found a man impaled on a turtle?"

"Sad to say but I did, luv. So many flies I thought at first he was a black man."

"You could see this from the air?"

"Of course not. I was on the ground right next to him. The spear that killed him punctured the turtle's shell, too, though it's not a cert that's what killed it."

What had the old ghoul done? Shooed the flies away and conducted a private postmortem? She didn't care to hear any more of the grisly details. "Have the police caught the killer?"

---- ★ ----

BONES
OF CONTENTION

JEANNE MATTHEWS

W🌐RLDWIDE®

TORONTO • NEW YORK • LONDON
AMSTERDAM • PARIS • SYDNEY • HAMBURG
STOCKHOLM • ATHENS • TOKYO • MILAN
MADRID • WARSAW • BUDAPEST • AUCKLAND

Recycling programs
for this product may
not exist in your area.

BONES OF CONTENTION

A Worldwide Mystery/March 2014

First published by Poisoned Pen Press

ISBN-13: 978-0-373-26889-4

Printed in U.S.A.

A very special, heartfelt thanks to Carl Lennertz,
who made this book possible.

And for all their help and encouragement, I thank
Jeanne Kleyn, Sal Gordon, Joe Winston,
Davis Lamson, Cynthia Hibbard,
Pat Snider, Dianne Eret,
and, of course, Sid.

To kill a man, point the bone of a dead shaman at him. An invisible force will shoot off the end of the bone, enter the victim's body, and draw his soul into the bone. Daub moist clay over the end of the bone, cover it with emu feathers, and bury it in the ground. After three full moons, dig it up and burn it.

As it burns, so burns the victim's trapped soul.

When it is consumed, the victim dies.

—Aboriginal Myth

PART I

ONE

DINAH PELERIN GAZED out the window of a tiny two-seater airplane as it lifted off from the airport in Darwin, Australia, and leapt into the hot blue sky.

"She's experimental," her pilot shouted above the drone. He was a craggy man with shoulder-length white hair, leathery skin, and a nose that swooped down his long face like an Olympic ski jump. His name was Jacko Newby, a rank stranger, and why she'd hitched a ride in his flimsy tin cricket could only be chalked up to jet-lag and poor judgment.

And momentum. She'd been gathering momentum since Seattle. The redeye to L.A., the long haul from L.A. to Auckland and Auckland to Sydney and Sydney to Darwin. She should have waited for the next regularly scheduled flight to the far-flung town of Katherine, but waiting wasn't her strong suit. So long as she kept moving, catching flights and mingling with strangers, she wouldn't cry.

"Can I buy you a beer?" Jacko pulled a cooler from under his seat and dug out a Foster's.

"Isn't there a law against alcohol in the cockpit?"

"Beer's nutrition, luv. Anyway, it's for you. I stay off the amber when I'm up in Sweet Petunia." He held out the can to her, but she declined.

The ticket agent had acted as if he knew the guy and the security guards called him by name and waved him through without a second look. Surely one of them would have warned her if he was a drunk or a loony. But in hindsight she shouldn't have made so much noise about need-ing to get to Katherine yesterday. She shouldn't have said it was a matter of life and death.

"How long have you been flying, Mr. Newby?"

"Call me Jacko. No worries, luv. What did you say your name was?"

"Dinah."

"Well, Dinah, I've been bending the throttle since be-fore you were born. This bird's not in full production yet, but I'm what you might say on terms with a bloke in the company, which is how I got one of the prototypes. She's state of the art, Petunia is. Flies herself."

In Dinah's world, there was no such thing as no wor-ries. Worries cropped up out of thin air, full-blown like toadstools after a rain, and her pilot's hands-off approach to aviation was one more hair-raiser she didn't need. Yes-terday her Uncle Cleon telephoned her at work to say he had decided to forgo chemo and end his life by assisted suicide. The news floored her. She didn't even know he was sick and all of a sudden he was dying. In less than a week. In the Northern Territory of Australia of all places. The man had been like a father to her, or tried to be. At any rate, he was family. She didn't think twice.

She went straight to her boss and asked for a leave. The little swine pitched a tantrum. He spewed a few obsceni-ties and, to emphasize his veto, heaved a statute book at her. It was the last straw. She quit, caught a taxi home, and walked in on her boyfriend in flagrante with a redhead. No worries? Did they make happy pills in that strength?

Jacko adjusted his headset, ran his eyes over what looked to be a bona fide flight plan, and rattled a string of headings into the mike. At least he showed some degree of competence. In a few minutes, Petunia leveled off. Her engine purred. Jacko's hands remained on the controls.

Dinah lowered the threat level to yellow, leaned her head back, and brooded on her other worries.

Perpetual motion and a kind of dazed numbness had kept her from thinking beyond the immediate, but this was the last leg of her journey. When she reached Katherine, she'd have to stop. And think. And speak. Speaking would be mandatory. Even in extremis, Uncle Cleon would ask if the cat had got her tongue.

On the phone he'd sounded resigned, upbeat even. He was determined to go out on his own timetable, "reared up on my hind legs and calling the shots like always." Bravado was all well and good, but she had nothing spunky or uplifting to say and the thought of making pre-suicide small talk creeped her out.

Busted love, no job, and death on the docket. She felt punch-drunk, too tired and traumatized to contemplate the fallout from any of it. Her eyelids weighed a ton. She stole a peek at Jacko. He wasn't flying upside down or doing loop-the-loops and, just for a minute, she closed her eyes.

SOMETHING BUMPED HER shoulder and she jerked to attention.

"Take a squiz out your window, luv."

She looked down and saw water. Water was wrong. The map in the guidebook she'd bought in the Sydney airport showed no major bodies of water between Darwin and Katherine. Shit. How long had she been out? Where was she?

"That's Van Diemen Gulf, an inlet of the Arafura Sea." Her pilot smiled.

Her groggy brain rebooted. Was he drunk? She saw no empty beer cans. Was he a lunatic? A pervert who preyed on jet-lagged women in airports and spirited them off to his lair to do God knows what to them?

Jerusalem in flames. How could she have been so gullible? She cast about for a weapon. She could cold-cock him with a can of beer, but then what? She eyed the controls. What were the odds of surviving a water landing? When she tore out in a fever all those long hours ago, she so hadn't planned on being plunged to her death in the what-ever sea and eaten by sharks. She envisioned her obituary:

Dinah Pelerin, 30, was eaten by sharks on the way to her uncle's euthanasia. Renowned for her habit of attracting weirdos, she accepted a ride from a stranger once too often. She is survived by a plan-etful of very much smarter people.

She said, "We seem to have strayed off course."

"A spot of sight-seeing."

"I'm not much of a scenery person. Really. Nature's wasted on me. Better take me back to Darwin."

"Keep your hair on, luv. You'll be in Katherine in jig time."

"Take me back to Darwin right now, you, or I'll…" she glanced down at the menacing waters, "I'll make trouble."

He lowered his woolly-bear eyebrows and mugged surprise. "Stone the crows! You're not afraid of old Jacko, are you, Dinah?"

"I'm afraid of anybody who refers to himself in the third person. Where the hell are you taking me?"

"I want to show you something before we loop back to Katherine."

"Like Jacko the Ripper wanted to show his victims his knife collection."

He laughed so hard he had to mop his eyes. "Strewth! You're too young to be so cynical."

"Obviously, I'm not cynical enough or I wouldn't find myself ten thousand feet over the ocean with a, a kidnapper."

"You've not been kidnapped, luv. Why, I'm harmless as a rubber ducky and that's the dinki-di. I'll take you to Katherine as promised so you can relax."

If he imagined she could relax, he was dinki-delusional. But until she was strapped into a parachute over dry land, the better part of valor was probably to humor him. "Do all Australians speak with as much flair as you?"

"It's not flair, luv. It's Strine, though I am laying it on a bit thick. Providing a dash of local color to go with the tour."

"Uh-huh."

"Who's going to cark it in Katherine?"

"What?"

"Hand in his dinner pail, cash in his chips, join the great majority. You told the bloke at the Airnorth counter it was life or death."

She slung him a look. Euthanasia was illegal in Australia. A slip of the lip could get the family deported. "Like you, I was laying it on thick. I just want to get there as soon as possible."

"The toey sort, eh?" She shook her head and he translated. "Restless. Keen to be on the go." His gray eyes assessed her with frank curiosity.

She said nothing and he turned away and attended to flying for a few minutes. Maybe this was some kind of publicity stunt or a Chamber of Commerce event to promote Australian tourism, like she was the millionth person through the Darwin Airport or something. She looked around for a concealed camera.

"So, then." Jacko fixed his inquisitive eyes on her again. "What occasion does bring you to Katherine, Dinah?"

"A family reunion." That much was true. Uncle Cleon had summoned his nearest and dearest to his vacation home in Sydney over a week ago. She'd been the last to get the call and, by then, the assemblage had moved on to Katherine for the main event.

"You can't go wrong in Katherine," enthused Jacko. "Snodger place. Where the outback meets the tropics, as the travel adverts say. June's a good time to tackle the gorges in the Nitmiluk. Water's calm. You're into the Dry."

"Do you live in Katherine?"

"Mailing address is Darwin, but Petunia and I call the whole Top End home. Wouldn't live anyplace else. What part of the States do you call home?"

"Seattle until yesterday, but I won't be going back."

"Born there, were you?"

"I was born in the opposite corner of the country from Seattle. In Georgia."

"Georgia in Dixieland? Bonzer!" He belted out a few bars of *Georgia on My Mind.* "Let me guess. Black hair, dark eyes, wound maybe a half-twist too tight. Some flavor of Latin. I'll guess Cuban. Am I close?"

"I'm part Seminole Indian."

"Strike me pink! One of the first people, eh? A proper American Aborigine. Well, you're grouse gear, luv. That's Strine for easy on the eyes."

That didn't sound like a Chamber of Commerce script. Was the old goat coming on to her? She looked down at the water and pictured an armada of killer sharks prowling beneath the surface. Where the hell was he taking her?

She consulted her watch. Terror agreed with her. She hadn't thought of Nick in almost five minutes. Soon the intervals would lengthen to hours and days and weeks and years. Eventually, if she thought of Seattle at all, her associations would be pleasant ones—the summer wildflowers on Mt. Rainier or the shoe department at Nordstrom.

"Where does your uncle call home?"

"Home is South Georgia, but when he was in the Marine

Corps back in the Sixties, he spent his R and R leave in Australia and fell in love with the place. He likes to vacation in Australia and he has some Australian clients, so a few years back he decided to buy a house in Sydney. He's been living there for the last six months."

"How many of your rellies plan to blow in for the party?"

If it weren't for the sharks, she'd tell him to mind his own beeswax. But until he set this bird down on terra firma, all she could do was keep him talking. "His children, his wives, and me."

"Wives? Polygamy, is it now?" He pulled a shocked face, which made him look even more farcical.

She had to smile. "Don't be too scandalized. One of them's an ex-wife, his first. The other is wife number three."

"Number two couldn't make it?"

"My mother had other plans."

"Your mother? Turn it up! I thought the gentleman was your uncle."

"It's more a term of affection for somebody there isn't a right word for. He's my mother's ex-husband. It's a complicated family."

"Where did your real father enter the picture, if you don't mind me asking?"

She minded, but there wasn't much she could do about it. "My mother divorced Uncle…the man I call Uncle Cleon to marry my father. But Cleon and my mom remained good friends and he's been an important part of my life for as long as I can remember."

"Well, whatever you call him, he's a brave bugger to stay on terms with one ex-wife, much less two."

"He's a very charming man. Sometimes the exes get snippy with each other. But numbers one and three spent a week together at his house in Sydney before they got to Katherine. I'm hoping they've made their peace by now."

"Well, it sounds like a rouser of a party. You must be fond of the old boy to come so far to see him."

Her throat constricted. There wasn't a right word for how she felt about Cleon Dobbs any more than there was a right word for what to call him. He was a fixture in her life, a primordial force not subject to categorization, and she would miss him terribly.

Assuming she didn't precede him in death. "Are you a pilot by profession, Jacko?"

"It's more a hobby, luv. Petunia lets me hop about the country fast and cheap and give a pretty girl in a hurry a lift." He didn't leer or wiggle his eyebrows, which she took as a hopeful sign.

She said, "That's kind of you. My brother Lucien's going to meet me in Katherine. I'm sure he'll want to thank you for getting me there safely."

"Beaut! Love to meet him. I take it Lucien's one of your uncle's offspring, so that would make him your half-brother?"

"That's right. My mother divorced Cleon when Lucien was four. She married my dad and I came along a year later."

"Are you and Lucien close?"

"Sure. We call the same woman Mom, we grew up calling each other brother and sister, and I call his father Uncle Cleon although Cleon Dobbs has been more of a father to me than my real one ever was."

He gave her another of his assessing looks. "Does it bother your real father that you think more highly of Mr. Dobbs than you do of him?"

"I wish he lived in constant torment. But unfortunately, he…carked, as you would say. When I was ten." All these years later and it was still hard to keep the anger out of her voice.

"I'm sorry, luv. An accident, was it?"

She did a slow burn. Was he just an innocuous old coot with a mania for Twenty Questions or was there something kinky behind his nosiness? The sharks began to seem refreshingly simple and straightforward. "Yes," she said without amplification.

He kept quiet for a minute, but his nosiness was apparently irrepressible. "Your uncle's other children and, um, wives one and three, are you close to them, too?"

Her fuse was getting shorter. "When I see them at holiday time, we get along well enough. Don't you have divorces and remarriages and extended families in Australia?"

"Well, of course we do."

"Then you shouldn't act as if it's some kind of stigma."

"I wasn't knocking your uncle, luv. It's the exceptional hubbie who can keep the good will of every woman he marries. He's inspired me to be more sporting when my old potato peeler throws me out again."

All at once, her fear and annoyance dissolved. The absurdity of the man and his lingo and the whole ridiculous situation triggered a gale of cathartic laughter. When she caught her breath, she said, "I'm glad I could furnish you with a role model, Jacko. Does your old potato peeler throw you…?"

"Look there ahead!" He pointed excitedly. "That's Melville Island." He flew in low across a rocky shoreline. "You see that outcrop just under us? That's where I discovered the body. Two if you count the water spirit."

TWO

DINAH STIFFENED. HE was a nut case after all. Her chest tightened. She slid her hand onto the door handle and nerved herself for a rendezvous with the sharks. Didn't all seat cushions double as flotation devices?

She tried to keep her voice amiable, play for time. "Was the water spirit you saw a mermaid?"

"No, it wasn't a…bloody oath, woman, I'm not daft. A bloke was murdered on the beach down there a week ago. Skewered through like a bloody kabob atop a sea turtle. I call the turtle a spirit because it's sacred to some of the clans, symbolizes one of their ancestral beings from the Dreamtime." His face was comical, but the intelligence behind his piercing gray eyes was indisputable.

She shivered. He made the macabre sound matter-of-fact. Like Nick. As if dead bodies were all in a day's work. "You're serious? You found a man impaled on a turtle?"

"Sad to say but I did, luv. So many flies I thought at first he was a black man."

"You could see this from the air?"

"Of course not. I was on the ground right next to him. The spear that killed him punctured the turtle's shell, too, though it's not a cert that's what killed it."

What did the old ghoul do? Shoo the flies away and conduct a private postmortem? She didn't care to hear any more of the grisly details. "Have the police caught the killer?"

"They're completely up a gumtree, can't work out the

who or the why. It's a grade A puzzler, all right, but I've noodled around with a few theories." He warmed to his subject. "The bloke was a well-known Pommie journalist—that's an Englishman to you. He wrote a series of articles about a gang of greenies who've been interfering with commercial dragnet fishing, setting off firebombs and causing a nuisance. Made them out to be a bunch of ning-nongs and thugs. In his view, every dolphin and turtle in the bloody seven seas could go extinct if protecting them cost an industry that feeds millions of people." He paused expectantly.

She picked up on his cue. "And you think that was the motive?"

"Bang-on! The turtle-huggers offed him to shut him up."

Suddenly, she got it. Jacko had discovered the body and now the murder was his personal property and claim to fame. How many times had he flown over the scene of the crime? How many hapless tourists had he lured out here with the promise of a free ride just to show off his special knowledge and expound his theory? Nick often said how some people relish their connection to a crime, especially a sensational one. They thrive on the attention and the fantasy of being indispensable to the police.

"Why," she asked, "would the so-called turtle-huggers kill one?"

"A bit of misdirection maybe, or an accident."

The radio crackled. "Robbery in progress, Bendigo…"

"Strewth!" Jacko shut it off.

"You have a police scanner?"

"How else would I keep tabs? But about the dead journo, here's another theory. It could've been one of the Tiwi people. They own Melville and the smaller island to the west. The land's not open to the public without permission of the

Tiwi Council. Could be one of the islanders took a scunner to this journo trespassing on their land, and whammo!"

"But an Aborigine wouldn't have killed the turtle. Not if it's a sacred totem."

"Not all Aborigines have the same totem, luv. There's no taboo against chowing down on another man's totem, especially if it's tasty. And green sea turtles are bloody tasty."

"Had anyone chowed down on the dead turtle?"

"Not so much as a chop." He looked so crestfallen she felt sorry for him.

"You know," she said, "some murders have no rhyme or reason. Maybe this began as a simple robbery, the victim fought back and the robber went berserk."

"What kind of a droob sets out to pull a hold-up armed with a spear? He'd have to be mad as a bloody meat ax."

"Are there no suspects at all who had a grudge against the guy? A jealous rival or…or a jilted lover?" She didn't like to think what she might have done to Nick if she'd been carrying a spear.

"His mates in Darwin have alibis as tight as a camel's arse in a sandstorm."

"Well, how about fingerprints then? The killer must've left something behind."

"Not so much as a gnat's nib. Any footprints or tire treads were washed away by the tide. Few vehicles allowed on the island and the dead man's name wasn't on the permit list. I'm thinking both killer and victim arrived and left by boat…but from bloody where?" He raked a hand through his white mane, rolled his shoulders, and turned Petunia back toward the mainland.

She breathed a sigh of relief and segued to a less bloody topic. "Do the Aborigines cling to their old customs or do they all carry cell phones and surf the Net?"

"Some are highly educated and up to the minute, but some haven't changed a whit in spite of all the Western civilization we've tried to cram down their throats. In their way of thinking, time's merged into one great bloody gob. Past, present, future— it's all the same. They believe the spirits of their ancestors live on inside the rocks and animals and trees and they can coax 'em out for a chinwag whenever they like."

"Every culture has myths. We all believe some things that aren't true."

"Fair enough, and we're none the worse for believing in the pixies. It's believing the hard-boiled, godless liars that does us up the bum and makes us cynical. Right?"

Did the nosy old codger expect her to volunteer a case in point from her own life? "I've never thought about it," she said.

"Well, take it from old Jacko, luv, they walk amongst us. The worst of them can hoodwink the best of us and they don't give a damn who gets caught in their graft."

First murder and now graft. His brain was a veritable police blotter. She prayed he didn't have another crime scene to show her. He looked at her in a sideways, calculating way as if he wanted to pry open her head and screw with the machinery, the way Nick looked whenever he tried to wangle her over to his way of thinking.

Nick again. She needed a mental escape key, a charm or incantation to ward off thoughts of him. What was that Latin phrase she was always misspelling when she temped at the law firm? Starry...no. It sounded like starry, but it was *stare*. *Stare decisis*. It meant that the matter was decided, over and done, finished, settled, kaput. And vis-à-vis herself and Detective Nick Isparta, the matter was *stare decisis* in spades.

She stared out the window at the walls of a spectacular escarpment fringed by tropical forest. They were over Kakadu National Park now. According to her tour guide and would-be crimebuster, it was the largest national park in Australia and home to Aboriginal people for the last 50,000 years. Maybe it was the aura of the place or the altitude or a vagary brought on by lack of sleep, but she thought she knew what the Aborigines meant by the merging of time. At the present moment she was buzzing into the future in a yet-to-be-produced airplane on a collision course with a past she'd made a specialty of forgetting. But with Cleon slated to die in a matter of days, one ancestral spirit in particular had reasserted himself in her consciousness and the time was now or never for a chinwag with the man who'd known him best. If Cleon didn't give her the lowdown on her father, that would be that. Her mother had stonewalled for years and gave no sign that she was saving the nitty-gritty for her memoirs.

"Give this theory a burl, Dinah. The Pommie bloke saw some skulduggery he shouldn't have seen, only what he saw happened elsewhere. He was brought to Melville by boat and murdered there to keep the other place a secret."

She couldn't believe the single-mindedness of the man. "Jacko, you've developed an unhealthy obsession. It must've been gruesome stumbling onto a dead body, but you need to do something to take your mind off it. Go on a holiday or read a book, maybe talk to a therapist."

"Think I've hopped the fence, do you?"

"If that means what I think it does, yes. You can't way-lay every tourist who walks through an airport and make them listen to you spitball a lot of whodunit theories."

"You're right to give me a taste of the curry, luv. You've places to go and things to do and I've delayed you long enough." He pointed out the window. "Look there below. We're over the Nitmiluk. That's the Katherine River."

The blue-green water shimmered like glass as it cut between the canyon walls. The fierceness of the sun gave the rugged cliffs a glazed patina—or was it her eyes that were glazed?

Ahead of them sprawled the town of Katherine. Soon she'd be on the ground, feet in the future, head in the past. Petunia descended and she caught sight of what appeared to be a large cemetery. She had a rush of second thoughts. Did she really want to delve into her father's felonious past? The sugarcoated version she'd been fed as a ten-year-old was painful enough. Why be a glutton for detail? You couldn't exhume a dead man's conscience or second-guess why he did what he did. If only she could make sense of his incongruities. If she could reconcile the kind, compassionate man she'd known with the callous, drug-running rotter he turned out to be, then maybe she could let go.

Stay away, Lucien had warned her. Let the dead bury the dead. But what did that stupid proverb mean anyway? Cleon wasn't dead yet and his memory was excellent. Why would Lucien discourage her from talking to him? Had Cleon told him something worse than what she knew already? Was he trying to spare her more shame and heartache or had there been something else in his voice? A note of…fear?

The runway zoomed up at her. She jammed both feet against the floor, threw her internal gears in reverse. She had a bad feeling, a foreboding, pins and needles in her toes.

Jacko whooped. The wheels clunked onto the tarmac, bounced, and clunked down hard again. "Bonzer ride, eh, Dinah?"

"Bonzer," she said, but she was thinking back to the sharks that didn't eat her with something like nostalgia.

THREE

DESPITE THE SURREAL detour, Petunia beat the Airnorth flight from Darwin, which according to a hand-printed sign taped to the Airnorth counter wasn't due for another half hour.

"Lucien knows how I hate to sit and wait," said Dinah, craning her neck around the terminal.

Jacko parked her suitcase and daypack next to a row of plastic chairs. "He must have called ahead and found out the flight was delayed."

"I suppose."

"Hard to tear himself away from the reunion, I expect. With his father living part-time in Sydney, they probably don't get to spend much time together."

"Not a lot. Uncle Cleon's used to having his own way and so is Lucien. They have a tendency to lock horns if they're together for longer than a couple of hours."

"All fathers and sons argy-bargy over one thing or another. Senior a bit of a tall poppy, is he?"

"If you mean does he have a big ego, yes. He bullies and browbeats and manipulates. He drives Lucien up the wall. But he can be caring and bighearted, too. At least, he's always been wonderful to me."

Jacko looked at his watch. "Cripes! I'm sorry to choof off and leave you to wait alone, luv, but it's later than I thought and I've some other goings-on to look into while I'm in town."

"Oh." She felt a shock of anticlimax, disappointment

even. Almost as if she were losing a friend. "Well, Jacko, thanks for the scenic tour and the crash course in Strine. It's been…unforgettable."

"It was my pleasure, luv. I hope your visit to the Land of Oz is a ripsnorter."

She watched him lope through the terminal barking Strine into a cell phone and an Alice-down-the-rabbit-hole feeling came over her. The Land of Oz was going to take some getting used to. As the flight she should have been on wasn't due for another half-hour, the bar seemed a logical place to wait for Lucien and start acclimating.

What she found was a chipped tile counter with four stools and an uncaged green parrot pecking seeds and raisins off the tiles. A Russell Crowe look-alike with a sexy grin and a diamond stud in one ear was unboxing bottles and lining them up on a shelf behind the bar.

"G'day." He wiped his hands on a bar towel and swaggered over. "What can I do for you? I've got vodka and beer. Tooheys New, Tooheys Old, and Hop Thief."

"Could I have a Bloody Mary?" Something with the word "bloody" seemed an appropriate finale to her adventure with Jacko.

"No worries. Take a load off while I do the science."

She sat down and he turned to his drink-making. She took a deep breath. With the emotional turbulence ahead of her, she could use a bracer. She hoped Lucien would come alone to meet her. She wanted to gauge his mood before wading into the larger family drama, find out why he'd been so dead set against her coming. He was probably just preoccupied and anxious when she phoned from Seattle. Thinking about how to say good-bye to his father would give rise to all kinds of knotty feelings. But he'd be glad she was there for him. The trick was to figure out the degree of "being there" Lucien would appreciate. He despised a bleeding heart and, as Nick once cracked, she wasn't a natural comforter.

Stare decisis.

The hunky bartender set her drink in front of her. "Where'd you fly in from?"

"Darwin."

"You're lucky you could land. The airport was closed until an hour ago. Wallies on the runway."

"What?"

"Wallabies. Pint-sized kangaroos. They're pests here at the airport." His cell phone trilled. He flipped it open and walked away out of hearing range.

Dinah took a sip of the Bloody Mary and gasped. This guy must've gone to the Molotov School of Bartending. As her taste buds acclimated, she remembered the incendiary cocktail Lucien had concocted for her thirteenth birthday—vodka, gin, applejack, and tequila. Afterward, she'd walked an abandoned railroad trestle across the Suwannee River as if she were performing on a balance beam and Lucien had dubbed her a full-fledged member of the Hundred Proof Club. It was the summer before he left for college and he and his pals had turned Cleon's peanut farm outside the town of Needmore, Georgia, into a training camp for life in the frat house. Cleon made sure she never crashed those parties, but she saw enough of the morning-after chaos to know they'd been wild. He let the boys get away with murder. Of course, he was between marriages then. He'd stayed single for a long time after her mother left him.

The passengers arriving on the flight from Darwin trooped through the terminal, kissing their meeters and greeters, handing off babies and bags. The singletons whipped out their cell phones and hurried on toward baggage claim and ground transportation. She set her watch to local time by the clock behind the bar. Three-thirty-seven. Back in Seattle, Nick was probably kissing his redhead good-bye, holstering his piece, and heading out to fight for Truth, Justice, and the American Way. *Stare decisis.*

Now that she'd quit her job at the law firm, she'd be beating the bushes for some other employment. When she was in college she'd been gung-ho about anthropology: primitive myths, bygone religions, vestiges of ancient beliefs that live on in curious superstitions. She'd wanted to revisit all the places and tribes described in *The Golden Bough.* She'd wanted to unearth a lost city in the Amazon or rescue some crucial fragment of a forgotten civilization from history's dustbin. On a dig in Macedonia during her senior year, she discovered a human skull with a neat round hole bored into the parietal bone—evidence of trepanation, the earliest known form of brain surgery. The early peoples of the region believed that epilepsy and other crazy or deviant behavior was caused by demon possession. Trepanation provided an exit hole for the demon to escape. The skull had been an exhilarating find. She was on her way to anthropological stardom.

But in late 2000, another of those Balkan insurgencies erupted. The ethnic Albanians attacked the Serbs, the Macedonians attacked the Albanians, her Bulgarian archaeology professor was caught smuggling weapons to the Kosovo Liberation Army, and Cleon dispatched a bodyguard named Mark Granger to bring her home.

In retrospect, it wasn't clear if her career had been Balkanized or Grangerized, but it had definitely been marginalized. She fell head over heels for Mark, a mistake for which she should have had her own head trepanated. And by the time she came to her senses and split, she'd lost sight of her dream. She drifted from place to place, job to job. Lounge canary and piano player in Atlanta, copywriter in Denver, paralegal in Seattle. She still read everything she could lay her hands on about myths and the magical stories people have dreamed up to explain the workings of the universe. Once in a blue moon, her old anthropology professor called with an offer of field work in some exotic place, but those assignments were temporary and led nowhere. Maybe this latest hiatus would galvanize her to set some long-term professional goals for herself. But even if she had to play "Stardust" ad nauseum for a room full of drunks or draft mind-numbing interrogatories for testosterone-crazed litigators, she needed a paycheck fast. She had less than $800 to her name.

Her Bloody Mary seemed to have evaporated and still no Lucien. What was keeping him? It suddenly hit her that she didn't have the telephone number of the lodge. Maybe there wasn't a telephone. She had the international cell phone number Lucien had given her somewhere. She grubbed through her purse. Wallet, passport, compact, lipstick, cigarettes. Boarding passes, overdue Visa bill, quart-sized plastic baggie with toothpaste and leaking blue mouthwash. Lucien's number wasn't there.

The parrot let out a ferocious squawk. "Where's my bloody munga?" It waddled down the bar to Dinah, cocked its head, and sized her up with one curmudgeonly little black eye. "Where's my bloody munga?"

She didn't know whether to laugh or take cover.

The bartender reappeared. "No scrounging from the customers, Speed." He brought out a banana, peeled it, and set it down at the opposite end of the bar. "Here's your bloody munga, mate. Come and get it."

Speed waddled off, squawking.

"Does munga mean banana?" asked Dinah.

"It's whatever there is to eat. Speed's not picky. How about you? Another Mary?"

"Sure." What the hell. If Lucien bloody Dobbs didn't show soon, he'd find her blitzed. But blitzed might be the best way to ride out this week. She predicted the atmosphere at the lodge would be combustible. In more crowded venues—Cleon's annual Christmas bash, for example—the wives tolerated each other with polite disdain. But in close quarters, in a situation fraught with so much emotion, repressed hostilities between the first Mrs. Dobbs and the third Mrs. Dobbs could flare into open warfare at the slightest provocation. Fortunately for all concerned, Dinah's mother, the second and most provocative of the Mrs. Dobbs, had sent her regrets.

The pain must be unbearable for a man who loved life as much as Cleon did to shorten it by even an hour. He'd always been so full of drive and gusto. She'd considered him practically immortal. It was hard to picture him weak and ailing, harder still to learn that he'd asked for assistance to end his life. The Cleon she knew would've shot himself without fuss in his own back forty. But having opted to die in this way, it was strange that he didn't go to Oregon or Washington or someplace more accessible where assisted suicide was quasi-legal.

She nursed her second Mary for half an hour, reorganized her purse, read a few sentences in her guidebook on Aboriginal myths, something about the physical contours of the country being encoded in "song lines." Only these "songs" weren't music, not in the ordinary sense. They were some kind of a divine navigational system, the energy currents generated by the ancestors as they traversed the land. It was too deep to fathom just now. Maybe after she'd rested and her own energy currents had regenerated.

She checked her watch, craned her neck. Maybe Lucien had a flat tire or a dead battery or an emergency of some kind. Oh, God. Maybe Cleon had passed away ahead of schedule.

"Did he stand you up?" The sexy bartender again.

"What?"

"You've been watching the clock ever since you sat down. I'll be off in a quarter hour. If you're staying in town, I'll give you a ride to your hotel." His eyes offered something way racier than a lift into town.

"Not today, thanks. Family obligations."

"I'll take a rain check. My name's Robbie. What's yours?"

"Dinah. From Seattle."

"Well, Dinah from Seattle, give me a call if you shake free and fancy a bit of night life." He jotted a number on her napkin and flashed a bad-boy grin.

"Maybe I will," she said. He looked like primo post-Nick therapy, but she'd had enough excitement in the Land of Oz for one day.

FOUR

"YOO-HOO! DINAH!"

She was on her way to ground transportation, ready to rent a car and look for a nearby motel, when an angular, loose-jointed character pranced out of the crowd waving his arms. He wore tan jodhpurs, a turquoise polo shirt, and a straw hat with a veil of wine corks bobbing from the brim.

"Eduardo?"

"C'est moi." He parted the veil and bussed her on either cheek.

"I didn't know you were coming."

"Of course you did. Lucien couldn't function without me."

She scanned the crowd. "Where is he?"

"He couldn't make it."

"What do you mean he couldn't make it?" Eduardo had been Lucien's partner for five years and she liked him a lot, but in the circumstances he was no substitute. "Doesn't he want to see me?"

"Don't be silly. I'll fill you in on the way to the lodge. Suivez moi."

He took her suitcase and breezed out the door. Feeling irritable and slighted, she followed him to the parking lot and a dusty black hatchback with a smiley face grill.

"What is this smirky little car?"

"A Daihatsu Charade."

"Did the Charade come with the chapeau? Or vice versa?"

"It's called a Ned Kelly, after some Australian desper-ado. It looks goofy, but it keeps off the flies. One of the thousand plagues infesting this godawful country." He loaded her suitcase in the back and opened the passenger door. "S'il vous plaît."

He pranced around, slid into the driver's seat and tossed the Ned Kelly into the back seat. "Fasten your seatbelt."

He peeled out of the parking lot and launched the Cha-rade southbound onto the Stuart Highway. It took her a heartstopping few seconds to remember that Australians drive like the British, on the left. The Katherine airport disappeared behind them and the sign ahead read "Mata-ranka, Tennant Creek, Alice Springs."

"Where is this lodge?"

"In the middle of effing nowhere. The drive will take over an hour."

"Doesn't Uncle Cleon need to be close to a hospital?"

"That would defeat the purpose, wouldn't it? Anyhow, his doctor is a guest at the lodge."

"The same doctor who's going to…?"

"Put him down? Mais oui." Eduardo spruced up his hair in the rear view mirror and wrinkled his elegant Roman nose. "Dr. Desmond Fisher is to Death as the robin is to spring. He chirps about it endlessly. He struts about in safari garb like a bad imitation of Ernest Hemingway, preaching about the right to die until you positively yearn to perish just to get away from the man."

"How did Cleon find a doctor willing to perform a sui-cide? Was he listed in the Yellow Pages under Physicians—Family Practice and Felonies?"

"He and Cleon met ages ago on a safari in Kenya and have been friends ever since, or so they say."

"You don't believe it?"

"Ha."

"What do you mean, ha?"

"Oh, I believe they've known each other a long time. Fisher lives in one of those to-die-for Harbourside mansions in Sydney, not far from Cleon's chateau, and he's visited Cleon in Georgia a number of times. I just don't believe they're all that friendly. Fisher joined our entourage as soon as we arrived in Sydney, which is a stunning city and very cosmopolitan, and why God put it on this continent passeth all understanding. Be that as it may, Cleon's given him an earful of his vintage abuse for over a week and if Fisher feels half as fed up as the rest of us, he can't wait to sink the fatal syringe."

"You seem to have your grief well in check."

"It's my manly façade. But even among the gentler sex, I think you'll find true grief in short supply."

Dinah kneaded her forehead. Eduardo was normally a blithe, sunny kind of guy. If he was peevish, the others must be foaming at the mouth.

She shifted her attention to the countryside, which was green and wooded, though not as verdant as the terrain she'd flown over with Jacko. To the south lay what her guidebook described as the Red Center, the arid and inhospitable heart of the continent. But here, the landscape wasn't all that different from South Georgia.

Her thoughts returned to family matters. "Eddie, why did Cleon invite Margaret? They've been divorced for thirty-five years. Couldn't he have said good-bye over the phone?"

"He invited Margaret to piss off Neesha. What else? Neesha plays the part of the adoring wife, but sharing the stage with the first wife is getting to her. Les femmes haven't come to blows, but the sound of rattling beads and ruffling feathers is positively deafening."

"I don't believe Cleon means to piss off anybody. He

still has feelings for Margaret and she is, after all, the mother of his firstborn. Maybe he just wanted to bring together all the people he loves for one last time. To tell us the things he should have told us, but never found the time."

"Lucien thought that's how he enticed you here."

She bristled. Lucien could blab her secrets if he liked, but there were some matters on which she did not desire big brother's opinion and most definitely she did not desire Eduardo's. "If Uncle Cleon's crotchety, it's probably due to the drugs he's on. Is he in a lot of pain?"

"Ha!"

"Come on, Eddie. Cut the man some slack. He must be suffering."

"He's certainly making everyone else suffer."

"You're prejudiced. You've never liked him."

He swerved around the bloated carcass of a dead kangaroo into the path of an oncoming tractor-trailer rig. Dinah looked up into the truck driver's furious eyes as Eduardo swerved back to the left with no room to spare. The trucker laid on his horn and the Charade was rocked by a series of concussive gusts as three long trailers filled with bawling cattle rumbled by in the cab's wake.

Eduardo thrust his arm out the window and pumped his middle finger. "Road trains! One pulling seven trailers passed me yesterday doing eighty. I barely kept from being blown off the road. The longer you're in this bizarre country, the more you'll understand why the Brits shipped their prisoners here as punishment."

Dinah had no doubt that she was being punished. When her heart rate came down from the stratosphere, she said, "I don't understand why he didn't want to go home to die. The logistics would've been much easier in the U.S."

"I don't think he's sick. He's up to something."

"What does he have to gain by dragging us here if he isn't dying?"

"You're the tea-leaf reader in the family, cherie."

She wished. Her intuition had been seriously off-line of late and she couldn't think why Lucien hadn't come to the airport to meet her. Maybe he and Cleon were busy telling each other those touchy-feely, father-son things they should have said before but couldn't. "How's the situation between Cleon and Lucien?"

"Lucien hasn't begun to gnash his teeth yet, but if Cleon keeps shooting barbs at him, it's just a matter of time."

So much for the feel-good scenario. "What kind of barbs is he shooting?"

"He heh-heh-hehs in that sly way of his and drops snarky little hints."

"Hints about what?"

"You'll have to decide for yourself."

"Well, I think you're making a mountain out of a mole-hill. You don't trust him because he's thrown his weight around a little bit in the past."

"A little bit?" His voice rose, mocking and querulous. "A little bit?"

"Okay, a lot. But how can he possibly jerk anyone's chain at this point?"

"Hello-oh? Are we talking about the same Cleon Dobbs? Chain jerker extraordinaire? Master manipulator? Redneck Machiavelli? Alpha hick?"

"You're being overly critical. Death changes people."

"The only thing Cleon's changing is his will."

"How do you know? Did he say that he was?"

"It's his constant refrain. He says he's still making up his mind who'll get what."

She'd prepared herself for friction between the wives and there was always the possibly of a dustup between

Cleon and Lucien. A money fight never crossed her mind. "Maybe he wants to distribute the estate more equitably. Fine-tune things, so to speak."

"He's fine-tuning, all right. Jabbing everybody up the ass with his tuning fork."

"And how, pray, is he doing this jabbing?"

"He hints about past crimes and misdemeanors without saying exactly what it was that we did to put his nose out of joint. He runs all kinds of vindictive possibilities up the flagpole. He's going to write off his children and leave all the money to their mothers, or he's going to lock up all the money in a spendthrift trust under the control of a trustee who'll make sure we don't blow it on anything that would make us even remotely happy. Every day it's something different. If he keeps it up, somebody will slit his throat before the doctor has a chance at him."

It must be the climate, she thought. Everyone seemed to have murder on the brain. "Do you have a particular throat-slitter in mind?"

"No, but you wouldn't believe the state we're in. Someone will snap."

"I'll snap if I don't get to a bed soon. How much farther?"

"The turnoff 's just ahead, but it's ten miles down a dirt road after that. And if you were expecting the Ritz, forget about it. Crow Hill Lodge is a pit."

"All I want is a shower and clean place to lie down."

"Well, the sheets are clean, but inspect them for spiders before snuggling in. The toilet seat, too. And if there are frogs in the toilet bowl, scream your head off. It's what I do."

He whipped an abrupt right-hand turn onto a rutted dirt track. The car lurched like a mechanical bull, her seat belt seized and her head flew back and down. When it came up, a flock of startled cockatoos exploded from a tree over-head. She examined her teeth. She still had the full set, no thanks to her chauffeur.

"You're in an awful damned hurry to get to this pit."

"There's an excellent single malt Scotch waiting for me at the end of the trail. The lodge has all the comforts and accoutrement of a gulag, but at least Cleon didn't stint on the booze."

Dinah still had a mild, palliative buzz from the Bloody Marys, but it was wearing off fast under Eduardo's hail of complaints. She watched the miles roll by in silence and conjured up visions of a gulag crawling with frogs and barb throwers and fork jabbers and bead rattlers and throat slit-ters. Thinking negatively never helped, but she suspected that her horoscope didn't bode happy times ahead.

Eduardo pursed his lips. "Did I mention that he brought those two little Winslow Homers that you like with him?"

"What?"

"When he moved to Sydney, he threw them in a suit-case he checked with the rest of the baggage. Carted them from Sydney to Katherine the same way."

"But that's nuts. You can't bounce paintings around like that. In this heat? Never mind the baggage handlers, the temperature and humidity might have ruined them. Have you seen them since they were unpacked? Has Lu-cien seen them?"

"No and no."

She could've wept. She loved that pair of Homer sea-scapes. They'd hung in the living room of Cleon's old farm-house for ten years like windows onto a storm-churned Atlantic. Just because Cleon owned them didn't give him the right to slam them about from pillar to post. They were irreplaceable.

The open landscape changed and walls of gigantic,

shaggy-barked trees closed in around them, blocking the sun. Dinah began to feel claustrophobic, as if she were being swallowed down the gullet of some strange animal. The trees, the colors, the smells—everything seemed alien and forbidding. Maybe that's why Cleon had brought the paintings with him. Maybe they reminded him of home. In any case, the paintings were his. If they soothed him or took some of the sting out of dying, who was she to criticize?

On the other hand, she felt amply justified in criticizing Lucien. "What was so all-fired important that Lucien couldn't trouble himself to meet me, Eddie? I mean, I know he said not to come. I know he doesn't want me emoting all over the place, but Cleon's been good to me. I owe him. Lucien should respect that."

"There was a small mishap the day after we arrived here from Sydney." He slowed down and his voice went flat. "Now don't freak out on me, okay? It's not as bad as it sounds."

A queasy sensation roiled her insides. "What haven't you told me?"

"Lucien was bitten by a death adder, Dinah. He's laid up with a catheter in his leg."

FIVE

CROW HILL LODGE loomed at the end of the track like a Wild West fort, a dark, near windowless box of rough-hewn logs seemingly carved out of the forest by somebody in a hurry. A few stumps scattered about the clearing added to the sense of frontier expediency. The only thing that looked modern was the white metal roof, agleam in the late afternoon sun.

Eddie pulled the Charade up close behind a line of other dusty cars and cut the engine. Dinah tore at the door handle.

"There's no need to be frantic. Lucien's going to be fine. He got the antivenin in time. I wouldn't have left his side for an instant if he were in danger."

"I know you wouldn't, Eddie. But I have to see him with my own eyes. Right now." She got out and started for the front door.

A gangling boy of about fourteen with rebellious eyes and an unruly mop of brown hair rounded the corner of the house. He'd grown a foot since she last saw him, but it was unmistakably Thad, the male half of Cleon's twins with Neesha.

"They're here," he called over his shoulder and chucked a rock at a cawing crow. The terrorized bird broke across the housetop and Dinah remembered why she'd never liked Thad.

"Hi, Thad. Long time no see."

"I'm cool with that."

Twerp, she thought as she bounded up the steps and onto the small covered porch.

Thad's sister, a smug-faced nymphet with long straight hair parted in the middle and an air of congenital entitlement, opened the door. As she did, a ball of yipping white fluff streaked out of the house and hurled itself against Dinah's legs.

"Cantoo, leave it!"

It crossed Dinah's mind that she'd been unwashed and uncombed for so many hours that she might actually be mistaken for an "it." She pushed on through the door with the yipping, sniffing dog riding on her shoe tops.

"Kate deBeau, you've shot up like a weed."

"That's such a cliché. Can't you think of anything else that's tall?"

Noxious weed, thought Dinah, reminded why she didn't like this one either.

"Mother thinks I should become a model, but I intend to be a famous writer and I'd prefer you call me K.D."

"Catchy." Dinah didn't anticipate enough social back-and-forth with the twit to call her anything. "Where's Lucien?"

"Upstairs." K.D. called out to her twin. "It's your turn to take Cantoo for a walk, Thad. Do be mature and accept responsibility."

"Eat snot," he shouted back and scuffed off down the lane.

Eduardo bustled through the door carrying her suitcase in one hand and his Ned Kelly in the other. He dropped the suitcase, yoo-hooed for somebody named Mackenzie, and took Dinah by the hand. "Allons, cherie."

He led her through a dusky foyer and up a flight of narrow wooden stairs. There was a dank, fungal smell suggestive of a long wet season, the other extreme of the

Dry that Jacko spoke of. They passed the first landing and headed up yet another flight. A rancid potpourri of mildew and must and dogginess emanated from the shabby carpet. When they topped out on the third floor, Eduardo ushered her down a long dreary hall with numbered doors on either side.

"He's in an artistic frenzy," he said. "Très bizarre." He rapped on the last door on the right and walked in without waiting for an answer. "Yoohoo! C'est nous."

Lucien sat in a wheelchair in front of an easel with a sullen frown and a loaded brush between his teeth. He didn't look up.

She said, "Hey, Dobbs. You don't have to gush, but a smile would be nice."

He turned, trance-like, and seemed for a moment not to recognize her. He had a square jaw and deep-set blue eyes like his father, but there was a protean quality about his features that subverted the camera's eye. No one had ever taken a good likeness of him. "Hey, Pelerin. Like a moth to the flame, huh?" Unlike herself, Lucien had never been self-conscious about his accent or tried to moderate it. His drawl was thick as grits.

He put down the dripping brush and held out his arms. She hugged him as best she could while keeping clear of his bandaged, outstretched leg and the wet paint. His color was ashen, but she knew better than to go all fluttery and exclamatory.

"How could somebody who was raised in the Okefenokee Swamp with copperheads and water moccasins for playmates let a little death adder sneak up on him? You should be embarrassed."

He grinned. "I am. Deeply."

Eduardo checked out his flawless appearance in the dressing table mirror. "I'll go and do the social thing with

Margaret and Neesha and leave you two to bemoan your miserable ancestry in private. Shall I send you up a snack from the kitchen?"

"No thanks," they answered in unison.

"Then bye-bye until happy hour." He blew a kiss over his shoulder and left.

Dinah sat down at the end of the bed next to Lucien's wheelchair.

He said, "Eddie begged and wheedled until I said he could come and now all he does is bitch."

"He's part of the family, too. He wants to help. We both do."

"Yeah, well. I couldn't convince either of you that the best way to help me was to leave me alone. But then you've got bigger fish to fry, don't you?"

She tried to sound blasé. "Have you talked to Mom? She hasn't changed her mind about coming, has she?"

"Not to my knowledge. She sent Dad a farewell letter. The way he goes on about it, you'd think he sleeps with it under his pillow."

"That must frost Neesha."

"I can't see how it wouldn't. Let's hope he doesn't put you in her cross hairs by treating you as Mom's stand-in."

"That's not why he asked me to be here. Or if it is, he's out of his gourd."

"Earth to Dinah. He's always been out of his gourd and if he keeps crapping on everybody, we'll all sing hosannas when he's gone."

"I won't. Jeez, Lucien, what's wrong with you? You've had your differences, but if there was ever a time to mend fences…" She dabbed at a drop of red paint on his chin. "You and Cleon are just too stubborn to admit you love each other."

He scowled. "Why'd you come, Dinah? Really?"

"I don't know. To comfort you. To comfort Cleon. You know how good he's been to Mom and me. I care about him. And I'm beholden."

"And?"

"Okay. And I want him to fill in the blanks about my father."

"Your father did what he did, Di. You need to get over it and move on. Anyway, what makes you think my dad would know anything about your dad's moonlighting? If Mom didn't know about it, Cleon sure wouldn't."

"Of course he wouldn't know about the drugs, Lucien. But he and my father used to talk a lot. Men confide in each other sometimes, don't they? Daddy might have said something to Cleon that he couldn't or wouldn't say to Mom. I have to know what was going on in his head that caused him to jeopardize everything he had for a sack full of money he didn't need."

Lucien curled his lip. "Why's everybody so fucking hung-up on the past?" He picked up his brush and slathered a thick stripe of carmine across the wet canvas. "What do you think of my new painting?"

Baffled by his lack of sympathy but happy for a change of subject, she searched for meaning in the swirling shapes and drunken colors on the canvas. This was a radical departure from his usual work.

"A monster? A red monster pointing a white stick?"

"It's a bone. You know about bone pointing?"

"You know me, Lucien. Myths are my thing. Bone pointing is an Aboriginal hex. A way to kill somebody from a distance. I've read that some people believe the superstition so strongly that, if a shaman points the bone at them, they actually get sick and die. Mind over matter."

He applied another layer of red on top of the violent impasto. "I've been reading some Aboriginal myths myself. The deadliest of the bone pointers was a snake god called Taipan. If he got you in his sights, it was curtains."

"So that red blotchy thing is Taipan?"

"You don't sound impressed."

"Just puzzled by your change of style."

"When in Rome." He leaned back and analyzed his handiwork. "It's a little short on method, but I'll get it. Anyhoo. This Taipan was a heavy-duty snake god. He could heal all kinds of ailments. He created blood and told it how to flow through the body so I painted him inside-out, all veins and raw meat."

"Lovely. What are those blue and green squiggles in the foreground?"

"The wives. He had three of them, two water snakes and a death adder."

"Not too subtle."

He dipped a clean brush into a blob of white and scrawled a jagged Z pointing down from the Taipan's other hand. "Maybe I've been possessed by the snake god. That's how it is with a lot of Aboriginal artists. They don't feel as if they're physically doing the painting themselves, but some metaphysical force is moving their hands and speaking through them."

"Like a Ouija board." She leaned back on the bed and propped on her elbows.

"Could be. I've been reading a lot about Aboriginal art, too. Have you met Mack?"

"No."

"Well, he's got some pictures of snakes that'll knock your eyes out. Speaking of snakes, there's an actual snake called a taipan that's fifty times as poisonous as a death adder. It would be a great way to snuff somebody."

"I hope your infatuation with snakes and death is a side effect of the meds you're taking and will soon pass."

"Is that a comment about my character or my painting?"

"It's a comment on the climate. Everyone I've met today has been harping on murder."

"Murdah, murdah, murdah." His voice rose to a girly falsetto. "Fiddle-de-dee, Miss Scarlett. This murdah talk is spoilin' th' fun at all th' pahties this season."

She laughed and fell all the way back on the bed. The show of humor reassured her. "Not everyone's obsessed. I met a hot bartender at the airport who bucked the trend."

"And are we meetin' this hot bartendah again?"

"Never you mind, big brother."

He grimaced. "Oh, I almost forgot. Nick called."

"Nick!" She sat up as if she'd been stung. "How'd he get your international cell number?"

"Beats me, unless you gave it to him."

Shit. She must have left it in the apartment.

"He says to call him back ASAP. How's ol' Nick doing? The last time we talked, things between you two sounded serious."

"They weren't. They're not. Nick and I are kaput. If he calls again, tell him I'm in the wind. No forwarding address."

"Another one bites the dust."

"None of your gibes about my checkered past, Dobbs. I walked in on this one banging a redhead. What was I supposed to do? Give him a medal?"

"Gosh, I dunno. Upbraid him severely?"

"If I'd had a gun I'd have shot him dead on the spot."

"Now who's harping on murder?"

They both laughed and she felt better. She didn't know how they'd gotten off on the wrong foot. "Now that I know the Taipan myth, the painting makes sense. Is that white zigzag coming out of his hand lightning?"

"Yeah. Too bad I don't have a tube of fluorescent white

for the thunderbolt. Taipan zaps the wicked before he turns into a snake and disappears into the earth."

The door burst open with a loud crack. "Dinah, darlin'."

"Uncle Cleon!"

"Come give us a kiss." He held out his arms.

She stood up and went to him. "Uncle Cleon, you look… fine." He wore a quilted maroon dressing gown, a blue silk scarf tucked around his oak-thick neck, and a grin as wide and taut as a crossbow.

"I ain't hurtin' none." He enfolded her in a python embrace and planted a kiss on her forehead. His ruddy complexion and robust strength didn't jibe with impending death.

"Come on downstairs with me, doll, and let's have a drink. We got ourselves some catchin' up to do."

"I'm really frazzled. A drink would wipe me out."

"Bullpucky. If I remember rightly, you've got a head for spirits. You take after your daddy in that way. Your mama now, she's apt to get a little too feisty on the firewater. I wish Swan could've been here. She'd sure liven things up." He let out a wistful sigh. "But, no use bellyachin'. Lucien, your paramour sends word he'll be up shortly to help you downstairs. Me and Dinah are gonna have ourselves a confab in the bar."

This wasn't the Cleon she'd bargained on. Suddenly, she wanted an ally. "We can help you downstairs if you'll join us, Lucien."

But Lucien shook his head and scowled at his painting of Taipan. "Y'all go on down and catch up. I'll be down in a while."

"Take your time." Cleon dragged her out the door. "Still woozy from the snakebite, I reckon. Or maybe he's allergic to weasel fur. Did you know that's what they make paint brushes out of? Weasels and squirrels. It can't be healthy."

SIX

CLEON TOWED HER down the hall, down the two flights of stairs, through the foyer and into a large, dim great room.

"Name your poison, doll. Bourbon? Vodka? Scotch? I got a kind of genius for the classic gin martini. Dry as a nun's fart. Will that do you? I asked the others to leave us to ourselves for a while. Too many mouths yappin' and nobody gets a word in edgewise."

He stepped behind a tarnished mahogany bar and dropped some ice cubes into the scarred old silver shaker she'd seen him flourish so many times before. He'd carted that from Georgia, too. While he busied himself with the rituals of the perfect martini, Dinah perched on a bar stool and took in the ambience. Across from the bar a pair of murky windows looked out on rotting porch columns colonized by moss. Framing the view, faded green draperies draggled on the dirty wood floor. A pair of stuffed boars' heads had been mounted on the wall on either side of the windows. Their dead eyes stared back at her with a penetrating hopelessness. A grouping of dilapidated leather chairs leaked gray stuffing onto the threadbare carpet and the dark paneled walls exuded the bleakness of a mortuary. Eduardo's description of the place had been kind.

Her reverie was broken by the sound of ice clattering inside the shaker.

"You gotta bruise the gin to bring out the flavor, but you don't want to inflict a mortal wound." He unscrewed the cap and drizzled the icy gin into frost-rimed glasses. He clinked his glass against hers. "Here's lookin' up your record."

"Cheers." Her initial plan to get blitzed and stay blitzed seemed the last best hope of cheer in this dump. She drained half the gin in a single gulp.

Cleon sat down on the stool next to her and savored his drink. "Yes, I wish your mama was here to see me off to the hereafter, but it's prob'ly for the best. Neesha don't mind poor ol' Margaret so much, but she's tetchy about Swan. Can't get it out of her head I loved her best."

Doesn't, thought Dinah. Neesha *doesn't* mind Margaret, you old liar. Did that slip out? The line between thought and speech had grown muzzy.

She said, "This isn't just another one of your all-inclusive Christmas parties, Uncle Cleon. At a time like this, any wife would want her husband all to herself. I'm sure that's how Neesha feels. I know you and Margaret are still friendly, but you've been divorced forever. Couldn't you have said what you had to say to her over the phone?"

"Margaret and I were high school sweethearts. She was in on the ground floor. Havin' her here with me now lends a kind of symmetry."

"You could've had your symmetry in Sydney and sent her home."

"We didn't finish discussin' our mutual creation, Wendell. Maggie frets that I don't dote on her boy like I oughta. Thinks I play favorites. I wanted to talk with Swan about *our* mutual creation, Lucien. She mighta helped Lucien and me iron out a little misunderstandin'. But…" He chugged his martini, "I reckon a man can't have everything he wants."

Dinah felt a pang of guilt. Her mother's being here would have meant a lot to him. But she would have squelched all discussion of Hart Pelerin, the co-creator of

Dinah. Call it symmetry or curiosity or plain old masochism, but once and for all Dinah wanted a discussion of her late father. There could be no reason to hold back now.

Her mother had loved her father deeply, of that she was sure. Even when Dinah was a child, centered on her own grief and loss, she'd recognized the anguish in her mother's eyes when the trooper told them he was dead. Swan hadn't screamed or cried or put on a show of her grief. Not then. Not ever. There was a tensile strength in her, Seminole genes that wouldn't surrender—to an invading army, to personal grief, to anything. She'd taken the hit, closed the wound, and gone on with her life. But for Swan, going on meant never looking back. She'd barred the door to the past. But the past didn't belong to her alone. Part of it belonged to Dinah and she'd put off exploring it until the only other link to Hart Pelerin was on a fast countdown to oblivion.

"What's the matter, toots? Cat got your tongue?"

"Why here?" she blurted.

He erupted in laughter. "You ain't changed a lick, doll. Run straight at it just like your mama. That's what I've always loved about you."

She didn't fault the man for his drawl, but the backwoods dialect was an affectation and after all these years it still irked her. Cleon was a senior partner in a prestigious international law firm with clients all over the world.

She said, "You didn't answer my question. Why not Sydney? Why not Oregon?"

"I've got unfinished business in this neck of the woods. What's on tap is gonna discombobulate some in the family."

"What kind of unfinished business?"

"You'll find out soon enough." His blue eyes twinkled with mischief.

Eduardo was right. He *was* up to something and he was enjoying it enormously.

She couldn't help but marvel at his zest for life, his determination to impose dominion over the House of Dobbs to his very last breath. For a few days more, he would hold Death at bay and exert his earthly powers. Well, God bless him. If he left one heir a little more money than another or put a few strings on how his young widow could spend her bundle, so what? Amending his will was the last power he'd wield in this world and anyone who begrudged him the privilege was being petty.

She said, "I hear you brought the Winslow Homers. What a beautiful idea."

"I reckon you're the only one who thinks so."

"If they bring you pleasure, that's all that matters."

"I ain't got around to hangin' 'em. We'll have us an unveilin' soon. Mack can scare us up some wine and cheese and make it festive like."

"Who's Mack?"

"He owns this place. I think of him as the cruise director for my final voyage. He keeps the deck chairs lined up, the liquor flowing, and our various druthers satisfied." He refilled their glasses. "Lucien informs me you've got yourself a beau up in Seattle."

"Not anymore. We split."

"What's the matter? He a dud in the sack?"

"As the attorney I used to work for might say, your question lacks foundation and it's way beyond the scope."

He cackled. "You'd be a hard witness to depose. Allow counsel to reframe the question. Are you well and truly shut of him or am I gonna miss your wedding?"

"You won't miss any wedding. Not mine. Not to… No, I'm definitely shed of him." She was touched that the thought of missing her wedding would bother him. If she had married while he was alive, he would have been the one to give her away.

"Uncle Cleon, I'd like to depose you about something. It doesn't have to be tonight, but I want you to tell me about my father. The truth behind the facts."

"That's a mighty fine distinction, sugah."

"You know what I mean. What was he thinking to botch up our lives the way he did?"

Cleon skewed his mouth to one side and rubbed his jaw. "You asked me why here. I'll ask you why now?"

"I wanted the truth twenty years ago, but everybody coddled and there-thered me and I taught myself not to think about him. I had a secret mantra, one of Grandma's Seminole sayings, and whenever his name popped into my head I'd say it three times to cast out his spirit." She took a fortifying sip of gin. "It wasn't very effective and, like they say, the truth makes you free."

"Truth ain't for sissies, sugah." He seemed to ponder the seriousness of her request. "When you get to my place in life and it's all behind you or fixin' to be, you may want to shade the truth a tetch for your own peace of mind or somebody else's. Knowing too much about the folks we love can lead to a mighty lot of bitterness. But if you gotta know…"

She faltered. Had her father's corruption gone even deeper than she'd imagined?

"Sorry to interrupt, sir." A stocky man with skin the color of wet sand and a close-cropped thatch of wiry hair appeared like a last-minute reprieve.

"Come on in, Mack, and meet my niece, Dinah Pelerin."

Mack smiled and shook her hand. "Ian Mackenzie. Everyone calls me Mack. It's a pleasure to meet you, Dinah."

"Likewise." It came out *lackwise* and she cringed. She was backsliding into the lazy vowels she'd grown up with.

Cleon said, "Don't let his British accent fool you. Mack's mama was a genuine Australian Aborigine. And Dinah's part Native American, Mack. Y'all should hit it off like gin and vermouth."

"I'm sure we will." He turned to Cleon. "You have a telephone call, sir. A private investigator, Mr. Kellerman. He says it's urgent."

Cleon polished off his olive. "When you ain't got but a week, it's all urgent. Show Dinah to her room, Mack. We dine late, sugah, so you can snooze for a couple of hours. I hope you brought a fancy dress. Me kickin' the bucket don't keep Neesha from insistin' on the proprieties."

SEVEN

BEING CRUISE DIRECTOR had its own urgencies. An agitated Aboriginal woman in a white apron flagged Mack down before he and Dinah had reached the stairs.

"There's no baking powder. Lady says follow the recipe, don't leave nothing out, it's his special favorite. How am I gonna follow the recipe for baking powder biscuits without baking powder?" She was short and stout and obviously on the brink of revolt. "You're the head man. You're the one buys all the fixings she wants. You be the one to tell her it can't be done."

"Calm down, Tanya." He tamped the air like a conductor trying to hush a rogue horn. "It's in the pantry."

"I looked there. No baking powder. Just soda."

"I'll take care of it as soon as I've shown Miss Pelerin to her room."

"I got the fish stock for her Charleston bisque simmering, parsnips to peel, cake to ice. Lamb needs watching all the time and her and that crazy doctor standing over my shoulder, do this, do that. You come now or I quit."

"Just tell me the room number," said Dinah. "Indians are born trackers."

He laughed. "Thanks. Room eight, third floor, directly across the hall from Lucien. I set your bag next to the armoire."

Mack and Tanya hurried off to the kitchen and Dinah trudged up the stairs. She'd been looking forward to a bed since the dawn of time and she'd been given two lousy hours to lie in it before they came to roust her out for a fancy-dress dinner. So far, nobody looked or behaved the way she'd expected and as soon as she was rested and thinking straight, she'd think about why. But not tonight. Definitely not in formal attire. She had a cache of Italian Valium tucked away in the bottom of her suitcase. That on top of Cleon's martinis would put her safely out of their clutches until tomorrow. Just let them try to wake her.

At the end of the hall, the lopsided wrought-iron 8 on the door reminded her of handcuffs, which reminded her of Nick, which reminded her what a fool she'd been not to break it off with him sooner. And he wanted her to call him? The monumental gall of the man boggled the mind. Call him? She could only hope he was holding his breath.

She shoved open the door to Number 8 and fell back in surprise as Cantoo threw himself into her shins, yipping and sniffing. "Leave it, Cantoo." K.D. lay on the bottom bunk, her long legs hiked up so that her feet pushed against the mattress above.

"Sorry. Wrong room."

"No, it's not. We're roomies. You get the top bunk."

Dinah ran her eyes around the seedy little room, made even less desirable by the pert, pink-jeaned presence of K.D. So much for privacy.

Hell, a bed was a bed. She didn't plan to be conscious for long. Her suitcase was next to the armoire, as promised. She hoisted it onto a luggage rack, unzipped the lid, and felt around for the Valium.

"I'm writing a short story about each of the seven deadly sins," announced K.D. A spiral notebook rested on her bare tummy and she waggled a pen between her manicured fingers. "My English teacher says they're the tools of the writer's trade. Can you name them?"

"Wrath," said Dinah. The Valium was gone. Surely

she'd packed more neatly than this. Had one of those Transportation Security goons rummaged through her suitcase and lifted it? Didn't they have to notify you if they confiscated your stuff? Or had somebody else…? She regarded her roomie with budding suspicion.

K.D. didn't notice. "I've already finished the Wrath story. Living with Thad makes that a no-brainer. The one I'm working on now is Lust. Mother says that ladies don't Lust, they only Love, but Mother is so Victorian."

Dinah shook a few aspirin into her palm. "Where's the bathroom?"

"There's a sink and a toilet in there." She nodded toward a warped door on the far side of the bed. "The shower's at the other end of the hall."

Terrific. She may as well have said the other end of the earth. Dinah yanked open the sticky bathroom door, found a clean glass above the sink and turned on the faucet. At the last instant, she saw the spider. Ruthlessly, she sluiced it down the sink in a torrent of scalding water and rinsed the glass. She downed the aspirin and examined the toilet seat on both sides for spiders before sitting down. Tomorrow she would light out for Katherine, on foot if necessary, and check into a hotel. She would phone the Russell Crowe guy, Robbie whatshisname, send Uncle Cleon a nice note and a box of cigars, and let the dead bury the dead.

When she emerged from the toilet, K.D. started up where she'd left off. "I've based all of my stories on Daddy's life, only I've given the characters different names and occupations. Daddy says I need to watch out I'm not sued for libel."

"Mm."

"That doesn't mean there isn't lots of verisimilitude, which means Truth. Verisimilitude and observation are the keys to great writing. My teacher says that a writer must be constantly observing Life."

"Sounds strenuous." Sneezing repeatedly, Dinah pulled a dress and a couple of shirts out of her jumbled suitcase and hung them in the armoire. Tomorrow, she thought. Tomorrow I'll tell Uncle Cleon I'm allergic to the dog and move into a hotel in Katherine.

"Envy's another of the deadly sins," continued K.D., failing to observe Dinah's conspicuous disinterest. "That story is mostly about Margaret. I called her Millicent. She's an aging movie star married to a brilliant film director, Charles—that's Daddy, of course. She gets fat after having a baby and he divorces her to marry Sybil. Sybil's your mother, Swan." The name Swan came saturated with condescension.

Dinah's hackles rose. "My mother didn't set out to wreck Cleon's marriage, you know. He pursued her. Relentlessly."

"She used her wiles on him," said K.D., supremely self-assured. "So. When Charles finds out that Sybil's cheated on him, he's devastated at first. But then he meets a beautiful model, Natasha, that's *my* mother, and falls passionately in love. Sybil's onto the next man and doesn't care, but Millicent envies Natasha's power over Charles because she wants her son Wharton to inherit his fortune. Wharton is my name for Wendell."

What a rigmarole, thought Dinah. Yet it wasn't so awfully far from the reality. The family mythology had soaked into her own imagination just as it had soaked into K.D.'s. Cleon forsaking his first wife, Margaret, and their son, Wendell, to run off with Swan Fately, a fiery Seminole beauty. His legendary crackup when Swan took their son, Lucien, and ran off with Hart Pelerin. Cleon's fight to win joint custody of Lucien. The period of reconciliation during which he offered his friendship to Swan and her new husband and showered gifts and attention on their daughter, Dinah. The shock and upheaval following Hart Pelerin's death. Cleon's strange and abiding alliance with Margaret and finally, his May-December marriage to a former Miss Georgia, Neesha Symms. K.D. had enough material for several potboilers.

Dinah sifted through her suitcase for a nightshirt and came up with an oversized tee with "Feel Safe Tonight, Sleep With A Cop" stenciled on the back. Shit. This is what came of hasty packing. Was this all she had to sleep in? If she'd been alone, she'd have set fire to it and slept in the nude. She gritted her teeth, stripped off her sweaty clothes and slipped into the damned thing.

The Constant Observer looked up from her opus. "Do you sleep with a cop?"

"No."

"Then why do you wear that?"

"Penance. I bought it in the hair shirt department at Nordstrom." Tomorrow she'd go into town and buy a replacement. Something with a picture of Russell Crowe or a wallaby. She climbed up to the top bunk and clasped a pillow over her chest. Why had Nick called? Was he arrogant enough to think she'd ever speak to him again?

"I haven't had actual sex yet," said K.D. "There aren't any mature boys in my school. They're all really short, and sooo dorky. I feel I'm ready for a sexual experience, but with an older man. Someone worldly and evolved. Like Aleksandr Petrovsky on *Sex and the City*."

Dinah squashed the pillow over her face. How long had Nick been cheating and who was that redhead? She'd seen her someplace before. How many others had there been? Tomorrow, she'd ask Cleon's doctor for a dose of Penicillin. Better safe than venereal.

The author prated on. "A name says so much about a character, don't you think? Wharton is stuffy and boring, like poor Wendell. Millicent is old-timey and strait-laced like Margaret and Sybil is sooo pagan. The perfect name for your mother. Of course, the story has lots of conflict and bitchy dialogue."

Dinah was tempted to give the little hack a one-on-one tutorial in bitchiness, punctuated by a few hard whaps to the derriere. But she hadn't defended her mother's honor since fifth grade when she lopped off Mindy Frye's pony-tail for calling her a squaw. A lot had changed since then and it was hard to explain her mother's flighty tempera-ment and serial, short-lived marriages. Even so, if K.D.'s stories were meant for Cleon's reading, she'd be well ad-vised to sheathe her claws. He had an old-school sense of gallantry about the women he'd loved and didn't like them meowing about each other.

"Daddy's old secretary, Darla, is the protagonist of the Lust story. He had an affair with her before he met Mother and they went to Paris together once or twice. She still writes to him. Mother doesn't like it, but Daddy just laughs. He cherishes loyalty. I call Darla Dierdre and she's an equestrienne, because I'm mad about horses. Write what you know. That's key. But I need a mysterious set-ting. Paris is so trite. What's the most mysterious place you've ever been?"

Kingdom Come! The torturers at Guantánamo could take lessons from this chatterbox. "I don't know. Istanbul."

"That's actually rather good. I just read about Turkey in my social studies class."

There was the sound of energetic scribbling. Dinah rolled over and thought about Turkey, where she'd gone to study First Century cave churches with her anthropology professor a few years back. The most prevalent superstition in Turkey is a belief in the evil eye. If a person looks with envy at another man's wife or his children or his orchard, the power of that envious look can cause illness or injury or even death. Everyone carries a talisman to stave off the evil eye. She wished she had a talisman to stave off the obnoxious author, something to cause sleepiness or writer's block or speechlessness. A gag and a roll of duct tape came to mind.

"Okay, how's this? Charles murders an evil imam and there's a fatwa against him. He flees down an alley, climbs over a wall, and drops into Dierdre's garden. He breaks into her house to steal some clothes and disguise himself and Dierdre walks into her bedroom and sees him undressed. So here comes the good part: *Dierdre's sultry, sapphire eyes devoured the glistening beauty of his naked, virile body and she lusted for him with every fiber of her being.*"

With every fiber of her being, Dinah wished she could strangle this pest. She strangled her pillow instead and tried to ignore her, but there was no ignoring K.D.

"Are you listening up there? What do you think? Is *every fiber* too much of a cliché? It's what Eduardo said to Lucien the other day. *You've cheated and you've lied and I'll make you regret it with every fiber of your being.*"

So that's what's eating them, thought Dinah, and fell asleep feeling even more down on love.

EIGHT

THERE WAS A racket. Knocking, barking, voices, a banging door. Dinah rolled over and nearly tumbled off the bunk. She held onto the edge and focused. K.D., in a rustle of fuchsia satin, pirouetted and preened.

"That was Mackenzie," she said and twirled in front of the armoire mirror. "You have a half-hour until dinner. Did you bring an evening dress? Mother says just because Daddy moved us into this horror doesn't mean we can't still be chic."

Dinah's self-restraint was waning fast. "I didn't know your father's death would be cause for a gala."

"You needn't be sarcastic. Daddy's made us all promise not to cry for him. He's lived a magnificent life and he wants no hearts and flowers." She glossed her lips and tossed her hair. "Anyway, you're not even his real niece." And she sailed out the door with Cantoo romping along behind.

"Shit." Dinah pushed herself out of the squishy mattress and climbed down from her roost. As she stepped onto the bottom bunk, something sharp dug into her foot. "Double shit!"

It was the wire binding of the Constant Observer's anthology of deadly sins. She picked up the notebook and leafed through it. In addition to the titled stories, K.D. had devoted a separate section to each member of the family. Cleon, Neesha, Margaret, Wendell, Lucien, Eduardo and an apparently recent entry for Dinah. After that bombshell about Lucien cheating, Dina couldn't resist reading what the little snoop had gleaned from her eavesdropping. Maybe lust was what was eating Lucien, and jealousy was what was eating Eduardo.

E. and L. fought every single day in Sydney, but E. was beside himself after the snake bit L. L. spent two whole days behind closed doors with Mack after we got here. E. totally postal after that. L. fought with Daddy last night, too. Both drinking. I think L. has something Daddy wants.

Uh-oh. Could Mack be the Other Man? That would certainly make an interesting triangle.
She skipped to the entry on herself.

I guess you could call her attractive in a dark, foreign way. (Her eyes are black as a voodoo spell.) Mother thinks she's sharp-tongued and pushy and she can't understand why Daddy is so attached to her. Everybody knows how slutty her mother is. And D. sleeps with a policeman. How plebeian is that?

Dinah threw the book down and stalked off to the toilet. When had she been sharp-tongued? Whenever she went home to Georgia and had to socialize, she talked so sweet her teeth itched. And as for her mother being slutty, Swan Fately might be fickle. She might marry and divorce too casually and too often. But she had more class and generosity in her little finger than Neesha had in her whole body. More than K.D. would have if she lived to be a hundred. More than I have, too, thought Dinah, sorry she hadn't stuck up for her. Lucien would have.
She appraised her voodoo eyes in the mirror above the

rust-stained basin. You shouldn't have come, she told her reflection. You should have sent a wreath or a headless chicken. Jeez!

The aroma of roasting meat wafted up from the kitchen. Her stomach growled. The last meal she remembered was a brick of kiln-dried lasagna and two sawdust breadsticks at 30,000 feet over the Pacific. Even more than sleep, she needed food. Just chill, Dinah. Put on your game face and go out there and strew compliments and congeniality like beads at Mardi Gras.

She donned her all-purpose little black dress, which was her only dress, pinned a pair of crystal shoulder-dusters in her ears, and pronounced herself passable. For a pushy foreigner. For a freaking wake. She squared her shoulders and marched downstairs.

On the second floor landing, a scratching noise arrested her attention and she stuck her head around the corner. Thad and a black boy of about the same age were picking a lock on a door at the end of the hall. She ducked out of sight and listened to them whispering and sniggering.

The punks. They must be ripping off the whole house on a room-by-room basis. And who rated a room with a lock in this fleabag? Looting her room had been as easy as turning the knob.

Well, if they thought they could get away with it, they had another think coming. There wasn't enough Valium in the bottle to do more than make them drowsy, but she'd make sure the next pills they swiped out of her suitcase would teach them a lesson. She added a strong laxative to her Katherine shopping list and continued downstairs.

In the great room, everyone milled about with a cocktail in hand. Dinah stood on the periphery and watched. Cleon was engaged in conversation with a thickset, silver-haired man in a belted safari jacket. He sported a full, salt-and-pepper beard and a cigarette in a plastic filter clenched between his teeth. By the process of elimination, she ID'd him as Dr. Desmond Fisher.

Neesha, glamorous in a clingy, floor-length mauve gown, sat enthroned in one of the leather chairs in the center of the room. Her platinum hair was hooked behind one ear and her plump lips curved in a rueful smile. She held out her right hand to Wendell, Cleon's eldest, and said, "It's from that elegant little shop in the Harbour Hotel. A keepsake from Cleon."

Wendell, balder and heavier than when Dinah last saw him, bent forward in his chair for a closer look. He'd been a football jock in high school and college, but time and the sedentary life of a banker had turned muscle to fat and his jacket strained at the seams. His face was solemn and stiff, as if he'd been botoxed from the eyes down, and his voice was sepulchral. "That's quite a rock."

Eduardo rolled Lucien's wheelchair to Neesha's side and the two of them bowed their heads over the ring like lapidaries. "Well, aren't we the pampered one," said Eduardo. "How many carats?"

"Ten." She dropped her chin and lifted her eyes, studiedly demure. "Of course, he shouldn't have."

"You deserve twenty," said Lucien, "after all these years putting up with the old tyrant."

She threw a nervous look around the room and took back her hand.

Eddie giggled. If he was steamed about Lucien's cheating, he was covering it well.

Cleon's first wife Margaret, a handsome woman in her early sixties with gray-blond hair sleeked back from a widow's peak into a bun at the nape of her neck, leaned her back against the bar and surveyed the room, alert as a raptor. She was that rare woman who actually looked good in gold lamé.

Dinah had to start somewhere and Margaret was the one standing closest to the champagne. Dinah went to say hello. "Margaret. It's good to see you."

"Dinah, Cleon must be tickled pink. He tried to woo your mother into coming, but she had too much sense. You'll be his consolation prize."

Grin and bear it, thought Dinah. Up to a point. She poured herself a flute of champagne. "It's just possible that Uncle Cleon likes me for myself, Margaret."

She smiled and put a hand on Dinah's arm. "I didn't mean that the way it sounded. I happen to know that Cleon likes you very much, indeed, and so do I. I'm overjoyed to have somebody with a brain to talk to." She shifted her eyes to Neesha. "The widow-in-waiting is blinging tonight. That bauble must've addled her brain or she wouldn't have let him Svengali her to this boondocks."

"You've got more sense than anyone I know, Margaret. How'd he Svengali you?"

"When I married him forty years ago I wanted the usual *'til death do us part* boilerplate. He overruled me with *so long as we both shall love*. Providence has finally overruled him and I wouldn't miss this parting for all the tea in China."

Dinah saw what Eduardo meant about grief being in short supply.

Margaret's out-of-context smile was disconcerting. "Cleon can pull the wool over Neesha's eyes. She's never looked any deeper than his pockets. But I know him down to the ground. He's plotting something."

"Changing his will, you mean?"

"There's that. I'd hate to see him do Wendell out of his rightful share of the estate. Wen's a good son, but he's a cream puff. He won't stand up to Cleon or compete for his birthright. But Cleon's nothing if not devious. Something tells me the will is a red herring." She gestured with her eyes toward Neesha. "Miss Georgia made a mistake by letting him come to Australia by himself."

"Hasn't she been with him in Sydney these last few months?"

"No, no. She didn't want to take the children out of school in Atlanta. She and the kids arrived in Sydney only a day or so before Wendell and I did."

K.D. hovered behind her mother's chair, no doubt gathering material for her little book of invective. Neesha kept up a conversation with Wendell while darting surreptitious looks at Margaret and herself. Eduardo and Lucien had gone off into a corner by themselves. They seemed simpatico, although Eduardo's smile appeared somewhat forced.

Margaret's eyes sparkled with malice. "Neesha and I declared a truce in Sydney, but I don't think she quite believes it."

The doctor emitted a braying laugh at something Cleon had said and Cleon clapped him on the shoulder and chuckled. Eduardo said that Cleon had given Fisher an earful in Sydney, but they certainly seemed chummy enough tonight. Margaret excused herself and moved off to listen in on their conversation.

In a black dinner jacket befitting a gig at Buckingham Palace, Mack sallied across the room with a tray of canapés. "The kitchen isn't equipped to handle a large number of hors d'oeuvres. I'm afraid the shrimp got a bit crusty under the broiler."

"They look great to me." Dinah helped herself to two.

"The place isn't officially open for business, but your uncle was adamant. Don't sweat the niceties, he said. But

I wish there was more and better help in the kitchen. Your party are the first guests."

She said, "I can live without some niceties, but I'm squeamish about spiders."

"You saw a spider?"

"It was tiny, but one roomie's enough."

"It was probably an assassin. They eat other spiders."

"Then I'm sorry I killed it. I'm also squeamish about snakes. I hope there are no more death adders lurking around."

"I'm sure what happened to Lucien was a oncer."

Maybe death adders weren't everyday callers at Crow Hill, but his offhanded certainty made her want to knock wood. "How long have you been running the lodge, Mack?"

"I bought it last year. The place had been derelict for a long time. I've been slow to renovate. More spiders than money, I'm afraid. Ultimately, I plan to turn it into a destination resort with original Aboriginal art in every room and art and cultural tours. Of course, I'll need to raise quite a lot of money. Your uncle's offer to pay top dollar for a week's stay was a godsend."

Dinah wanted to ask if the price covered the risk of allowing an illegal suicide on the premises, but self-censored. Mack might not know. And if he wondered why a wealthy American sought out his spidery, no-niceties inn in the boonies, top dollar had evidently allayed his concerns.

Tanya, the disgruntled Aboriginal cook, came around with a tray of stuffed mushrooms. Mack took one for himself and one for Dinah. "You can manage two trays at once, can't you, Tanya?" He pressed the shrimp tray into her free hand.

She glared mutinously and stumped off with a tray balanced precariously on either arm.

Dinah foresaw employee relations issues in Mack's future. "What did you do before taking on this place, Mack?"

"I was concierge at the Godfrey Arms in London. When the hotel went bankrupt and closed its doors, I decided to return to Australia, reconnect with my roots, and track down my birth mother." He glanced around the room. Everyone was deep in conversation and Tanya was circulating with the shrimp. "If you'd like, I'll show you some of what I have in mind for the place."

"Sure." Maybe he had a private room in mind for her.

He led her back into the foyer, past the stairs, and turned left down a long, dismal hallway. A few paces along and another, shorter hall turned left again and doglegged behind the stairs. Dinah followed Mack to where it dead-ended at a dwarf-sized door. What was this? A storm cellar? A storage room? The pit where he kept his pet snake?

He opened the door, switched on the light, and motioned her inside.

She looked at the diminutive door and balked. "You know, Eduardo is wild about interior design. He'd just love to see your ideas. I'll run back and get him."

Mack's chin jutted. "I assure you I'm thoroughly domesticated and trustworthy." He turned a cold, indignant shoulder, stooped, and went inside.

Oh, for crying out loud. She was probably being paranoid.

"Geronimo," she said under her breath and followed him three steps down into the basement.

NINE

"Wow!"

The room was windowless but beautifully lit and redolent of fresh paint. Shelves lined the back wall and Aboriginal art adorned the other three. A campaign table in the center of the room was stacked with books on Aboriginal art, culture, and mythology.

"This is my study." He smiled broadly, mollified by her admiration.

"I can see where Lucien's been learning about Aboriginal myths and art."

"He's been in to browse every day. He's going to buy two paintings and Neesha's also expressed a strong interest. The paintings are all by highly respected local artists, and all based on Aboriginal myths."

It sounded like a sales pitch. She said, "Aboriginal mythology seems so much more esoteric and mystical than other mythologies I've studied. My Western bias, I guess." She stroked the feathers on a pair of brightly painted poles. "What are these?"

"They're morning star poles, used in burial ceremonies. The morning star connects the feathered string to the deceased's soul to guide it to the Land of the Dead."

She spied a quartet of intricately painted sticks in the corner. Each stick was different, whimsical, like figures in some children's game. "These are fun."

"Burial poles. The more ornate the pole, the more important the dead man."

Was she hypersensitive or did the Top End overdo the death motif? She ambled around the room taking in the art. There were crocodiles and crocodile men in a design of wavy lines and diamonds. There was a kangaroo with x-ray bones being speared by an elongated striped man. There were leaves and flowers and arcane symbols in a complex mosaic of dots, all in the vivid ochres and browns and reds of the Australian earth.

"It's a fascinating collection. A fine start toward re-connecting."

He riffled through some papers on the table and handed her a magazine article titled *The Stolen Generation*. "Until nineteen-seventy-one, it was the policy of the Australian government to assimilate their Aborigines through a pro-gram of eugenics until the race died out. This agenda en-tailed, among other things, the removal of mixed race children like myself from their black mothers and place-ment in detention centers. I was one of those children."

"You grew up in a detention center?"

"After a year I was adopted by an English couple. They took me back to England and I grew up with only a vague awareness of my origins."

She supposed from the relatively light color of his skin that Mack's non-Aboriginal parent was white. "You have no idea who your real father might have been?"

"None. He was probably just some drunk who raped an Aborigine woman and went cavalierly on his way." His tone was caustic.

"How old were you when you were adopted?"

"About three."

"And now you're back to reclaim your Aboriginal iden-tity."

"Well, I won't chant or dance or do any body painting. Not while your family is visiting anyway."

Dinah laughed. "Wise decision. Neesha would brook no body painting. She's really pouring on the pomp."

"She wants to make the last few days of Cleon's life a celebration rather than a prelude to death, something she and the children can remember in a positive way."

So he did know. Not finicky about the nation's laws, she decided.

She paused in front of a large serpent coiled around what she assumed were eggs. "Snakes seem to figure prominently in Aboriginal art and mythology. Is this the Taipan?"

"Not necessarily. The Rainbow serpent is known by many names. He's the father who gave healing powers to the shamans. He could create or destroy. The painting next to it is the mother deity who gives us our monsoons here in the North. Her travels across the land during the Dreaming formed the topography of Kakadu National Park. It's a World Heritage site. For cultural as well as natural reasons."

"I had an anthropology professor in college who'd be enthralled by your myths."

Clearly, Mack was enthralled. He could scarcely contain his enthusiasm. "There are thousands of stories handed down orally from generation to generation. These last few months I've immersed myself, compiling my own dictionary of deities and symbols."

"Then maybe you can explain song lines to me. I was reading about them, but I can't quite grasp the concept."

"Try to think of them as footprints, the trails of the ancestors who created the land. In the beginning of the Dreaming, there were no visible landmarks. As the ancestors traveled and assumed different shapes, the world took on shape. Their songs brought the land into existence and each geographical feature retains their spiritual essence and perpetuates it."

She said, "It sounds similar to the Native Americans' reverence for the earth."

"Similar, but song lines are more than that. These paintings, the ceremonies, the storytelling and dancing—all Aboriginal art forms are song lines. The ancestors live on in everything around us and continue to impart their wisdom to those in a receptive state of mind."

Dinah envied the Aborigines their rapport with the dead. She had a hard time gouging information out of the living.

A painting of a turtle stopped her cold. "Mack, did you hear anything about a journalist who was murdered on top of a sea turtle on Melville Island last week?"

"Oh, yes. The papers were full of it. The fact that he died on Aboriginal land brought the local population a lot of unwanted publicity. Tourism is a growing part of the economy. Anything that scares away visitors is a problem."

"Was there much speculation about who might have killed the man?"

"One paper speculated that he was killed by pirates. Piracy's become more common of late. Another tried to make a case against the Tiwis. Completely unfair. In fact, the coverage came perilously close to racist."

"What was the murdered man's name?"

"Hambrick, I believe. Bryce Hambrick."

"I understand he made some enemies in the green movement. A man I met in Darwin thought the killer was a greenie terrorist."

"Strange things have been happening in several of our coastal areas. I've heard rumors of poaching and vandalism and thefts. But I don't believe environmentalists had anything to do with Hambrick's murder."

"Why not?"

"Because they are by and large nonviolent people who respect the earth and want to make it a better place. Like the Aborigines. But the police have turned a blind eye to other groups, people with far more reason to kill anyone who got in their way."

"What groups?"

"The boat people."

"You mean illegal immigrants?"

"That's right." His delivery grew animated. Obviously, Jacko wasn't the only one gripped by the Hambrick murder mystery. "Some from Indonesia. Some from the Middle East by way of Indonesia. Iraqis, some of them, people habituated to war and violence."

"Are boat people a problem in Australia?"

"Enough so that the government has detention camps and sponsors TV ads warning asylum seekers against debarking in certain coastal areas. They could find themselves a midnight snack for sharks or crocs."

She was surprised that Jacko hadn't considered the boat people. Maybe he'd been too fixated on the relevance of the water spirit. Did the turtle have any bearing on the Brit's murder, or was it just in the wrong place at the wrong time? "Mack, do you know any Aboriginal myths about sea turtles?"

"Let's see." He communed with the ceiling for a few seconds. "During the Dreamtime, there were two turtle sisters who had a secret reservoir of water under their shells. They were selfish and tried to keep all the water for themselves, but a kangaroo rat kicked them in the chest and water geysered out all over the place and formed the lagoons and creeks and rivers."

Dinah didn't think the man who speared the turtle on Melville Island was looking for water. The poor creature was probably just an unlucky bystander. She halfway wished Jacko were here to "noodle" a few more theories with her. Unless the police solved the crime soon, she might never find out what happened.

"Mack, thank you so much for sharing all this with me. I truly hope you're able to locate your mother."

"It's rather a forlorn hope. The adoption records were destroyed and I don't even know which clan she belonged to."

"Your adoptive parents don't know anything at all?"

"Only that my father was an American serviceman. The records at the time contained a note that my birth mother had contacted the American Embassy to ask them to intervene because I was half-American."

Dinah judged Mack to be somewhere in his mid-to-late thirties, which would place this putative American serviceman in the Vietnam age bracket.

A wild thought sprang into her mind. Oh, Jesus. Oh, Jericho and Jerusalem. Could this be the answer to *why here*? Was former Marine Lieutenant Cleon Dobbs's decision to change his will and do himself in at Ian Mackenzie's middle-of-nowhere hostelry a coincidence, or was he going to announce over dinner that he'd fathered an Aborigine son out of wedlock?

"You looked perplexed," Mack said.

"What? No, no. It's just hard to believe how heartless a…a government can be."

He said something, but she didn't hear. She was gnawing on Cleon's remark about unfinished business in this neck of the woods. She was mulling the implications of the verb *discombobulate*.

TEN

"DEAR DINAH. WE'RE so happy you could be here." Neesha simpered and held out her arms.

Dinah squeezed out an answering smile, steadied herself, and forged into the dining room. "You look well, Neesha. The strain doesn't show."

"You're sweet to say so. We're all under a dark cloud, of course."

Dinah frowned. Was it possible she knew about Mack's origins and was making a bad double entendre?

"What a darling little dress you're wearing. I told K.D. that you'd wear something simple as pie and make it look chic. I know you think we're puttin' on the dog, but the finery is for Cleon. I want his last hours to be filled with beauty, even in this depressing place."

"He doesn't seem depressed," said Dinah.

"Oh, he is. We all are. We're just trying to make it easy on one another. It's what Cleon wants."

Cleon had already ensconced himself at the head of the long, rectangular dining table. "I trust you ladies won't take umbrage if an old invalid don't rise for y'all."

"Of course not," said Neesha. "Here's my place card. Don't you want me next to you, Cleon?"

"Not tonight, darlin'. I told Tanya to shuffle us up, give a couple of the others a chance to partake of my companionship."

Wendell held out Neesha's chair for her, one seat removed from Cleon.

"Thank you, kind sir." Neesha patted the chair to her left. "And dear Dinah's gonna be right here next to me."

Wendell held out the chair for Dinah. She exchanged a look with Cleon and sat down with a nebulous sense of dread. There was enough tension without the introduction of a brand new Dobbs.

Eduardo flitted around the table humming tunelessly, reading the place cards. "Here you are, Lucien, in the hot seat again." He moved a chair out of the way and parked Lucien's wheelchair between Cleon and Neesha. "Voilà."

Cleon said, "But for your fine manners elevatin' the tone, I don't reckon we could call ourselves civilized, Eduardo."

Eduardo sashayed around the table and found his place card in the middle of the table directly opposite Dinah. He leaned across the table and mouthed, "See what I mean?"

Wendell seated Margaret and Little Miss Hatchet Job, K.D., and took his place at the foot of the table opposite Cleon.

Cleon said, "You fairly outdo yourself bein' chivalrous, Wendell. We shoulda named him Lancelot, shouldn't we, Maggie?"

Lucien laughed and Cleon turned his mischievous eyes on him. "On the subject of names, I hear tell that in Da Vinci's paintin' of the Last Supper, nobody knows if it's John or Mary at the right hand of Jesus."

Dinah couldn't believe her ears. Cleon never dissed Lucien or anybody else for being gay. He had stood against bigotry of all kinds for as long as she'd known him. It was one of his most endearing qualities. Was he trying to provoke a fight?

Lucien scowled. "Since when did you give a damn about art or religion?"

"Don't underestimate me, son. I could have a death-bed conversion."

"Lucien." Neesha diverted his attention. "Is your poor leg simply excruciating? Eduardo says you're back painting already. Tell me about it, do."

Seemingly relieved by the distraction, Lucien jockeyed his wheelchair closer to the table and started to regurgitate the Taipan myth.

Dr. Fisher entered the room carrying a highball and looking deeply self-satisfied.

He walked around the table and found his place on Dinah's left. "You must be Dinah. Desmond Fisher. Call me Dez. Everybody does." He gave off an effluvium of cigarette smoke and the Hemingway beard could have used a thorough wash and a trim. His Australian accent wasn't nearly as broad as Jacko's, but he had an irritating, staccato speaking style.

"Nice to meet you, Dez."

"You don't remember me, do you?"

She acknowledged that she did not.

"Wouldn't expect you to. You were climbing trees and chasing a pair of wild kittens around the yard back then. I went hunting with your father once or twice."

"You knew my father?"

"Crow Hill's not the most luxurious place to carry out your uncle's last wishes, but Big Brother prohibits suicide so we had to improvise."

"Right. I never knew my father hunted. When was this?"

"Government nannies putting their beaks in everybody's business, protecting us from ourselves. If we're not careful, they'll regulate what we can eat and drink. Can't even lie in the sun without catching a scolding. And look how they've pared away the rights of smokers. You a smoker, Dinah?"

"Once in a while. About my Dad, what can you...?"

"Good girl. Don't let the stickybeaks tell you what to do."

"You've drunk too many Scotches, Desmond." Margaret's voice was freighted with disapproval. "Don't harangue the girl."

"And don't you be a killjoy, Margaret. We're here to give Cleon a rousing send-off, isn't that right, Cleon?"

"That's the plan," said Cleon. "Wouldn't want anybody killin' the joy."

Eduardo rolled his eyes.

Lucien uttered a short laugh and resumed his conversation with Neesha. "Tell me about your plans for the gallery, Neesha."

"Well, it's got a super location right on Peachtree Road near the Phipps Plaza and it's just a fabulous space. Cleon's already paid for the first year's lease. I've got several pieces on consignment from a great Atlanta artist, Laura Mitchell. Do you know her? But I'd love for you and Eduardo to introduce me to some of your artist friends and acquire some good pieces. Of course, I'd be happy to hang your work. And would you help me pack the Homers for the return flight? I think I should buy extra insurance, don't you. I simply couldn't bear to lose them."

Dinah tried to steer the doctor back to the subject she was interested in. "You were telling me about my father, Doctor...Dez."

"Hart Pelerin?" He put away the last of his Scotch and looked around as if he needed a refill. "Yes, sorry to hear about his death. Untimely. Couldn't have been much past forty. Young or old, we all die. Trouble is, people don't accept the reality. Cleon's got the right idea, leave on your own terms. You have a living will, Dinah?"

"I don't have a will of any kind."

"Well, you should, and a medical directive that prescribes how far they should take resuscitation efforts when you're in a vegetative state and unable to speak for yourself like that woman in Florida. What's her name?"

"Terri Schiavo?"

"That's the one. Keeled over brain-dead at twenty-six. If she'd had a medical directive and a living will, she'd have saved her family and the whole country a lot of hoo-ha. They'd have pulled the plug. It pays to plan ahead."

Dinah suppressed a whimper. It was going to be a long evening and the doctor was going to ride his hobbyhorse from soup to nuts. Or until she went nuts. Maybe in the morning when he wasn't soused, she could get him to share his recollections of her father.

"Shall I pour the first wine, sir?" Mack had lined up a row of wine bottles on the sideboard behind Dinah's chair.

"I reckon we're about settled," said Cleon. "Let Neesha be the taster. She chose it."

Mack took a white wine out of a tub of ice and poured an inch into Neesha's glass.

She swished it around and tasted. "Pouilly Fuissé. It's scrumptious."

"At the price, it oughta be," said Cleon. "Pour it all around, Mack, and sit down." He thumped the plate to his left. "You've got my left wing."

The seating arrangement confirmed Dinah's suspicions that Mack was due for a genealogical eye-opener. When he finished pouring, he took his assigned seat beside Cleon. A vacant chair remained between himself and Margaret.

Thad. Dinah felt a twinge of alarm. Where was the little perp? Had he boosted more drugs from other people's rooms? A doctor could have narcotics or opiates in his bag. He'd have the lethal drug meant for Cleon.

As if reading her thoughts, Cleon demanded, "Where's Thadeus?"

"He'll be down in a minute, dear." Neesha's smile turned hectic. "You know how he gets caught up in whatever he's doing and forgets the time."

"Only an idiot forgets to feed hisself. He havin' one of his squirrely days?"

"He's not an idiot, Cleon. He's just not punctual."

"He's damned peculiar is what he is. We got the psychiatrist's bills to prove it."

"Thad's coping with a lot of confusion and this, this suicide you're subjecting us to is too much. He has attention deficit disorder. What did you expect?"

"All right, Neesha, you've made your point. Lord knows, his peculiarity don't stand out none in this family."

Doesn't, thought Dinah. His peculiarity *doesn't* stand out *any*. But the news that Thad had psychiatric problems ramped her stress level into the red zone. She was on the verge of declaring an emergency when the kid shambled into the room and flopped into the chair between Margaret and Mack.

Cleon said, "You gonna tell us why you're late to the table, Thadeus?"

"If I'd known you'd be raggin' on me I wouldn't be here at all."

"You'd be here if I had to hogtie you. Push your hair out of your face and straighten your necktie. You look like a heathen."

"Oh, for chrissakes," said Lucien. "Don't take out your spite on the kid."

"Discipline ain't spite, but what do any of my young'uns

know about discipline? It ain't a trait that runs rampant in our family."

Wendell said, "Don't be too hard on him, Dad. He didn't mean any disrespect, now did you, Thad?"

Neesha smiled her gratitude.

But Lucien was off on a tangent. "If we lack discipline, it's because you never noticed us when we were good. The only times you notice us are when we raise hell."

Here we go, thought Dinah. The customary Lucien-Cleon headbutt.

Neesha tried pouring oil on troubled waters. "Neither you nor Cleon is feeling well, Lucien, but this isn't the time or the place for such talk."

Wendell said, "Dad's work was very demanding. He did the best that he could and he's been openhanded and generous with all of us. To say otherwise is ungrateful and downright mean-spirited." He had a ponderous speaking style. It wasn't just his Southern accent. It was as if each word labored under a heavy weight of gravitas.

"Money," said Lucien, "was what he gave us instead of time. When did he ever ask how your life was going, Wen, or give you a pat on the back for being such a Boy Scout? It's not like he supported our interests or talents."

K.D. piped up. "You're being childish, Lucien. Daddy is extremely supportive of my writing. And your plebeian paintings are all over the house in Atlanta."

"If they are," said Lucien, "it's because of Neesha. Dad's only interested in dead artists."

Margaret said, "It surprises me, Lucien, that you think Cleon didn't pay you enough attention as a child. He was so smitten with your mother, I'd have thought you got the best of his fathering. I hope he apportions his estate more impartially."

"For heaven's sake," said Wendell, "don't go down that road again, mother."

"He deserted you when you were in diapers, Wen. It wounded you emotionally."

"He deserted you, not me, and I'm not wounded."

"Can't we please have a peaceful dinner together without all this bickering?" pleaded Neesha.

Cleon chortled as if the bickering entertained him hugely. "Now people, don't y'all be perturbed by Lucien mouthin' off. He was just playin' a broken-winged mama duck to draw my ill humor away from Thad, and so he has. Top up everybody's wine, Mack. The gang's all here. Let's carpe this fine diem."

ELEVEN

DINAH WOKE UP clammy and disoriented. A spider roved across the ceiling, not two feet above her face. The smell of mildew and dry rot and dog dander clogged her sinuses. From somewhere deep in the recesses of the architecture, Willie Nelson and Julio Iglesias sang, *To all the girls I've loved before, who've traveled in and out my door...*

Last night's dinner came back to her in a reflux of disagreeable flashbacks. Fisher maundering about death. Lucien whining about ancient injustices. Eduardo rolling his eyes. Wendell acting the goody-goody, Neesha fawning, Margaret gloating, the twins being their usual insufferable selves. Cleon pushing everybody's buttons and chortling. He hadn't sprung the news about Mack's parentage and Mack seemed unaware that his status was about to change. Maybe the private eye who'd telephoned Cleon with the urgent matter had other things to check out before he could validate Mack's bona fides. Or maybe she'd guessed wrong. Anyway, the evening was about as much fun as a blister. A whole passel of blisters. So far as she could see, the only plus at this end of the globe was a minus: there was no Nick.

Keeping a wary eye on the spider, she sat up and dangled her feet over the edge of the bunk. How long before she stopped thinking about Nick when she woke up in the morning? How long before she stopped missing his hands and his mouth?

A wave of mortification engulfed her. She jumped to

the floor, threw off the odious Sleep With A Cop night-shirt, and dressed for a hike down the hall to the shower. She took some comfort from the fact that K.D. was already out and about. One crack from that piss-ant this morning and she'd skin her alive.

The hall was dark and empty and the communal wash-room unlocked. She slipped inside and slid the bolt. The room smelled of some eye-wateringly potent disinfectant. She hung her clothes on the door hook, whisked aside the white plastic shower curtain, and inspected the area for spiders. The shower was the size of an upright coffin, dis-colored and leaky, but spider-free. She ran the water from cold to lukewarm, stepped inside, and tried to project the course of her life post-Crow Hill.

As present, her debts exceeded her assets by just a few hundred. But if she didn't get her act together soon, she'd be destitute, busking on street corners and passing the hat. She didn't need or want a lot of money, just enough to af-ford a measure of freedom. She liked to think of herself as an intelligent woman who hadn't yet found her niche, and that someday she would do big things—*Golden Bough*-ish things. That lost city, the myth-laden relics, they were out there just waiting for her to show up and reveal them to the world. Or so she'd once believed. Lately, she was beginning to fear that the greatest myth of all was her own potential.

Well, why fight it? She had no prospect of doing any big things in the near term, and choosing so poorly in the romantic line demolished any conceit that she was an in-telligent woman. The pressure was off and she might as well own up to the fact that she was hoping Cleon would leave her a few thou, or enough at least to pay off her bills and give her a fresh start.

She had to believe he'd come through with a little some-thing. Would he have asked her to travel all this way if he didn't have at least a token bequest in store for her? As Neesha had sniped via K.D.'s journal, he felt an attachment to her. And Dinah cared about him, too, although her feelings were muddled. There was affection and gratitude and admiration, diluted in no small measure by exasperation and embarrassment and generational misunderstanding. He'd been especially unlovable last night, although Lucien had said some pretty mean things back to him. The tensions between them must have been building like steam inside a volcano during that week in Sydney.

There was no fan in the bathroom. The mirror fogged and the towels felt damp and rough against her skin. She dried and dressed in the steamy mist and admonished herself not to count her chickens before they hatched. Even if Cleon left her some money, it wouldn't be available for weeks, maybe months, while the will went through probate. She hated to touch Lucien for a loan. But she needed cash to tide her over and with sales of his art flourishing, he and Eduardo were rolling in the green.

It was noon when she passed Lucien's door. Should she knock? She wavered. He'd had a lot to drink last night and if he was hung-over or poring over that dreadful Taipan painting, he'd be a bear. Maybe this afternoon would be a more auspicious time to talk money, after a bite of lunch and a few sociable preliminaries.

She didn't see or hear anyone on her way downstairs. The house was quiet. Not a creature was stirring, not even Cantoo. Willie and Julio had ceased their warbling and no sounds from the outside world penetrated the musty silence. Had she slept through a neutron bomb? A massacre? The Rapture?

She peeked into the great room. "Hello?"

Empty. Just the boars' heads mounted like sentinels over their private tomb. She tried the dining room. Nobody there either. She followed the stale smell of fried meat into the kitchen. The room was dark. She scouted around and found the light switch. There was a pan on the cold stove with a piece of mutton in a lake of congealed grease. On the counter, she espied a glass pot with a couple of inches of either crankcase oil or coffee. She took a chance, found a cup and heated it in the microwave.

Where was everybody? She took her cup, retraced her steps through the foyer and looked out the front door. All the cars were gone. Had there been another crisis? Another snakebite? Why had they skipped out en masse? She didn't crave human company, but she didn't like being left alone with the spiders and snakes either.

Maybe Mack was sequestered in his hideaway. She traipsed down the hall to the midget-sized door and knocked.

"Mack?" She opened it a crack and hit the light. As she entered, the colorful array of painted lizards and snakes and kangaroos jumped out at her like spooks. They seemed to be the only ones at home today. Involuntarily, or so it seemed, she gravitated to the painting of the turtle. The specter of the dead man on the turtle had lodged in her brain like a squatter. She wondered if Mack had clipped any articles about the case.

She sat down at the table and perused a few magazine articles. They were mostly about the lost generation and the resulting cultural alienation of those forcibly removed from their Aboriginal homes. There was one article on contemporary Aboriginal art. Of the 30,000 Aboriginal people living in the Northern Territory, an astounding 6,000 of them were artists producing some kind of art or crafts for sale. Her eyebrows shot up. Could all of this output be telepathically communicated from an ancestral spirit? There was nothing in his stockpile of articles about the murdered Brit and she felt a bit let down. She made another circuit of the room, pausing in front of each painting, receptive to whatever wisdom the spirits might bestow. But if these spirits were talking, they were talking in a language she couldn't parse.

She soon lost interest and went to reconnoiter the veranda. She found Tanya sitting on an upended wooden keg grinding some sort of yellow-brown substance to a powder in a large stone mortar. There were a dozen tin cans lined up in front of her. Dinah pulled up a chair and watched. As each batch was pulverized, Tanya funneled it into an empty can, dropped a fresh clump of the stuff into her mortar and began working her pestle.

"What is that?"

"Limonite oxide."

The mineralogical exactitude took Dinah aback. "What's it for?"

"It's ochre."

"For paint, you mean?"

Tanya's snort was obviously Aboriginal for *duh*.

Dinah laughed. "Are you an artist?"

"I find the ants' nests and dig out the limonite for the ones that paint. Not much money, but not that much work either."

"My brother's an artist, but I guess you know that already."

"Hmmph."

Dinah considered explaining that the work currently on Lucien's easel wasn't nearly as good as the rest of his work, but thought better of it. Tanya wouldn't have occasion to view Lucien's other work and maybe her contempt had more to do with the subject matter of the piece than the style or execution. Taipan was, after all, one of Tanya's ancestors and a god, to boot. Who knew how much leeway she'd grant to a foreigner to portray him?

The sun felt warm and reenergizing. Dinah shaded her eyes and gazed across the untended yard at the encroaching woods, no doubt teeming with ancestral fauna. Wombats and bandicoots, Tasmanian devils and deadly vipers. And painted trees. "What are those red and yellow bands on the trees about, Tanya? Is it part of some Aboriginal…" she thought twice and edited the word superstition…"tradition?"

"Wouldn't mean anything to you."

Ooh-kay. From the moment she slopped the Charleston bisque into the bowls last night, Tanya had made it plain that sociability was not her nature and food service was not her first love. Dinah held neither of these aversions against her. She closed her eyes, turned her face to the sun and listened to a medley of unfamiliar birdsong and the rhythmic grating of Tanya's pestle. It took her back to her childhood, sitting beside her Seminole grandmother on her ramshackle back porch beside the Okefenokee as she shelled beans or wove reeds and reminisced about her childhood on the Big Cypress Reservation. There was a beauty in that placid, simple way of life. Of course, it would bore anyone under the age of ninety wild.

Tanya didn't look much past fifty, but there was an intimation of antiquity about her, as if she'd been misplaced in Time. Perhaps it was her serenity. She was a lot more serene grinding limonite oxide than she was cooking and serving.

Dinah's curiosity finally got the better of her and she tried to draw her out. "Will you stay on with Mack or is this a temporary position?"

Tanya didn't deign to respond.

Dinah tried again. "I worked for a caterer once, drudging all day in a hot kitchen. It was miserable. I'd rather work outside in the fresh air anytime."

Still no comeback.

"It must be a good feeling to know you provide the artists with their colors. It makes what they paint partly your creation."

"Don't be a nong." She whanged her pestle on the side of the mortar a few times and surprisingly, her stolid face cracked into a smile. "I'm the yellows."

Dinah felt the thrill of conquest. She'd broken the ice. "You're a whole spectrum of colors—yellow to brown to orange to red. The artists would be lost without you."

"Not all of them use the true ochre."

"Still, the demand must be high. So many people in the Territory are artists."

"Not many jobs around. People need money. Most do woodcarving or painting or some kind of art. Some I could name take advantage. Commerce men. They buy cheap and sell high to rich tourists who don't know what they're looking at."

With the frame of reference between them this small, naming names wasn't necessary. Dinah let a minute go by. "Mack certainly has a beautiful collection of paintings."

"Hmmph."

Was that a judgment on his principles or his taste? Or was *hmmph* just a verbal tic, no more pejorative than *I hear you*? Whatever it meant, Tanya didn't explain.

Dinah persevered. "It's terrible that he was taken away from his mother and deprived of his Aboriginal heritage, but he seems dedicated to learning everything he can about the culture and reintegrating himself into the community."

Tanya emptied the last of the ochre into a can, stood up and brushed off her apron. "If you're hungry, there's bread in the pantry and cheese in the refrigerator. I got no time to cook for you special. Have to start dinner soon as Mack and the lady come back from town with the groceries. Soup, two kinds of fish, beef in red wine, some kind of meringue pie and she'll want it all poshed up and garnished with flowers and leaves. Too much to remember and people in and out all the time. The old man wanting olives for his martinis, the cripple wanting a poultice for his leg. Always somebody wanting something."

Neesha's insistence on four-course, gourmet dinners mystified Dinah as much as it aggravated Tanya. Much as he loved his martinis, Cleon had always been a meat-and-potatoes, no-frills kind of eater and the rest of the family should have gotten its fill of haute cuisine in Sydney. But Neesha had been living in Atlanta unconstrained by Cleon's likes and dislikes for the last six months. She fawned and kowtowed to him still, but maybe these banquets were a passive-aggressive statement that she intended to spread her wings when he was gone and do as she pleased.

The thing that would please Dinah right now was a heart-to-heart with Lucien. "Did Lucien and Eddie go into Katherine, too?"

"Them, the old man, the doctor. They all went. Wendell took my nephew, Victor, with him and the young ones. Victor sees them spending money like water, he'll think we should be able to do the same. He'll come home wanting an iPod and forget who he is."

Dinah felt a stab of guilt. Tanya had no rich relatives to mooch off, no one to hit up for a loan, no inheritance to hope for. It put Dinah's troubles in perspective. She resolved to stop sniveling about her little setbacks and be thankful she didn't have to raid ants' nests or bake meringue pies to make ends meet.

TWELVE

Bored and at loose ends, Dinah hung around on the veranda thinking about the many twenty-first century amenities, diversions, and time killers not on the menu of services at Crow Hill. She couldn't zone out in front of a mindless soap opera because there was no TV. She couldn't pop around the corner to a Baskin Robbins and choose from 31 flavors of brain freeze. She couldn't read a newspaper or surf the Net or go window-shopping. There was a deck of cards on the bar, but she was too antsy for solitaire. She should go for a jog and work off some of her pent-up nervous energy, but the sun was too hot.

She kicked around the backyard for a few minutes, on the *qui vive* for death adders, and had a closer look at the colorful bands painted on the trees at the edge of the woods. In Native American mythologies, trees were sometimes regarded as ladders to the Sky World. She'd have to ask Mack if there was a similar belief among the Aborigines.

Around the side of the house, partially hidden by brush and trees, she spotted a green shed and went to investigate. The door was padlocked. There was one window, but it had been boarded up. Next to the shed, someone had stacked a hodgepodge of empty wine crates bearing the names of various Australian wineries. Balthazar, Kellermeister, VineCrest. The ones on the ground looked as if they were about to disintegrate. There was an old tabletop, also disintegrating, and a large metal dumpster.

Archaeologists loved middens. You could learn a lot about people by the things they threw away. Mack's dumpster didn't rank up there with the middens of ancient Mesopotamia, but it didn't stink and Dinah's curiosity was whetted. Using a stick to lift the dumpster's lid, she stood on one of the sturdier wine crates and peered inside.

She pushed a raggedy cotton throw rug out of the way and dug among the discarded artifacts. A broken cornice, a dried-out bucket of paint, a small lamp in the shape of Michelangelo's David with a risqué on-off switch, an empty economy size box of Omo Laundry Detergent. If there was a washing machine hidden away in the shed, she'd ask Mack for a cup of Omo and the key. This was probably the detritus of a serious housecleaning as Mack rushed to get ready for his first guests.

Stuffed around the sides was a miscellany of old magazines and newspapers. Since her arrival, she'd seen no evidence of mail delivery to the lodge. She pulled out a not-too-moldy issue of the *Northern Territory News* and noted the label. It was addressed to Mack at a post office box in Katherine. There were also quite a few issues of the *Katherine Times*. She sat down on her wine crate, and dipped into the news that had transpired in the Top End over the last few weeks. Politics, bush fires, power outages. Queensland was teed off at the Top End for letting droves of wild swamp buffalo range into its territory. The Top End was teed off at Queensland for letting a scourge of toxic cane toads overspread its territory.

A report of a suspicious death caught her eye. A young woman had been found dead in her home and her boyfriend was being detained for questioning. But the police wouldn't name the community or the woman "because of cultural reasons." Dinah presumed that the culture in question was the Aboriginal culture. Was the *Times* bending over backwards to avoid any imputation that the community was violent or unsafe or did Aboriginal culture inhibit the mention of death? Mack hadn't been inhibited from talking about the Melville Island murder, but then he was a Brit. His cultural sensitivities weren't so easily bruised. From what he'd said, there'd been reams of stories about that murder. Of course, the victim was also a Brit and a newspaperman, besides.

With so much coverage, surely one of these papers would have something about the murder. She began to sort through the stack of papers, skimming the front pages for anything about Melville Island. When she finished with one stack, she went back into the dumpster for another. Her fingers were black and her butt tired of the wine crate, but finally she hit pay dirt.

NO LEADS, NO ARRESTS, NO SUSPECTS IN JOURNALIST'S MURDER

A full week following the discovery of the body of noted British journalist Bryce Hambrick on an unfrequented beach on Melville Island, the police have found no witnesses and no evidence. Without either, hopes of solving the crime dim with each passing day. The police are asking the public to come forward with any information they may have concerning Mr. Hambrick, who had no permission to be on the island.

There have been many rumors about why Mr. Hambrick was murdered. One NT politician has advanced the idea that Hambrick was one of the thousands of commercial and industrial spies working throughout Australia for Beijing and Moscow and that his murder was the work of foreign agents. The minister has submitted a letter to both the Chinese and Russian Consulate-Generals in Sydney demanding full disclosure.

Others in government and the media blame extreme elements of the conservation movement. Mr. Hambrick was a harsh critic of environmental activists and, in some quarters, that does for a motive. There have been numerous instances of ecotage in recent years, including the sugaring of trucks by groups opposed to logging, and damage and destruction to fishing boats and nets by groups opposed to the use of seines. Environmentalists counter that unsubstantiated claims of ecotage by industry officials and politicians are rubbish disseminated to incite violence against lawful protesters.

Dinah thought, the poor man's murder has spawned a national guessing game. There were several other stories about the murder, one or two with photographs of Hambrick. He looked to be in the neighborhood of forty, with a pudgy face, a cumulus of pale, flyaway hair, and pronounced laugh lines around the mouth. Not the staid, censorious Brit she'd imagined.

She stood up and tossed the newspapers back into the dumpster. She was about to close the lid when she noticed a painted pole like the burial poles in Mack's library. She pulled it out and turned it around and around in her hands. It looked as if it had been whittled by a novice and the painting was careless and only half-finished.

THIRTEEN

As THE SUN dipped behind the enclosing wall of trees, a caravan of dusty cars rolled up in front of the lodge. Dinah looked up from her sixth game of solitaire, which she'd laid out on an itsy-bitsy table on the itsy-bitsy front porch. Wendell, Neesha, the twins and the Aboriginal boy she'd seen lock-picking with Thad piled out of the first car. No doubt this was Tanya's nephew, Victor. The kids' hair was wet and the outline of their damp swimsuits showed under their clothes. Thad and K.D. shoved each other and traded insults. Each carried a shopping bag. Victor walked behind them cradling a bag emblazoned "Wizard of Oz Video-tronix." His euphoric smile proclaimed that he was now Podded up or otherwise on his way to becoming a typical adolescent cyborg. Tanya could blame Wen if Victor coveted more expensive toys in the future.

Neesha wore a beige linen pantsuit, an Hermes scarf tied under her chin, and huge, retro-chic white sunglasses. She had a sort of Jackie Kennedy-fleeing-the-paparazzi apprehensiveness about her.

Mack got out of the second car and called out to Victor to help him unload several sacks of groceries and boxes of wine. Victor's smile drooped. He entrusted his prize to Thad and sulked off to do the servant thing as Neesha and the privileged twins continued into the house.

"What a retard," sneered Thad, jostling Dinah out of his way. "Like a stupid camera phone is so cool it's off the chain."

Dinah sighed. Loathing Thad had been so satisfying before she found out his problems had a clinical cause. As she watched him flaunt his faux-faded, designer-ripped, Abercrombie-jeaned ass up the stairs, she decided that some prejudices were worth the extra guilt.

K.D. and Neesha jogged up onto the porch. Dinah held open the door and K.D. charged in toward the kitchen. Neesha tipped Dinah a small, automatic smile and hurried after K.D.

"Where's Cantoo?" cried K.D. accusingly. An outbreak of frenetic yipping ensued. "Oh, no! How could you keep her penned up in there all day?"

Dinah was still standing against the open front door as Cantoo spurted outside and disappeared around the side of the house in the tall grass.

K. D. charged out of the kitchen and up the stairs. Before the kitchen door banged shut, Neesha wailed, "Oh, Tanya, you've curdled the remoulade!"

Dinah's heart went out to Tanya, but she didn't have the stomach or the standing to get between the chatelaine and her cook.

Alone in the third car, Margaret alighted with a testy hauteur and called out to Wendell. He went back to her and they swapped what seemed to be divergent views. He followed her into the house with an uneasy diffidence, as if fearful she might turn and lob a grenade.

"You were smart to stay here," Margaret said as she swept past Dinah. Over her shoulder, she said, "Wendell, I'd like to see you in my room. Now."

Wendell's face was frozen and impassive. He gave Dinah a curt nod and followed his mother meekly up the stairs.

Dinah continued to hold the door open for Mack and

Victor as they schlepped in the groceries. She wondered if she should add "doorman" to her résumé.

Mack was chipper and full of pleasantries. "G'day, Dinah. Beautiful day to lay back and bask in the sunshine, isn't it?"

"Lovely, so long as a cool drink is within reach."

"It's normally much cooler at this time of year. After all my years in London, I'm still getting used to calling June winter." He scurried off to the kitchen after Victor.

Cleon and Dr. Fisher sat talking together in the fourth car. Neither looked as if he were enjoying the fellowship. After a minute or so, the doctor got out and walked toward the house carrying an old-fashioned medical bag. It must have been weighted with rocks because he listed to the side like a mast in a storm. Cleon followed, head down as if lost in thought.

Dinah couldn't hack another of the doctor's sermons on death and, after Cleon's surliness last night, she had no desire to cross his path before she had to. She crept inside, ducked into the great room, and hid behind the bar, remembering too late Cleon's proclivity for gin.

He strode into the room and stepped behind the bar. "What're you doin'?"

She grabbed an ice bucket off a shelf. "Getting some ice."

He reached for the cocktail shaker. "Well, you're just the gal I want to see."

"Why's that? Am I on your list of people in line for a whuppin' today?"

"Naw. What makes you think that?" He was all surprised innocence.

Now that she'd admitted to herself that she wanted something from him, it was hard to be completely artless. But she couldn't bring herself to brown-nose or act as if his bullying behavior was hunky-dory. "You weren't exactly adorable last night, Uncle Cleon. You should be shoring up relationships with your children, not tearing them down."

"I know, I know. The boys and I got crosswise of each other, but we'll work things out in the next day or so. It ain't no biggie. Now let's you and me mix ourselves some refreshment and go upstairs. I got somethin' to show you."

"I was waiting for Lucien. Where is he?"

"Out vulturin' up the culture, I expect. Dez removed the catheter and changed the dressin' on his leg this mornin' and I ain't seen hide nor hair of him since." He sprayed a fine mist of Vermouth into the cocktail shaker, added ice, emptied in a pint of gin and shook twice. "You fetch the glasses and that jar of olives there."

Holding the shaker in front of him like a lantern, he propelled her upstairs to the second floor. He led her down the hall to a numberless room, adjacent to the room she'd seen Thad and Victor burgle, and opened the door. He turned on the overhead light and pushed aside the flowery chintz curtains over the window. She looked around and again thought, why here? The room was larger than hers or Lucien's, but a far cry from luxe. The bedspread was a tatty blue, the walls a dingy gray, and the furniture oppressively dark and grimy. On the floor next to the bed was a newspaper and a biography of Mark Twain with the edge of a letter poking out. She wondered if it was her mother's farewell letter.

Cleon set the shaker down on a marble-topped dressing table, dragged a large suitcase from under the bed and pulled out two, bubble-wrapped squares. He ripped the plastic off and propped the Winslow Homer watercolors side by side against the dresser mirror.

"Well, what do you think?"

Most watercolors seemed washed-out and sickly to her, but Homer's were rich and radiant, almost as intense as oils. "I can almost feel the spray," she said. "It's like looking through an open window onto the ocean."

"They're fine examples of the master's oeuvre, I'm told. Did I pronounce that right?"

"You know you did. You only mangle words when you want to. For effect."

"Now, sugah. I hope I ain't that transparent, but if I was gonna be, I'd sooner it be you who sees through me than anybody else." He poured the martinis and they stood together admiring the paintings for a while. "Neesha and your brother gave me a lot of heat for bringin' 'em, but it was worth it. Lookin' at 'em bucks me up."

"They buck me up, too. They're wondrous."

"I'm glad you like 'em, doll, 'cause they're all yours."

"What?"

"I'm bequeathin' 'em to you in my will."

"Me?" She was blown away. "But they're worth, I don't know, maybe millions."

"I got millions. It's no skin off anybody else's nose if that's what you're thinkin'. Wen doesn't know Winslow Homer from Homer Simpson. Lucien's house is overflowin' with fine art, his and all his up-and-comin' artist friends', and Neesha…" His face twitched as if from pain.

Not sure if the pain was physical or mental, Dinah reached for his hand.

He brushed her comfort aside, looking abashed by the momentary weakness. "Neesha's gonna open her own art gallery when I'm gone. She'd sell 'em to the first customer that walked in. As for the rest of the family, they want my liquid assets, not my aesthetic ones. Irregardless, nobody deserves these more than you do."

"I don't know what to say. I'm knocked out." She didn't

care how he butchered the language. Irregardless, she threw her arms around him and gave him a kiss on the cheek. "Thank you, Uncle Cleon. Thank you millions."

"If they persuade you to stop gallivantin' around the world and come to light someplace where you can hang 'em up and enjoy 'em, that's all the thanks I want. I wish I could've seen you married and happy before I go. Leastways now I'll know you'll have assets to fall back on. Don't feel like you can't sell 'em off if you need to. I sure as shootin' won't care where I'm goin' so it's strictly up to you. If you sell 'em, the only string is that you get full market value in cash up front."

He finished his martini and eased himself down on the bed. "You best skedaddle now, doll, and let me nap for an hour or two. Tonight's dinner's gonna be a lulu."

FOURTEEN

GIDDY WITH EXCITEMENT, Dinah returned to the great room to wait for Lucien and tell him the good news. She was a millionaire, heiress to works of one of America's premier artists, emancipated from the grind of crummy jobs. She could take charge of her life, pursue her anthropological studies, maybe even finance her own expeditions.

Much as she loved the paintings, marvelous as it would be to have them all to herself to look at whenever she liked, keeping them just wasn't practical. It was so good of Cleon to say that he didn't mind if she sold. With the money she got from the sale, she could do anything, go anywhere, indulge her every whim. Or, she could sell one and keep the other, a cake-and-eat-it solution. Lucien would know what to do. He had a friend who owned a gallery in New York City. St. Jean Dupree. It was in his gallery that Neesha found the Homers and Lucien had helped Cleon negotiate the purchase. Maybe St. Jean could exhibit the paintings for her and one of his well-heeled clients would snap them up in record time.

From the kitchen came a hubbub, clanging pans and strident voices. A door slammed. Dinah stuck her head out and saw Neesha storm up the stairs.

Dr. Death bopped out behind her. "Not a multi-tasker, that Tanya," he said through a plume of cigarette smoke. "Rigid, plodding, one thing at a time. Grumbles when you offer her advice. I'm off for a pre-dinner jaunt to work up an appetite. Come along?"

He was probably about as sober as he was ever likely to be and she did want to gather whatever knowledge he had about her father for her mental casebook. But she was too keyed up right now. "No. No thanks, I'm waiting for Lucien."

He rambled out and she went back to the bar. She ought to go help Tanya out, but Tanya didn't need another know-it-all standing over her shoulder, however well-meaning.

Waiting was Dinah's least favorite thing, especially when she had earthshaking news to report. She needed to say it out loud to believe it herself. "I'm stinking rich," she told the boars on the wall. Their dead eyes stared back at her, underwhelmed, and her feelings of elation began to dwindle. It was premature to start celebrating. She was still broke. She'd still need to touch Lucien for a floater until the paintings were legally hers and the proceeds of their sale in her hot little hand.

The sound of a car sent her dashing to the front door. She flung it open, saw the Charade, and went running down the stairs. Eduardo got out, pulled a pair of crutches out of the backseat, and helped Lucien to his feet. Once Lucien had balanced himself on the crutches, he swung toward the house like a trapeze artist gaining amplitude to fly to the next bar.

"You're pretty spry on those things," she said.

"There've been some dicey moments, but I've been practicing most of the day."

"Can I fix you a drink? I need to talk to you."

"Sure. Eddie can take his shower first."

Eddie's magenta Polo shirt showed underarm perspiration marks and his hair was damp and tousled. "How does anyone live in this inferno? Mon Dieu!" He blotted his dripping brow with a monogrammed blue hanky and betook himself upstairs.

Dinah followed Lucien inside to the great room, helped him settle into a chair and went behind the bar. "The usual?"

"Two jiggers, please. Lots of ice."

Without measuring, she glugged a couple of inches of Makers Mark over ice and handed it to him.

He said, "You wouldn't believe how much Aboriginal art there is in little ol' Katherine. There's a lot of really cool stuff about the Dreamtime. With your pash for mythology, you should check it out before you fly the coop."

She waited until he'd had a couple of sips of bourbon. "I have big news, Lucien."

"What's that?"

She took a huge, pregnant breath. "Uncle Cleon gave me the Winslow Homers."

"To hang in your room? That oughta brighten the décor."

"No. In his will. They're mine to do with as I please."

His expression conveyed something less than unalloyed joy. In fact, it was seriously alloyed.

"What's wrong?" she asked.

He shook his head. "Don't you see what he's done? He's pitted you against Neesha. She wants the paintings."

"Tough cookies. Her decorator can find her something else to match the French wallpaper."

"At least she has a spot on her wall. Where the hell would *you* hang them? You said yourself you're in the wind."

"I don't know where I'd hang them. Lucien, aren't you happy for me?"

"You want me to do handsprings? Sure, I'm happy for you. I know you've always liked them. But liking them's one thing, keeping them's another."

"I thought I could sell one and use the proceeds to buy a house somewhere."

"That'd be a mistake. You wouldn't realize a tenth of its worth. The market for American art's no good right now. You should hold off for at least five years."

Her excitement fizzled. "You really think so?"

"I know so. Sotheby's had to pull a John Singer Sargent from their catalog just last week because there were no bidders. Wait 'til the demand for realism rebounds. I could keep your paintings for you at my place until the time's right. Five years down the road, their value will shoot through the roof and you'll be filthy rich. By then, you'll be married and living in a McMansion with more rooms than the Louvre."

Five years down the road was a stupefyingly long time, and marriage and a McMansion were highly dubious milestones along the way. But at least he didn't take the position that selling them was a sacrilege. She'd heed his advice for now. In the meantime, she'd have to live.

"While my masterpieces are appreciating on your wall, could I borrow a couple thousand until I get resettled? I'll pay you back."

"Take as long as you need. I'll write you a check first thing in the morning."

So that was that. Oh, well. All the more reason to embark on a serious career. She gave Lucien a hug and, before she went upstairs to dress for dinner, she stopped by the kitchen to see how Tanya was bearing up. If the proletarians couldn't afford to revolt, they could at least commiserate.

FIFTEEN

REGULAR AS THE TIDE, the family rolled into the great room for the de rigueur cocktail hour. Dinah picked up emanations of wariness, but everyone presented a smile and a veneer of conviviality. Wendell chatted with Lucien about art, Eduardo chatted with Neesha about the plans for her new gallery, Margaret chatted with Cleon, and Dr. Fisher lectured Tanya—something about the importance of the liver and kidneys.

K.D. sipped a pink mocktail while she bent Dinah's ear. "Daddy never obeys the rules of grammar except, of course, when he's in trial or handling a big case. But he can be incredibly profound. When I was writing my Envy story, I asked him if he had ever envied anyone and you know what he said? He said, 'Everybody's like the moon, sweetness. We all got our dark side.' Daddy speaks his mind so openly, even when he knows it upsets people, that I can't imagine him hiding anything. But it was a beautiful thing to say, wasn't it?"

It was certainly an interesting thing to say. Dinah thought that Mark Twain or Pink Floyd or somebody famous had said it before Cleon, but it was interesting that Cleon would quote it. Interesting that he would evade K.D.'s question. Interesting to muse on how many of the perfectly calibrated smiles in this room hid dark feelings.

Cleon interrupted the conviviality to announce the unveiling of the Homer watercolors. Mack brought Lucien's easel downstairs and set the small, unframed but beautifully matted pieces at the end of the bar where the dim light from a pair of sooty sconces did nothing to enhance their beauty. Tanya brought around little nuggets of Brie and crudités and the crowd clustered around the paintings for a better view.

"I've promised 'em to Dinah," said Cleon, raising his glass in tribute. "She can keep 'em or auction 'em off to the highest bidder. You don't care, do you, Neesha? They'd stick out like corn pone at a sushi bar in your new gallery. You're into more avant garde artists, right, darlin'?"

"Do what you like," said Neesha. "You always do." She shot Dinah a weaponized smile and moved as far away from the usurper as possible. K.D., looking more titillated by the mini-drama than angry, followed her mother.

Margaret gloated. "Your bride's in a sour mood this evening, Cleon."

"She's in mournin'," said Cleon, topping up her martini. "Nerves all to shreds, worried how she'll get on without me to baby her."

Neesha's snit and Cleon's sarcasm extinguished the remaining smiles. Dr. Fisher slapped his pockets and went outside for a smoke. Mack excused himself to go and see about something in the kitchen. Wendell moved off to an armchair in a lonely corner and appeared to check his cell phone for messages. Quaffing an evil-looking brew he called a Lord Byron, Eduardo plopped down in one of the club chairs and gave Lucien the evil eye. Lucien slouched in his wheelchair, swilling bourbon and jiggling his healthy leg up and down on the footrest. There was definitely discord between the two, but Dinah couldn't tell if it related to sex or the family dynamics.

Seeing no friendly port in the storm, she loitered at the end of the bar listening to Margaret lambaste Cleon.

"You're holding your money over our heads like a

piñata. It's not right, keeping us blindfolded and playing us off against each other. You should make your intentions known."

"Your avarice is showin', Maggie."

"*My* avarice?"

"All right, I know you ain't out for yourself. But don't badger. I mean to be fair. I'd be loco to short your boy, Wendell. You'd come after me hammer and tongs."

"That wouldn't be feasible once you're dead." She said it lightly, almost flirtatiously, and rushed on before he could retort. "You've never bonded with Wendell. You needn't deny it. But he's always done you proud. Good grades, football scholarship, respectable job. He's a fine son and a good man. He deserves more than a pat on the head. More than your gold-digging beauty queen."

"Ease up now, Maggie. The law compels a man to provide for his widow."

"The law guarantees a widow a third of her husband's estate unless the prenup states otherwise. If I know you, your prenup has an airtight cap on what she can inherit."

He laughed. "The bar lost a crackerjack when you didn't go to law school."

"I don't need a law degree to know how your mind works, Cleon Dobbs. You'd make damn sure that when the merry widow remarries, your replacement doesn't live high, wide, and handsome on your money." She finished her martini, smacked her glass down on the bar, and seemed suddenly to notice Dinah.

"Your brother Lucien looks lonely, don't you think?"

Chagrined, Dinah took her glass of wine and drifted over to see if she could eke some conversation out of Lucien. She dragged a metal folding chair close to his and sat down. She said, "You were right about Neesha wanting the Homers. She's shunning me like the pox."

He rattled the ice in his empty glass. "You don't much care, do you?"

"I won't after I leave here. It'll be awkward until I do."

"It's in Neesha's interest to gloss over any unpleasantness. Keep your head down and she'll be her usual cloying self." He shook an ice cube into his mouth and munched. "Have you sounded out Cleon about your father?"

"Not yet. It's hard to find the right moment."

"You will. Just remember, the coward dies a thousand deaths."

Mack stole up behind her. "Congratulations, Dinah. Those Homer watercolors are a treasure."

She said, "If I listen to Lucien, they're not going to generate any spendable treasure until I'm old and gray. He's been touting the pleasures of delayed gratification."

Lucien ignored her little dig. His eyes rested on the paintings. "Homer may be America's greatest artist. What he did with light and water is near miraculous."

A bothersome thought occurred to her. Could it be that Lucien wanted the Homers for himself? Could his advice not to sell be tinged with self-interest?

Mack had a different view of the artist. "He was good. But to my eye, he's rather austere. Too literal. Limited by the apparent reality."

Lucien grinned. "You're a chauvinist, Mack. Admit it."

"Okay, I admit it. Aboriginal art is deeper and more spiritual. It's a manifestation of some creative act of the ancestors. It involves you, pulls you into the story and the symbolism. It's like going to church."

Mack seemed to have vanquished Lucien's funk. As Dinah listened to the two aficionados riff on symbolism and the ritual power of art, she glanced over at Eduardo. He was watching their interplay with a look of pure malevolence.

"Heads up, all of y'all!" Cleon motioned everyone to gather around the bar. "I got another bequest to announce."

When they were all dutifully gathered, he clamped an arm around Wendell's shoulder. "Your mama and I have been talkin' about your love of the water, Wendell. I want you to have somethin' personal from me, somethin' more meanin'ful than money. And so I've decided to leave you my yacht, the Suwannee. She's a fifty-five footer, a peach of a boat, moored down in Sydney. You can cruise home like a tycoon."

Wendell's face registered surprise and a slow, cautious dawning of pleasure. "Well, that's wonderful. Awesome. Thank you, Dad."

"You're welcome as the flowers in May, son." Cleon set down his martini, clamped his free arm around Neesha and squeezed. "Promise me you'll take Neesha and the family on a cruise. Help 'em through the grievin' process."

"Of course," said Wendell. "Of course, I will." Looking strangely discomfited, he disengaged from Cleon and turned to Dinah. "Do you do much boating around Puget Sound, Dinah? It's the most fun in the world. I have a little Bayliner, the Wave Walker, back home in Brunswick. I take her down the Florida coast a few times a year. But a luxury yacht. It's unreal. Out of this world."

Margaret said, "The yacht isn't all you can expect from your father, Wendell. He's promised to be fair and evenhanded with the rest of the estate, haven't you, Cleon?"

"I'm as good as my word, Maggie. Count on it." He chuckled and picked up his martini. "Now you mind you don't have more fun than's good for you, Wendell. They say a boat's like a mistress. If a man ain't careful, she'll be his undoin'."

SIXTEEN

"SETTLE DOWN, Y'ALL. I want to make a toast."

They had assembled around the dining room table in their same seats as the night before. Cleon had asked Mack to display the Homers on the sideboard. Small as they were, their stormy waters gave the room an unstable, billowy feel. Neesha looked as if she were fighting off seasickness and Lucien wore a faraway, absent expression. When Mack popped the champagne cork, he flinched.

"Daddy, may I have a glass of champagne for the toast?" asked K.D.

Cleon chuckled. "Mack, pour K.D. and Thadeus a glass of bubbly. This is a momentous occasion."

Mack poured all around and when everyone was seated, Cleon lifted his glass. "First and foremost, to my beautiful wife, Neesha, for keepin' her chin up and puttin' on such a brave face."

Neesha frowned and fidgeted with her ring.

"Next up, to my long-sufferin' ex-wife, Margaret, for forgivin' me my scoundrelly ways and comin' so far to commemorate my passin'."

Margaret's eyes held about as much forgiveness as a rockslide.

He turned a doting smile on K.D. "To my gorgeous and brainy daughter, K.D., the writer. She's gonna give us all literary aliases and divulge our deep dark secrets. Y'all best beware."

"You'll always be my inspiration, Daddy." K.D.'s brattiness melted away in the warmth of her father's praise and she looked almost lovable.

"And last but not least, to my true-blue niece, Dinah. When it's crunch time, she turns on her siren and comes runnin'. To all my fair ladies, let's drink."

Everyone drank, but K.D. was the only one who appeared to enjoy it.

Cleon made a wry face. "Tastes kinda limp to me. Of course, I'm partial to the kick of gin." He peered over the rim of his glass at Eddie. "You're the highbrow, Eduardo. Is this French fizz worth the exorbitant price Neesha paid for it?"

Eddie's eyes narrowed. "I hardly think my opinion is the one you want."

"Sure, it is. You're too ticklish, Eduardo. Aw, hell, it don't matter. I'm rich as Croesus. We'd be lappin' liquid gold if it complemented the viands. Right, Neesha girl?"

Neesha's cheeks blazed. "I never knew you to be such a tiger for thrift, Cleon. Quite the contrary."

Everyone but Cleon and Thad looked ill at ease. Mack brushed imaginary crumbs off the tablecloth. Wendell dropped his eyes and picked at a hangnail. K.D.'s eyes washed back and forth inquiringly from Cleon to Neesha, but neither took note.

Cleon laughed. "Darlin', I'm full of contradictions. It's what gives me my edge."

There was an uncomfortable silence during which Dinah noticed that the chairs on Mack's side of the table had been moved closer together to make room for a chair to his left. Had somebody miscounted or was Neesha incorporating a spiritual element into tonight's proceedings, setting a place for the prophet Elijah or something?

Cleon lifted his glass again. "And now a toast to the gents. To my old huntin' buddy Dez Fisher for bein' here in my hour of need and helpin' me dodge around his country's boneheaded laws. To old times, Dez."

"Maybe I'll run for Parliament," said Dez. "Change the bloody law from inside."

"You'd never be elected, Dez. Your platform's too morbid." Cleon drew out the last word as if he were pulling taffy.

"Maw-bid." Fisher's braying laugh reverberated off the rafters. "Mawbid."

"To Ian Mackenzie," continued Cleon. "For your hospitality, good sir, which under the law amounts to aidin' and abettin' but it's in a good cause and we'll soon be outa your hair."

"I wish you could be here next year," said Mack, "to see all the upgrades and changes I have planned."

"Maybe I'll come back as a ghost. Swan's a great believer in ghosts and hauntin' and such. We'll soon know if she's onto something."

Wendell said, "We'd rather have you alive, Dad. If you underwent another few months of chemo, you might beat this thing. Other people have."

"That train's left the station, I reckon. But I raise my glass to you, Wendell. No matter how harsh a view your mama took of my philanderin', no matter how many of your ballgames I missed or how many birthdays I forgot, you stood up for your old man, loyal to a fault, and here you are standin' by me at the end."

Wendell's face softened and he seemed sincerely moved. "You've always been a larger-than-life figure to me."

"Larger than life." Cleon guffawed. "I like it. Reckon I can be larger than death, Thadeus?"

Thad flipped his hair out of his eyes. "You're no Bionic Commando."

Cleon's shoulders shimmied with mirth. "I'm sorry I

ain't gonna see you grow up, Thadeus. You're a right interestin' boy with more candlepower than you let on. That ain't a bad thing. Keep 'em guessin'.

"And now to Lucien. What can I say about my second son?"

"Isn't 'second' enough of a testimonial?" asked Lucien.

Cleon's eyes danced with amusement. "To Lucien. A gifted artist, a freethinker, a wonderful human bein' and a straight arrow in most every way but Nature's Way."

"Couldn't pass up the cheap shot, could you? Couldn't miss an opportunity to tell me how short of your Southern ideal of manhood I fall."

"That dog won't hunt, Lucien. You can romance the front line of the Pittsburgh Steelers for all I care so long as you play straight with me. Straight, as in on the level, in case you forgot the alternate meanin'." He gave Lucien's shoulder a conciliatory shake. "Why's everybody so touchy? What we all need is a good laugh. Like Swan says, if it's somethin' you'll laugh about later, you may as well laugh now. Enough of this fizz. Pour us a splash of still wine, Mack. Nothin' like a few bottles of wine to wash away a man's sorrows and start him to thinkin' maybe that woeful prognosis the specialists handed him is hogwash and there's no such thing as death."

"Wishful thinking, Cleon." The mention of death was catnip to the doctor. "When the quality of life's gone, there's no point holding on. No sense prolonging…"

"Oh, look," cried Neesha. "Our first course."

Tanya scudded into the room like a thundercloud and wrestled her squeaky serving cart toward the head of the table.

Neesha said, "The first course is minted English pea soup with lobster and orange. It's a Martha Stewart recipe."

Tanya snorted. "Cost more than a week's tucker for some."

Mack ahemmed uncomfortably. He didn't seem to know whether to reprimand her and risk her leaving him in the lurch or let someone else assume the risk. He got up and went to the sideboard. After a rather fussy show of cork sniffing, he selected one of the open bottles of white wine and engrossed himself with pouring a perfect two inches for all of the adults.

Tanya ladled the green soup from a tureen into double-handled white bowls and garnished each with a bit of lobster. She plunked a bowl down at every place, threw a basket of biscuits on the table and rolled her trolley back toward the kitchen.

Mack finished his wine service and sat down. "Tanya's new to the service industry. I hope you'll excuse her outspokenness." Cleon gave the matter the back of his hand. "There's no call to excuse honesty. It's too seldom heard as it is."

Dinah's toes prickled. Why was Cleon so hipped on straightness and honesty and why had Tanya set a bowl in front of the empty chair? The missing diner must be expected momentarily. Maybe Cleon wanted his investigator, Kellerman, on deck when he dropped the paternity bomb. Or maybe he'd asked a local acquaintance to dinner.

"Incidentally," said Mack, "Tanya came across a Gympie-Gympie tree in that row of taller trees behind the lodge. She says it has heart-shaped leaves and is very poisonous. Anyone walking out back should stay clear of it."

"I wouldn't leave the veranda without a hazmat suit," twitted Eduardo.

The doctor said, "If you're ever stung by a Gympie-Gympie, you'll wish you were dead. It has tiny, hair-like spines that slide under the skin and start to release a neurotoxin. A man will feel like he's on fire for days, sometimes weeks or even months afterward. But when the poison wears off, there's no lasting damage."

"Unless in his pain," said Cleon, "he'd asked you to put him out of his misery." His eyes were teasing.

"I'd do that with steroids," riposted Fisher. "Suicide is a last resort of the terminally ill." He climbed back on his soapbox. "In ninety-five, physician-assisted suicide was legal here in the Top End. Then the churches complained and the Aborigines chimed into the debate. Kill doctors, that's what they call doctors who assist a suicide. They say they'll run a spear through anybody who helps one of their own to die."

"Did you ever get speared?" asked Thad.

"I've not assisted an Aboriginal suicide, so I haven't run afoul of the taboo."

"It's called payback law," said Mack. "But the Aborigines have never made any threats against doctors."

"Balls." Fisher patted his pockets and stood up. "I need a fag." He threw Mack a contemptuous look and walked out of the room.

"I don't think I'll ever get used to the Australian patois," said Eduardo.

"The main concern about the euthanasia law," said Mack, rather starchily, "was that Aboriginal people would be afraid to seek medical help of any kind. After the inhumane treatment they've received at the hands of Westerners, they have cause for mistrust."

Who doesn't, thought Dinah. Her eyes kept returning to the empty chair. Maybe Mack had invited one of the Aboriginal artists he'd been hyping and the guy had missed the turn-off. Or maybe Cleon had located Mack's mother. She nudged Eduardo under the table with her foot. "Who else is coming?"

"Je ne sais pas. There's no place card."

Margaret rested her elbows on the table and steepled her fingers under her chin. "You've promised to allocate the estate fairly, Cleon, and I believe you. But handing out the goodies piecemeal is a cop-out. If we don't talk about the terms of your will while you're alive, there'll be nothing but hard feelings and lawsuits when you're gone."

"Talking money is so tacky," said Neesha. "How common can you be, Margaret?"

Cleon held up a hand. "Feelings may run high, but there'll be no grounds to contest my will, Maggie. I'm gonna elaborate the whys and wherefores on videotape so as to demonstrate my sound reasoning and steel-trap mind."

"If a man's not careful," said Margaret, "the old bones he leaves to rot in that steel trap of his will be his undoing."

Cleon held her eyes for a long, loaded moment. She had obviously struck a nerve. Finally, he threw back his head and laughed. "All right, Maggie. I'm on a tight schedule for hearin' y'all's gripes and I want everybody to have their say. How do you think I should divvy up my money?"

"K.D. and Thad are too young to manage their inheritance and their mother, no offense intended Neesha, is too extravagant to manage it for them."

Neesha flushed. "Why, you insulting old…"

"Shush," ordered Cleon. "What is it you're proposin', Maggie?"

"Put their share of the estate and Lucien's in a trust and name Wendell the executor. He'll administer it fairly and prevent Lucien and Neesha from frittering it all away on fine art and bric-à-brac before they're forty."

Lucien jeered. "You're out of your tree if you think I'd go groveling to Wendell for my allowance."

"No one questions Wen's fairness," said Neesha, "but

I can manage my own money and I'll thank you not to intrude in matters that don't concern you, Margaret."

"It concerns my only son. Let's be blunt, people. Cleon's decision to change his will has made you all adversaries."

"We're not adversaries," said Wendell. "There's more than enough money to go around. He's just given me a yacht, for heaven's sake. And anyway, money's not the important thing. It's not why we're here."

"Ha!" said Eduardo and everyone stared at him as if he'd broken wind.

"Don't be naïve," scoffed Margaret. "He's pledged to be fair, but what does that mean precisely? Cleon Dobbs is scheming at something. Just look at his face."

Dinah looked. He was grinning like the Cheshire cat, the one whose grin remained after the rest of him had vanished.

No one had the temerity to agree with Margaret or to disagree. After a longish interlude of soup and silence, she said, "This suspense over the will can only cause dissension, Cleon. You want us to be straight with you? You be straight with us."

"She has a point," said the doctor, returning with a bottle of Scotch. "No cause to be so tight-lipped about it, mate. Your legatees have a right to know where they stand."

"I ain't dead yet and my legatees can cool their jets and wait 'til I am."

Fisher sat down and poured himself a tumbler of Scotch. "It won't be long now."

"Oh, splendid," said Mack, jumping up as Tanya trundled her squeaky cart in from the kitchen. "The fish this evening is barramundi."

Thad perked up. "Like the tribe on 'Survivor?'"

Mack looked blank.

K. D. elucidated. "'Survivor' is an American television show about people stranded in a horrible place."

Thad sniggered. "Like us."

"Don't be rude, Thadeus." Neesha darted a skittish glance at Cleon.

"Barra is a prize catch in the Top End," said Mack. "It puts up a tenacious fight."

"Fitting fare for this family," quipped Lucien.

Mack brought another bottle of wine to the table and replenished everyone's glass. Tanya cleared away the empty soup bowls and began serving the fillets of barra on individual plates. Dinah frowned as she set a plate in front of the empty chair. Was she being perverse? If she was so conscientious about the cost of food, why did she persist in serving a guest who wasn't there? Why did no one ask who was expected?

"The fish is sauced with my special remoulade," said Neesha. "I hope we got it right this time, Tanya."

Tanya humphed. "Barra should be steamed in paper-bark and gum leaves."

Mack's brow furrowed. "It's not your place to critique the food, Tanya."

"Hmmph." She served the doctor last, a different fish in a different dish.

"Black cod," said Fisher. "Good for the hepatic system. I have a liver condition."

"Lot of extra work," said Tanya. "Too many things to remember."

This time, Mack took a stern line. "That'll be all, Tanya. I'll ring when we're ready for the meat course."

She gave him a stony look and pushed her cart back toward the kitchen.

Fisher bent over his plate and inhaled. "Ahhh. Like spring rain on a warm rock."

Dinah had never seen an uglier piece of cod, but it was the barra going begging in front of that vacant chair that worried her. She searched Cleon's face. What would make a dying man's eyes twinkle like that? What would make this particular dying man so happy? Oh, God. What if he'd sweet-talked her mother into putting in an appearance after all?

Minutes went by and the only sound was the plinking of cutlery against plates. Neesha picked at her fish. Lucien played with his, drawing scallops in the remoulade with his fork. K.D. minced. Fisher gourmandized. Margaret sawed angrily at her fish and masticated each mouthful very slowly without taking her eyes off Cleon's face.

Dinah couldn't stand another second of his cat-and-mouse game. Whatever discombobulation he planned to spring on them, he should man up and get it over with.

"Uncle Cleon, do you have another heir, or what?"

His jaw dropped. "Well, if that don't beat all. Did you have one of those witchy premonitions of yours, Miss Dinah?"

Neesha clutched her throat melodramatically. "Another heir?"

Cleon hefted himself out of his chair. "Well, the cat's out of the bag, so I may as well fess up. It seems I got a son I didn't know I had. He's another peculiar duck—no address, prone to wanderin' around in strange places. But I hired me a detective and like Eduardo's wont to say, vi-ola. I was expectin' him in time for dinner this evenin', but…"

"You're changing your will for a bastard?" Margaret was livid.

"Reparations to the wronged," said Lucien. "Money's all he knows how to give."

Cleon pounded his fist on the table making the glasses and flatware judder. "I can see how my sins stick in y'all's craw." Glowering, he pointed his spoon around the table. "Neesha blushin' and flushin' like she's comin' down with the diphtheria, Maggie squabblin' over my money and her lingerin' emotional wounds, Lucien spoutin' off about how I neglected him, Wendell so mealymouthed I can't hardly stand it, Thad sassin' me, Dez dancin' on my corpse. It's a sorry verdict on a man's life."

He squinched up his face and rubbed his jaw, as if reconsidering, and slowly his glower morphed into a grin. "Aw, but y'all are overwrought. A man forgets how disturbin' his death can be to the ones he's leavin' behind. There ain't nothin' I can do now about your old wounds and grievances, but rest easy about the 'reparations.' Everybody's gonna get his just deserts. Bastards notwithstandin'."

SEVENTEEN

"SEEMS LIKE MY news has killed y'all's appetite," said Cleon. "We may as well adjourn this powwow to the bar in the big room."

Chairs screaked against the floor as everyone pushed back from the table and stood up. Thad bolted out of the room like a paroled convict and charged noisily up the stairs. Cleon pulled out Neesha's chair for her. Dinah diagnosed the glint in her eyes as stark hatred, but her back was to Cleon and it was gone in a second.

Tanya began to clear the table, scraping the uneaten pieces of barra into a pail. "Waste of life," she muttered.

The doctor blundered to his feet, swaying dangerously. He reached for his bottle of Scotch and staggered backward into Tanya. "Clumsy Abo! Wash what you're doing."

Tanya fell hard against the table. A glass tipped over and Dinah caught a lap full of red wine. She jumped up, dripping.

Cleon said, "Help him up to his room, Mack, and let him sleep it off."

"Sod off, Cleon. I'm done taking orders from you. Shz—time…time you're dead."

Mack hastened around the table and took the doctor firmly around the shoulders. "Come with me, Desmond."

"Bloody hell, I will." He shook off Mack's arm.

"Dez, you're way over the line," said Margaret. "Let Mack help you."

"Shtick it up your jumper, Mags." He regained his

balance and reeled toward the door, bumped into a chair, reoriented himself, and staggered on.

Tanya righted herself and glared after him. "Galka."

Mack flashed her a look of such alarm that Dinah did a double take. Whatever the word meant, it must be vicious.

He said, "We can clean this up later, Tanya. Please go and make us some coffee."

"Temperance ain't Dez's for-tay," said Cleon, shaking his head. He wrapped one arm around Neesha and the other around K.D. and squired them out of the room.

Like a vapor off dry ice, Margaret huffed out of the room behind them.

Mack gave Dinah's dress a helpless, afflicted look, handed her a stack of paper napkins, and hustled Tanya out of the room as if he saw snakes crawling out of her hair.

Dinah sopped up as much of the spilled wine as she could, but the dress was done for. It was her big Christmas splurge, and she was still paying for it.

Wendell said, "You realize, don't you, Lucien, that this could reduce our share of the estate big-time?"

"I realize," said Lucien. "I thought you didn't care about the money."

"I wouldn't if he were going to leave it all to Neesha and the kids. But for all we know, this Johnny-come-lately is a confidence man."

"What if he is? There's not much we can do about it if Dad decides to leave him the whole caboodle." The worry lines above Lucien's nose belied the airy reply.

"Don't be too sure," said Wendell. "He hasn't changed anything yet."

Lucien's eyes met Dinah's briefly as Wendell left the room.

She said, "What did Cleon mean about you not playing straight with him?"

"Nothing. What is this? Get Lucien Day?"

"I would pay to see Wendell slug it out with Cleon," said Eddie, rolling Lucien's wheelchair away from the table. "But I don't care who's dying or how utterly shattered you are, pumpkin. Next year we're summering in St. Tropez."

"Christ Almighty." Lucien batted away Eddie's hands and rolled himself toward the door. "I'm going to see what other surprises the patriarch has up his sleeve."

Eddie rolled his eyes, made a moue of martyr-like forbearance, and went after him.

Left alone, Dinah sat back down and rubbed her tight neck. She'd once watched Nick hot-wire a car. She wondered if she could do it right now. She could be up and dust before anyone noticed. Tempting. But, to cite the estimable K.D., not very mature.

Shit. She pushed herself up, pulled her sticky, wet dress away from her thighs and followed the crowd. She straggled into the great room as Fisher, standing apart from the others, blew a low, wheezing noise through a long, cylindrical tube with Aboriginal symbols painted in shades of ochre.

Cleon was mixing martinis behind the bar. Margaret and Wendell leaned across the barricade, breathing fire.

"You've gone too far this time, Cleon," said Margaret. "How old is this alleged son? Who's his mother?"

"Have you tested his DNA?" demanded Wendell. "How do you know he's not conning you?"

Neesha sat across the room, her lips compressed. Her eyes jumped hither and thither as if mapping the fastest route to the exit. It might be in her interest to gloss over unpleasantness, but she was clearly at pains to put a shine on this puppy.

K.D. was nowhere to be seen. It must have taken a dire

threat to oust the Constant Observer from the center of the action. Probably off drilling a peephole, thought Dinah.

Lucien had parked his chair beside Neesha. He jiggled his good leg and looked daggers at Cleon. Or was it Eddie?

Eduardo rifled through the liquor bottles, murmuring epithets. "Espèce d'idiot. Espèce de merde."

Not knowing from which direction the fireworks would come, Dinah installed herself on one of the bar stools.

The doctor wrapped his swollen lips around the long pipe and wheezed again just as Mack appeared in the door.

"Put that down, Desmond." Mack marched up to him and wrested the instrument out of his hand. "Have some respect."

"Gimme the bloody thing." Fisher fumbled the instrument out of Mack's hands.

Cleon poured himself a martini and sauntered across the room to join Mack. "He can usually hold his liquor better than this."

Mack was outraged. "You've lived in Australia, Cleon. You know the didgeridoo is like a deity to many Aborigines. It represents the phallus of an ancestor."

"Is blowing it fellatio?" taunted Eddie.

Mack gave him a dirty look and so did Lucien.

"Buncha bloody meddlers," said Fisher, mouthing the didgeridoo again.

"Here, now, Dez." Cleon set down his drink and grabbed at the instrument. As he did, Dez began to drool and choke.

"Kkcchhh! Kkcchhh! Kkcchhh!"

Margaret started across the room. "Something's wrong with him."

"He's skunk-faced is what's wrong." Cleon righted him and slapped him on the back. "Scotch go down the wrong way, Dez?"

"Kkcchhh!" Fisher's eyes bulged. He tore at his beard and his throat.

Lucien leapt out of his chair on one leg. "Somebody give him the Heimlich."

Mack tried to get his arms around him, but he flailed and rasped and writhed, hitting out wildly, fighting for air.

"Kkcchhh! Kkcchhh! Kkcchhh!"

"It's a fishbone!" cried Margaret.

"Or a heart attack." Wendell elbowed her aside as Fisher toppled to the floor.

"Does he take digitalis?" Eduardo knelt down and loosened his collar.

"I don't think so," said Wendell. "Does anyone have aspirin?"

"I'll get them," said Dinah, running for the door.

"No, here." Lucien took a bottle out of his pocket and pitched it to Wendell.

Wendell pried apart the doctor's jaws. "His tongue is huge. He can't swallow."

"Somebody start CPR," cried Margaret. "Clear his throat."

"I'm CPR certified," said Mack. He pushed Eduardo and Wen out of his way and knelt beside the doctor. He tilted his head back, held the doctor's nose closed and blew into his mouth. Nothing. He pumped the doctor's chest, counting each compression aloud. When he got to thirty, he stopped.

Nothing. The doctor lay stone still, his eyes staring up at the ceiling.

Mack laid an ear against the doctor's chest, felt for a pulse. "He's dead."

Margaret slumped onto the sofa, her hands over her mouth.

Cleon leaned over the body for what seemed a very long

time. He closed Fisher's eyes and when he looked up, his own glittered with vitriol. "One of you geniuses poisoned the wrong man."

PART II

EIGHTEEN

DINAH WOKE WITH a crick in her neck and a muddy taste in her mouth. She opened her eyes. Motes of suspended dust glinted in the gray sunlight and a prodigious cobweb glistened in the corner of the ceiling. The smell of mothballs assaulted her nostrils. Somebody had covered her with a stinky wool blanket. She sat up and flexed her neck. Nothing looked familiar. She swiveled her eyes around the room and met the glassy stare of a stuffed boar.

Jerusalem's bells!

She threw off the blanket and stood up. How could she have fallen asleep in her wine-drenched dress three feet from the spot where Desmond Fisher had died in agony? How could Lucien have let her? The fiasco came back in a flurry of confused images—the doctor's purple face, distended tongue, and rasping breath. Then shouting, the futile attempt at CPR, the interminable wait for the police who never came.

She heard Cleon's voice outside the window.

"Since nobody had any quarrel with the doctor, I reckon I was the one supposed to die."

She hurried to the window. Keeping out of sight behind the frowzy-smelling curtains, she looked out onto the veranda and saw him gesturing and orating as if he were summing up to a jury. He was unshaven and had dark circles under his eyes, but his voice resonated with confidence and conviction.

"I've let it be known that I mean to alter my will. I

expect somebody tried to put the quietus on that plan and bungled the job."

She moved to the other side of the window for a look at his audience. The cavalry had arrived, or two of them anyway. One sported three white chevrons on his sleeve and a pair of horn-rims on his nose. He looked serious and intellectual. His colleague had two chevrons, sloping shoulders, and ropy arms. He kept his head down and took notes.

The extra chevron asked the questions. "Do you have reason to suspect a specific individual, Mr. Dobbs?"

"No. I can't hardly stand to think…no."

"If it was poison, as you think, sir, do you have any idea how or when it was administered?"

"We did have a house full of open wine and liquor bottles. But I'm just an ol' country lawyuh, constables. I'll defer to your forensic experts."

Dinah stifled a sneeze and left the window. Cleon's poor-old-country-boy shtick sounded affected and phony in the circumstances. If he believed somebody had tried to poison him, he needn't be coy about the rest of his assumptions. Whatever the cause of the doctor's death, one thing was certain: without him, Cleon's suicide was a no-go. Cleon would be forced to go home and avail himself of one of his guns, or stay here and die on God's clock. And if an autopsy of Fisher's body did detect poison, how could they know who the intended victim was? Every member of the family including Cleon, himself, would become a suspect.

You're having a nightmare, she told herself. In another minute you'll wake up in Seattle and every rotten thing you think has happened over the last three days will have been a figment of your sick imagination.

The smell of coffee seeped into the room. It's part of the dream, she told herself. The verisimilitude part, like the plastic cigarette holder she descried on the floor next to her foot. Had it been poisoned? For no sane reason, she kicked it under the sofa.

Her dress was a mishmash of stains and wrinkles and her hair felt like a rat's nest. She hoped she didn't encounter any policemen before she had a chance to make herself decent, but what the hell. The need for caffeine trumped vanity.

She followed her nose to the kitchen. It was deserted. There were three pots labeled reg, decaf, and tea and a tray of mismatched mugs. She helped herself to a mug of reg and sat down at the wooden table in the center of the room. The sun burned through the dirty windows and the caffeine began to burn through the fog in her brain. Sadly, she had to conclude that she was awake in real time, in the Northern Territory of Australia, in what was shaping up to be a very nasty predicament.

Why was Cleon so sure it was murder? Desmond Fisher was well into his sixties. Old birds dropped off the twig every day for all kinds of reasons—salmonella, for example. Maybe his cod had gone off. And hadn't he mentioned a liver condition? He drank like a fish. Maybe it was a case of self-poisoning by alcohol.

But if it was murder, who was supposed to die and how and when had the poison been administered? There'd been lots of wine breathing on the sideboard, but they'd all drunk from the same bottles. And if it was the liquor that was poisoned, everybody knew that Cleon drank gin and Fisher drank Scotch so there could be no mistake there. Maybe the didgeridoo was poisoned. She tried to recall whether anyone had done anything furtive or odd at dinner, but it was all a blur.

Her eyes fell on a large metal box at the end of the table with the words "POLICE PROPERTY" stenciled in black. She got up, tore off a paper towel from the roll beside the sink and used it to lift the lid. Inside were two long-bladed knives bagged in plastic.

Knives? She must be hallucinating. Why would the police bag knives? Had somebody been stabbed while she dozed? Surely Lucien would have woken her up for a knife fight.

Knives. She racked her brain. The kitchen was Tanya's jurisdiction and she'd be the one in charge of the knives. Could she have shivved the doctor when he plowed into her in the dining room and he was too drunk to realize it? But that wasn't possible. There'd have been blood. The doctor choked. He gagged. He turned purple and wheezed, but he didn't bleed. She'd definitely have noticed if he was bleeding. So why did the police bag these knives?

"What're you doing?"

"Nothing." She swung around as a rangy guy with uncanny green eyes strolled into the room.

"Nothing's an underrated occupation. In relation to the infinite, we are as nothing. But in relation to nothing at all, we're everything." He smiled an enigmatic smile. "Even after we die, we're something. Me, I believe in karma. What you do in this life determines your phylum in the next. Reincarnation. I see myself coming back as something friendly and vegetarian, maybe a koala. I didn't have the pleasure of meeting the murder victim. What do you think he'll come back as?"

She arched an eyebrow. "Are you a policeman?"

"Not in this lifetime. I'm Seth Farraday, long-lost son of Cleon Dobbs."

Fisher's death had driven the new heir completely out of her mind and at this hour of the morning, she didn't have the bandwidth for this egotistical sage-of-the-Orient. She went back for more coffee. "What do you want?"

"In the cosmic sense?"

"In the kitchen sense."

"Tea. And you needn't look so guilty."

"I don't. I'm not."

"You do, even if you're not."

He was annoyingly attractive. She raked her hair out of her face and tried to bring off an air of nonchalance. "There's the pot. Pour it yourself."

He poured himself a mug of tea and sat down, smiling. She sat down across from him. "When did you arrive?"

"I don't know. Two-ish. I got delayed."

"And the police? When did they arrive?"

"Around five-thirty, I think."

Over an hour ago, according to her watch. She drank some more coffee. "Have the police questioned you already?"

"Oh, yes. Caught hell for moving the body. Of course, everyone thought the old geezer had died of natural causes."

"That isn't what Cleon thinks."

"Everyone except Cleon. Isn't that what you think?"

"I don't know. If Cleon thought Fisher had been murdered, why did he let anyone move the body?"

"Margaret sent up a hue and cry. *Don't let him just lie there, Wendell. Close his eyes, take him to his room, cover his body, the children mustn't see this.* A compulsive tidier-upper, the first Mrs. Dobbs. Classic anal personality."

"You psychoanalyze people rather quickly."

"I find most people are pretty scrutable. I'd say Wendell is a textbook mama's boy and Lucien is an aging paradigm of the angry young man." He nodded toward the metal box. "What's in there?"

"I don't know." Maybe it wasn't his mouth that smiled so much as the corners of his eyes. She resolved to concentrate extra hard on disliking him. "What was it that delayed you, Mr. Farraday?"

"Seth. Or call me cousin if you like."

"No thanks."

He shrugged. "My meeting with Cleon's P.I. ran late and, truth to tell, I wasn't all that eager." He turned his mug around and around in his hands, a thoughtful look on his face. "Do you believe somebody in the family tried to kill Cleon before he could change his will?"

"No." She sounded more emphatic than she felt.

"Maybe Wendell or Lucien liked their get under the old will better."

"Maybe you want Cleon to think that so he'll leave their share to you."

"Kill the doc, delay Cleon's death, and throw suspicion on the rest of the field. That's clever. Are you a lawyer?"

"No."

"Detective?"

"No."

"Fiction writer?"

"Very funny."

"What then?"

"I do a lot of things." Why did she feel so defensive? She couldn't care less what this supercilious article thought of her or her career path. "And what, pray, do you do?"

"I'm a freelance photographer. I mostly take pictures of clear-cut left by unscrupulous loggers, mountain gorillas butchered by poachers, elephants slaughtered for their ivory. That sort of thing."

By extreme dint of will, she kept her face neutral.

His eyebrows went up. "Sorry if I've grossed you out."

She'd obviously overshot neutral. The addition of a greenie to the plot hit her like a wind shear. Not that a few photos and an aggrieved tone made him a fanatic. He was probably citing a few random examples from his portfolio. A butchered gorilla would stick in anyone's mind. But he probably took pictures of weddings and horse races, too. "You must work for a lot of different people and take a passing interest in whatever they're paying you to photograph."

"Protecting the earth isn't a passing interest. It's a core value and it has nothing to do with money. I only work for people who care about the planet, and against those who don't." His eyes had hardened and his tone was devoutly aggrieved.

Dinah had one of her bad feelings. "I don't suppose you care for dragnet fishing."

"It sucks. Why?"

"Forget it. I'm going upstairs to shower."

NINETEEN

Once she herded the assassin spider up the bathroom wall and out the window, it was a routine shower, considering. Considering a dead crusader for the right to die and an out-of-the-blue greenie on a jihad against polluters. Considering a spoon-pointing Cleon full of hints and allegations. Considering a resentful Lucien possessed by a bone-pointing snake god. Considering sexual undertows and sibling rivalries and somebody who, just maybe, went haywire enough to commit murder. Considering a house full of adversaries who didn't trust each other and a coming swarm of policemen who never trust anyone.

These considerations orbited her head like killer asteroids as the water orbited the shower drain counterclockwise. When her life was going down the drain back in the Northern Hemisphere, at least it was going down in a clockwise, predictable direction with nothing more disheartening than a crummy job and a plebeian boyfriend. Here in the Southern Hemisphere, everything went down the wrong way, even the water.

She blow-dried her hair, dressed, and slunk back to her room. K.D. was out, thank God. She sat down on the lower bunk, fished a cigarette out of her purse and lit up, trying not to think about the doctor's purple face.

Somebody knocked at the door. If her caller didn't shout "Fire" or "Police" she wasn't budging. And even if it were the police, she could stall them, plead a migraine or post-traumatic stress disorder. Maybe she should plead the Fifth.

If it turned out to be murder, she'd be as much a suspect as anyone else.

"Open up, cherie. I know you're in there. I bring important tidings."

Shit. She got up and opened the door.

"Mon Dieu, but you do look ragged. Would you like to borrow my Aqua-Pac eye mask? It'll take care of that puffiness."

"Stuff it, Eddie."

"Woke up on the wrong side of the sofa, did we?"

"How could you have let me crap out like that?"

"You outlasted Neesha, although she did make it upstairs to bed. Give me one of those." He flicked a cigarette out of the pack and held it between his teeth for her to light. She did and he took a deep drag. "Have you seen our newest family member yet? Ooh-la-la. Dommage he isn't gay."

Eddie's insouciance had begun to grate. She went to the mirror and combed her hair. "What did you come to tell me?"

"A majestically bizarre policeman is waiting for you in the great room."

"All policemen are bizarre. They all have two faces and an ulterior motive that's hard-wired into their stunted little hearts."

"Of course, you're bitter about Nick. But this one's a pussycat."

"Leading you down the garden path, no doubt. Setting you up for the ambush. And by the way, I don't appreciate Lucien telling you about my breakups or any other personal business."

"Well, if that's how you feel…"

"Don't make it about you, Eddie." She was being a blister, but she didn't care. "Do you think Fisher was murdered?"

He exhaled voluptuously. "Probably some tropical virus."

Maybe she'd lived with Nick too long, but it didn't compute that a man who'd forecast a slit throat two days ago would be ambivalent now that there was an actual corpus delicti. And up to the time she passed out last night, Lucien had maintained the cause of death was cardiac arrest.

"How's Lucien feeling this morning?"

"Hung-over like everyone else. Very gruff and sans joie."

"A man's dead, Eddie. Don't act so flaming Maurice Chevalier."

"We all have our strategies." He stubbed out his cigarette and gave her a chilly look. "Alors. Tanya's on strike this morning so I'm the chef. When the inspector's done with you, come have a piece of my quiche Lorraine. Maybe that will restore your joie."

She doubted that very much. She followed him down the hall at a distance, reciting Nick's advice on how to skate through a police interrogation. Be confident, but not overly. Be cooperative, but don't donate your own theories. Be polite. Don't let the cop bait you. Keep your temper. Remember what you say and keep your story consistent. Cops listen for inconsistencies and discrepancies. They'll jump on anything that sounds hinky. The main thing here was not to say anything they could construe as a motive for murder, particularly anything that might suggest that Lucien had issues with Cleon. Then, if it did turn out to be murder, the police would have to look for somebody with a grudge against Desmond Fisher, which wouldn't be Lucien because the doctor had saved his life.

By the time she reached the first floor, she was ready for the Spanish Inquisition. She arranged her face, not too downcast. She barely knew Desmond Fisher. But she would show a respectful gravity. Policemen were suckers for gravity. She took a deep breath, steeled herself, and stepped into the room.

"You!"

"Hello, luv. Now don't come the stunned mullet on me. Didn't I tell you I was the chief walloper in the Top End?"

This was bad. This was the iceberg dead ahead, this was the stalled bus on the tracks, this was the yawning chasm where the bridge used to be and she was hurtling toward it, strapped in, helpless as a crash test dummy. Why did Fate lavish her with so many unnerving coincidences, so many dots she didn't want to connect?

She replayed her meeting in the Darwin Airport with Jacko Newby, a garrulous old eccentric who just happened to overhear her asking for an earlier flight, who just happened to have a private plane at his disposal, who just happened to have a bee in his bonnet about a murdered journalist and a yen to show her the scene. She replayed the questions he'd peppered her with, questions that zeroed in on her family and their comings and goings. She tried to replay her answers, but the only thing she remembered telling him for sure was that Lucien and Cleon didn't get along.

And here he was again, with police insignia on his sleeves, in a coincidence so towering she could scarcely comprehend it. A coincidence, the implications of which could only mean one very bad thing. The Australian police suspected that a member of her family, or somebody who purported to be a member of her family, had something to do with the murder of a British journalist on a lonesome beach on an island populated by Aborigines. And now Desmond Fisher was dead. Murdered, if Cleon was right.

"Come have a seat, luv. You look a bit green about the gills."

She sat. Or rather her knees buckled into a club chair.

Jacko circumnavigated the room, his eyes seeming to sweep in every detail. "Too much of the alkie last night like the rest of the bunch? Understandable. A man drops dead at your feet, it would give anyone a thirst. Have you had your morning cuppa?"

"Yes."

"Well, I've met your family and they're pearlers, one and all. Razor sharp and all with the gift of gab. Your Uncle Cleon especially. My kind of bloke. Lays the oil on a bit thick, but hits his main point like a mallet."

Dinah tried to muster her thoughts, remember Nick's catechisms. Don't donate an opinion was one. She didn't.

"Yes, I've chatted them all up. Amazing the variety of ideas. But I couldn't hie off to Katherine without hearing your skull fruit. What do you think? Did the doctor pop off naturally or was he murdered?"

"I don't know."

"A smart cookie like yourself, I'll wager you've a good hunch."

She contrived a tight smile, but she was seething. The cunning old bastard had lied to her from jump, beguiled her with his quirky charm and played her for a fool, and now he was going to beguile her into tattling on her family? He was as conceited as Nick. They were two of a kind, Detective Nick Isparta and Inspector Jacko Newby. Brothers in tradecraft, hiding their twisty machinations behind would-I-lie-to-you grins.

"You're the pro, Jacko. What's your hunch?"

"It's another puzzler, Dinah. Desmond Fisher crossed swords with a lot of people here in Oz with his views on the right to die. Of course, he came from a long line of kooks and quacks. His grandfather fancied himself God's Gift and tramped about the scrub preaching hellfire and telling whoppers."

"Oz seems rife with whoppers."

"I can see you've got your back up, Dinah. Maybe I should've told you I was a copper. I thought you'd guessed. I thought you were two moves ahead of me."

"Like you said, it's the hard-boiled liars that make us cynical."

"I'm sorry for misleading you, luv. Truly, I am."

"Right. So why exactly did you latch onto me in Darwin?"

"Dr. Fisher has a shady reputation. I wanted to know what business he might have with your family."

During their flight to Melville Island, he hadn't asked her a single question about Fisher. Did he think she was such a ditz she wouldn't remember? "What do you want from me?"

"I'd like your slant on what happened during dinnies last night."

"What?"

"The dinner. I understand there was a bit of a blue over the arrival of Mr. Farraday, sharp words were exchanged, and you didn't get past the reef to the beef."

She said, "After the fish, everyone was full. We moved on to the great room."

He walked over to the window and seemed to meditate on the view, leaving her to smolder in silence. What did he expect her to say? What was he after?

After an eon or so, he turned around and gave her an ingratiating smile. "I'd welcome any insights you might have about the doctor."

"I only just met him. What possible insights could I have?"

"Did you have any discussion with him?"

"I sat next to him during dinner the past two nights. He suggested I get a living will."

"That how he jollied his way into the family bosom? Pushing the idea of living wills?"

"I don't know what he pushed on the others. You'll have to ask them."

"Did the doctor say anything to you about not feeling well?"

She weighed the question. It would be to everyone's advantage to play up the doctor's poor health, wouldn't it? The sicker he was, the likelier he died from natural causes. "His liver wasn't right. He didn't say what the condition was, but he looked unwell. He smoked and drank too much and he couldn't eat the barramundi. Tanya prepared a separate fish for him. Black cod."

"It was fugu."

"Fugu? The poisonous fish?"

"No flies on you, luv. Has to be prepared just so. The entrails are toxic, especially the liver and sexual organs, and they're not destroyed by cooking."

If Dinah had looked like a stunned mullet before, she must look even more stunned now. Fugu. Wasn't that the toxin they used in voodoo ceremonies to turn people into zombies? The fish was a gastronomic treat in Japan, but chefs had to apprentice for years before they could serve it. What manner of moron would let a part-time Aborigine cook who preferred her fish à la paperbark and gum leaves prepare his fugu? That must have been what he was lecturing Tanya about—the liver and kidneys can cause death.

She said, "It had to have been an accident. Tanya must've failed to clean out all the entrails."

"That, or maybe somebody came along after she'd gutted the fish and reinserted a morsel. It's more than a thousand times as poisonous as cyanide and almost a thousand times pricier."

Who'd been in the kitchen besides Tanya? Neesha and K.D., Mack, Lucien asking for a poultice, Cleon asking for olives and she, herself, commiserating with Tanya over the meringue pie. At some time, probably everybody had wandered in. Seth Farraday, too? What if he'd arrived at the lodge earlier than he claimed? He could have nipped into the kitchen and tampered with the fish while Tanya was in the dining room serving the soup. Was he also a suspect in the Melville Island murder? Was he the reason Jacko had glommed onto her in Darwin? Had he known that Seth would be joining the Dobbs party and assumed that she knew something about him?

It would be a sad coda to Cleon's life to find a son he didn't know he had only to learn that he was a murderer. She said, "Until after the autopsy, you can't be sure Fisher didn't die from old age."

"Anything's possible, luv, but it's odds-on for the fugu. The doctor had another of the fat little blighters hidden away in the freezer. There's no mistaking blowie. I've sampled it once or twice on a dare. Tastes a bit like chicken, blowie does, and makes a man feel immortal. There's some will tell you that a dollop of fugu gonads in a shot of hot sake is the best aphrodisiac in the world."

"I won't need to remember that recipe. But if it's odds-on for the fugu, it's odds-on that it was an accident. Accidents happen far more often than murder. Statistically."

"Your uncle's not a one for statistics, luv. He's flogging the theory that it was murder and he thinks that he was the intended victim."

"Well, if it *was* murder and if fugu *was* the cause, then the doctor had to have been the target because he's the only one who ate the stuff."

"But why kill Dr. Fisher? You see what I mean about it being a puzzler."

Apart from a general desire to shut him up, Dinah could think of only one reason. Killing Fisher postponed Cleon's death. "Have you told Tanya about the fugu?"

"You're the only one I've told."

There he went again, trying to con her into thinking she was his Watson and privy to inside information when all he really wanted was to dupe her into revealing family secrets. "What makes you think I won't tell everybody else?"

"Call it professional instinct. I trust you. And I'd hate to see you get hurt trying to cover somebody else's bum."

She didn't know whose bum he was talking about and a still, small voice told her she didn't want to know. The more she thought about it, the more this whole mess seemed like Desmond Fisher's own stupid fault. "Why would a doctor, of all people, trust an untrained cook to prepare a potentially lethal fish for him?"

Jacko slipped on a latex glove, took a half-empty bottle of Scotch off a side table, and added it to a box of open bottles on top of the bar. "Some men are chancers. Addicted to risk. It could be that for Fisher a bit of extra risk added to the thrill."

"I can't understand why he'd be so harebrained. He was going to run for Parliament. He was on a mission to reform your euthanasia law. Death was all he talked about, not that everyone else in this place isn't gaga on the subject."

"Now why is that?"

She bit her tongue. "Dr. Fisher wouldn't stop talking about it."

"Everyone agrees he was a bit of an earbasher," said Jacko, letting her off easy. "A bit of a boozer, too, from what I hear."

"That's right. And after he got loaded, he became belligerent. He stammered and slurred his words."

"The slurring was probably worsened by the fugu. It numbs the lips, puts a man in an expansive frame of mind right up until the convulsions and the respiratory paralysis." He crossed the room, picked up the didgeridoo, and secured a plastic baggie over the end. "As for the belligerence, who did the doctor go off on?"

"Everybody." She didn't know what information the others had disclosed, but she saw no reason to call undue attention to the fact that Fisher had told Cleon to sod off and Margaret to stick it up her jumper. Somebody else would no doubt have recounted Mack's angry tug-of-war with Fisher over the didgeridoo and their odd little tiff over whether doctors had been threatened by Aborigines. But Fisher's most unsettling run-in was the one with Tanya. What was that word she spat at him? Galka. Was it a curse? A threat? It had certainly jolted Mack. But if it was the fugu that killed Fisher, Tanya had served it long before that incident.

She said, "Fisher was a complete jerk to Tanya. But if it was the fugu that killed him, I'm sure it was an accident. Tanya was flustered, too many pots bubbling on the stove. And her nephew? He's a handful. Keeping track of him would've exacerbated her stress. Her mind must've wandered."

Jacko took off the plastic glove and stuck it in his pocket. "She'd prepared it for him correctly once before. She says he gave her a demo on how to clean it and cook it as soon as he lobbed in at the lodge."

"Well then, he should have quit while he was ahead. Anyone who's eaten even one meal here would know that Tanya's no master chef. She's not to blame if a sliver of gonad ended up on the doctor's plate."

"You've an aptitude for the tidy closure, luv."

"Will you let us know the results of the autopsy?" she asked.

"I'll keep you informed. And if you see or hear anything sussy, I'd appreciate it if you'd give me a call."

"Sussy?"

"Suspicious, whiffy on the nose."

"You're asking me to spy on my own family?"

"Not all are related by blood, are they? You'll have to decide for yourself. I'm asking you to consider the possibility that somebody in the house is a killer."

A knee-jerk defensiveness boiled out of her. "I know something about the police mentality, Jacko. You assume the worst about everybody because you spend your life rubbing shoulders with lowlifes and scuzzballs and floozies. You're disrespectful and deceitful and you have the power to wreak havoc in people's lives."

"He was that sort of a bugger, was he?"

"Who?"

"The policeman who disappointed you."

"And another thing about policemen, they think they hear significance behind every casual remark. My point is, what happened to Dr. Fisher was a tragic accident due entirely to his own negligence. And furthermore, I don't know what connection you think there is between my family and that dead journalist, but none of us has so much as set foot on Melville Island. If one of us killed him, we had to do it by remote control."

"Like pointing the bone," he said.

Her attitude crumbled. Looking into his steely, seen-it-all eyes, it was impossible to mistake him for anything but a cop, and a cop who meant business. Anyone who failed to take him seriously or who willfully obstructed his investigation would do so at his or her peril.

She said, "I accidentally kicked the doctor's cigarette

holder under the sofa. You'll probably want to check it for poison.

"Just in case."

TWENTY

DJANG IS THE Aboriginal equivalent of the Big Bang. It formed the world and is the constantly recharging energy that sustains it. Djang is the collective spirit of the whole race, the stored-up powers of the ancestors, a latent creative force that resides in certain sacred objects and places and, like the power of the atom, it can be tapped and released in frightening ways. Cyclones. Floods. Earthquakes. Death by remote control.

The book didn't say that in so many words, but death by remote control is what Dinah made of it and she had no time to get bogged down with semantics. She shut *The Illustrated Atlas of Aboriginal Storytelling* and replaced it on the shelf. When you're tossing a man's study, you can't let yourself be sidetracked by his mythology, although she had hoped to find in Mack's extensive library some reference to payback law and the Aborigines' animus toward kill doctors.

Seth had gone off by himself to photograph the morning light through the foliage; Tanya had gone AWOL; Mack had gone to Katherine to restock the now-empty bar; and Dinah had made sure everyone else was gathered around the dining room table comparing notes about their recollections of last night and their interviews with the police before she slipped out of the room to snoop. They'd be finished soon and dispersing throughout the house and she didn't have time to dip into every tome.

She couldn't articulate just what it was about Mack that

aroused her suspicion any more than she could articulate why she kicked Fisher's cigarette holder under the sofa. Everything was in turmoil and she was operating on nerves and her iffy intuition. There'd be time to rationalize and reflect when the dust settled. With any luck, this would not take place inside an Australian prison.

In the corner, covered by a cloth screenprinted with Aboriginal symbols and a cairn of art books, she found a two-drawer metal filing cabinet. She flipped through the folders in the top drawer. Most contained information on the various clans in the Northern Territory and there were a few poignant, handwritten narratives telling of children removed from their families.

The bottom drawer yielded a basket full of shells and stones and tree bark and underneath, a permit to visit Melville Island dated May 15, some three weeks ago. Well, well, well. It was a leap to infer that a man who'd merely visited a place committed a murder while there, but the fact did confer a certain distinction. She tried to picture the dignified and rather punctilious former concierge spindling a man on top of a sea turtle with a spear. The image didn't jell.

When did he arrive on Melville and how long did he stay? From the way Jacko had described the body, it had already begun to decompose by the time it was discovered. She didn't know anything about forensic medicine, but it was probably impossible to pinpoint the exact time of death. She could only pray that her assertion held true and the family hadn't arrived in Australia until long after the deed was done.

There was a leaflet detailing the history and artistry of pukamani burial poles, for which the Tiwi people apparently were renowned, and a bill of sale for twenty poles, twelve pots, and four bark paintings. As there were only a couple of burial poles in this room and no pots or bark paintings, the rest must either have been resold or stored someplace else. She thought about the crude, half-painted pole in the dumpster. Was Mack trying to become an artist, himself?

He was clearly out to hoover up native art, probably with the aim of reselling at a higher price to affluent tourists. There was nothing illegal about being a "commerce man" unless Australia had some kind of anti-exploitation law or something. But what if Mack had sold pukamani poles that weren't carved by the Tiwi people and Fisher found out about it? Maybe to keep Fisher quiet, he poisoned him in a house full of people who'd known the doctor from way back in order to spread the suspicion around.

It went against Dinah's grain to spread suspicion to people she hardly knew, people she liked and wished well, but she couldn't conceive of a member of the family doing murder and she felt bound to provide Jacko with a viable alternative. Her allegiance, first and foremost, was to her kin and Jacko was wacko if he thought that being kin was only about blood.

She had never doubted that Cleon and his wives and children were her family. They were family for the same reasons that anybody takes root in another person's life—fate, custom, history. Choice, too. In spite of their many warts, she'd chosen them and nobody had the right to dictate who did or did not deserve her loyalty. She might not agree with the Dobbses on much. She didn't even like them half the time. But they were formative and familiar and, however much they feuded among themselves, they weren't the bloody Borgias.

It would be sad if Mack or Tanya turned out to be a murderer, but they weren't the only candidates nor were they the best. Seth Farraday gave rich new meaning to the word whiffy. How whiffy was it that he turned up just hours after Fisher hit the floor dead? Seth had no motive to kill Cleon. Not before he'd changed his will. But if the doctor was the intended victim, as Jacko seemed to believe, the possibilities broadened. She wasn't at all convinced that Seth was Cleon's son. Maybe he and the Kellerman guy who vetted him had a scam going to search out ailing rich men and foist Seth off as a missing heir. Maybe Fisher had run into them before and Seth killed him to keep from being recognized. And hanging over all of their heads like a lowering phantom was the dead man on Melville Island.

Jacko had searched Fisher's room, but for whatever reason probable cause or its Australian counterpart—he hadn't searched any of the others' rooms. Maybe he needed the results of the autopsy before he brought the full weight of the law to bear. But her hands weren't tied. As soon as she found out which room was Seth's, she'd give it a going-over for evidence of a prior acquaintance with Fisher and a recent visit to Melville.

She looked at her watch. Time was wasting. She closed the cabinet, replaced the cover cloth and books, took a last gander around, and oozed out into the hall.

Jittery from her sleuthing, she headed to the veranda for a steadying fix of nicotine. Through the cloudy panes in the back door, she saw Cleon and Wendell talking. She opened the door a crack.

"How can you think such a thing?" protested Wendell. "That one of your children would murder you for a few thousand more? It's preposterous."

Cleon shielded his eyes with a sheet of paper and squinted into the sun. "As many chances as you've had at me over the years, I'm inclined to believe it wasn't you or Lucien."

"That leaves Seth Farraday," said Wendell, sounding

portentous. "That dossier you've got there is ludicrous. No P.I. in the world could verify that stuff. It's like he cribbed it from *Soldier of Fortune* magazine."

Cleon folded the piece of paper and put it back in his pocket. "Things have come to a pitiful pass when a man's obliged to verify what his own flesh and blood tells him."

"Well, if Farraday is your flesh and blood, which I very much doubt, he must hate you for the way you treated his mother."

"You don't hate me for the way I treated yours," said Cleon. It wasn't exactly a question, but it finished with an un-Cleonlike inflection.

At first, Wendell seemed nonplussed. Finally, he said, "Of course, I don't hate you. I, I revere you."

"Revere me." Cleon smiled an odd, bashful smile and draped an arm around his shoulders. "Let's mosey down the lane a ways and talk. After last night, I could use a mite of reverence."

Dinah watched the two disappear around the side of the lodge. It was a sweet moment. She wished that Lucien could repair his relationship with Cleon before it was too late. Maybe he would yet. Maybe Fisher's death would shake him up and bring about a rapprochement, or at least a state of affairs where Lucien could speak Cleon's name without snarling.

Curious about Seth Farraday's Soldier of Fortune dossier, she cancelled her cigarette break and went straight to the kitchen to find somebody who could give her the scoop. Margaret was the only one still at the table.

"I just ate the last piece of Eduardo's quiche, but there's bread and butter and there's some fried mutton in that skillet on the stove if your digestion's up to it."

Dinah looked at the slab of meat in a pool of grease. "I'll make do with toast and jam."

Margaret buttered a chunk of bread and smeared on a half inch of jam. "Our Martha Stewart has ordered duck à l'orange for dinner. She's acting like one of those characters in an Agatha Christie mystery. The dinner must go on."

Dinah saw no benefit in taking sides. "It's her way of coping, I guess."

"True. I shouldn't criticize poor Neesha. Cleon hectoring, Thad rebelling, Dez dropping dead."

Not to mention your campaign to steer Cleon's money away from her to your son, thought Dinah. She wondered if eating was Margaret's way of coping.

She poured herself a cup of coffee and sat down. "Margaret, have you seen the P.I.'s report on Seth Farraday?"

"No. Cleon has kept the Farraday person and anything to do with him away from me. Doesn't want me dumping cold water on his happiness."

"Happiness?"

"Oh, yes. He may not look it, but he's a new man this morning. Something's put the spring back in his step—maybe the arrival of Farraday. More likely, it's the moratorium on his own death."

Dinah had had misgivings about Cleon's health from the minute she first laid eyes on him. "Is he really and truly dying, Margaret? He doesn't act like a man about to face his maker."

"What maker? Cleon made himself." One corner of her mouth turned up slightly, like a grapefruit knife. "Yes, he's dying. He could probably live five or six months if he went through another round of chemo, but he nixed that. Said the time for torture's when he gets to hell, not before."

"Why did no one tell me that he had cancer?"

"He didn't tell anybody, not even Neesha, until two weeks ago. His Australian client wasn't the only reason he moved to Sydney. He didn't want anyone to see him go through chemo. Dez made sure he got the best care available, but the cancer had spread. You didn't see Dez at his best. He was an extraordinary man in many ways, but full of contradictions. Like Cleon. Like they all are, I suppose." In the strong morning light, she looked careworn. Her skin had a crepey texture and her eyes were rimmed red. She'd been glib about not missing Cleon's final parting. Could it be she was more broken up by Dez Fisher's?

"Did you know Dr. Fisher well, Margaret?"

"As well as he let anyone know him. Dez and Wen are… were business partners. They co-owned a fish processing company in Brunswick."

Fish again, the leitmotif of Fisher's life. "I didn't know Wen had any business other than his job as bank manager."

"The plant's more of an investment."

"Investment requires a lot of extra capital lying around, doesn't it?"

Margaret's eyebrows climbed toward her widow's peak. "Anyone with the sense God gave a goose invests. And don't you poor-mouth, young lady. You have a trust fund."

Dinah did not suffer allusions to her father's ill-gotten gain gladly. The little pile of dirty money he'd left her in an offshore trust was an open secret, but not one she cared to have thrown in her face. Her quarterly stipend was a posthumous communication from her father, important to have, but shameful to spend. She'd never told anyone that after she graduated from college, she began to donate the money to tsunami relief or whatever other catastrophe happened to be in the headlines when the check arrived.

In deference to Margaret's emotional strain, Dinah let her breach of manners pass. "Did Dr. Fisher have a family or is Wen now the sole owner of the business?"

"I hadn't thought about it, but I guess he is. Dez was a

widower with no children. He used to come to Georgia several times a year to visit Cleon and check on his business and I visited him a few times in Sydney. I guess you could say that Dez and I...dated." A wisp of sadness skirred across her face. She banished it instantly. "We shared an enjoyment of food and wine. I don't know if it was because of our friendship or because Cleon recommended it, but last year Dez made Wendell a partner."

"Does Wen participate in the business?"

"No. The way Dez explained it, Wen's the go-to man in the event there's a strike or an immigration problem or some trouble at the plant and he couldn't get there from Australia quick enough to handle it. Nothing like that's come up. Cleon prepared the legal documents. There was a nominal buy-in, but it's been all gravy for no work. Almost a gift. It allowed Wen's highfalutin wife to hire an au pair and a full-time maid."

"Do you think Dr. Fisher was murdered, Margaret?"

She expelled a derisive phtt, almost a belch. "If he was, it was Seth Farraday who killed him."

"Why? Did he know Seth before he came?"

"Whether he did or didn't, it's irrelevant. Farraday needed more time to get his hooks into Cleon. He's a designing piece of work, but he may luck out. One thing about Cleon Dobbs, he's captivated by fly-by-nights and flibbertigibbets." She scarfed down a last bite of bread. "Wen and I are off to Katherine in an hour to arrange for Dez's cremation as soon as the police release the body. We plan to have lunch in town and discuss what to do about Farraday. You may be a legatee, yourself, Dinah. The paintings may not be all Cleon leaves you. Do you want to sit in with us?"

"No thanks. I'll hang here with Lucien and Eddie."

"Lucien said he wasn't interested either, but then you're

Swan's cygnets. Cleon would never shortchange you." And on that note, she scorched out of the room without a backward glance.

One of these days, thought Dinah. One of these crazy, flaming days.

TWENTY-ONE

DINAH WASHED HER cup and peered out the kitchen window. Twenty yards across the weedy lawn, sublimely oblivious to the risk of death adders, a half-naked Seth went through a sequence of slow, stretching motions. T'ai chi, she assumed. She hung over the sink entranced as his lithe body flowed through each movement with a sinuous grace. God, but he was sculpted.

Tanya clumped into the kitchen, muttering darkly. "Has to get out of the house, she says. Pack a lunch, she says. Stuff some eggs. Make sweet iced tea. Make sandwiches. Skinny boy wants roast beef, sliced thin. Her and the girl want pimento cheese with the crust trimmed off the bread. Probably want a side salad of dollar bills."

Dinah wondered what sweetener had induced Tanya to return to work. Perhaps Mack had doubled her pay or Jacko had cajoled her to stay on and spy for him. "Tanya, is there a roster of who's staying in which room?"

"Why?" She clumped into the pantry and lugged out an armful of jars, mayo and mustard and pickles, and dumped them on the table.

"I have some old family photos. I thought I'd slip a few under everyone's door."

"How come you don't hand them out at dinner?"

"They're sentimental. Best enjoyed in private."

Her forehead pleated with suspicion, but it was clear from her snort that she didn't give a rat's patootie what

Crow Hill's troublemaking guests found under their doors.
"No list."

"Well, do you know who's where?"

"Who you think makes the beds?"

Nobody had made up Dinah's rumpled aerie, but this
was hardly the time to complain. "Will you please tell me?"

"Eight, you and the snooty girl. Seven, the no-good
painter and the poofter. Six, my Victor and the boy that
hoons around with his video games and his iPod. Five,
the glum one."

"Wendell?"

"Him, yes. His bossy mum's next door in four." She
turned on the tap full force and filled a kettle. "Gotta be
Darjeeling. Gotta seed the lemons and slice 'em just so."

"What about the second floor?" prompted Dinah.

"Old muckety-muck and Lady La-de-da are in the big
room at the far end. No number. Mackenzie took three
for himself. He put the new son doing the crazy dance
out there in one."

Dinah had to hand it to her. The woman had a knack
for the concise putdown. Was it a reluctance to speak ill of
the dead that kept her from tagging the former occupant of
Room 2 a scumbag? Or a galka? Dinah wanted to ask her
what it meant, but something volatile in the air between
them stopped her.

Tentatively, she asked, "Where do you sleep, Tanya?"

"In the shed behind the house. Where'd you think, the
captain's suite?" As she clanked a pan with last night's
leftover roast beef onto the stove, she radiated antagonism.

Dinah had nothing to say in the face of her withering
stare. It was pot-bangingly clear that the fellow feeling
they'd established beating egg whites for meringue had
expired. Dinah didn't have to ask why. If Tanya had poisoned Fisher, she'd be afraid to say anything that could give

her away. But if she believed she'd prepared the fugu correctly, she'd assume that one of the Dobbs clan had murdered Fisher. She'd worry that the family would try to lay the blame off on her. And she'd be right, thought Dinah, smarting from guilt.

She left Tanya to her clanking and muttering and went out into the foyer. In the great room, the only voices she heard were Lucien's—raw and edgy. "For the love of Christ, if he knows, why doesn't he come straight out with it?" And Eduardo's—querulous, "Because he positively revels in goading you."

The *he* was obviously Cleon. Dinah was torn. If Cleon knew what? Should she go and beat the truth out of Lucien or give Seth's room a whirl while she had the chance?

She skulked to the back door to see if he was still t'ai-chiing. K.D. dallied on the veranda, ostensibly brushing and grooming Cantoo. Her eyes were hidden behind her pink Juicy Couture sunglasses, but Dinah had no doubt that she had staked herself out to observe Seth. He was still feinting and thrusting and pivoting with a contained, balletic grace. A towel and gym bag lay on the lawn near where he was exercising. When he finished, he'd probably head straight to the shower. But he'd have to get past K.D. first and shaking loose from that cocklebur would take time.

Her thoughts racing, Dinah padded back down the hall and tiptoed upstairs to the second floor. A quick glance to make sure no one had seen her, a twist of the door handle and she was safe inside Room Number 1.

Like everything else at Crow Hill, it was comfortless and dingy and the furniture looked as if it had been salvaged from a junkyard. The bed was a rickety single with a split headboard. Moths had pastured on the meadow-green upholstery of the only chair and a battered hulk of

an armoire balanced on three bun feet and a ratty copy of
Plato's *Collected Dialogues*. A satirical drawing of a pig
holding a "Welcome to the Trough" sign had been tacked
haphazardly on the wall above the bed. It was limned in
exquisite detail, which meant that the artist had to be Lucien. She groaned. Either he or, more likely, Eduardo on his
behalf, had gotten here ahead of her. But had he searched
the room or merely left this memento to haze Seth?

In the tiny water closet was a rusty basin with a medicine chest above it. Nothing incriminating inside—razor,
shaving gel, toothbrush, toothpaste. She moved on. A canvas satchel lay open on the bed. Underwear—crew necks
and packers, a pair of Nikes in a clear plastic sack, a bottle
of Wild Turkey and a carton of Chinese cigarettes. Chung
Hwa. She would have pinched one, but the cellophane seal
hadn't been broken.

On a luggage caddy next to the armoire was a water-
stained suitcase. It had been patched with duct tape and
plastered with markings and stickers indicative of numerous border crossings. She inventoried the outside pockets
first and came up with a couple of year-old boarding passes
and a wad of strange currency spendable in no country
she'd ever been to.

She sorted through a stack of neatly folded shirts, socks,
cotton slacks. At the bottom, wrapped in a nylon windbreaker, was a handgun. A Glock. Black. Compact. Sexy.

But telling? The murders in question had been per-
petrated using a spear and a fish. A weapon as techno-
logically advanced as a Glock didn't fit the pattern. She
carefully rewrapped it and opened a large camera bag.
Inside she found a dog-eared copy of Al Gore's *Earth
in the Balance* and a U.S. passport. Jason Seth Farraday,
born in Fresno, California, February 14, 1975. The photo
was definitely him, but a more prosaic him. The Brooks

Brothers-ish suit and conservative blue necktie clashed with the persona of a man who wanted to come back as a koala. The Seth in this picture looked like he might come back as a predator. A panther, maybe. He had an intimidating countenance. Like a litigator or...or a man backed up by a badge.

No! She shook the thought out of her head. She was seeing cops behind every tree. She noted the issue date, six years ago, and thumbed through the pages of exotic stamps and visas.

She took out a Canon digital camera and hit display. Up popped a picture of a large boat. There were several more shots of the same vessel. A close-up of the bow showed the name, Suwannee. Cleon's yacht.

Something whumped against the door. Shit.

Voices, hushed and urgent. The door handle turned.

Unthinking, she tore open the armoire door, which creaked, and clambered inside. Instantly, she felt stupid. Stupid and scared. It was pitch black in here and she could practically feel the spiders foraging up her pant legs. She swept a cobweb out of her face and groped about for something soft to put under her knees. Why did she always react like a guilty child? No matter how humiliating, she wished that Seth would fling open the doors and let her out. Surely he'd heard that creak. She'd rather be caught red-handed than to have a herd of hairy spiders grazing on her flesh.

"Oh, God, what are we going to do? He knows. Did you hear him last night? I tell you, he knows."

Neesha? What the hell was Neesha...?

"Shhh. It'll be all right, darling. He can't possibly know. We've been discreet."

Holy Shit. It was Wendell. Wendell calling Neesha darling.

"Oh, Wen, I could've stood three more nights. Three

and then…but he's saying he can't go through with it now, not 'til the police have finished investigating the doctor's death. How could this have happened?"

"I don't know, but he can't last many more weeks. I've asked him not to change his will until we learn more about this Farraday character. The man's obviously an impostor."

"Not Cleon's son?"

"I don't know. He's a fraud. I just don't know what kind of a fraud."

"What if he walks in on us?"

"He won't. He told me he does that t'ai chi stuff for an hour every morning."

"Oh, Wen."

There was an interval of quiet during which Dinah inferred kissing. During which her skin tickled and crawled. During which she brooded on infidelity and the parameters of incest and what seemed a remarkable lack of curiosity on the part of the kissers about the cause of Fisher's death. During which she debated whether to burst out of the box and scream "Aha!" or "Small world" or "Somebody get the assassin out of my shirt."

The smell of dry rot and mouse droppings made her want to retch. How many thousand years had she been trapped in here? There were Egyptian mummies who hadn't been shut up this long.

"Your mother's being horrid to me, Wendell. I know you have feelings for her, but the way she's hounding Cleon to take away what's mine…Can't you stop her?"

"Not as long as Dad puts up with her nagging. She acts like she's lobbying for me, but I think she just enjoys sparring with him. In some dark cranny of her brain I think she still loves him. Whatever her idea of love is."

"This is my idea."

Presumably, there was more kissing. Fondling, too, if Neesha's ardent little moans were any indication.

A zipper whished and Wendell began to moan.

"Oh, Jesus. Oh. Oh."

Dinah didn't like to think what the Victorian lady was doing to her wooden-faced stepson to elicit such noises. Could he be panting that hard? That close?

Cantoo. Cantoo was snuffling and scratching at the door of the armoire. Sweet Jerusalem, she'd been treed. She massaged a cramp in one knee and tried to envisage a far distant time in a far distant place when this would seem funny.

The dog gave a sudden, frustrated yip.

"Damn it, Neesha."

The zipper whished again.

"Leave it, Cantoo."

The scratching and snuffling stopped. Neesha must have picked up Cantoo.

"Can we meet in town this afternoon, Wen?"

"Too risky. We have to sit tight for a few days. Trust me, darling. With the money you and the kids get from Dad and my share of Dez's business, we'll be fine."

"None of it matters as long as we're together."

Dinah couldn't stand the armoire or the lovey-dovey any longer. Her hand was on the door.

"Give it back!" K.D.'s high-pitched shriek cut through the thin walls like a chain saw. "Give it to me this instant, Thad."

Cantoo barked, Neesha and Wendell whispered urgently, and what sounded like a herd of buffalo thundered up the stairs.

"He has bedroom eyes the color of jade and his body is like a glorious temple that cries out to be desecrated." Thad, very loud and with that intrinsic sneer in his voice.

"Thadeus Dobbs, if you don't give it to me this minute, I'll kill you."

"In your dreams, fugly. I'm gonna read this shit to everybody."

The sounds of battle passed by the second floor and moved on to the third.

After a moment, Neesha said, "When can we talk again?"

"We'll have to play it by ear. Don't let him rattle you."

A few more inaudible whispers and the door snicked open and shut again.

Dinah scrambled out of her cubbyhole mussing and brushing her hair like a mad thing. Her skin felt itchy and her already jaundiced opinion of mankind was in a nosedive. Wendell fornicating with his stepmother. It made Nick's two-timing seem tame. Unless the redhead was his sister. Nothing was beyond the pale. Life was a masquerade. No one was who or what he pretended to be.

And K.D. wasn't where Dinah assumed she'd be, which meant that Seth wasn't either. She put his passport and camera back where she found them and repaired to her room to shake the spiders out of her shirt and reassess.

TWENTY-TWO

A TIZZY IS what her mother would have called it. A twitchy, distracted, hair-on-fire feeling that could only be alleviated by moving. Preferably at full tilt. Cooped up in that spidery hutch with a head full of refractory emotions, Dinah had a tizzy. She went back to her room, but she couldn't sit still. Her thoughts were in ferment. She had to move or go mad.

Heedless of the noonday sun, she twisted her hair into a ponytail, changed into her running togs, laced up her Nikes, and went out for a run. She'd discovered the release valve of running when she ran track in high school and she'd been a runner ever since. When she ran, life's upsets and letdowns seemed to fall away from her mind, left behind in the dust. Her grandmother believed that running was an affirmation of her Seminole blood. Seminole was what the Spanish had called the Cimarron Indians. It meant either "wild" or "runaway." In Dinah's present tizzy, it meant both.

The lane at midday was brutally hot, but she set out at a furious pace, pursued by a posse of thoughts she didn't want to think. Whatever Cleon's defects as a husband and a father, he didn't deserve to be betrayed in so sleazy a fashion. All that lovey-dovey baloney from Neesha, all that bogus loyalty from Wendell—they were hypocrites of the highest order. All they wanted was to see him dead so they could snaffle up his money and feast on each other's flesh. And Wendell's wife and children back in Brunswick? Collateral damage, evidently not worth mentioning. And lo and behold, Wendell had expectations from Fisher's will.

She checked her watch. She was running six-minute miles, sweating profusely and the upsetting thoughts weren't falling behind. If anything, they were gaining on her. She slowed to a walk. After a few minutes, a previously unnoticed walking path angled off into the trees. It had a smooth, well-beaten look, not too snaky and more shaded than the road. Impulsively, she turned onto the path.

Breathing more easily now, she began to jog and to think more constructive thoughts. Wendell had nullified any allegiance she might have owed him. The important thing now was to help the police nab Fisher's murderer and put this sick-making episode behind her. Much as she hated to rat, she would tell Jacko about Wendell's sordid affair with Neesha and their financial incentive to hurry both Fisher and Cleon out of this world. For good measure, she'd throw in a tip about Seth Farraday's Glock.

"You've spoiled my shot!"

Her heart caromed off her chest wall so hard she bent double.

Seth Farraday materialized out of the trees like a ninja, camera slung around his neck, and pointed. "That was a Gouldian finch. They're nearly extinct."

Heart hammering, she sagged against a tree. "What the hell are you doing?"

"You're always asking me the same question. What does it look like I'm doing? I'm taking pictures. What are you doing?"

"Wishing you were extinct." Breathing hard, she straightened up and glared at him. He was exasperating, but if she were going to find out more about him, she'd have to mind her tongue. She wiped the annoyance off her face. "Just kidding. I was about to turn around and walk back to the lodge. You're welcome to join me."

He reprised the enigmatic smile. "Thanks, I will."

They fell into step and she asked, "Are you a birder as well as a photographer?"

"I encompass multitudes. You know Walt Whitman?"

"I read some of his poetry in school."

"He was a nature lover, a transcendentalist who valued the spiritual above the factual. He believed in the affinity between man and his environment, mind and soul in perfect harmony with Nature."

She stemmed the poetical drift. "Where did you go to school, Seth?"

"I dropped out of Berkeley in my junior year, built a concrete skiff, and sailed it across the Pacific."

"You sailed solo?"

"To Penang on the Malay Peninsula. I bummed around Thailand for a couple of years logging teak up north. I had my own elephant until the assholes who ran the company modernized and replaced the elephants with hydraulic grapple skidders."

She tried to picture him working an elephant. It seemed a throwback to another age. Obsolete. Like hunting with spears. "What did you do after Thailand?"

"I dropped anchor in Papua, New Guinea, for a year to photograph the initiation rituals of the crocodile people."

She felt a pique of jealousy. Studying the rituals of such an obscure tribe would be an anthropologist's dream. "What are the rituals like?"

"The men make rows of cuts on their bodies and when they heal, they look like the raised nubs on a croc's hide. A man with no scars gets no respect from his tribe.

"Shhh." He dropped his arm in front of her like a railroad gate and raised his camera. "It's a willy wagtail."

The little black and white bird seemed almost tame as it hopped about on a fallen log and cheeped at them. Seth took a few sunflower seeds out of his pocket and sprinkled them on the ground. The bird seemed to regard this offering as its rightful due. While Seth snapped pictures, Willy cavorted about like a star ready for his close-up. Funny little character that he was, Dinah couldn't help but feel a stirring of disquiet. In her book of Aboriginal myths, the willy wagtail was a harbinger of bad luck.

When Willy had flown, she returned to Seth's bio. "Where did you go after you left New Guinea?"

"Oh, I trekked through Burma and across the Gobi, photographed some camel races for National Geographic. I lived for a year in the mountains in Kyrgyzstan, but it started to get too touristy. I moved on to Ninghsia where I entered a Buddhist monastery as a novitiate monk."

"You're a monk?"

He gave her a playful biff on the arm. "I didn't take the final vows."

The needle on her truth meter fluctuated between *what beautiful eyes you have* and *what a crock*. She almost asked why a monastic dropout found it necessary to pack heat, but that would've given away her snooping.

They had reached the road and Dinah's feet itched to start running again. She felt toey, as Jacko would say. Toey and ready to toss the hot potato of Wendell's perfidy and the unharmonious fact of Nature Boy's Glock to somebody who could do something about it.

There was just one thing she had to do first.

She turned to Seth. "I'm sorry. I just remembered I have to be someplace really fast." She took off like a gazelle and did six-minute miles all the way back to the lodge.

"Lucien, let's go for a drive." Dinah had showered too soon after her run and she was still perspiring.

"It's too hot. Sit down under that fan and cool off." He'd been holed up in his room for hours, apparently absorbed in his painting. The Taipan monstrosity had been replaced on his easel by an elongated polka-dot man with elongated polka-dot baskets hanging on his arms. Weird, but a bit more in the style of the paintings in Mack's library.

She stood in front of the electric fan and plucked at her damp shirt. "The car's got air-conditioning."

"It's two o'clock already. Time to go downstairs and rustle up some lunch."

"We could stop somewhere on the road and have lunch, a picnic, just the two of us. It'll do us a world of good to get away from the lodge and talk."

"You can talk all you want right here."

In front of Eduardo isn't what Dinah had in mind. She didn't want to insult Eddie by saying that her business with Lucien was private, but he refused to take a hint. He lay propped up on the bed doing needlepoint. The abandon with which he plunged his needle in and out of a half-finished yellow bird was painful to watch.

She said, "You could do with some fresh air and sunshine, Lucien. Wouldn't you like to go sightseeing?" She didn't know how she'd disinvite Eddie if he made a pitch to come along, but one name might taint the idea of an excursion for him. "Mack told me about this really fascinating place, Manyallaluk or something, not far from here. There's an arts and crafts center and lots of rock art. We could do a self-driving tour. Maybe you'll be possessed by a Dreamtime spirit who'll guide your paintbrush metaphysically like you said before. Please?"

Eduardo plunged his needle through the bird's wing

with a savage jab. "He's already possessed. By Ian Effing Mackenzie. You mark my words, Lucien. The primrose path he's taking you down will lead from bad to worse. De mal en pis."

"Manyallaluk sounds like a great idea," said Lucien, angrily jamming his brush into a jar of turpentine and reaching for his crutches. "In fact, Mack downloaded a story about the place for me on my Nano. He knows a couple of the guides. Maybe they'll give us the royal treatment."

They left Eduardo pouting and started for the car. Dinah had a hundred questions. She wanted Lucien's input about the Wendell-Neesha liaison before she told Jacko and she was also turning over in her mind how to broach the subject of Lucien's rift with Cleon. Cleon had it in his head that Lucien had been dishonest with him about something. It was probably a tempest in a teapot, but forewarned is forearmed. It was time for Lucien to come clean with her. If there was a doubt that Cleon had been the poisoner's intended victim, they would have to shoot down any suggestion that Lucien had a motive.

But when they got to the car, Lucien handed her his crutches, pulled his Nano out of his pocket, and insisted on stretching out in the back seat.

"But Lucien, I wanted to…"

"It's a podcast about Manyallaluk." He plugged his earphones into his ears. "It'll give us some background, help us make the most of the experience. Anyway, my leg will be more comfortable back here."

"Fine." Having committed herself to the trip, she could only hope an opportunity for conversation would present itself as the day progressed.

She looked over the map Mack had sketched for her, adjusted the seat and the mirrors, and set off. The drive, much of it on dirt roads, was longer than she'd expected and her optimism flagged. Rocks pelted against the undercarriage of the Charade and she couldn't get anything on the radio but static and soccer. At one point, she had to stop for a half dozen wild donkeys which stood brazenly in the middle of the road, unfazed by her honks and shouts. Lucien offered no help, not even an encouraging word, and she began to resent his aloofness, to feel that he was deliberately ducking her. Why would anyone need that much background on this godforsaken place unless he was planning to join the tribe?

At last she saw a big green gate with Welcome to Manyallaluk on one side and The Dreaming Place on the other. She pulled in and parked and, to her considerable irritation, Lucien hopped out, grabbed his crutches, and vaulted off to the reception building. She trailed along behind him, chafing inwardly. They were greeted by a smiling Aboriginal man in a broad-brimmed hat and khaki shirt. The name on his pocket was Peter. Lucien immediately dropped the name Ian Mackenzie and, sure enough, the royal treatment commenced.

The entrance fee was waived and Peter, a mustachioed man with laughing eyes and irresistible dimples, took Lucien under his wing and led him off to the art center. Dinah couldn't face another dissertation on art and asked a pretty young woman with a pixie hair cut and a professional smile if she could just wander around the grounds.

"Yes, of course. But please stay within the grassed tourism area." She handed her an information sheet and wished her a pleasant afternoon.

Dinah began her tour, reading as she walked. Manyallaluk, she learned, means the Frog Dreaming because it occupies a site along the song line, or creative journey, of the frog ancestor. The people of the Frog Dreaming passed through the area as part of their pilgrimage to places sacred to their "moiety" or clan. Mines and cattle stations established by "white fellas" once predominated, but the land was eventually returned to its traditional Jawoyn owners and Manyallaluk is now an Aboriginal owned and operated tourism venture.

A list of cultural guidelines advised visitors how to comport themselves.

Aboriginal people dress conservatively, please respect their culture by avoiding flamboyant or revealing clothing.

She was wearing long pants, but she had rolled her sleeves up above the elbow. She rolled them down to her wrists and turned up her collar.

Our guides are used to "Western" ways, but do not take it as impoliteness if other residents of the community do not make eye contact or accept your offer of a handshake. If an individual appears uncomfortable with eye contact, avert your eyes.

She repositioned her Wayfarers more firmly on her nose and focused on the didgeridoos rather than the elderly men who were blowing them, and on the pandanus baskets rather than the elderly ladies who were weaving them.

Cultural information is provided to a certain "public knowledge" level, but more information may be forbidden to be told by traditional law. If you are given an answer that doesn't make sense, the guide is trying to avoid the question for cultural reasons.

These people were as stingy with the truth as her family. As she was accustomed to people avoiding her questions, she moved on to the next rule.

Please avoid asking questions about "Sorry Business" (death, funerals, etc.), "Secret Men's/Women's Business," and cultural stories.

That puts a lot of business off limits, she thought. How did Jacko go about investigating the Melville Island murder if it was culturally verboten to mention death? She remembered the story she'd read about the woman found dead under suspicious circumstances, but the newspaper hadn't printed her name or her community for cultural reasons.

A trio of Aboriginal women sat under a large mango tree tending a cookpot suspended over a campfire. They were encircled by a group of onlookers. Dinah stopped for a while to watch and listen. One of the women explained that the red meat they were chopping was kangaroo tail. It would be stewed with some bush herbs and eaten with damper bread, a hard-crusted bread baked in the ashes of the open fire. The strong, gamy smell of the meat didn't entice Dinah to wait around for a sample.

She was growing bored and impatient. Somehow the day had gotten away from her without talking to Lucien or Jacko and she felt stymied and increasingly antsy.

Against a backdrop of bright green trees, a black man with a painted face and chest was demonstrating the art of spear throwing. The target was at least 120 feet distant and he hit the bullseye with a powerful thud. Dinah took off her sunglasses and stared at him. How strong, how deadly accurate, how motivated did a man have to be to ram a spear through another man's body? As murder goes, it was the very antithesis of poisoning, which required no physical strength. Maybe she'd been overthinking things. Surely there could be no connection between two murders so disparate in method and location as the Melville and the Fisher cases except for the fact that Jacko was investigating both at the same time.

She spent another sweaty hour sitting on the steps of the reception building shooing flies and ruminating on the myriad ways in which she wasn't having fun. When Lucien finally reappeared, she was in a waspish mood.

"Your leg looks fine to me. I'd like the pleasure of your company in the passenger seat. Or else."

He grinned. "Or else what?"

"You don't want to find out."

He climbed into the front seat, she tossed his crutches into the back and before they had cleared the gate, she hit him with the Secret Man/Woman Business that had been burning inside of her all day. "Wendell and Neesha are lovers. They plan to marry as soon as Cleon's dead."

"That's pretty far-fetched, baby sis. You've been sitting in the sun too long."

"I've definitely been sitting in the sun too long, but I know what I know. And Wendell's a beneficiary under Fisher's will."

"That's no surprise. The doc set Wen up as a junior partner in his business."

"Well?"

"Well, what? You want me to think that Wen killed Fisher for his money?"

"Why not? It's thinkable."

"No, it's not. Wendell's a big wuss."

She maneuvered the car around a couple of immovable donkeys and almost offered an unflattering comparison to present company. "It doesn't take a he-man to poison somebody, Lucien. And unless Seth Farraday had some beef with Fisher that we don't know about, Wen's the only one with a motive to kill him."

"Why not Dad? He and the doc mixed it up pretty good once or twice."

"About what?"

"I don't know. Who listens to a pair of old roosters ripping each other? Politics maybe. Cleon called Fisher a goddamn bloviating gasbag. Fisher called Cleon a sod-ding bloody autocrat. You couldn't say either of them got it wrong."

She dismissed Cleon as a suspect. "Cleon needed Fisher to assist his suicide. And anyway, creepiness by itself isn't a motive for murder. Not like money or sex." She thought about Wendell and Neesha necking outside that armoire and Neesha's little sob of revulsion that Cleon might go on for weeks.

"Lucien, Cleon's life may be in danger."

He laughed. "You're a regular stitch, you know that?"

"Okay, he has terminal cancer and he wants to commit suicide. But he doesn't want to be murdered."

"Maybe he does want to be murdered. Maybe that's why he's been needling us."

"Why are you being such a dick? And why does he think you haven't played straight with him?"

"Who knows? Some youthful peccadillo."

"What peccadillo would he hold over your head to his dying day? Stolen hubcaps? A shot-up mailbox? Erotic graffiti on the Welcome to Georgia sign?"

"He's a spiteful old man, Dinah. I know him better than you do. There's plenty you don't know."

"Yeah, well, you could remedy that problem. What don't I know?"

"Look, Dinah, I've seen Dad's dark side. He's a user. He's using Farraday, he's using that clown Newby, and he'll use you."

"Use me how?"

"To get at me."

"Lucien, I would never take sides against you. You're my big brother. In my book, you hung the moon and stars."

"Don't turn me into a paragon of virtue, little sister. The last star I hung was the tinsel doodad on last year's

Christmas tree. And I thought you'd learned your lesson about men with feet of clay."

"Thanks for the reminder. I just hope Jacko doesn't misinterpret your secret peccadillo as a motive for murder."

"Jesus! You know what your problem is, Dinah? You turn everything into a crisis, like it was fucking nine-one-one. I don't know what lies your dad told to cover up his illegal sideline or what lies Nick told to cover up his redhead, but I'm not your lab frog and if you want to dissect something, go and dissect your own fuck-ups."

She drove the rest of the way to Crow Hill with her throat choked from road dust and what felt like the smoke from burning bridges.

TWENTY-THREE

DINAH HID OUT in her room during dinner and when K.D. returned at ten with a moony look in her eyes and began rhapsodizing about Seth, she closed her book, sprayed her neck and arms with DEET, and hoofed it downstairs to hide out on the veranda.

The great room was quiet as a morgue. Apparently, everyone had turned in early for a change. She stopped by the bar, poured herself a snifter of brandy, and went to the back door and looked out. The coast was clear. There was a small, battery-powered lantern next to the door. She turned it on and went outside.

The cool night air was like a tonic. She lit citronella torches and walked gingerly around the perimeter holding the lantern. Seeing no snakes, she set the light on a makeshift wine-box table, brushed off a deck chair, and lay down to unwind.

She sipped her brandy and reflected on the day's developments. If she were Cleon, she'd want to know if her spouse was cheating on her. Would he? What was it he'd said? When you're near the end, it may be better to shade the truth for your own peace of mind or somebody else's. Maybe it was better to let him die with his illusions intact. But were they? She thought back to his toasts, to Neesha for keeping her chin up, to Wendell for being loyal to a fault. Was he being ironic? And there was that business of the spoon pointing and his comment about everybody getting their just deserts. Was he warning the lovebirds that they'd pay a price for their infidelity?

She spotted a pack of cigarettes on the floor next the table. Winfields. She picked it up and held it under the lantern. The package showed a hideous gangrenous foot with putrefied black toes under the caveat *Smoking Causes Peripheral Vascular Disease*. The Aussies didn't mince words. I'll quit tomorrow, she thought, and leaned over to a citronella torch to catch a light.

It was a beautiful, star-studded night. Cicadas chirred and fireflies flickered. She couldn't remember the last time she'd seen a firefly. It seemed years. She and Lucien used to capture them in Mason jars when they were kids. They'd had a lot of fun together. Now they were virtual strangers.

She blew smoke rings like little white lassos around the stars and watched the smoke evanesce. Like all her human bonds. She couldn't hold onto the people she loved anymore than she could hold onto a star.

Well, so be it. She could be philosophical. What was one more disconnect? She wasn't going to cry about it. The brandy and the vessel-destroying cigarette had cauterized her throat.

"That's the Southern Cross up there."

Jerusalem. Seth Farraday was quiet as snow.

He appeared out of the shadows at the edge of the veranda and pointed upward. "It looks more like a kite than a cross. The Aborigines here in the Top End say it's a stingray being chased by a shark."

"Sailor, photographer, astronomer. You're like that old nursery rhyme, Tinker, Tailor."

"I couldn't tailor a suit, but I'm a pretty fair hand with a yurt."

His exaggerated opinion of himself was becoming irksome. "It must be heady to excel at so many things."

"I'm just a dilettante. Like you."

The back door opened and a bright light strafed the darkness like a heat-seeking missile.

"Well, looky who else can't sleep." Cleon stepped outside and shone a flashlight in their faces. "I've been exiled from the conjugal bed, y'all. Neesha's up walkin' the floor and boohooin' to beat the band. Wants to send the children home to her mama. Thinks their little lives are gonna be permanently blighted by poor ol' Desmond's murder." He shined his light on a chair at the far end of the veranda. "Drag that chair over here for me, Seth."

Seth brought the chair over and set it down next to Dinah.

"Thank you, son." Cleon turned off his light and lowered himself into the chair. "Well, what do y'all think? The young'uns seemed sprightly enough dealin' with *my* death."

"Children are a lot more resilient than their mothers given them credit for," said Seth. "I know I was."

If there was an implied criticism, Cleon ignored it. "My opinion exactly. Kids got their own agenda in this life and their own modus operandi for gettin' what they want. They ain't apt to fall apart because a couple of old farts cash in their chips."

Seth shook a Winfield out of the package, caught a light off one of the candles, and sat down across from Cleon. "Aren't you going to ask me what my agenda is?"

"I reckon you're about to tell me."

"It's to take you for a shitload of money and forget you ever existed."

Dinah became acutely aware of a chorus of frogs. She listened to them for what seemed an eternity before Cleon spoke.

"At least you're honest," he said.

She tried to see his face, but it was in shadow. She felt a swell of sympathy for him. He had done so many good things for her over the years. He hadn't been a faithful husband or a model father to Wendell or Lucien, but he hadn't molested anybody or let them go hungry and there was such a thing as forgiveness. With so little time left to him, it seemed ineffably sad that he would reap nothing but resentment and enmity from his sons. He was lucky to have K.D., who would never forget that he existed or let anyone else forget.

"Yes, four strange children already and now I got me a fifth. Interestin' all the odd things you've done. Tell us what you did at that monastery. Did y'all distill spirits and herbs like some of 'em do, or make cheese, or bake little loaves of nut bread?"

"We got by mostly on alms."

"You were a beggar?" Cleon was shocked into subject-verb agreement.

"A monk's needs are simple—a bowl of rice, a straw mat to sleep on."

"Lord love a duck." Cleon laughed so loud it must have woken the house. "It goes to show, don't it? Enough temptation and a man's agenda can turn on a dime." He pushed himself out of his chair, still laughing. "I'm gonna go and have me a nightcap. Gotta gentle my nerves for the big meetin' in town tomorrow."

"What big meeting?" asked Dinah.

"I've arranged a consultation with a young estates and trust attorney who used to do some work for me down in Sydney before he moved north and hung up his shingle in Katherine. I recommended him to Dez and evidently they got on like a bush fire. Not only did Dez have the boy prepare his will, he chose him to be the executor. It'll be a good while before any of the assets are released, but at least we'll get a general idea what Dez had in mind. Me and him bein' old cronies, he'll have left somethin' to me."

"Too bad you won't have time to spend it," said Seth.

Cleon had no comeback.

Dinah watched him disappear inside the house and got up to go in, herself. At the door, she turned around. "You don't know anything about him, Seth."

"I know he walked out on my mother."

"Then you should ask him why while you have the chance. Maybe his reasons are forgivable. Understandable, anyway. Take it from one who knows, it's a terrible thing to go through life hating your father."

He didn't answer and she went inside and climbed the dark stairs to her room.

TWENTY-FOUR

"THERE YOU ARE! I been lookin' high and low." Cleon found Dinah in the great room playing solitaire. "You look tight as a string on a fiddle. Something worryin' you?"

"Oh, no." Since absurdity knew no bounds.

"Your motor's been idlin' too long, child. Ride into town with me for the readin' of Fisher's will. Neesha's gone on ahead to do her shoppin' and I could use some female companionship."

The day had unfolded on a geologic timescale. Breakfast was epochs ago, in the Precambrian period. While the earth's crust slowly solidified, she'd read one of Mack's mythology books and struggled with the concept of song lines. At ten, she phoned the number Jacko had given her, but he wasn't in. Sometime during the Paleozoic period, she decided to accost Lucien and tell him just what she thought of his hurtful outburst yesterday, but she chickened out at the door to his room and took a jog instead. At two o'clock, she'd tried Jacko again. The woman she spoke to said he'd be in the Katherine office around four. The world seemed determined to make her wait.

"Cat got your tongue? What d'ya say?"

She wasn't sure if he was inviting her to the reading or just for the drive, but either way she had no desire to sit around here waiting for the dinosaurs to come and go. And if she did attend the reading, she'd have even more information to pass on to Jacko. "A drive into town would be lovely."

"Then let's roll."

In no time at all they were on the road, tooling down the rutted dirt track in Cleon's plush, black Mercedes with Dinah rethinking Lucien's advice to hold onto the paintings until the market improved. Why should she follow his advice? So what if she didn't wring every last cent out of the sale? If she didn't net the max, it would be, as Lucien so churlishly put it, her fuck-up.

She thought, I'd get more from the sale of just one of the paintings than I ever dreamed of having. I could hold one back until a more propitious time and if Lucien apologizes and shows a little respect for my needs and my opinions, he can keep it for me in his house.

Of course, a painting that valuable would have to be insured. That would cost a pretty penny and eat into her profits from the sale of the other one. But no, even if the timing was wrong, she would sell them both. She wondered what an apartment in London would cost. Or Paris. She visualized her life in Paris. It wouldn't take long to dispel the noir of Nick in the City of Light.

Dispelling the noir of Lucien would be harder. He and Cleon had banged heads many times before and, up until now, they'd found a way to smooth things over. But she and Lucien had never fought and his hostility came as a shock and a betrayal. Again, she was beset by the thought that he wanted the Homers for himself. It couldn't be for the money they'd bring, because he had oodles. Did he read Cleon's decision to give the only good art that he owned to her as a repudiation of him? Surely their wires weren't that crossed. But even if Cleon was dissing him, how could Lucien be so flippant about her fear that Cleon might be murdered?

A film of dust enveloped the Mercedes. Cleon turned on the windshield wipers.

She didn't want to offend him or start an argument. But if giving the Homers to her was what had stoked Lucien's resentment, if that was Cleon's intention, she needed to know.

She said, "Lucien told Mack that Winslow Homer is America's greatest artist."

"That should make you feel good about your pictures."

"It does, only…Has Lucien said anything about wanting them himself?"

"Naw! He thinks they're blah."

"He can't have said that."

"Yes, he did. Changed his mind since, I reckon."

"But why would he say they were blah one time and miraculous the next?"

"Could be he was just showin' off his superior ah-tistic discernment for Mack. It don't matter. You and me like 'em and we ain't feebleminded."

You and I, she thought reflexively. You and I like them. She gave up on delicacy. "Uncle Cleon, if you're using those paintings to get at Lucien by giving them to me, I won't stand for it. If he wants them, I'll give them to him after you're dead."

"Listen, doll, I know you think I'm a shit-stirrin' old bastard and I oughta kiss and make up with your brother. But Lucien and me, we're at loggerheads right now. We'll thrash things out before I croak. It ain't my purpose to stiff him out of what he wants. I swear on my life, what's left of it, that Lucien'll be very happy with his legacy. Wendell, now. Wendell may not fare so well."

She studied his face. "Why? Why won't Wendell fare so well?"

He mashed her hand in his big, red-knuckled mitt and winked. "You know, it ain't as much fun defendin' corporate crooks and tortfeasors as it was defendin' regular folks. Did I ever tell you about Luther Jones?"

"No." He was obviously avoiding her question, but that wink kindled suspicion.

"Luther was a tenant farmer, worked a few acres of corn and collard greens outside of Mayday, Georgia. He was a deacon over at the Baptist church, never caused any trouble. Everybody thought well of him until he got drunk as a wheelbarrow one night and shot his wife dead. There was never a question he'd done it."

"Did he get the death penalty?"

"Naw. I get a letter from him every once in a while. Says prison ain't half bad. He's too old now for hard labor and the prison dishes up three squares a day."

If this story had a point, he was taking his sweet time getting to it. She said, "There must have been extenuating circumstances."

Cleon chuckled. "At the trial, the jury looked kinda mean-eyed and I didn't have much choice but to call Luther to the stand to see if he couldn't cultivate a little sympathy. I asked him, 'Why'd you do it, Luther?' He said, 'She took up with a back-door man.' 'And who was this back-door man?' I asked. Luther scrunched up his face, mournful as a whipped hound, looked straight at the jury and said, 'It was my brother.' After that, you could've heard a pin drop."

Dinah stared at him. The point of the story was, he knew. Cleon knew about Wendell and Neesha.

"I reckon Luther would've killed his brother, too, if he hadn't run like a jackrabbit. Yessireebob. The fact it was his own brother is what saved Luther from the needle. That and Luther's winsome way of speakin'. He said, 'I shot her, all right, and no denyin'. But I pulled the trigger real slow, bein' as how I'd had tender feelings.'"

Dinah's thoughts weltered. Was it conceivable…well,

of course it was conceivable because she just conceived it, that Cleon had tried to kill Neesha and killed Desmond Fisher by mistake? Or more diabolical still, did he poison the doctor to foil his suicide and confound the adulterers?

"What have you done, Uncle Cleon?"

"About my will, you mean?" He took a card out of the glove box and handed it to her. "That's the bub we're goin' to see, Stephen Geertz. When I get around to it, he's gonna videotape me readin' my will. I was thinkin' I'd leave the Mercedes to Eduardo. He enjoys the trappings of wealth and if things don't work out with him and Lucien, he deserves a souvenir of his time with the Dobbses."

She tried to erase the thought of Cleon as murderer. It was hysterical. Against all reason. But there was no doubt in her mind that he was wise to Wendell. Maybe cutting him out of his will was Cleon's way of pulling the trigger real slow. "You promised Margaret that you'd divide your money fairly among the children."

"Fair means different things to different people. You heard Wendell say how he don't care about money. I should take him at his word. That'll teach him not to palter."

Dinah no longer took anyone at his word, Cleon included. She said, "Margaret takes it for granted that Wendell will get all of Dez's money."

"Does she now? That's a right strong motive for murder."

"Not so sure anymore that you were the intended victim?"

He screwed up his face and rubbed his jaw. "Old moneybags like Dez and me, it coulda been either one of us. I'd be lyin' if I didn't say I was right pleased to wake up and smell the coffee this mornin'."

Margaret was right about his improved outlook. Fisher's death seemed to have given him a new lease on life.

She said, "You don't seem much distressed by your old friend's death."

"Our friendship was wearin' thin since he became such a Johnny-one-note on death and politics. A man ain't got much sense of humor about his own demise."

Dinah had seen no aspect of Fisher's character that would appeal to Cleon. It was a strange relationship, made stranger by Margaret's affair with Fisher. "When did he become so enamored of euthanasia? And why?"

"First off, he was enamored of a young nurse. Married her and, before they had time to get sick of each other, she came down with a rare wastin' disease. No cure, no letup from the pain. Watchin' her shrivel up and die a slow death and not bein' able to help her put Dez off doctorin' for a while. I think it made him a little careless of his own life."

That snippet of history explained the man's obsession, but it didn't make Dinah like him any better. "How," she asked, "did an Australian doctor come to own a fish processing plant in Georgia?"

"He had a fair amount of money and he was always on the lookout for investment opportunities. The Brunswick plant came on the market at a time when he was in town visitin' Maggie. He bought the controllin' interest, ponied up fresh capital, and handed over the runnin' of the place to the people who knew what they were doin'."

"Not Wendell?"

"Dez wasn't that boneheaded. He let him put in a few dollars and call himself an owner, but Wen couldn't pull the fire alarm without a memo from headquarters."

She began to wonder if she'd misread that wink. If he believed Wendell was so timid and inept, would he think him ballsy enough to seduce Neesha?

Cleon said, "As his drinkin' got worse, Dez started to

lose his rudder in more ways than one. He quit takin' care of business like he oughta have done."

That rang a bell. "At dinner that last night, he said something about not taking orders from you anymore. Were you in business together?"

His face contorted. Either he was in pain or the question required a grueling intensity of thought. After a while, he said, "We threw in together from time to time."

He clammed up for the next mile and she took another tack. "Dr. Fisher mentioned that he went hunting with my dad. Did you introduce them?"

"I seem to recollect your daddy joinin' in a quail hunt with us one time. Wouldn't shoot the birds, but got a kick out of watchin' the dogs work. Hart didn't have much of a stomach for huntin'. Miss Margaret now, she's a huntress if ever there was one. She went on a number of hunts with Dez and me. She could outshoot the both of us."

"I gather she and Dez were an item once upon a time."

"It's true. Maggie set her cap for him a long while ago, but Dez never requited her affections, not to the point of matrimony anyways. I toyed with the notion that she's the one who tried to poison me. She's got a backlog of mighty hard feelings against me. But maybe I'm too self-centered. Maybe she got the right man. A woman scorned is apt to do something drastic, especially if it gives her only son a big payday."

Dinah didn't doubt the siren song of money, but if being scorned could send Margaret over the edge, she'd have murdered Cleon years ago. "Do you really believe Margaret's capable of premeditated, cold-blooded murder?"

"I don't know if you could rightly call Maggie cold-blooded, but she can do what needs doin' and not bat an eye. She's got sangfroid." He pronounced it correctly, without the drawl, absent-mindedly erudite.

He stopped at the intersection with the Stuart Highway and turned his face to her. He might be grateful for a brief extension of his lease on life, but age and illness had etched deep lines in his forehead and for the first time, she saw the pall of death behind the mask.

"I've agonized over this, Dinah. Whoever that poison was meant for, I hope to God it wasn't one of my children that served it up."

TWENTY-FIVE

THE OFFICES OF Arnold, Rutledge, and Geertz were located in a modest brick building in a quiet street lined on either side by extremely wide-spreading trees with ugly, tangled roots and a pervasive smell that reminded Dinah of Vicks VapoRub. A bronze plaque on the sidewalk next to their parking space identified them as coolabah trees.

Cleon's gloomy spell had passed or at any rate, he'd gotten back some of his color and put on his game face. As he escorted her into the lobby, he sang. "*Once a jolly swagman camped by a billabong, under the shade of a coolabah tree.*"

They took the elevator to the second floor and Cleon announced himself to the receptionist as if his entrance must mark the high point of her career.

She was a slack-mouthed girl of about twenty with frizzy yellow hair, cherry-red talons, and a starchy blue suit no one her age would be caught dead in after five. "Please take a seat, sir. I'll let Mr. Geertz's secretary know you're here."

"We'll stand," said Cleon. "Geertz won't keep me waitin' long." He pulled Dinah a foot or so away to the end of the reception desk. "That Inspector Newby's a peculiar pheasant plucker, don't you think?"

An elderly man sitting on the sofa behind them looked up from his magazine.

Cleon took no notice. "Fortuitous him runnin' into you

at the Darwin Airport like that. What d'ya suppose got him interested in us?"

"Another murder. The murder of a British journalist on Melville Island."

The man on the sofa leaned forward.

Dinah dropped her voice. "Did Jacko ask you anything about it? I don't know why, but he seems to think there's a link between the murdered man and somebody in our family."

"He asked me if I knew him. I never heard of the fella 'til now. What was his name again?"

"Hambrick. Bryce Hambrick."

"How does Newby figure he's connected with us?"

"I don't know. He didn't say."

"That figures. Newby can talk the hind legs off a donkey and not say a cottonpickin' thing you can hang your hat on. You reckon his elevator goes all the way to the top floor?" His eyes twinkled. He was testing her.

Her temper flared. It dawned on her that Jacko Newby and Cleon Dobbs might have been twins separated at birth. Disarmingly rustic, deeply calculating, and determined to use her to their own ends. She had no doubt that Cleon was using her, but to what end? Did he want her to pass on his suspicions about Margaret to Jacko? Tell Wendell and Neesha he was on to them? Had he brought her to the reading of Fisher's will so she could inform Jacko who benefited from his death? Or was he plotting against Lucien in some Byzantine way she didn't quite capiche? And not to get too carried away by suspicion, but Hambrick's murder would have led the TV news when it was first discovered and every newspaper in the country would have carried the story. How could Cleon have missed it?

She said, "I don't think anyone gets to be Detective

Chief Inspector of the Territory if his elevator doesn't go all the way to the top."

"You're probably right." He ticked a finger against his watch dial to telegraph his impatience to the receptionist.

The girl was saved when a woman with a helmet of gray hair and an air of brisk efficiency stepped into the lobby. "Mr. Geertz will see you now, Mr. Dobbs. This way, please."

"Madam, your charmin' backside will be my beacon."

The lady drew in a sharp breath and preceded them down the hall to an open door.

A dapper man with nervous eyes and a small, melancholy blond mustache stood·to greet them. "Good to see you again, Cleon."

"How's tricks, Steve? It's been a while."

The men shook hands and the helmeted lady spanked the door shut behind them.

"This is my niece, Dinah."

"Pleased to meet you." Geertz shook Dinah's hand and bade them sit.

"May I offer you a drink? Beer, Scotch, water?"

They both asked for water and he poured two cups from the dispenser in the corner. Cleon fished a bottle out of his pocket, shook two pills into his palm, and tossed them down.

"I appreciate you takin' the time to meet with us, Steve. I know there's no requirement to read the will, but as I explained on the phone, how Dez left things in his will may affect how I write my own. If Wendell scores big off Dez, I ain't gonna lumber him down with still more money."

"Glad to do it," said Geertz. "I'll be filing the will in Sydney in the next few days and apply for a Grant of Probate. I know Wendell will have to travel back to the States soon and it's best that everyone be apprised of the terms.

Paying the debts and taxes and managing the transfer of assets, it'll necessitate a lot of work."

Cleon said, "I'm sure you put in a clause that guarantees your hourly rate."

Geertz laughed uneasily. "I was surprised to hear of the doctor's death. He was in fine fettle when he came into the office last month."

"He want you to sue somebody?" asked Cleon.

"No, no. He was here to add several codicils to his will."

Dinah pricked up her ears. Was it whiffy on the nose that will changing had become such a fad? She wondered if Cleon had something to do with the changes. Had he inveigled Fisher to cut Wendell out of his will? That would certainly give the lovebirds a nasty surprise.

Cleon frowned at his watch. "Where is Wendell? You told him four o'clock sharp, didn't you, Steve?"

"I'm sure he and the others will be here soon. Wendell had a few more arrangements to tend to at the funeral home. Dez left detailed instructions regarding the cremation. He felt that anything other than a cardboard casket would be a waste of money."

Cleon reared back in his chair and crossed his arms over his paunch. "I'm havin' my body preserved cryogenically in a freezer in Houston, Texas. Might come back to see y'all one of these days when they get the bugs out of the defrostin' part."

Geertz smiled. "I understand your other son is handicapped and unable to be with us in person, so we'll get him on the speakerphone as soon as the others arrive."

"He ain't too handicapped to gad about lookin' at art."

Geertz cleared his throat and twiddled with one end of his mustache. A knock on the door brought him out of his seat like a jack-in-the-box. "Come in, come in."

Wendell, Margaret, and Neesha walked into the office

together. There was a lot of handshaking and shuffling of chairs and passing out of drinks. When everyone was introduced and settled, Geertz buzzed his secretary and asked her to put through a call to Lucien.

Dinah got why Wendell and Neesha and Margaret would want to be here. But what interest would Lucien have in Fisher's estate?

"Now," said Cleon. "Let's hear how old Dez decided to treat the world in his absence."

Geertz cleared his throat again and opened a green file folder. "There's the usual legal verbiage."

"Unless he's left it all to famine relief or a bunch of do-gooders, we'll stipulate he was of sound mind," said Cleon. "Leastways he was when he was sober."

Margaret said, "I think Mr. Geertz should read the document in its entirety. There may be restrictive clauses."

"Don't be a stickler, Maggie. We can hash over the fine print if any of us decides to contest the will." Cleon leaned across Geertz's desk. "A while back, Dez represented to me that my minor children would come in for a goodly sum when he died. Did he come through?"

"Yes, he did. Thadeus James Dobbs and Katharine De-Beau Dobbs will each receive fifty thousand dollars to be held in trust for their college educations."

"That was dear of him," said Neesha.

"Dear? Why, it ain't enough to cover their freshman year. Miserly son-of-a-bitch drinks my liquor and sponges off me for twenty years and that's the best he could do?"

Geertz looked flummoxed. "If carefully invested now…"

"Did he leave me anything else?"

"Er, well. Actually…Were you expecting a devisal to yourself, personally?"

"Sure I was. Does that hangdog look mean I didn't get one?"

Geertz loosened his tie and worried his mustache. "I'm afraid not."

"Is that one of the changes he made last month?"

"I'm not really at liberty to say, Cleon. Lawyer-client privilege. You understand."

"I understand, all right. All I did for him and the bozo left me squat."

"Be gracious, Cleon," implored Neesha. "It was kind of him to leave money for the children."

Cleon refused to be appeased. "It's the principle of the thing, Neesha. He knew anything he left me would go to you when I passed or, hell, he coulda left it in your name. It's a snub is what it is. I hope he wasn't as miserly with the rest of y'all."

"Moving on then," said Geertz. "To Mr. Wendell Paul Dobbs, I hereby devise and bequeath all assets of Fisher Industries, Incorporated, and full ownership of bank accounts and properties in Switzerland, the United States, Mexico, Costa Rica, and Australia as follows: In Zurich, Switzerland…"

"Switzerland?" Wendell seemed surprised.

"The corporation has diversified holdings throughout the world," said Geertz. "When the various currencies are tallied and converted to dollars, it will be worth over five million. Likely a great deal over."

"There has to be some mistake," said Wendell, seemingly bowled over. "I mean, the fish plant's worth five or six hundred thousand, tops. And his house in Sydney, I know it's worth a lot, but…"

"Approximately two million in Australian dollars," supplied Geertz.

Cleon whistled. "No fear your boy will come up short,

Maggie. He's hit the jackpot with your old beau." He reached over and gave Wendell a congratulatory knuckle bump on the arm. "Did the doc leave Miss Margaret a remembrance, Steve?"

"There *is* a bequest to Mrs. Margaret Dobbs," said Gertz. "To my special friend Margaret Dobbs, in appreciation of our many years of shared epicurean pleasures, five hundred thousand dollars and the Louis the Fourteenth epergne she's always longed for."

Cleon ooh-eed. "Half a mil. You came out golden in the end, Maggie."

Margaret's eyes widened, but her composure was all sangfroid.

Geertz's phone rang. "Yes, yes. Put him through." He pushed a button. "Are you there, Lucien?"

"Yeah, I'm here." Lucien's disembodied voice had a hollow ring. "I don't know why you want me in on the meeting."

"Then you're in for a happy surprise," said Geertz. He reddened and rephrased. "I mean you may find some solace in the late doctor's regard for you." He flipped through several pages and cleared his throat.

Dinah tensed for the happy surprise.

"Here we are. To Lucien Osceola Dobbs, I hereby bequeath the following works of art. *The Hermaphrodite* by Jackson Pollock; *Berlin at Night* by Marsden Hartley; *The Wrestlers* by George Bellows; and two watercolors by Winslow Homer, *Moonlight at the Cape* and *The Sea Sprite*."

There was a protracted silence. Dinah felt as if she'd been swept out to sea by one of Homer's storms. Her thoughts capsized and splintered into a flotsam of wild surmise. If Lucien knew about this, if he had any idea, then he had five stupendous reasons to kill Fisher.

Finally, Margaret spoke up. "Dez had a collection of

antique table appointments and serving utensils, but the only paintings in his house were inexpensive reproductions."

"I can only read to you what's stated in the will," said Geertz. "The paintings are stored in a fire-resistant, temperature and humidity-controlled facility in Sydney. According to the bills of sale and certificates of authenticity, they must be quite valuable. I'd guess this makes you a multi-millionaire, too, Lucien."

"Well, I'll be a Chinaman," said Cleon. "You can found your own museum, boy."

The speakerphone was silent.

"Are you still with us, Lucien?" asked Geertz.

"Maybe he fainted," said Cleon.

A slow, sibilant "shhhit" issued from the speakerphone.

"Well," said Geertz, with a benedictory smile, "other than a small charitable gift to Exit International, that about covers it. Unless there's something else you'd like to know?"

"Just one thing." Cleon chuckled and prodded Margaret in the ribs. "What in hell's rich emporium is an epergne, Maggie?"

TWENTY-SIX

The Mekhong Thai Café & Take-Away on the corner of Katherine Terrace and the Victoria Highway was jam-packed and the commotion in the kitchen augured slow service. Dinah didn't care. For once, she didn't mind waiting. How happy she'd be to sit in limbo forever and never learn another fact or communicate with another living soul.

The meeting with Geertz had overloaded her circuits. And from the speed with which everyone had scattered when it was over, the effect had been unanimous. She'd told Cleon she needed to pick up something at the drug store and shoved off down the street, ignoring his shouted injunction to meet him back at the law firm in an hour. Her thoughts in a tailspin, she'd walked around the town until twilight. As the streetlights began to wink on, she drifted into the Mekhong where she sat with her chin in her hands, forgotten in the dinnertime rush.

"One galloping horses, one Mussaman curry, one dom yam gung," cried the man behind the counter.

"Ma ho!" yelled a voice from the kitchen. "Gaeng Mussaman!"

A man at the table behind her sounded petulant. "Order the bloody fried bananas, Sonya. You're fat as a match."

A party of raucous young men with "Socceroos" printed on their shirts argued good-naturedly. "Even blind Freddie could've told you they wouldn't get away with kicking the Strikers out of the League. The bloody Pride, now, that's a different kettle of fish."

Dinah had lost her taste for fish, possibly forever, but she roused herself and pored over the menu. The spicy smells coming from the kitchen stimulated her appetite. The Siamese fried chicken looked good, maybe with a side of mangoes and sticky rice. And there was a pork dish called rum, which unfortunately did not list the spirit as one of its ingredients. She was, however, gratified to see that the menu listed a number of beer and wine selections. If a waiter ever got around to taking her order, she would order enough wine to anesthetize a hippopotamus.

She didn't want to think about the hairball of fresh complications coughed up in Fisher's will. She didn't want to think about a fish plant with a Swiss bank account or the ominous excess of fine art or the growing suspicion that Cleon had engineered things from the start. She didn't want to think about any of this, but she couldn't stop herself. Why did Fisher hoard his art in a warehouse instead of hanging it in his home? Why had he not said anything to her about Cleon's Homers if he owned some of his own? And why had he willed his bonanza to Lucien, who didn't even like him?

She had a brainstorm. Maybe Fisher had a secret art fetish and required paintings as remuneration for his services in lieu of cash. What if Cleon brought his Homers, *her* Homers, to Australia as a payment to Fisher for helping him die? Cleon and Fisher had been arguing about something in Sydney. Maybe Cleon had decided to give the paintings to her and reneged and Fisher threatened to sue Cleon's estate. Could that be another motive for murder? A motive for Cleon?

"I didn't mean to sling off at you, Sonya, but make up your mind. What about a nice mango mousse or the pineapple jelly supreme?"

"Another round over here," shouted one of the Socceroos. "We're drier than a Pommie's bath towel."

Dinah wondered what the Socceroos would do if she marched over to their table, pulled up a chair, and started talking about murder. She needed a sounding board, somebody to bandy ideas with. Somebody like Nick. A hairball of lies and secrets would be right up his alley. That she missed him infuriated her. That it wasn't just because of the talk mortified her.

A hand stroked the back of her neck. "Found you."

Her heart stuttered. It was Seth.

"Who'd you have to screw to land a table in this joint?"

It was Seth, channeling Nick. He sat down and gave her that odd, transcendental smile. This was not helpful. He was not a safe person to happen by in her present mood, not if he were going to sound like Nick.

"What are you doing here?"

"Cleon sent me to find you. He's holding court at a bar down the street and you're truant."

"I'm eating here. I've decided to stay in town tonight at a motel."

"If you stay in town, your Uncle Cleon will blow a gasket."

"Let him. What's the worst he can do to me?"

"Snap your bones? Drink your blood? I don't know my new papa well enough to hazard a guess." He looked over her menu. "Shall we order a bottle of wine and run a few ideas up the flagpole?"

"Regarding my punishment?"

"Regarding who murdered the doctor and why. How's your investigation progressing?"

"I'm not investigating."

"Sure you are. Don't you want to grill me?"

"Okay. Are you some kind of environmental extremist?"

"Whoa! You're loaded for bear."

"An animal lover shouldn't use hunting metaphors. And if you won't answer, it's obvious you don't want to be grilled."

"My kind are not the ones who're fouling the environment and using up the planet's resources, Dinah. I'm a nice, back-to-the-Garden guy."

"Don't patronize me, Seth. I'm sick of being patronized and used and punked. What's your game, exactly?"

"Jesus. You're into some bad yang." He ran his eyes over the menu and looked up at her with an invitation she just knew was going to lead to trouble. "What do you say we drink some wine and kick back?"

It was no surprise he caught the eye of a waitress right away. Every woman in the restaurant, fat-as-a-match Sonya included, had turned their heads like heliotropes to ogle him. He must be inured to female attention, or if he noticed, he didn't let it show. He ordered a bottle of white wine and when the waitress had gone, returned his magnetic gaze to Dinah. "Let's start over. I don't sabotage housing developments or torch SUV sales lots. How's that?"

"A journalist who happened to be an apologist for dragnet fishing was found murdered on Melville Island last week. What do you know about that?"

"Nothing, although if I did, I'd probably lie about it."

"I'd expect nothing less of you. It's the Zeitgeist. Everybody's doing it."

"What was it? Finding out there was no Santa Claus, no tooth fairy, no weapons of mass destruction? What made you such a cynic?"

"All of the above." His mouth had the most tantalizing curve, making it impossible not to smile back, and his eyes had little gold flecks around the iris, like pyrite. She drank half a glass of ice water.

He said, "Don't you have an intuition about who's telling the truth?"

"I thought I did. I thought I was practically clairvoyant. Apparently, my extrasensory powers only work on civilians, i.e. people outside the family."

"Why do you think of anyone other than Lucien as *your* family?"

Now he was channeling Jacko.

"They just are. It's a Southern thing. You wouldn't understand."

He shrugged. "I understand ancestor worship, but I can't see why you'd hold an old ham like Cleon in such high regard."

"Well, I do, so don't take any potshots. I don't know anybody who's squeezed as much out of life as he has and even if he's a jerk sometimes, he has his reasons." She didn't want to go into those reasons with this green-eyed operator, or face up to the fact that some of Cleon's reasons might verge on the diabolical. "Anyhow, I owe him. He helped my mom and me out of a bad situation once."

The wine came. She sipped and watched as Seth read the menu. There was definitely something clandestine about him, but he didn't fit Dinah's idea of a poisoner. Besides, the kitchen was a mob scene all day on the day of the murder. It would've been impossible for a stranger to waltz in, ascertain that the doctor would be dining on fugu, find it, spike it, and waltz out without somebody seeing him.

"Know what you want to eat?" he asked.

"Number thirty-one and number fifty-two, extra spicy."

He waved and a pretty Thai waitress appeared instantly. Before Dinah could open her mouth, he ordered in fluent

Thai. The waitress could scarcely conceal her enchant-
ment. Dinah could scarcely conceal her surprise. Not that
speaking a language proved anything.

The waitress toddled off with a blissed-out smile on
her face.

Dinah said, "You don't act like a man who's just found
his biological father."

"How does such a man act?"

"I don't know. You've made it plain you don't like him
or respect him, but you should at least be curious. Why
aren't you pestering everyone for stories about Cleon?"

"I'm learning things indirectly. You should try it. When
you're angling for information, lull your subject into a relaxed state of mind. Use your feminine side, the yin. Be
oblique and slowly feel your way inside his head."

"Does your curriculum vitae include a stint with the
CIA?"

"I read about interrogation technique in a spy novel."

In her mind's eye, she flashed to the intimidating face
in the passport photo. Who was this guy really? "Who are
you really?" she asked.

"Maybe I'm who I say I am."

"I doubt that. I see no family resemblance between you
and Cleon."

"His investigator Kelliston took my DNA to the best
lab in Singapore for testing."

Dinah thought about Cleon's audacity, his belief in himself, and the righteousness of his stands. "Maybe there is
a resemblance, just not a physical one."

Seth pinged his chopsticks against his wine glass. "Lucien sure is a chip off the old block. Is he bent out of shape
because he wants a bigger piece of Daddy's pie?"

She bridled. "Unlike yourself, Lucien's not mercenary."

"Everybody likes money, Dinah. It's a matter of degree.

I'll bet that even you could think of some pleasurable things to do with a liberal transfusion of money. The sale of those paintings, say."

A vision of a light-filled apartment in Paris winged through her mind.

He said, "I heard Lucien and Eduardo talking about your good fortune. They didn't sound too pleased."

The wine soured in her mouth. When had Lucien turned into such a rotter?

Seth knitted his brow. "Lucien seems like one of those still-waters-run-deep types. He hides a lot under the surface, the way your Mr. Homer hides little crosses under the waves."

"You're seeing him at a bad time. He's normally very extroverted and friendly."

"I once read a book about a guy who staged an attempt on his own life so he wouldn't be suspected for the murder he planned to commit."

"Your point being?"

"Don't you think it's odd that Lucien would be bitten by a poisonous snake one day and the next thing you know, his doctor's been poisoned?"

It hadn't occurred to her. Embarrassed, she said, "It's a coincidence."

"Obviously, you can't be objective."

"Maybe I can't, but I know Lucien wouldn't murder anyone."

"I hear he spent two years in the Marine Corps."

"That makes him a patriot, not a poisoner."

"I'm not accusing him, Dinah."

"Good."

"But his body language tells me he's hiding something heavy."

"His body language tells me his leg is sore. And who asked for your psychological analysis?"

"I thought you were beginning to warm up to me."

"It was only a partial thaw and you've reversed it."

"I think you're afraid Lucien's in trouble, but you won't face up."

"You're wrong. You don't know the first thing about Lucien or me or anybody else in this family."

"There's a burning reason for me to learn, wouldn't you agree? I'm under suspicion like everybody else." He refilled their glasses and held his up to the light as if truth were a tangible particle that might float to the surface. "What if it's the other way around? Suppose the murderer first tried to kill Lucien?"

She was dumbfounded. "But nobody's said...nobody's even considered..."

"Snakes can be handled by somebody who knows what he's doing."

"But why would anyone want to kill Lucien?"

"I don't know that anyone does." He reached across the table and covered her hand with his, shooting sparks up her arm. "What do you say we put our heads together and bat around a few ideas?"

TWENTY-SEVEN

THEIR DINNER ARRIVED and Seth ordered another bottle of wine. He loaded his plate with rice and helped himself to the shrimp and the steamed crab cakes. His karmic sensibilities didn't diminish his appetite for crustaceans.

"Okay," he said. "Here's my two cents. I helped Wendell carry the doctor's body upstairs to his room and while everybody was arguing about what to do next, I had a look around."

"Other people's rooms, you mean?"

"Not all of them. Lucien's and Wendell's."

"What were you after? Money? Jewelry?"

"A head start. A little inside skinny on my half-sibs."

"In a pig's eye."

"Dinah, just hear me out, okay? In one of the bags in Lucien's room there was a book on herpetology, a primer on the poisonous reptiles of Australia."

"That's easy to explain. Lucien's doing a painting about some snake god or other. He obviously wanted a photo to go by."

"From what I've seen of his painted snakes, he didn't go by any photo. He's better at drawing porkers."

She almost agreed, but caught herself. "I don't know what you mean."

He smiled. "Lucien and Eduardo share the same address, right? The luggage tags carried Lucien's name, but not all of the bags are his. Eduardo could have corralled a snake and placed it where he knew Lucien would step on it."

"Eduardo couldn't handle a snake. He'd have a conniption if he even saw a snake."

"He saw the snake that bit Lucien. Did anybody say he had a conniption?"

"No. But it's only natural that he and Lucien would want to learn about the snake that bit him. They probably bought that book in Katherine."

"Is Eduardo a named beneficiary in Lucien's will?"

"Yes." Lucien had shown it to her once. He'd left her his painting of their Seminole grandmother in a traditional dress and enough money for a first-class ticket to just about anywhere. But the house and the bulk of his estate went to Eduardo. She said, "Even if Eduardo wanted Lucien dead, he wouldn't be dumb enough to kill him before he receives his inheritance from Cleon."

Seth poured more vino and gave his glass that searching-for-veritas look. "Not all domestic murders are about money, you know."

Dinah's thoughts coiled around Eduardo. What did she really know about him? He had a B.A. in theater arts and he'd spent a year abroad where he picked up a smattering of French and a passing acquaintance with an art student who later introduced him to Lucien. Her conversations with Eduardo had always been superficial and impersonal. She had no idea what passions percolated under those brightly colored Polo shirts.

Had Eduardo tried to kill Lucien? It would have made more sense to wait until Lucien came into his inheritance from Cleon. But if Lucien were to die beforehand, from something as off-the-wall as a snakebite, no one would suspect Eduardo. Tomorrow she would ask questions about the death adder episode. Until then, she had questions enough for Seth. "What did you find in Wendell's room?"

"A diamond earring and, unless I'm very much mistaken, it's not his style."

"It's Neesha's," she said. "They're having an affair."

His eyebrows slanted up. "That doesn't shock you? You Southern belles are a lot looser than I thought."

"Don't be snide. I found out by accident, but I'm pretty sure Cleon knows."

"How does Cleon feel about it?"

"He hasn't admitted that he knows." She hesitated. But for whatever reason—the wine, the need to talk, the color of his eyes—she let down the drawbridge. "He's angry enough to cut Wendell out of his will, but it won't hurt Wendell too badly. Dr. Fisher left him a business worth millions."

"Sweet. Did Wendell know he was due to inherit from Fisher?"

"Yes, but he acted surprised by the amount. Of course, he's acted like the epitome of Christian rectitude and family values for years and we now know that was BS."

"Sounds like Wendell's not one of your faves. What's his life like back in Georgia?"

"Ordinary. He has an imitation Tara in the burbs. He does whatever it is that bankers do. Golfs. Boats. His wife's a member of the Garden Club and the Daughters of the Confederacy. They're well-to-do, but not rich. Until now."

He passed up the chance to ridicule. "How do you suppose the doctor was poisoned?"

"Fugu, improperly cleaned. At least, that's what Inspector Newby thinks."

"Fugu! Now that's ingenious. Fisher must have been off his rocker to let a novice cook prepare fugu for him."

"The Inspector says he was kind of a quack, and probably addicted to risk."

The corners of his eyes lifted. "You're kind of cozy with that old copper, aren't you?"

"He'd like to think so."

"Use it. Play him for everything you can get from him."

She felt a qualm. Is that what Seth was doing? Playing her for all she was worth? "It's only a guess really, very provisional until Inspector Newby gets the autopsy report."

"Don't worry. I won't tell him I know." He reached across the table and covered her hand with his. The resulting heat was distracting in the extreme.

She took back her hand. "You've traveled all over. Do you know much about Australian Aborigines?"

"Some."

"Do you know any of their languages?"

"A word here and there. Yolngu refers to somebody from an Aboriginal clan. Balanda is a non-Aborigine."

"What does galka mean?"

The word seemed to startle him. "Where'd you hear that?"

"Tanya. Is it some kind of Aboriginal expletive?"

"It means doctor."

"That's it?"

"Bad doctor, witchdoctor. A galka can hypnotize a man and cause him to kill himself."

That was it. Tanya had called Fisher a kill doctor. She must've found out that he was going to help Cleon kill himself. But would she have cared that much about the death of a non-Aborigine? Used Fisher's craving for dangerous munga to save a Balanda's life? Dinah didn't see why not. Tanya was a good person in a bad situation, a situation fraught with aggravations and condescensions and impossible demands and, on top of everything else, she'd been ordered to prepare a high-risk delicacy for the delectation of a witchdoctor who was about to kill a man.

She said, "Tanya must have believed that Dr. Fisher was a witch-doctor and she poisoned him to keep him from killing Cleon."

Seth looked skeptical. "Superstition's a lame motive for murder."

"No, it isn't. People act out of superstition all the time. Maybe she thought the fish would only make him sick so he couldn't hurt Cleon." She sounded presumptuous and self-serving, even to herself. The results of the autopsy hadn't even been announced. Was she so anxious to be out of this quagmire that she was willing to scapegoat a woman on the basis of a word flung in anger?

She tossed off the rest of her wine. Cleon was right about wine. It made you forget there was any such thing as death. Or want to forget.

Seth's gold-flecked eyes were staring at her. Psychoanalyzing her. "What's on your mind, Ms. Pelerin?"

"Let's get out of here."

TWENTY-EIGHT

THE DIRT TRACK to the lodge at two o'clock in the morning was black as the inside of a well. Dinah strained her eyes and gripped the steering wheel with both hands. There'd been a dead wallaby at the turnoff, right in front of a yellow sign with a picture of a wallaby, and she was worried that one would jump out in front of her. Seth's car wallowed from rut to rut, its puny headlights groping the road ahead like the antennas of a blind bug.

He lounged unbelted in the passenger seat, his bare feet braced against the dash. He was smoking a Chung Hwa and giving them both lung cancer. After dinner, they'd gone for a walk beside the Katherine River to clear their heads, but a cloud of mosquitos harried them back to the car. Once inside, as they swatted and slapped at the invaders, touching was unavoidable. Dinah wasn't quite sure how, but touching had led to kissing, which led to more purposeful touching and more fervent kissing. This ex-monk could do things with his mouth that would melt stone, or at least impair cerebral function to a high degree. But as he unbuttoned the tortoiseshell buttons on her shirt, she remembered the dead tortoise on Melville Island. The dead tortoise with the dead man shafted on top.

It was more chilling than a cold shower. She'd called an abrupt halt and commandeered the car keys. Seth hadn't seemed unduly disappointed. Rather like being told the restaurant was out of a dish he didn't want anyway.

She glanced across at his smoke-wreathed profile.

When exactly had he arrived in Australia and where had he come from? His debut at Crow Hill was just too coincidental for comfort. Did he have a record? If Jacko was already aware of Seth's connection to the family when he picked her up in Darwin, he must have. Bombings? Arson? Monkey-wrenching? Murder? And what if the beans she'd spilled tonight helped him to get away with his crimes?

Why had she been so to quick to brush off her suspicions and let down her guard? Denial, that's why. Denial and disbelief. How could she have gotten herself tangled up with so many deceivers and dissemblers?

She said, "This car drives like a boogie board."

"You should've let me drive."

"You'd have driven us to a motel."

"I thought that's what you wanted."

"I changed my mind."

"Your prerogative. My yin and yang are in harmony."

"Lucky you." She'd gone nuts for a little while, but she was back in control now, and ready to do a little deceiving and dissembling of her own. "Seth, can you help me get a handgun? Talking about the murders like we did, the reality has finally sunk in and I don't feel safe. I need protection."

"From Tanya? Get real."

"What if it's not Tanya? Like you said, superstition's a lame motive. What if it's Mack? Or Eduardo?"

"Whoever did it, he can't possibly be interested in you. Hang loose. In a week or so, Cleon will drown himself in the Katherine River so it doesn't look like suicide and you and I will inherit a sack full of money. Maybe we can do Phuket together. You'd like Thailand."

"Humor me, okay? Please? I'd just feel better if I had a gun."

"You'd have to apply for a license and go through

a long waiting period. This'll all be over long before you'd qualify."

"Isn't there a shortcut? Some way around the red tape? Can't you buy one for me or something?"

"The only guns I've seen in the Territory are hunting rifles and air pistols. Nobody has a handgun in this country. Stop worrying. I have a black belt in t'ai chi. I'll protect you from the bad guys."

She sighed. Whatever germs they'd swapped while kissing, the germ of truth obviously wasn't one of them. She steered around a large rock and picked up speed. She'd been overtaken by events and, once again, failed to carry through and call Jacko. In the circumstances, she supposed tomorrow would be soon enough.

"Look out!"

"Jesus!" She stood on the brakes, skidded on loose gravel and the car did a screeching one-eighty.

Heart pounding, she swiveled her head around and stared into the blackness behind. "What was it?"

Seth blew out his cheeks and rubbed his elbow. "A cat, I think. Lots of feral cats in the bush. Or maybe a quoll. You okay?"

"Uh-huh." Her teeth were chattering. The sight of those yellow animal eyes had petrified her.

Seth put on his shoes and got out of the car. He took a last pull off his Chung Hwa, crushed it underfoot, and walked around to the driver's side. "I'll drive."

She scooted over and he took the wheel. She had a premonition. "There's something out there. Something bad."

"It was just a cat, Dinah. You didn't hit it. You've got good reflexes."

"It was an omen. Trust me. I get this tingling in my toes, like a warning. It's neuroscientific. A glitch in my anterior cingulated cortex. Really. I once had a boyfriend who did brain research."

"Does this warning system tell you what direction the bad thing is coming from?"

"No."

"Well, until your toes get GPS, we'll keep going in the direction of the lodge. Unless you want to go to a motel."

"No."

"Just know that wherever you want to sleep tonight, mi cama es su cama."

"You speak Spanish, too?"

"Un poquito." He backed the car around, managing to stay out of the ditch on either side of the road, and drove on toward Crow Hill.

She rolled down the passenger window to clear the smoke out of her lungs. The night air smelled resinous. Gigantic trees towered over the road, obliterated the moon and stars, enclosed the car between walls of sinister darkness. "What are these trees with the whitish bark?"

"They're a type of eucalyptus. Ghost gums."

Terrific. Even the trees suggested death. Was it Raymond Chandler who'd compared the smell of eucalyptus to cat piss? She wished she could summon the ghost of Raymond Chandler for a bit of advice, but Ray had very sensibly stayed put in the good old U.S. of A.

A tandem of shadows streaked across the road.

"Seth, stop!"

He pulled to the side of the road and they jumped out of the car at the same time.

"Thad?" She called after the fleeing figures as they crashed pell-mell into the woods.

"Thad, you've been made. You may as well come out."

There was a spate of impressive profanity and slowly, Thad stumbled out of the trees. He wiped dirt off his knees, flipped his hair out of his face, and nearly lost his balance. "Who d'ya think you are, five-O or something?"

Dinah wondered if Thad had picked up the gangsta slang for cops from rappers he listened to, or whether the crowd he ran with in Atlanta had firsthand experience being hassled by cops. She felt bad about his mental kink, whatever it was, but her stolen Valium still rankled and his smart-ass attitude made her want to wring his neck.

Seth asked, "What are you doing out here in the middle of the night?"

"What's it to ya?"

Dinah said, "He reeks of gasoline. For God's sake, don't light a cigarette, Seth. You'll immolate your new step-brother."

Seth pulled Thad close and smelled his shirt. "Were you trying to start a fire?"

"No." He wobbled like a dying top.

"Then what?" Seth jerked him up by the collar. "Were you sniffing petrol?"

"What if I was?"

"Where'd you get it, Thad?"

"Siphoned it out of Dad's car."

Dinah looked up and down the road. There was no car in sight.

She said, "You didn't walk all the way from the lodge in your condition. Where's the car?"

"We jacked it and drove a few miles down the road. It hit something and got stuck back there." He waved his arm drunkenly in the direction of the lodge.

She scoured the dark palisade of trees. "Who was that with you?"

"Victor."

"Tanya's nephew?"

"Yeah."

"Is he high on gas fumes, too?" asked Dinah.

"I guess."

Seth shouted out Victor's name. "Come talk to us, Victor. Time to call it a night."

"He won't come out," said Thad. "He's an Abo. He knows how to hide in the bush."

Dinah didn't know the effects of inhaling hydrocarbons, but she didn't like the way Thad was wobbling. "What about pills? Did you guys swallow any pills?"

"One or two."

Seth tightened his hold on Thad's collar. "What kind of pills?"

Thad answered with an insolent flip of his hair.

Oh, Lord. Dinah envisioned a long night ahead, tracking Victor through the ghost gums with a thousand snakes slithering underfoot. If he passed out alone in those woods, he could die. They had to do something, call Tanya, call somebody. "Call an ambulance, Seth. Call the police. Call Cleon."

He pulled out his cell phone and walked a few paces down the road.

"No, please," whined Thad. "Don't rat me out. We're not so messed up, just a little dizzy. And it was Victor who siphoned the gas. I never sniffed it before he showed me how."

Dinah resolved never to have children. "I'll bet Victor never took pills before you showed him where he could steal…" She stopped. It was the doctor's room she'd seen the boys slip into. Her foreboding intensified. "These pills, did you steal them from Dr. Fisher's room?"

"No."

"Don't lie to me, Thad. I saw you sneak into the doctor's room the night I arrived. What kind of pills did you take? Show me the bottle."

"They're yours, okay? There weren't any pills in the doc's room."

"Help's on the way," said Seth. He closed his phone and rejoined the interrogation. "What else did you do besides sniffing, Thad?" He took the boy by the arm, pulled him into the car's headlights, and studied his pupils.

"Honest," said Thad. "The doc didn't have any pills. All I took out of his room was money. I swear."

"Well, you'd better fork it over," said Dinah. "Or did you spend it already?"

"I don't have it with me. It's too heavy to carry and we couldn't have spent it here. It's American."

"Too heavy? How much money are we talking about?" asked Seth.

"Three hundred thousand."

"Fisher had three hundred thousand U.S. dollars in his room?"

"Yeah, I counted it."

Dinah remembered the heavy medical bag that caused Fisher to list to his right.

Seth cuffed Thad on the side of the head. "No bullshit, Thad. You took it all?"

"Yeah."

"When?" asked Dinah. "Did you go in the doctor's room more than once?"

"Yeah. When Dad was telling y'all about Seth and ran me and K.D. out of the room, I went back. I was gonna klepto a couple packs of cigarettes, but I looked in his bag and when I saw the cash…"

"You took that instead." In the glare of the headlights, Seth's eyes gleamed like phosphor. "Where is it now?"

"That can wait," said Dinah. "Thad, you'd better pour yourself into the backseat of Seth's car and pray the EMTs get here pronto."

No sooner had she spoken than a Land Rover with flashing red lights barreled down the road straight at them. It stopped behind Seth's car and Jacko climbed out on the passenger side.

Seth didn't seem all that pleased to see him. "How'd you get here so fast?"

"I was already on my way when I got your SOS."

"Why?" asked Seth. "What brings you to the lodge at this hour of the night?"

Jacko shone a flashlight in Thad's eyes. "Haven't you heard? There's been a robbery."

TWENTY-NINE

JACKO ORDERED THE two men traveling with him to set up flares on the road and comb the scrub for Victor. He asked Thad to spell his name and count to twenty forwards and backwards. To Dinah's surprise, Thad performed like a whiz kid and Jacko pronounced him fit to go home. He called the dispatcher and ordered a backup police vehicle in addition to the ambulance. Brusquely, he ordered Dinah into his Land Rover.

She wanted to go with Seth to keep an eye on him, but did as she was told. Jacko ordered Seth to drive Thad back to the lodge, then climbed behind the wheel of the Land Rover.

"Getting to know your new rellie, are you, Dinah?"

"Somewhat."

He gave her a sardonic look, cranked the engine, pulled around Seth's car and took off at speed, indifferent to the danger of darting cats and wallabies and the blizzard of dust and stones thrown back into Seth's windshield.

"You'll want to put your buttons in their proper holes before we blow in at the lodge. I understand the family's bashing about in a bit of a lather. Wouldn't want to give them a scandal."

Hot-faced, she turned away and corrected her buttoning. Jacko didn't know the meaning of the word scandal. She stewed for a minute, but common sense kicked in. She'd been chomping at the bit to tell him about her own scandalous discovery and air her fuzzy suspicions, and here he was.

His radio blared and a voice said, "I think I see him. There, on the far side of that fallen tree."

Jacko turned down the volume. "The lad's probably too wonky to get far. I just hope he doesn't take a header and crack his skull."

Dinah thought about Victor floundering around in the dark. "Is sniffing petrol very dangerous?"

"Not for the Dobbs boy. He'll not do it after he leaves the Territory. But make a habit of it, as some Aborigine lads have done, and it rots the brain."

Dinah wished she could help Victor. She wished she could help Tanya. Instead, she was about to add to her misfortunes. "Did you get the results from the autopsy?"

"It was the fugu like we thought."

Perhaps that "we" meant he was back in a friendly mood.

"Tanya may have had a motive to kill Dr. Fisher." She recapped the scene where Tanya called Fisher a galka, giving Seth's definition.

"Why would the poor woman think Fisher was a galka? He'd not hypnotized anyone to kill himself, had he?"

She didn't know if anyone had clued him into Cleon's planned suicide and she was beyond caring. "You'll have to ask Tanya why she said it. I'm not accusing Tanya. Other people had motives." She told him about Wendell's and Neesha's affair.

"You saw them pashing?"

"No, but I heard them talking. Wendell was anticipating a windfall from Fisher's will." Jacko would find out soon enough about the provisions of Fisher's will. She decided to earn Brownie points by being first with the news. "Fisher left Wendell millions and it turns out the doctor collected some valuable art, which he left to Lucien."

"Your brother gobsmacked by his good luck, was he?"

She tried not to sound defensive. "He was surprised."

"I'll bet."

She disregarded the sarcasm. "You said that Dr. Fisher had crossed swords with a lot of people, Jacko. Were there any rumors linking him to stolen art?"

"Starve the lizards! You must have psychic powers. I was just thinking of stolen art. Would you believe it? It's fine art that's gone off from the lodge."

"You have every reason to be fed up with all the chicanery, Jacko. So am I. I don't know what's going on, but I guessed it was the Homer watercolors that were stolen. They're the most valuable things in the house."

"And yours, I hear, or will be at your uncle's death. We've had a long yack, your Uncle Cleon and I. I hope this doesn't come as too great a shock, luv, but he may cark it sooner than later. Cancer, he tells me. Inoperable. So little time to spend with the son he didn't know he had. It tears the heart."

They passed Cleon's Mercedes with the left front tire stuck in a ditch. Jacko pulled off the road and, as he did, Seth drove past them with Thad hunched in the backseat. Dinah didn't have to be a mind reader to know what Seth was thinking. Where's the money? And from the way Thad sneered when Jacko said there'd been a robbery, she assumed he was thinking he'd hidden the cash too well for anyone to find it without his help.

While Jacko inspected Cleon's car, Dinah revolved the series of crimes and possible crimes through her mind. Thad had ripped off Fisher's cash, which Fisher must have brought home from Katherine on the day of his death in his medical bag. Where did the money come from? Had

Cleon paid him $300,000 to help him commit suicide or was it payment for something else? For changing his will in favor of Wendell and Margaret and Lucien? For inflating his assets to make them think they'd be getting more than they would?

She thought about all that art the doctor owned but didn't hang. Did it actually exist? And if it did, where had it come from before Fisher acquired it? Had Lucien procured it for him? He'd procured the Homers for Cleon and Neesha. Dear God, was it possible that her paintings were hot and that's why Lucien didn't want them on the market? Had he stolen them to make sure she didn't try and sell them?

Jacko returned to the Land Rover and growled into his radio. "What's the good oil, Norton? Any sign of the boy? Well, keep on it. I don't want to have to tell his aunt he's gone walkabout with a herd of pink elephants lolloping about in his head." He told Norton the location of Cleon's car. "Have it pushed out of the ditch and, if it's drivable, drive it on to the lodge. I'll want you there in any event. For mob control."

He signed off, turned on the overhead light and gave Dinah a crimped smile. "All right, luv. Let's have your guess at who took the bloody pictures."

"I don't know."

"But you've an inkling."

"No."

"Crikey!" He whammed the steering wheel with the heels of his hands and she winced. "Don't try my patience, Dinah. I'm not out here at three in the bloody morning for a lark." There was a bite in his voice, an announcement that beneath the codger act was a hard-nosed cop who'd crack heads if he had to.

"I have inklings about a lot of things, Jacko. Most of them have been pretty unreliable over the last few days."

He turned off the light, started the car, and drove on toward the lodge. When he spoke again, he sounded like the old, affable Jacko. "You asked me why I latched onto you in Darwin. Fair crack of the whip, I'll tell you. The feds have been monitoring a group called Earth's Turn for over a year. We think they're the push that's been dynamiting docks and disrupting fish harvesting operations in the area. Just after the Melville murder, one of the heavy hitters for the group turned up in Sydney in the company of your Uncle Cleon."

"Seth?"

"Spot on. Mr. Farraday's a man of many facets. We don't know if he's the demolition man or just an errand boy and spotter for the big hammers. I thought you'd be his wife flying in for a get-together."

"He's married?"

"The missus is a Cuban girl from south Florida. She's the group's roving ambassador. Looks quite a bit like you from the photo we have on file. Not knowing your uncle's relationship to the Farradays, I had to find out if she was the one he'd wired the ticket to. If so, she'd be entering Oz under a false name."

A headache began to drum dully at her temples, like elephants lolloping. "Did Seth know Dr. Fisher before he arrived?"

"They were in Sydney at the same time. We don't know if they ever met."

"Was Seth on Melville at the time of the murder?"

"There's no proof. The bloke assigned to follow him shot through a red light and had a nasty bingle. Landed in hospital, himself, and we lost Farraday for a few days."

"Can't you arrest him for something? He has a gun, you know."

"His permit is in order. There aren't any outstanding warrants."

"How about fraud or misrepresentation? Is he really Cleon's son?"

"Your uncle's better placed to answer that and he says that he is."

They had reached the lodge. He pulled the Land Rover close up in front of the porch as if to block the escape route and radioed Norton again. This time there was good news. Victor had been found, fuddled and scrappy, but otherwise all right. They were taking him to the hospital for eval to be on the safe side.

"One fire put out." Jacko turned on the overhead light and eyeballed her for a long minute. "I don't believe Tanya poisoned the doctor, accidentally or on purpose, and it's a dead cert she's not rapt about the brushwork of Mr. Winslow Homer. You know who's left, luv. And in case you didn't know, Mr. Eduardo Conti spent a year in chokey for drug possession and your half-brother Lucien was bailed up for assaulting an art dealer in New York last month."

"Lucien was in jail?"

"Overnight. The charges were dropped and I know what you're thinking. What does a skerrick of cannabis or a little punch-up have to do with murder or stolen art? Maybe bloody everything, or maybe bugger all. But when you're deciding whether to cooperate with the police and dob on your rellies, keep in mind there's a law against impeding a police investigation."

THIRTY

THE WIVES AND K.D. sat shoulder-to-shoulder on one side of the dining room table, each in a different colored robe. Like a lineup of surly parakeets, thought Dinah. K.D. held a panting Cantoo in her lap and jotted notes in her little book of smears.

Thad moped in a chair in the corner, temporarily out of the spotlight. Petrol sniffing and car jacking apparently ranked lower in priority than the theft of the Homers. Seth stood over Thad with his arm on his shoulder, possessive as a prison guard.

Wendell languished against the wall at one end of the sideboard, his hands balled in the pockets of his tartan robe. Lucien leaned heavily on his crutches at the other end. Cleon stood in the doorway, arms folded across his chest like a teacher facing down a classroom of cutups, and frowned at the naked wall between them where the Homers had hung. Eduardo, dressed as if for a day at the races, puttered about with the coffee service and helped his nemesis, Mack, pass around cups and saucers.

As Dinah sidled past Seth, she whispered, "I'm going to tell Jacko about Fisher's bag of money, so don't think you can get your paws on it."

His eyes crinkled at the corners and her skin itched with loathing. She sat down next to Neesha and tried to catch Lucien's eye. He kept his head down. Seth was right about his body language. He looked guilty as hell, but of what? Was he an art thief? A fence for stolen art? Had he heisted a shipment of major art works and sold them to Fisher? Were the Homers he'd fobbed off on Cleon hot?

Jacko shook hands with Cleon and the two of them ducked into the kitchen for a private tête-à-tête.

"You've got some nerve," hissed Neesha.

Never a dull moment, thought Dinah. "What did I do?"

"While the men are taking care of this embarrassing situation, let's have ourselves a toddy, shall we?" She snapped on a frosty smile, linked her arm in Dinah's, and dragged her up and out of the room.

When they got to the great room, she dropped Dinah's arm like a dead possum. "First, you talk Cleon into leaving you my pictures and, knowing he'd change his mind, you steal them."

"I was out of the house all afternoon, Neesha, first with Cleon and tonight with Seth. I couldn't have stolen them."

"You probably enlisted that impostor to help you." She swept her long hair around to one side of her face and fiddled with the ends. "It's intolerable. Margaret trying to chisel me out of my money on one side, Seth Farraday on another. And I should have known you'd worm your way into the will. Your mother probably put you up to it."

It cost Dinah no small amount of willpower to restrain herself. "You can't blame me for how your husband chooses to leave his money. And certainly, not my mother."

"Why not? Depravity runs in your family like a disease. You get it from both sides, don't you?"

Dinah saw red. This two-faced viper was asking for it. "Oh, Wendell, darling, I could have stood three more nights…sob, sob. Oh, darling, this is my idea of love… zip, zip."

Neesha blanched and Dinah felt a frisson of triumph. "How's that for depravity, Neesha?"

"You spied on us?" Her voice was tremulous, but defiant.

"The walls have ears."

She gave Dinah a venomous look. "Have you told Cleon?"

"Do you really think I'd have to? But just so you know, I did tell Inspector Newby."

Remarkably, her old beauty-pageant poise rallied. She raised her chin and struck a pose. "There's nothing anyone can do to us now. Cleon can't disinherit his minor children and as Margaret says, I'm entitled to a third of the estate and all the gifts he's given me. Including those Homers. And if you stole them, I'll see you do time for it."

Dinah clenched her fists. If she ever let her inner Injun loose on that platinum scalp...

The front door bumped open and there was an irruption of voices in the hall. Dinah turned her back on Neesha and went to see what was happening. The three-chevron deputy she remembered as Norton and a black deputy walked in, their radios sputtering, and met Jacko as he ushered the family toward the great room. Cleon marched past Dinah and went straight to the bar, followed single file by Margaret, Wendell, K.D., Thad, Lucien, Eduardo, Seth, and Mack.

Jacko ordered the black deputy to find Tanya and break the news about Victor, then drive her into Katherine to the hospital. He took Norton aside. Dinah watched as they huddled at the end of the hall for a few minutes. When they finished their parley, they returned to the great room. Jacko stood in the doorway and announced that he would be interviewing each member of the household separately in the dining room. They could wait in the great room until called or move about the house, if they liked.

"Norton will find you when it's your turn," he said.

"Will you be searching the house?" asked Margaret.

"As soon as the warrants arrive." He leveled his gun-barrel gaze on Thad. "I'll start with the youngest Mr. Dobbs. Follow me, please, sir."

Thad cast an appealing look at his mother. "Don't you have to be present, Mom?"

"Not this time, Thad. When Inspector Newby has finished questioning you, go up to your room. I'll be up to say good-night in a little while."

He looked to Cleon, but Cleon was rattling his martini shaker next to his ear like a maraca and paid him no mind.

"Fine. Sure, okay." Thad curled his lip and scuffed out of the room behind Norton and Jacko.

"What? Say again?" Wendell moved as far from the noise as possible, his cell phone glued to his ear. "I know it's an important closing, Bud, but I'm out here in the sticks. Can't it...what?"

Violating his rule on how to treat good gin, Cleon rattled the ice in the shaker so hard it sounded like small arms fire.

Neesha said, "I have a splitting headache. K.D., will you please tell Sergeant Norton I'll be waiting in my room." She cinched her robe more tightly and steamed out the door.

Wendell's eyes trailed after her. "All right, Bud, I'll try, but I can't promise anything." He pocketed his phone. "I'm going upstairs to get my laptop. When the inspector's ready for me, I'll be in the kitchen trying to get a dial-up connection."

He left and Mack and Seth and Eduardo sat down to wait. Lucien stood in the corner scowling.

Margaret settled herself on a bar stool. "Make one of your silver bullets for me, Cleon. And tell me why you're shaking the bejesus out of the gin."

Cleon poured himself a drink and started shaking up another one for Margaret.

Lucien exploded. "Will you stop that noise? You've brought all this on yourself, you know that? It's your own goddamn fault, all of it, for riding roughshod over us and digging the spurs in at every chance. What did you expect?"

Cleon looked up, deadpan. "Not this."

"Oh, the hell with it," said Lucien. "Tell Norton I'll be on the veranda." He made a disgusted face and vaulted out the door, legs kicking out from between his crutches like battering rams.

Cleon reached for a bottle of Makers Mark. "Here, Eduardo." He held out the bottle. "Your paramour's got hisself wrought up. Better go see if you can revive him."

Eduardo didn't reply. He took the bottle and two glasses and went after Lucien.

Dinah sensed that the tension between Cleon and Lucien had come to a head. She wasn't sure what they'd just said to each other, but whatever it was, they knew. Eduardo knew, Margaret knew, Seth knew. Even K.D. had a knowing look on her smug little puss. Everyone seemed to be on the same page but Dinah and she didn't feel she was even in the same book. In frustration, she stalked out into the hall and began to pace.

Before long, Norton came out of the dining room with Thad. The kid didn't seem as cocky as he did a few minutes before. He peeled off from Norton and went obediently up the stairs. Norton continued into the great room and called for K.D. Dinah watched them march toward the dining room and, spontaneously, she about-faced and headed for the veranda. Lucien was going to tell her what was going on if she had to beat it out of him.

She opened the back door and he and Eduardo broke off in mid-sentence. Pretending she hadn't noticed, she stepped outside. One of them had lit the citronella candles and placed the lantern on a wine crate with the bourbon. Eduardo stood at a distance, his back against a column. Lucien slouched in a chair nursing his bourbon.

Dinah took a deep breath and planted herself in the chair next to Lucien. "Another eventful day, huh?"

Lucien sighed. "I feel a third degree coming on and if it's all the same with you, Torquemada, I'd rather wait for Newby to put me on the rack."

"We're out of sorts," said Eduardo. "De pis en pis."

"For chrissakes, Eddie, will you can the faggy French? We're not in Paris."

"We would be if you'd listened to me," said Eduardo.

Dinah saw no gain in being tactful. "It might behoove you to talk to me before the inspector gets to you, Lucien. It'll give you a chance to trump up a better bunch of lies. I'm sure he'll have a number of questions about that bonanza of Pollocks and Hartleys and Homers you just inherited. They give you a jim-dandy motive for murdering Dr. Fisher."

"You think I don't know that?"

"Well, then, get your head out of the sand, big brother, and help me figure things out."

"You want a crisis, figure out who stole the Homers, why don't you?"

"Okay," she said, dismayed that a couple of little pieces of pilfered art outranked a murder in his mind. "We can start there. Who first noticed the paintings missing?"

"I did," said Eduardo. "When I passed by the dining room around ten this evening, I saw they were gone. At first, I thought Cleon had taken them down. I asked him and he hit the roof."

Lucien was pessimistic. "They could've been lifted anytime during the day. By now they could've been bundled off to Katherine and sold to a private collector or a pawn broker or the Russian mob."

"Famous paintings aren't that easy to sell," said Dinah. "You know that. A buyer would want certificates of authenticity and a bill of sale. But even if they're not found, Uncle Cleon must have insured them."

"Fuck the insurance. It doesn't matter."

Dinah threw up her hands. "Okay, Lucien. I get it. You want the paintings for yourself and if they're found, you can have the damn things. Just tell me what it is you're hiding. Did you steal them from your dealer friend in New York? Is he the guy you beat up last month? What the hell is going on?"

"Tell her," said Eduardo.

Lucien put his head in his hands.

Eduardo came and put a hand on Lucien's shoulder. "If you don't tell her, I will."

Her fear magnified. "Lucien?"

"They're forgeries, Di."

"What?"

"Your Homer watercolors are forgeries. Some of my best work."

"You? You forged them?" She felt as if she'd been blown off a cliff.

"I copied them from the originals."

She stared at him in complete shock. This was a turn-up she couldn't have imagined. The one person whose honesty and integrity she'd have staked her life on was a liar and a scammer, apparently from way back.

He said, "They started out as a joke."

"A man walks into a gallery. Ha-ha." What did he want from her, absolution?

"Neesha walked into a gallery, the one belonging to my old art school friend, St. Jean. It was just after she and

Cleon married and he'd given her a blank check to refurbish the farmhouse. She and her decorator were in New York trolling for antiques. They met St. Jean and me for lunch and I just happened to be showing the pieces to St. Jean. They weren't for sale. They were like, exercises. Experiments. Neesha's decorator saw them and went wild. They'd be the crowning touch for the new drawing room."

Dinah cut to the crux. "And you and St. Jean got dollar signs in your eyes. You strung them along and cashed in."

"Things got out of hand," put in Eduardo, in a sort of proxy apology. "Lucien didn't know how good an artist he was."

"How good a con artist, you mean." She got up and stomped around the veranda. What offense against the gods had she committed to deserve so many pretenders and connivers in her life?

"I was in my early twenties," said Lucien. "Fresh out of school and experimenting with lots of styles and media. It wasn't the crime of the century. Neesha and Dad are philistines. They didn't know the difference."

"From the stink bombs he's dropped into the conversation lately, I'd say Cleon knows the difference now. How'd he find out he'd been flimflammed?"

"I don't know. He never came right out and said that he knew until tonight when the things went missing."

"Did you tell Mom? Maybe she put him wise."

"I told her when Cleon first bought them, but she'd never blow the whistle on me."

"A tad lackadaisical of her, wouldn't you say, sitting quietly by while her son fleeces his father out of millions?" Her tone was scathing, as she meant it to be.

Lucien answered in kind. "You know something, kiddo, I'm tired of being your personal coloring book where you get to color me however you like, inside your lines. And for your information, Mom didn't think what I did was much of a swindle. Those pictures are damn good. They wowed Neesha and, as far as I knew, they were going to stay in the family indefinitely."

"Maybe it was Mom's indulging your big fat ego that led you to think you could outshine Winslow Homer in the first place."

"Just what is it you're…?"

Eduardo said, "I'll be happy to referee this family spat later. Right now, we need to concentrate on finding the paintings."

"Fine." Lucien finished his bourbon and picked up his crutches. "Neesha is the only other person who wants them. If what you told me about an amour with Wendell is true, then maybe he stole them for her. It was either Wendell or Neesha. I'm sure of it."

"Maybe they're in the trunk of Wendell's car," said Eduardo.

Lucien pooh-poohed the idea. "Too risky. They're probably in a locker at the Katherine Airport."

"With the key safe and warm in Neesha's cleavage," said Eduardo.

"And she accused me of stealing them." It wasn't hard for Dinah to transfer some of her anger onto Neesha. But the woman had sounded so convincing. "What if it was Cleon who took them?"

"Why would he do that?" asked Lucien.

"I don't know. To get your goat. To get Neesha's goat. He certainly got mine." She felt more galled by Cleon's deception than by Lucien's. Cleon had made her believe he was doing something special for her because he loved her when, in fact, he was just turning the screws on Lucien to make him fess up. "I was a sap to believe he was leaving me millions."

"I told you he'd use you," said Lucien.

"Oh, right. The way my high-minded, selfless big brother never would. You've had only my best interests at heart."

"Berate me all you want, Dinah. I deserve it. But if Neesha hangs those pictures in her gallery for the world to see or tries to sell them, I'll be up the proverbial creek."

"Didn't you paint some little tell or anachronism on them? Something to show they weren't intended to pass for the originals?"

"No. I matched the colors, even the watermarks in the paper. Everything's exact."

A second wave of anger hit her. "Lucien, why don't you just tell everybody they're fakes and then nobody will want them?"

Eduardo said, "Neesha would have him thrown in the Bastille, Dinah. It would ruin his reputation as an artist."

She pictured Lucien in an orange jumpsuit with shackles around his ankles. However much of a blister he'd been, whatever he'd done to get himself into this pickle, he was still her brother. Clan loyalty was in her genes.

Sergeant Norton opened the door. "Mr. Lucien Dobbs, Inspector Newby will speak with you now, sir."

Lucien pushed himself up on his crutches. "I'm on my way, Sergeant."

Norton held the door open and Lucien hobbled off to his interview.

Eduardo said, "He feels really bad about letting you down, Dinah, but you put him on a pedestal he never wanted to be on."

"Well, he's off it now."

"Be careful you don't get a nosebleed standing on such high ground, cherie. You must've done things you're not proud of."

"Yes, but my peccadillos aren't likely to land me in the slammer."

"Touché."

"And why did I have to hear it from Jacko Newby that you'd served time for drug possession?"

"I brought a teensy amount of mu over the border from Mexico a long time ago. Tout le monde does it. You know how Draconian the drug laws are. There was no reason to prostrate myself with regret."

She had a glimmer of intuition. "K.D. overheard you accuse Lucien of cheating, that you'd make him regret it with every fiber of his being. But it wasn't about sex, was it?"

"Sex? No, no, no. I meant that Cleon would make him regret cheating *him*."

"But if Lucien's not two-timing you, what's your problem with Mack?"

"He's trying to persuade Lucien to copy some Aboriginal art."

THIRTY-ONE

EDUARDO SAID HE needed coffee and went inside to brew a pot. Dinah stayed on the veranda watching the shark in the Southern Cross chase the stingray across the sky and thinking about the stolen paintings. They were small and unframed, but enlarged by the mats, they would be too big to hide in a sock drawer and too fragile to stick behind a piece of filthy furniture for the mice to nibble. Lucien's idea that they'd been taken away from the lodge was probably right.

A strong case could be made against Neesha, but Mack was shaping up as a promising culprit even if Lucien didn't see it. A man who'd commercialize the spiritually inspired paintings of his people or collude with a foreigner to paint knock-offs might not be averse to a quick killing in Western art if the opportunity presented. And there was Seth. He wouldn't turn up his nose at a chance to score a couple of valuable paintings, all proceeds to save the planet.

She held her watch under the lantern. Jacko must think that the longer he kept everyone from sleep, the likelier it was that someone would crack. She got up and followed her nose to the coffee.

The dining room door was closed as she passed by on her way to the kitchen. Wendell was sitting at the kitchen table, his laptop open in front of him and plugged into the land line. He was talking on his cell phone, which he held between his neck and his shoulder, and his voice sounded stressed.

"Bud, it's not going to work. I tell you the modem doesn't…well, sure. Sure. Yes, I'll try that."

Dinah poured herself a cup of coffee and, seeing that Wendell had a half-drunk cup next to the computer, poured him a warm-up. He mouthed a cursory thank-you and she sat down across from him and studied him over the rim of her cup. It was hard to believe that behind that bland exterior beat the heart of a lying back-door man. But a man who could lie so ignominiously about one thing could lie about another. She wondered if Neesha had slipped him the word that Dinah knew about their affair or if his little business emergency had delayed the inevitable. He seemed friendly enough, albeit very distracted and a shade haggard just now. With all the millions he'd inherited from Fisher, he wouldn't be toiling away for the Bank of Brunswick much longer.

"It's the network connection, Bud. It keeps failing. Can't this wait until…?"

Sergeant Norton appeared in the door. "Mr. Dobbs, the inspector's ready to see you now."

Wendell held up a finger, like be-with-you-in-one. "Right. Right. Because of the numbers. I understand. Look, Bud, I have another emergency here. I'll try to send it again in a few minutes."

He turned off his phone, executed a few quick clicks on the computer and closed the lid. "Sorry to keep you waiting, Sergeant. It never rains but it pours, eh?" He gave Dinah an absent-minded nod and got up and followed Norton out of the room.

Dinah slid the laptop around and opened it. Strange that he would turn it off when he meant to come back in a few minutes and try to re-send the whatsit with the numbers to Bud. Banking in Brunswick, Georgia, must be classified Top Secret. Or…or maybe he was afraid she would sneak a peek while he was out of the room and find a batch of salacious e-mails from Neesha, explaining her idea of love in non-Victorian language.

If the computer contained e-mails between him and Neesha or anything not kosher in his dealings with Fisher, maybe she could ransom it for Lucien's forgeries. If he had them. Even if Cleon knew about the affair, it would be embarrassing if Bud and the folks back in Brunswick found out what kind of hanky-panky old Wendell was up to. And compromising e-mails could be highly detrimental when it came time to divorce his wife.

She wished she could be sure no one would walk in on her and she'd do a search, but it would be too time-consuming and risky. She definitely didn't want to have to explain to Jacko why she was dipping into Wendell's e-mails. Maybe she'd have a chance tomorrow.

She looked at her watch. Shit, it was already tomorrow and had been for hours. She was tired to the bone. If she didn't get a time-out soon, she'd start to gibber and Jacko still hadn't called her in for her interview. She folded her arms and put her head on the table. Just as her eyes were closing, she saw the briefcase standing open under the table.

She pulled it toward her and looked inside. The padded compartment where the laptop would be carried was empty. On the other side she finger-walked through a calendar, a copy of Forbes magazine, a plastic envelope with Wendell's passport and a few American bills inside, and what appeared to be photocopies of documents detailing the various properties in Desmond Fisher's estate. Loose in the bottom of the case were a couple of ballpoints and a little black doohickey, maybe two inches long. She took it out and examined it. Flash Voyager was printed in yellow on one side. It was a flash drive, a computer memory stick.

There were people who recorded their entire lives on these little gadgets with the capacity to hold about a bezillion bytes of potential embarrassment. Had Wendell downloaded any embarrassing secrets?

She rolled the little stick between her palms as if she could absorb its secrets through osmosis. If she took it, she'd be guilty of theft and maybe blackmail. And if it contained information relating to Fisher's murder, she'd be guilty of withholding evidence, subjecting herself to criminal prosecution. Subjecting herself to God only knew what retaliation from Wendell and Neesha.

She slipped the Flash Voyager in her pocket. If Jacko found the paintings before he left, she'd put it back where she found it and no one would be the wiser. If not, she'd take it to town with her tomorrow, find a computer somewhere, and look for something damning. If there was nothing there, she might still be able to return it without anyone's knowledge.

You've sunk to blackmail, she thought sleepily. Neesha got one thing right. The D in my DNA could only stand for depravity.

THIRTY-TWO

MACK WAS IN a state of high dudgeon. Wendell and Neesha had made pointed references to his interest in art and insinuated that he might have had something to do with the theft of the paintings. Mack denied this vociferously. But what really threw the fat in the fire was Eduardo's contention that if anybody knew where to hide the paintings where they wouldn't be found, it was Mack. Eduardo had tagged after the police exhorting them to look for loose floor boards, false walls, and secret panels. No hidey-holes were found, but Mack was incensed. As soon as Jacko and his men had left, which was just after sunup, Mack announced with icy indignation that he, too, was leaving and would not return until after the Dobbses had packed up and moved out.

Dinah's status as an American Aborigine seemed to have immunized her from the worst of his ire and, before anyone could object, she grabbed her things and cadged a lift into town with him. She intended to rent a car, check into a snug, spiderless, and spotlessly clean motel, and get a good night's sleep. Maybe with distance, she could gain some perspective on all the craziness.

"It always comes down to class," Mack said as they drove away from the lodge. "When the nobs and the swells are looking for someone to blame, it's either the butler or the black man."

"Completely unwarranted," said Dinah, careful to stay on his good side. "Very insensitive." She didn't discount the possibility that Mack had filched the paintings. He had no compunction about counterfeiting art. Stealing was no great leap. But Jacko and his men had searched the lodge and all the cars from stem to stern and come up empty.

"I've shown your family every courtesy, jumped through all their hoops, given Lucien a crash course in Aboriginal art, played nursemaid to Cleon and manservant to Wendell and Neesha and those cheeky children and this is the thanks I get."

"We've brought a lot of trouble on you, Mack. You don't deserve it."

"And the police? I won't say that Inspector Newby talked down to me exactly, but he flattered and blarneyed and led me on as if he were talking to a child. It was demeaning. Completely uncalled for."

"Completely." His bleating about injustice was tiresome, but his leisurely pace made Dinah want to take a whip to him. He snailed along, swinging wide around the potholes as if the very soil beneath his tires were sacred. She picked dog hair off her slacks, polished her Wayfarers, and watched the trees grow another foot.

"I've done the best I could to make everyone comfortable, catered to everyone's wants and needs."

"You should demand more money. Hazard pay."

"And I kept your uncle's illegal plans to myself."

"You didn't tell Inspector Newby about Cleon's suicide plan?"

"That would make me liable under the new suicide law."

"There's a new law?"

"It's a crime to discuss end-of-life options by telephone or e-mail. Unfortunately, I did both. Dr. Fisher contacted me by telephone and offered me a tidy sum if I'd allow an assisted suicide under my roof and your uncle e-mailed me later to confirm. I don't know if the law is retroactive and I don't want to find out."

"You can't even talk about suicide? Isn't there a constitutional right to free speech in Australia?"

"No."

"Well, I'm sorry we've put you in a spot, Mack." She thought about his reaction to Tanya's galka remark. "Did you tell Tanya about the suicide?"

"Certainly not. Suicide is taboo for Aboriginal people. If Tanya learned what he was planning, it wasn't from me. Your family talked about it among themselves, you know, Cleon loudest of all. It's all of a piece. If you're black, you're guilty. Neesha even blames poor Victor for Thad's mischief with the petrol-sniffing."

It was hardly a surprise that Neesha could overlook her son's petrol-sniffing. Dinah's mother could apparently overlook forgery and fraud in her son. She said, "Lucien doesn't blame you for anything, Mack. He doesn't think you took the paintings."

"I should hope not. But Eduardo, well. If you want my opinion, he's a fool. I can't understand why a serious artist like Lucien would pair up with someone so frivolous."

Better frivolous than fraudulent, thought Dinah, not as trusting of Mack's blamelessness as Lucien. "Where are you off to today?" she asked.

"I'm meeting a Jawoyn acquaintance who runs a tourist camp on Aboriginal land to the south. My adoptive parents conjectured that my mother might be Jawoyn. Maybe he can suggest the name of an elder who might remember a young girl whose baby was taken about that time. She'd be in her late fifties or early sixties by now."

It crossed Dinah's mind what an irony it would be if Tanya turned out to be Mack's mother. Her age was hard to gauge, but she had to be past fifty. If they should someday discover that they were mother and son, Dinah didn't think the news would bring either one of them much joy.

"Will Tanya continue to work at the lodge after we're gone?"

"I think so. She needs the money. Victor's parents are dead and she's saving to buy a house in Jabiru."

She let a mile or so go by and asked, "What does galka mean?"

He eased the car over a rock as if he were afraid it would cry out in pain. "What was the word again?"

"Galka. Don't you remember? Tanya called Dr. Fisher a galka after he fell into her."

"It doesn't sound like any word I've heard. She was probably saying, don't gawk. Something like that."

Dinah awarded him points for verbal gymnastics and didn't labor the point. "Jabiru is near the entrance to Kakadu National Park, isn't it?"

"That's right."

"Have you been to the Park?"

"No. I'm told that it's a true natural wonder. Wetlands, mostly. Thousands of birds and animals. The rainbow serpent stories of the region are beautiful. The most powerful spirit is Kuringali. She can be tempestuous when crossed. Some legends have her sending earthquakes and floods, some have her eating people alive."

"Don't go into advertising, Mack. The habitat of a quake-sending, people-eating snake woman doesn't fit most folks' definition of Paradise."

He laughed and at long last, they turned onto the non-sacred Stuart Highway and he speeded up. "There's a small Aboriginal town in the park, Oenpelli, that I'd like to visit. It's famous for its bark paintings and pandanus weavings. Screenprinted fabrics, too."

"Have you ever visited the Tiwi Islands? Melville?"

"No. I've been meaning to go. It's just across Van Diemen Gulf from the Cobourg Peninsula, but the Tiwi people don't issue permits unless you've booked a tour. A friend with a boat would come in handy, but alas, I haven't met one yet."

Dinah enjoyed a lie as much as the next person. The nimbleness of conception, the round, plausible feel of it in the mouth, the pride of accomplishment when you deliver a beauty and watch it swallowed whole. Being lied to was considerably less enjoyable but, of late, it seemed her lot in life.

Why would Mack lie about visiting Melville? She hadn't asked him if he stole a load of burial poles or killed anybody. All he had to say was that he'd been on the island wheeling and dealing close to the time Bryce Hambrick was murdered and, alas, wasn't it awful. His inexplicable lie, combined with his scheme to sell sham artworks, bumped him into the top tier of suspects.

When they reached Katherine, she asked him to drop her in front of the library.

He pulled the car into a space in front of the bright and cheerful mural that graced the front of the library. "How will you get back to the lodge?"

"Lucien's meeting me later this afternoon," she lied. "He says his leg feels well enough so he can drive now and he wants to show me a few of the galleries."

"I don't know if I'll see you again before you and your family leave," he said. "Perhaps, I should say good-bye to you now."

"Oh, I'm sure we'll see each other again, Mack. Inspector Newby will probably bring us all together for the climax of his investigation and the thief and the killer will be unmasked."

His eyes flashed with indignation and he drove off without further adieu.

THIRTY-THREE

DINAH DROVE HER blue Toyota Rav 4WD Cruiser away from the Thrifty Car Rental thinking how much she had missed the freedom of having her own wheels. The Rav's ABS, EBD, VSC, Traction Control, air-conditioning with dust filter, dual sunroof, and throaty vroom were neat, but it was the mobility that pepped up her spirits. Mobility was one of life's most empowering feelings—the option to vamoose if a relationship or a job or the general course of events went bad. She'd vamoosed many times in the little Porsche Boxster that Cleon had given her when she graduated from college. It finally conked out in Seattle and she'd done without a car for the last year. If Cleon had left her anything other than forged paintings, she'd have bought another one as soon as she got back to the States. Alas, as Mack would say.

She wondered about poor, ill-treated Mack and the missing Homers. He wasn't as up on American art as Aboriginal art and wouldn't realize they were fakes until he tried to sell them. Even then, he probably had contacts who could help him peddle them to some unsuspecting soul. In fact, if he held onto them until the Dobbs clan left the country, he'd be sitting pretty. But Lucien was positive that Wendell had taken the paintings for Neesha and Dinah had no choice but to start the recovery effort with him. Any other shakedowns, whether of Mack or anybody else, would have to wait. Today she would review the material on Wendell's Flash Voyager, see if it provided any leverage, and go from there.

She meandered through Katherine looking first for a comfortable place to spend the night. The lush and palm-shaded Katherine Lodge Motel on the banks of the Katherine River on Giles Street seemed the best of a limited lot. The lobby was clean and modern, the price reasonable for a place with an ensuite bathroom *and* insect screens, and she registered for one night. She would've gone straight to her room for a nap, but it was too early for check-in. She left her suitcase and started toward the in-house restaurant, the Cheeky Croc, for a quick lunch. A diffuse, institutional smell that reminded her of a school cafeteria stopped her at the door and she decided to scout out something more appetizing. On her way out, she asked the woman at the front desk where she might find an internet café. As luck would have it, that was in-house, too.

The woman showed her a small room just off the reception area with a row of clunky old computers and dial-up access only. Dinah was beginning to feel like a frontiersman. But doubtful she'd find anything better, she postponed lunch and sat down to begin the tedious process of connecting. After a century or so, she was on-line.

Before inserting Wendell's flash drive, she checked her e-mail. The first four messages were from Nick and she deleted them unread along with the airline promotions and bookstore coupons.

There was a newsy note from her friend, Mallory, full of excitement about her new boyfriend and the cool new clothes she'd bought to go with him, and there was a blast from the past from her boyfriend before Nick.

Dear Dinah,
Every day I look out across the Valley to the mountains and wonder if today's the day you'll come back to me. The folks at the book exchange over in Butte ask after you whenever I'm in town. Hope you're

*moving up the ladder in your new job, but don't for-
get I love you. xxx, Ty*

Tyler Colby. She hadn't seen the guy in over a year,
hadn't told him she'd been living with another man, hadn't
told him her job ladder was a step-stool to nowhere. Eddie's words rained down on her head like hot coals. She
had done many things she wasn't proud of and letting Ty
go on loving her when she'd long since relegated him to a
historical footnote was one of the worst.

*Dear Ty, I miss you, too, and think about you every
day.*

E-lies required no skill. No shifty eyes, no shaky voice,
no hemming or hawing to give you away. But she felt guilty
anyway and deleted "every day." There was a grain of
truth in "miss you." At least, she wished that she missed
him, which was almost the same thing. It wasn't as if she'd
ruled him out of her life plan. There was a Native American Studies department at the University of Montana.
Maybe she could finagle a job as a teaching assistant or
something and in her spare time, put together an encyclo-
pedia of Native myths.

*As a matter of fact, Ty, I quit my job. I'm in Australia
juggling a poisoning, an impaling, a derailed euthanasia, and the theft of forged art.*

It sounded as if she were hyperventilating. She scratched
the last sentence.

*I'm on vacation with my brother dealing with family
issues. My plans right now are iffy, but I promise I'll
call you soon. xxx, Dinah*

She had hoped there'd be an offer from her anthropology professor—an immediate assignment in Timbuktu or Kizil Arvat or the International Space Station. But it probably wouldn't do her any good. Jacko hadn't confiscated her passport yet, but it was just a matter of time before he grounded the whole family.

She inserted Wendell's flash drive into the computer. The good news, he hadn't installed password protection. The bad news, he hadn't copied his E-mail onto the Flash Voyager. She brought up the list of files. Baltimore, Barranquilla, Black Point, Brunswick, Cayenne, Davao, La Guaira, Manado, Miami, Montevideo, Surabaya, Tampico, Veracruz.

It was like Jeopardy with only one category—geography. She didn't know where all of them were, but water seemed to be the common denominator. Baltimore and Brunswick were U.S. ports on the Atlantic, Veracruz was situated on the Gulf of Mexico and wasn't La Guaira the seaport town next door to Caracas? Black Point. Hadn't she seen that mentioned in her *Northern Territory Lonely Planet Guide?*

She signed onto Google Earth and called up a scan map of the Territory. Black Point was a small dot on the tip of the Cobourg Peninsula northwest of Kakadu Park in Arnhem Land, which was owned by the Aborigines. From the descriptions she'd read, Black Point was little more than a wide spot with one store where you could charter a boat and buy fuel and basic provisions. But on Wendell's flash drive, Black Point kept company with some heavyweight ports. Why?

She opened the Brunswick file. The Port of Brunswick was one of the busiest on the east coast, importing and exporting automobiles and agri-products of all kinds. It was also where Wendell lived and worked and, presumably, the center of Fisher's business empire. She scrolled down a list of numbers that appeared to represent dates. After each date, if it was a date, there was a row of letters, possibly representing the name of the buyer or seller. Next to each name, if it was a name, was another number and a small k—kilobytes? kilometers? kilograms? And next to that number were more names. Lucky Rascal, Sea Rover, Windcheater, Aces Full, Wave Walker. Boats. The Wave Walker was what Wendell had named his Bayliner, the one he took his kids to Florida on.

Did fish processing plants keep their records in code? Did professional fishing boats usually have such frolicsome names? Wouldn't the plant have to designate the type of fish it was purchasing and wouldn't there be a different price for each variety? She looked at the k again. Wouldn't American fisherman sell their fish by the ton rather than by kilograms?

She opened the Black Point file. BH-PROB. DF2GO5317BP. If this were a simple abbreviation, PROB would be problem. A problem with BH. Bad Hair? Boat House? Boat Hitch? Bags of Heroin? Heroin was sold in kilograms.

Drugs. Desmond Fisher owned a necklace of waterfront properties perfect for smuggling drugs. The fish plant was a perfect front and Wendell, the drab and respectable banker, was his perfect front man and accomplice. If this all meant what she thought it did, he and Wendell were involved in a criminal enterprise on a massive scale. Seth might also be involved. He had a passport with stamps from the most prolific drug producing countries in the world and she had a feeling he knew more about the doctor's still-missing satchel of cash than he'd admit.

BH. What if BH-PROB stood for Bryce Hambrick problem? DF—Desmond Fisher to go May 31, 2007, Black

Point. Holy Moly. She felt the exhilaration of certainty. Jacko had been right. Hambrick was murdered somewhere else and brought to Melville to keep the other place secret. To keep Black Point secret. The clues, if there were any, were in Black Point.

If Wendell was operating a drug cartel, it was a fire she didn't want to play with. Her head told her to call Jacko, but if she did, she might inadvertently blow the gaff on Lucien's forgery.

She removed the flash drive and pushed it through a small hole in the lining of her tote. She sandwiched a pad of the motel's stationery between K.D.'s journal, swiped while K.D. slept this morning, and the Manila envelope containing Cleon's original Last Will and Testament, which he'd left lying on the sideboard. For no particular reason, she'd also lifted a snapshot of Wendell and his son at the helm of the Wave Walker out of the side pocket of his briefcase last night.

On impulse, she'd snitched one other item. Seth's Glock lay camouflaged in his navy windbreaker under the rest of her plunder. After Jacko had searched all the rooms, while Seth was making himself scarce and everyone else was clamoring for Jacko's attention, she'd crept into Seth's room to see if the gun was still there. It was. Given all that Jacko knew and suspected about him, it seemed like an oversight. An oversight she corrected. At the time, she couldn't have imagined that she would be dickering with a drug lord for the return of Lucien's paintings. Maybe her ESP was back on track at last.

THIRTY-FOUR

THE T-SHIRTS on sale in the Katherine Oasis Shopping Center ran the gamut of Australian icons. The Sydney Opera House and Harbour Bridge, Ayers Rock and the Great Barrier Reef, kangaroos and koalas, Akubra hats and vegemite. Dinah was drawn to a shirt with an erect, open-jawed crocodile in red boxing gloves—The Boxing Croc of Humpty Doo. The woman at the sales counter informed her that Humpty Doo was a small town near Darwin and the giant Boxing Croc was a famous landmark in the Territory, one of the country's Big Things.

"What kind of big things?" asked Dinah.

"Oh, there's the Big Beer Can, the Big Mosquito, the Big Banana, the Big Prawn. There's lots of Big Things in Oz. It's kind of an art form. The tourists love 'em."

"Is Humpty Doo an Aboriginal name?"

"I'm not sure. Some say it means fine and good. But whenever things turn out wrong or upside down, my mum says they've gone humpty doo."

"Perfect," said Dinah. "I can always use another name for trouble."

With her new boxing croc nightshirt in the bag, she had a taste for hot Italian sausage and Chianti. She drove through the town in search of a trattoria and ended up at a place called Diggers Den—a rather unprepossessing pub that claimed to serve Italian food. She had just been seated and handed the menu when who to her wandering eye should appear but Margaret. She spotted Dinah at the same time and turned to leave, then about-faced with an expression that seemed more a nod to the inevitable than a glad hello.

"I had to get away from that place for a few hours. As we used to say back in the sixties, it has bad vibes."

"It's still said today, Margaret, and I agree. Crow Hill has very bad vibes."

"I drove Lucien's car. He said that he and Eduardo wouldn't be needing it for the next couple of days. Lucien doesn't look well. I hope it's not a relapse."

"He's on edge like the rest of us." Dinah was happy to see Margaret and hoped she could update her on the scene at Crow Hill. "Have you had dinner? You're more than welcome to join me. I haven't ordered yet."

"Why, yes. It'll be good to talk with someone who isn't having histrionics." She sat down and blew out a heavy sigh. Her face showed the strain of the last forty-eight hours, but her eyes still had that hawk-like vigilance. She was a full-figured woman and gravity was winning out, but she held her chin high and her posture was finishing-school perfect. She'd obviously turned heads thirty years ago and even now, there was a knowing quality about her that some men might find attractive.

"Who's having histrionics?"

"K.D.'s having a hissy because Thad stole her journal. Wendell thinks the Inspector overreached his authority and took something he had no right to. Lucien and Eduardo are saying hateful things about Wen behind his back. Neesha has locked herself in her room and the Farraday person is prowling through the house like a cat burglar. Of course, Tanya's with Victor at the hospital and Mack's absconded, could be with your paintings."

"What's Cleon doing?" asked Dinah.

"Making out his new will."

A hurried young server arrived and spieled off the evening's specials: camel croquettes, buffalo kabobs, and meat pie. They ordered drinks—Dinah a glass of Shiraz and Margaret a martini—and pondered the menu.

"Cleon's way with a martini is the first thing that attracted me to him. All the other boys I'd gone out with in high school and college guzzled beer, but Cleon aspired to sophistication even in the backwater he came up in."

"He grew up in Needmore, right?"

"He used to brag it was Tallahassee. But after he won a few big cases, he lost the sense of inferiority and started embroidering on his countrified past, regaling the tony Atlanta crowd with stories about the bumpkins he'd known back in Needmore. It called their attention to how far up the ladder he'd risen, how much higher he still might rise."

Dinah said, "I've always been curious about Cleon's early years, what he was like when…when he was just starting out as a young lawyer."

"Don't pussyfoot. You want to know what your mother saw in him."

"That, too."

"Did she never talk to you about him?"

"She's never talked to me about Cleon or my own father, even. Nothing that wasn't self-evident. She's pretty frugal with details about the men in her life."

Margaret dabbed her lips with her napkin and turned thoughtful. "Cleon was a well-built, athletic boy, sure of his abilities and ambitious as hell. He believed he could conquer the world with one hand tied behind his back. Nothing was going to stop Cleon Dobbs."

"The drive hasn't changed," said Dinah.

"But there's nothing left to drive for." Margaret was pensive. "All that fire and charisma and he didn't get the grail. He didn't get…"

"Our drinks are here," said Dinah, cutting her off. The waiter offloaded the martini and the wine and took their food order. Margaret went for the beef rib-eye, rare, with fries and an extra cupful of blue cheese dressing for the salad. Dinah ordered the pasta arrabiata and a side Caesar.

As their server was walking away, Margaret tasted her martini. "Vodka! I don't know what's wrong with bartenders anymore. I wanted a martini, old school with gin, not this odorless, tasteless potato water."

"Send it back. I'll run and catch him."

"No, no. This is just the aperitif. I'll make myself plain on the next round. I don't care if I get snockered tonight. I'm in pit city. That's another thing we said in the sixties. Pit city." Her mouth quirked up on one side. "We had no idea. No idea at all."

Dinah couldn't see Margaret as a murderess. She wasn't a soft woman, and she made no secret of her lasting anger toward Cleon for dumping her after four short years of marriage—anger, Dinah imagined, in direct proportion to how much she'd once loved him. It was obvious that she'd cared about Dez Fisher, too, and Dinah was probably the only person on the continent who could condole with her. "Get as drunk as you like, Margaret. It's girls' night out."

"All of Cleon's women should get drunk together. Me, Neesha, his old secretary Darla, Seth Farraday's mother. I'm sure there were a lot more. But there was only one woman who gave him heartburn."

So much for condolence. "Don't start in on her, Margaret. Please."

She started in. "Cleon wanted Swan Fately the minute he laid eyes on her. He chased after her and courted her like she was a princess. She didn't scruple to remind him he was already married, but it wouldn't have mattered.

He had the bit between his teeth. He wasn't going to let a wife and child stand between him and the Holy Grail."

"Margaret, I understand why you hate my mother, but don't belittle her to me. She *is* my mother and I've heard more than I care to hear about her foibles."

"From Neesha?"

"Yes, of course. K.D., too."

"Neesha's lived in Swan's shadow longer than I'd have predicted. She married Cleon for his money, of course. With Cleon away from home so much, I expect she has a handyman on the side." She laughed. "All the Viagra in the world is no substitute for youth."

With his doughy physique and dour disposition, Wendell didn't seem like the stud of anyone's dreams, but there was no arguing with sexual chemistry. And Margaret was obviously in the dark about her boy's semi-incestuous love life. She imbibed the last of the potato water and raised a hand for the waiter. "Your mother never seems to age. She must have a pact with the Devil."

"She doesn't have a pact with the Devil, Margaret. She's not an ogre."

"I know she's not."

Conversation lapsed for a few minutes until their server arrived with the salads.

Margaret ordered an "honest" martini. "Mind you, that's gin, Tanqueray if you have it, and tell the bartender I'll just imagine the vermouth."

"No worries, missus. And you, miss? Will you have another glass of Shiraz?" It rhymed with pizzazz.

"Of course, she'll have another," said Margaret. "Keep 'em coming every twenty minutes 'til we cry uncle."

Dinah had to laugh. Margaret was in rare form.

"It's true I hated your mother once. But give me some credit for the wisdom of age. Wisdom's blinking all that comes with age. That and the spotty hands and sagging boobs. No, Swan couldn't help the effect she had on Cleon and I admire the way she held onto herself. She didn't let him take possession. She's the only person, male or female, who's ever brought him to his knees. He never owned her the way he's owned everyone else, myself included. You can't imagine how I cheered the day she ditched him and ran off with your father. It nearly killed Cleon. He drank himself sick on my back porch and cried like a baby." She sat ruler straight and her eyes sparkled with schaden-freude.

Their main course came, along with the honest martini and the Shiraz. Margaret swigged the Tanqueray. "Ahh, now this is more like it." She reminded the waiter to hit her again in twenty-minutes and salted her steak. "It's a relief to eat a simple meal for a change and not have to rave about the back taste of fenugreek or a soupçon of am-choor in the sauce. I never really liked all those outlandish dishes Dez set such store by, but I acted like shark's fin soup was the nectar of the gods. My Southern upbring-ing. You know how it is. But gin and red meat, those are the essential food groups."

She sucked down half her martini. "Yes, Cleon stayed drunk at my place for two weeks after Swan shagged off to Miami with Hart Pelerin. Lost a big products liability case because he couldn't keep his mind on his facts. I tried to help, but the man was a basket case for six months. It nearly wrecked his career."

Everybody knew Cleon had a breakdown after Swan left him. But he'd gotten over it. He won joint custody of Lucien, made peace with Swan and, over time, won the friendship of Dinah's father.

Dinah said, "Cleon likes to tease you and Neesha about

his deathless love for Mom and how marvelous she is, but he got over her years ago. He befriended my father. They played cards, went to football games, barbecues. Apparently, they went quail hunting together at least once with Dez Fisher."

"And when your daddy got himself killed, Cleon was Johnny-on-the-spot to represent your mother in court."

"As a friend. To keep the feds from railroading her."

"It wasn't just that. He thought he could win her back. He found out the hard way, what goes around, comes around."

Unrequited love, it seemed, was the bane of almost everyone's life. Dinah wondered if her mother had ever loved a man who didn't love her. Would she understand what it was like to watch a man she loved cry his heart out over another woman, or catch him in bed with a redhead?

"Don't spoil our dinner by dredging up old calamities, Margaret. Desmond Fisher's murder is calamity enough to have to contend with."

"Yes. I'll miss Dez."

"He must've cared a lot for you to leave his businesses to Wendell and so much money to you."

"I suppose. We never dreamed how valuable it was or that Wendell would own it someday, lock, stock, and barrel. Of course, Wen will have to sell it. He's not bold enough or savvy enough to run a company. He's a good man, a good husband and great with the children. He's been especially good with Thad. But Wen's not gutsy. Nothing at all like his daddy."

Dinah felt sorry for Margaret. She was due for a serious reality check and daughter-in-law trouble wasn't the half of it.

"What do you know about this fish processing plant, Margaret? Did you ever meet any of Desmond's employees?"

"No."

"Did Wendell or Dez talk about the business at all?"

"Wen had nothing to do with it and Dez became withdrawn whenever I asked him questions. Our relationship stayed in the shallows." Her voice thickened. "At least he cared enough to leave me some money."

"Plus the epergne," said Dinah, not sure what to say or how Margaret would take a pitying squeeze of the hand.

"And the epergne!" She laughed. "It would be the perfect receptacle for his ashes."

"Were you in love with him, Margaret? Really in love?"

"I'd have married him if he asked. He found me witty and desirable, which was balm to my clobbered ego. But love?" She blew a mordant little puff through her nose. "Cleon broke me of love the way Swan Fately broke him."

Dinah felt a touch of irritation. Loving someone who doesn't love you is a heartbreak and two, three months, even a year of breast-beating in the worst cases was understandable. But Margaret and Cleon had had three decades to get over their disappointments. She said, "Mom's past sixty now, Margaret. If she caused you pain, I'm sure she's very sorry. I don't need to hear anymore about her disastrous impact on everyone's life."

"I don't believe she set about deliberately to cause anyone pain. But she knows that she did and she's no more remorseful about it than the moon is for shining."

There was no point arguing. Like everyone else, Margaret had her own impression of Swan. It sometimes seemed that Swan was nothing but a collage of other people's impressions. Dinah loved her mother, but she had given up trying to understand her. She had been a benign and lenient parent, charming, but not much engaged in her children's moral or social development. Especially after Dinah's father died, she was off in her own world. Like a Dreamtime being, thought Dinah. The Swan Dreaming. She had given her children life, imbued them with nice table manners and a penchant for denial, and retreated into the mythical realm. Without being present, she was everyone's excuse for something. It was an open question how many of those excuses were hidden lies.

"My mother has feelings, Margaret. But probably no one knows her well enough to say exactly what they are."

"Don't you want to know her secrets before she's dead and gone?"

"Everybody knows the facts of her life. It's her interpretation of the facts that she's kept secret. I'm not sure she knows, herself, what to make of all that's happened. I was hoping Cleon could give me some idea what my father was thinking when he…" She hadn't meant to bring her father into the conversation, but it wasn't as if Margaret didn't already know the gory details. "Cleon is more analytical than Mom. He might have seen or heard something that would help me understand my father's actions, or the demons that drove him to do what he did."

Margaret kept her eyes on her steak, cutting it into prissy little bites and chewing each bite very slowly. She seemed to be chewing her way toward some delicate decision. Finally, she said, "When you talk to Cleon, ask him about your trust fund."

"What's to know? My father stashed a measly few thou of his illegal booty offshore for my college education."

"Your father died penniless. The government seized his farm, his bank accounts, everything they deemed to be proceeds of his illegal drug trafficking. It was Cleon who set up that trust."

Suddenly, Dinah was ten years old again, bewildered by

the news that the father she adored was dead, smothered under a half ton of Acapulco gold when his pickup flipped on a midnight-black road outside of Brunswick. She hadn't known what Acapulco gold was. Mexican coins? Chains and bangles? And before she'd absorbed the finality of his death, U.S. marshals came and arrested her mother for aiding and abetting. While her mother was in jail awaiting trial, she'd lived with her grandmother in a shanty next to the Okefenokee Swamp and become a pariah in the fifth grade.

The thing she'd held onto was the belief that however bad her father was in the eyes of society and the law, he'd loved her. He'd concerned himself with her future welfare, outwitted the feds, and squirreled away a nest egg solely for her benefit. It wasn't a lot and she'd never spent a penny on herself. But it had been important that it was there, a lasting proof of his love. And now he'd betrayed her all over again, from the grave.

"Why?" she asked. "Why didn't Cleon take credit for his charity?"

"You'll have to ask him," said Margaret, washing down the steak with the last of her martini. "But don't say I told you about the trust."

"Why not?"

She examined the back of her left hand and rubbed the naked ring finger. "Cleon wasn't born with a silver spoon in his mouth. He started out a lowly sole practitioner with a big student loan, a mortgage, his sick mama's nursing home bills to pay and after we divorced, he was into me for alimony and child support while buying mink coats and trips to Paris and Rome for your mama. Not two years after he made partner at that hotsy-totsy Atlanta law firm, he went on safari to Africa, bought a six hundred acre farm, and built himself a great ol' big house. When Swan ran out on him, he was on the hook for child support for Lucien, too. But that didn't stop him from buying a penthouse in Atlanta, a fifty-foot yacht, and setting up your trust fund. You think about it."

PART III

THIRTY-FIVE

SETH ANSWERED THE phone at the lodge. "Dinah, where are you?"

"On the path to Enlightenment. Let me speak to Wendell."

"It's after midnight. He's in bed. Speak to me. We've had some other disturbances here."

"They're going around. Wake Wendell up. Tell him it's important."

"Your uncle wants to talk to you. He's threatening to put out an APB."

"Let him." She wasn't sure if she hated Cleon for his lifelong charade or herself for being too stupid to see through him. She couldn't begin to sort through her feelings for her mother just now, but if she knew...if she had known...

Seth said, "We've had some more items go missing. K.D.'s journal, for instance."

"Thad."

"He says he didn't take it."

"Have you noticed? Saying a thing very seldom makes it true."

"Did you take it?"

"Why would I? Come to think of it, there was a pink spiral notebook in the backseat of Mackenzie's car." She surprised herself with the alacrity of the lie. I've been assimilated into the dominant culture, she thought. My depravity is complete.

"What would Mack want with K.D.'s journal?"

"I haven't the foggiest. Now please put Wendell on the line."

"Look, Dinah, you'd better..."

"Don't you *you'd better* me, you. Not unless Fisher's three hundred grand is present and accounted for in Jacko's evidence room."

"There is no money. Thad's story didn't pan out."

"I don't believe you. Get Wendell."

He let out an exasperated breath. "Cleon's original will is also missing."

"So what? He's making a new one."

"And a handgun. My handgun."

"There are no guns in the Territory, remember? Let me speak with Wendell."

There was silence, which she assumed would culminate in either Wendell's voice or Cleon's. Either way, the lodge didn't have caller ID and she wouldn't be tarrying in Katherine long enough for anyone to find her.

She pulled Cleon's soon-to-be-changed will out of the Manila envelope, pressed it open on the bed and skimmed the legalese. Neesha and her children were the primary beneficiaries, but Wendell and his children and Lucien received healthy bequests of stock and property. Margaret and Swan had been remembered with courtly words and $100,000 apiece "in atonement for my sins." None specified, the old devil.

There was no mention of the Homers, but he'd left Dinah $25,000 "mad money" and the contents of a safe deposit box in Panama. His attorney would provide her with the location, the number, and the key. What fresh hell would that open?

She folded the will and tried to stuff it back in the envelope. It caught on something. She reached her hand inside and drew out a smaller envelope. It was a letter addressed to Cleon from Swan Fately.

Her forehead felt warm and the arrabiata wasn't sitting well. She was coming down with something. Too bad it wasn't amnesia.

"Dinah?" Wendell's voice jarred. "What's wrong?"

The question would seem to fall into the category of duh, but she was beyond sarcasm. "That little item of yours that's gone missing? I have it."

He made a sound like a tire going flat. "Live and let live, Dinah. It can't mean anything to you."

"What it means to me is a quid pro quo. You have something I want. I'll trade you."

"For what? What could I have that you would want?"

"The Homers."

"You're off base. I don't have them."

"Either you do or Neesha does. Give them to me and I'll give you the gizmo."

"Gizmo?"

"The item with your sins spelled out in black and white."

She felt his hatred through the receiver. She hoped he felt hers.

"All right. Where are you? I'll meet you."

"Tomorrow morning at the Katherine Airport in front of the Airnorth counter. Nine o'clock. Bring the paintings and I'll bring the…"

"I can't get them by then. I left them with someone for safekeeping. I can't get in touch with him."

"When can you have them?"

"I don't know. Look, can't we talk tonight?" His voice lightened. "I'll come to you, wherever you are. I can explain everything. Just tell me where…"

She slammed down the phone. That last glass of Shiraz had clouded her thinking. Margaret was too looped to drive after dinner and Dinah had checked her into the motel to sleep it off. But what if she phoned Wendell to say nighty-night? What if she happened to mention that her drinking buddy Dinah was two doors down the hall?

Suddenly, Dinah wasn't so eager to confront Wendell. The lines of demarcation between who did what to whom blurred, but one thing was sure. She was up against a murderer, and she'd just given him a reason to murder her.

It took her less than twenty minutes to pack up and beat feet. Less than an hour later, Mallory Hayes stretched out on her bed at the Kookaburra Motel, reading K.D.'s journal and formulating a new plan. It began with a visit to the Katherine Public Library first thing in the morning.

THIRTY-SIX

SPEEDING NORTH OUT of Katherine on the busy Stuart Highway, Dinah revved the Rav 4's air conditioning as high as it would go and clawed at a fresh mosquito bite on her left ankle. The fever she'd been flirting with for the last three days seemed to have spiked. Her insides felt frothy. Her skin felt as if she'd slept in a bed of nettles. In fact, she couldn't remember sleeping at all. Maybe she was asleep right now and the traffic whizzing by on all sides was a particularly vivid dream. Maybe she'd contracted malaria from the mosquitos. Maybe she was delirious.

Dinah Pelerin, who might one day have unearthed lost cities or owned an apartment in Paris, dead of fever. Ashes to ashes.

She blew past the entrance to Nitmiluk National Park and Edith Falls. She was in full flight, no time to dawdle. Over the long, sleepless night, doubts besieged her. Sounds outside her window made her cower. Shadows made her jump. She must have reached for the Glock a hundred times. And leaving the library this morning, she thought she saw Wendell in one of those Akubra hats lurking behind the reference shelves. But with all the fear and anxiety, one thought had crystallized to a certainty. Wendell didn't have the Homers. The one who had them had flat out confessed and she'd been too psyched out by all the theatrics to take it in.

Another bug splatted against the windshield. It was a Rorschach of bug juice, gooey yellows and whites. She flicked the windshield washer lever, squirted a few jets of blue cleaner fluid over the carnage, and turned on the wipers. The resulting mess reminded her of a Jackson Pollock abstract.

She thought about Lucien's talent for painterly imitation, his predilection to fraud. And he had the unmitigated gall to brag about the "miraculous light" he'd achieved in his copies, the gall to blame Cleon for holding him accountable for bilking him. This wasn't the Lucien she knew. Had he deceived her or had she deceived herself? Had she invented a perfect brother to make up for her outlaw father?

Somehow, Cleon learned that Lucien had foisted off a pair of fakes on him and he'd rubbed Lucien's nose in his trickery by pretending to will them to his vagabond sister who'd be sure to sell them at the first opportunity. But it was pure theater. Lucien was Swan's cygnet, like Margaret said. Cleon wanted to punish Lucien for not playing straight with *him*, but he must have gone to great lengths to redeem Lucien's other forgeries. How he found and acquired them would probably constitute a whole litany of felonies. And the fact they'd ended up in Desmond Fisher's will was proof aplenty that Cleon had known that Fisher would cark before he did.

Lucien had an equally fine talent for euphemism. Peccadillo. That was rich. She could handle peccadillos. But in her world, sins didn't come in a size small. Infidelity. Forgery. Robbery. Murder. And churning in the pit of her stomach was the growing suspicion that Cleon had been in the drug business for years, that he might actually have recruited her father to mule for him and gotten him killed for his trouble. She pictured her father's pickup with its load of contraband flying hellbent down the road. It was coming right behind her. The past was worse than she could ever have dreamed and it was catching up fast. No kudos to her character, but her first instinct was to try and outrun it.

She went around a speeding road train and thought was swallowed up in the noise. It was like being inside a whirlwind. She became the noise. She became the speed. And still she couldn't outdistance the rolling avalanche of revisionist thoughts.

If both Cleon and her father were drug smugglers, then ipso ugly facto, her mother had been a co-conspirator. She must have known. How could she not? She'd been married to both men. No wonder she never talked about them. If they were the king-pins, she was their queen. Either she'd been actively complicit in their corruption or she'd condoned it. It didn't matter. Dinah was moving too fast to split hairs.

Strange as it seemed to her now, she had never considered her own complicity. For at least a dozen years, she'd known that her little trust fund was founded on drug money and not once had she considered turning it over to the government. She'd rationalized. At this point, they'd probably arrest her as an accessory after the fact. And as for the harm posed by the marijuana her father had been hauling, why, compared to the cornucopia of killer drugs on the street today, it was practically wholesome. Weed had medical uses, for crying out loud. Besides, her father had paid for his crimes with his life. That trust money was compensation for what the government had taken away from her. It was *old* drug money, not some nouveau, degenerate pile derived from hooking kids on heroin or meth.

Or so she'd thought. But what if marijuana wasn't the only drug in the pipeline from Barranquilla to Black Point to Brunswick? What if the money that Cleon had set aside for her came from smack or coke or some virulent pharmaceutical that ate men's brains?

A bird hit the windshield with a sickening splat.

"Oh, God!"

The mop of feathers slid down the glass leaving behind a thin line of red. She slowed to a crawl and it dropped onto the hood and fell on the road. Eyes streaming, she shuddered and pulled off onto the shoulder. She got out of the car and walked back to the pile of gray-blue feathers in the middle of the road. Tanya's voice echoed in her ear, *waste of life*. In her worldview, this bird probably symbolized somebody's ancestor.

She took a step into the road, but the road train she'd passed lumbered over the horizon like a juggernaut. The shiny steel cowcatcher mounted on the front looked big enough to stop a T Rex. She jumped out of the road and the driver smiled and waved at her. She held onto her wind-whipped hair as four bright green trailers boomed by and by and by and by. It was like watching a football field in locomotion. When it had passed, the bird was nothing but a greasy spot and a few scattered feathers eddying in the train's draft.

The Seminole prayer for the dead she'd learned from her grandmother came back to her. "They are not dead who live in the hearts they leave behind."

She walked back to the car, blew her nose, and cleaned off the windshield as best she could. She had to snap out of stampede mode. If she was going to fall to pieces over a dead bird, she might as well throw in the towel and call Jacko to come get her. He'd probably have some choice words for a buttinski who makes off with the evidence and then goes all weak-kneed and blubbery because her mommy neglected to inform her that Cleon was dirty as sin and so was she.

And in spite of Cleon's contempt for him, Wendell had followed in his footsteps. Father and son had probably conspired in their illegal trade for years along with Desmond Fisher, but with Cleon's health failing, Wendell had taken over the operation. Had he and Fisher wrangled over who would take over the reins? Smashed on Scotch, Fisher said he was through taking orders from Cleon. Was he also unwilling to take orders from Wendell? Was that unwillingness the reason he was killed or did his sortie to Melville Island and the murder of Bryce Hambrick lead to his own murder? The flash drive didn't answer those questions.

The phrase "chain of custody" sprang to mind. Belatedly. Like most of her rational thoughts these days. It would be her word against Wendell's that the gizmo belonged to him. He could claim it belonged to Fisher or to Lucien or to her. By running off with it, she'd probably made the prosecutor's job impossible. She should've returned to Crow Hill after she'd read the thing, sneaked it back into Wendell's pocket, and dimed him out to Jacko. But waiting wasn't part of her skill set and anyway, what could Jacko do with the information? At this point, her interpretation was pure supposition. It would take the police time to decipher the code and afterward, there'd be legal red tape.

She walked around the car a few times and tried to think what to do next. Her meddling had compromised the flash drive's usefulness, but there was no turning back now. If she were going to make amends, she'd have to ferret out fresh evidence against Wendell. This was no time to go off the deep end over ancient crimes. Sufficient unto the day is the evil thereof. What she had to do was concentrate on nailing Wendell.

Nobody in the world knew where she was right now. This was an advantage. She would take a break in the next town, chill out for an hour or so and clear her head. She threw a last look over her shoulder at the splotched feathers, climbed in the car, and drove away subdued, but dry-eyed and determined.

Where the Kakadu Highway branched off to the east toward Jabiru and the Kakadu National Park, she drove west. In a kilometer or so she pulled into the town of Pine Creek. After the rush and roar of the highway, it was like entering a chapel. The tranquility was unsettling. The boy at the petrol station where she pulled in to hose off the windshield and buy a pack of cigarettes was soft-spoken and friendly. There were flower boxes under the windows and a bird feeder above the door with two birds whose brilliant plumage took her breath away.

"Are they parrots?"

"Rainbow lorikeets," the boy informed her. "Never shy about taking a handout, those bludgers."

She sent up a silent thanks that the bird she'd hit wasn't a lorikeet and then felt guilty for valuing one creature over another just because its feathers were more beautiful.

Leaving the station, she tootled along the sun-dappled main street with her windows rolled down, listening to the birds and soaking up the tranquility. A few cars poked along as if they had no particular place to be and no time by which they had to be there. She drove under a banner advertising GOLD RUSH FESTIVAL, but it had apparently come and gone and today nothing seemed to be happening in Pine Creek but sunshine and birdsong.

She parked the Rav on Main Street and walked. The pedestrians she met smiled and asked, "How are ya?"

She smiled back. "Fine, thanks." Who knew? A few hours in this flowery, friendly town might actually make it so.

An antique steam locomotive sat on the grass going nowhere in front of an old railway station. Old mining implements rusted quietly in the sunshine. How restful it

must be to just lie in the grass and rust, build up a thick
ferrous scab of forgetfulness over the old hurts. Maybe
when this ordeal was behind her, she'd settle down in Pine
Creek under her new alias and steep herself in the humid
air until all tracks to the past had rusted out.

Old photographs and placards on display in shop windows sketched the history of the town. Posthole diggers
for the Overland Telegraph Line had discovered gold in
the 1870s and thousands of prospectors descended on the
town to "fossick" for gold. Chinese laborers were recruited
to work in the mines and the population grew. A lot of
people made their fortunes during the boom. A lot more
lost their lives, either in the fire that razed the town or the
malaria epidemic that ravaged it. When the gold petered
out, most of the miners and the merchants who supplied
them moved on.

Dinah followed the signs to the Enterprise Pit Lookout
above the town. It was a steep climb up an asphalt road
and there were no other walkers, but the physical effort
felt good. Breathing in the pine-scented air felt good. Returning the waves and how-are-yas from passing cars felt
good. Spotting another lorikeet felt really good.

The higher she climbed, the calmer she felt. Under this
warm mantle of sunshine, a plan began to sprout. Last
night, before her courage had wilted, before she lammed
off to the Kookaburra Motel in a cold sweat, she'd con-
cluded that the likely point of departure for Bryce Hambrick was Black Point, just a few nautical miles around
the tip of the Cobourg Peninsula from Melville Island.
Why not go and have a look-see? If Hambrick traveled
there overland, he would have passed through Jabiru and
Oenpelli en route. She'd appropriated from the Katherine Library's archives the relevant copies of the *Northern
Territory News* and the *Darwin Star* with his photo on the

front page. Some alert resident might remember seeing him. If she could place Fisher or Wendell in Hambrick's company, Jacko might have what he needed to solve the murder. It was a long shot, but worth a try.

At the top of the hill she looked out over the open-cut pit, some 800 feet wide and filled with water the color of green antifreeze. She sat down on a shaded bench and mused on the consequences of digging too deep.

An hour went by. Her stomach grumbled and she stood up and stretched. It didn't pay to get too metaphorical. Sufficient unto the day...

Back on Main Street, she bought a copy of the *Katherine Times* from a vending machine and wandered into a cutesy café, the Leaping Flea. It had blue-checked curtains and blue-checked tablecloths and a sign that said Seat Yourself. No sooner had she sat than a smiling, round-faced woman wearing a blue-checked apron appeared.

"I'll just clear the shrapnel out of your way," she said, raking the preceding customer's tip into her pocket before laying a fresh placemat and a roll of flatware. "There now." She handed Dinah the menu. "Specials are on the blackboard, dearie. Take a squiz and I'll be right back."

Dinah glanced over the bill of fare. Kangaroo pot pie, Tasmanian possum and beans on toast. The menu supplemented this selection with meat pie and meatburger, no attribution to a specific animal, something called spag, and something called snag.

Snag? She was feeling better, but not kangaroo or possum better, and snag sounded like an intestinal parasite. When the waitress returned, she ordered the spag, enunciating the p very clearly, and a glass of lemonade.

While she waited, she paged through the newspaper. There was a report about toxic chemicals in imported furniture endangering Australians' health. Three human skulls had been dug up on a roadworks site. A sex shop had caused a kerfuffle with its advertisement to entertain kids with coloring books while the parents shopped. A feature captioned *KNOCK DOWN THE BIGGEST GRUNTERS* advised boar hunters how to maximize bullet penetration.

She skipped to the obituaries.

Desmond Fisher's face stared back at her. *EUTHANA-SIA DOCTOR DIES. Desmond Fisher, 66, vocal proponent of assisted suicide, died suddenly while visiting friends at a lodge near Katherine. No cause of death was given.*

"Arvo!"

Dinah jumped. A lanky man in a Padres Football cap was smiling down at her.

"How are ya?" he asked.

"Fine. Thanks."

He kept standing there, smiling. She closed the paper and smiled back, which seemed to ease his mind. He doffed his cap and moved off to a table next to the kitchen.

The waitress beamed. "Arvo, Fred. How are ya?"

"I'm feeling crook, Em. Up half the bloody night playing poker with Tom's gang of crunchers and when I got home, the ball and chain gave me a right roaring-up. No need to show me the bloody card. Just bring me a meat sanger and a cold stubby. Hop Thief if you've got it."

Fred's lingo reminded Dinah of Jacko. He would already have deduced that she was the one who swiped K.D.'s journal and Cleon's will. She didn't think that Seth would report his missing Glock or Wendell his missing flash drive, but their antsiness and unease wouldn't be lost on Jacko. She wondered if he'd made any headway in winnowing out the suspects for Fisher's murder. She didn't know what part Seth had played, but Wendell and Cleon were in it up to their necks. It hardly mattered which one meted out the poisonous entrail.

She went back to Fisher's obituary.

Fisher, who lost his license to practice medicine in 1990 following accusations that he administered lethal drugs to an elderly patient, espoused the right of the terminally ill to die at the time and place of their choosing. Over the past two decades he has urged passage of a national law permitting assisted suicide. In the last year, his essays and opinion pieces have become more frequent and more vehement.

If Cleon was telling the truth, Fisher's wife had died a lingering, painful death. Dinah wondered if he'd loved her as much as Cleon loved Swan. Was their grief over lost and irretrievable women what had drawn the two men together all those years ago? She remembered Cleon's leeriness when she asked if they'd been in business together. It was obvious now. They'd been in cahoots in the drug business.

Em came out of the kitchen carrying a tray. She set a bottle of beer and a glass on Fred's table. "Your sanger will be out in a tick, Fred. I put a fresh basket of chips on to fry."

She set a plate of spaghetti on toast and a pint of lemonade in front of Dinah. "Would you care for the dead horse, dearie?"

Dinah hesitated. She was on her own in the Land of Oz. No interpreter. No net. If she were going to get along with the local populace, she'd have to adapt, learn the lingua franca, go with the flow. She smiled. "Yes, please."

Em grabbed a bottle of ketchup off an adjacent table and put it down next to the spag. "Save room now for the lamington."

"Sure thing," said Dinah.

Enriched by several shakes of ketchup, the spag wasn't

half bad. Lots of sodium. Lots of carbs. And the lemonade, while it seemed to have no actual lemon in it, had lots of sugar and yellow dye. Tucker of champions. And a lamington next up. She was on a roll.

Em brought Fred's sanger, which looked like an ordinary sandwich, and a plate of French fries—a/k/a chips. Easy-peasy. Dinah congratulated herself on adding several words to her Strine vocabulary.

A shaven-headed man in dark glasses walked in and took a seat toward the back. He had a gaunt build and frowned as if he had a mouth full of vinegar. Fred and Em said "arvo" and smiled. He didn't return their smiles or arvo back. Em showed him the blackboard specials, but he hardly looked. He ordered a green salad and an omelette in a nasal, American twang. Dinah pegged him for a bloke who couldn't adapt.

She finished her spag and Em brought her a gargantuan wedge of sponge cake dipped in chocolate and coconut. The lamington. Bloody good munga. Life was looking up. She cleaned her plate, tucked Fisher's obituary into her tote, and left an Australian ten spot with a picture of Banjo Paterson and a fistful of shrapnel on the table.

On her way out the door, she turned and said, "Bonzer lamington."

"Ta," said Em, beaming. "You have a nice day now, dearie. Oo-roo."

"Oo-roo." Dinah smiled at everyone and, high on sugar and renewed self-confidence, hit the road toward Black Point.

THIRTY-SEVEN

SHE WENDED HER way northeast along the Kakadu High-way at a calm and moderate speed. Her plan was to spend the night in Jabiru on the eastern edge of Kakadu National Park, obtain a permit from the Northern Land Council to cross the border into the Arnhem Land Aboriginal Reserve, and start asking questions. If she couldn't nose out anyone who'd seen Hambrick or Fisher or Wendell in Jabiru, she would press on to Oenpelli tomorrow and camp in the Rav. Depending on how fast she could get a permit, going on to Black Point from there would take half a day and she'd have to turn around almost as soon as she arrived as it wasn't permissible to overnight on Aboriginal land.

She wondered if she'd have a problem getting the permit. Surely if you were there already, a smile and friendly how-are-ya would suffice. If not, she could bluff her way in. She'd claim she was a World Heritage anthropologist, there to evaluate some newly discovered cave art or invasive species. Hadn't they received the letter? There must've been a mix-up at UNESCO's Paris headquarters.

At the entry gate, she remitted the fifteen dollar fee and an Aborigine gentleman gave her a park map and a brochure. From this, she learned that the park boasted 280 bird species and 4,500 varieties of insect. She'd already met quite a few of the latter, kamikazes whose parti-colored remains slimed her windshield. The brochure further informed her that there were 128 species of reptiles in the park and three rivers named Alligator: the East Alligator, the West Alligator, and the South Alligator. Apparently, Alligator was a misnomer as there were no alligators in Australia, only crocodiles of which there were two kinds—salties and freshies. It seemed excessive. Were they that thick on the ground?

The map showed a uranium mine near Jabiru, probably salting the entire region with polonium-210, turning the flora into flesh-eating mutants and the crocodiles into Godzillas. She pictured the inscription on her headstone.

Dinah Pelerin, beloved daughter and sister,
she lit up our lives.

She sighed. In light of recent revelations, "bamboozled" was closer to the truth than "beloved."

Traffic was heavy. There were tour buses and campers, mud-caked bangers hot to pass, and lallygagging SUVs that pulled off the road at every turnout. There were groups of bicyclists and at one point, a wild boar trotted across the road. Black cockatoos with fantastic yellow tail feathers flashed through the trees like escapees from a Disney cartoon. Sundry other tufts of red and blue flickered in the treetops. Were the colors really that brilliant or did her Wayfarers distort them?

She'd expected a mist-shrouded, primeval rain forest, but the road undulated gently across open savannah woodland with a thick undergrowth of grayish grass. In spots, the grass had been burned, probably to prevent the spread of wildfires. The eucalyptus trees, recognizable by their waxy green leaves, weren't as tall here as the ones around Crow Hill. Some had dark, stringy-bark on the trunks with smooth white bark on the upper branches. Probably what the brochure called woollybutts. Some had a pinkish bark. Some were thorny and gnarled. The eucalypts were interspersed with low shrubs and wispy bushes, lesser cousins perhaps of the multifarious eucalyptus family.

Side roads led to waterfalls, billabongs, wetlands, walking trails, and boat excursions. She wondered if the Suwannee, Cleon's big honking boat, had been chocked full of drugs for Wendell to take back to the States. She willed herself to by-pass that mental side road. Later, she told herself.

Sections of the highway had been washed out in the not too distant past leaving mounds of mud and debris, but erosion couldn't explain a twenty-foot dirt minaret girded with elaborate turrets. She pulled over for a closer look. A sign at its base identified it as a Cathedral Termite Mound. The Land of Oz got weirder and weirder.

In the late afternoon, she reached the intersection of the Arnhem Highway. Left led to Darwin, right to the Ranger Uranium Mine and Jabiru. The thought of driving through a fug of deadly polonium didn't bolster her confidence. She waited at the stop longer than she had to. Maybe it wasn't too late to turn back.

Don't wimp out now, she told herself. If the townspeople glowed in the dark, the guidebook would have mentioned it under Points of Interest. She turned right and after a short distance, Jabiru Drive branched off from the main highway and she followed it into town.

Jabiru was a neat, orderly little town with what seemed like about three times as many gawping tourists as residents. She drove around and located the Northern Land Council, but it had already closed for the day. She parked and idled through the village shopping center. At the supermarket, she purchased a couple of Cadbury bars, a bottle of water, and a bottle of Schweppes tonic. She'd been looking forward to a gin and tonic for the last hour. She cursed herself for not buying the gin in Pine Creek. Alcohol was an intractable problem with many native peoples and she hoped Jabiru wasn't a dry zone.

"Is there a liquor store in town?" she asked the man at the checkout counter.

"Hotels and restaurants serve alcohol, but the only place to buy takeaway is the golf course. You can buy a membership in cash at the bar."

"Thanks." She hadn't planned on joining any clubs while she was here, but why not. She'd seen the Jabiru Golf Club sign on the way into town and decided to go back for a bottle and assess its potential as a place to pick up information.

When she returned to the car, it felt like an oven. She threaded her way through the traffic and back onto Jabiru Drive. When she turned into the club entrance, she was struck by the lushness of the greens. She knew nothing about golf, but the course looked beautiful. She proceeded directly to reception and applied for membership. The woman at the desk asked to see her driver's license and she was forced to join under her own name. It didn't matter. No one would think to look for her at the golf club.

In the bar, she purchased a fifth of Tanqueray from a busy, cheerful man who, according to a rather prominent sign, had passed the Responsible Service of Alcohol course. There were a lot of people in the bar, laughing and gassing about their eagles and their bogeys. They all looked like tourists and she decided to find a place to spend the night and an eatery where the locals hung out.

The dorm-like facilities at the Kakadu Frontier Lodge were okay, but the place was overrun by friendly Australian tourists and her purpose was to hobnob with locals. The Gagudju Holiday Inn on Flinders Street was her next stop. It was obviously a tourist Mecca, but who could resist a building laid out in the shape of a crocodile? She entered its open jaws into an airy lobby with crocodile-green floors and crocodile green chairs. It came as no surprise that a standard room cost an arm and a leg, but she was hot and road weary and it offered air-conditioning and a bed that didn't require a ladder.

She filled out a registration card and the white-bearded, turbaned gentleman at the front desk asked for a credit card.

"Silly me," she said. "I wrote down the wrong license plate number. Could I have another registration form please?" The Mallory Hayes nom de guerre wouldn't work if she had to use her credit card. She handed over her Visa and hoped the bank hadn't revoked it because of one missed payment.

The man looked at her askance, but gave her another form.

"What's a good place to meet the local people?" she asked as she filled in the form.

"The Jabiru Sports and Social Club down by the lake is very nice."

"There's a lake?" Suddenly, a cool dip sounded heavenly. The motel had a pool, but it was small and when she'd passed by, it was occupied by two clucking mothers and four infants in water wings. "Is swimming allowed in the lake?"

"It's not advisable. Inspectors pulled a nine-foot croc out of the lake yesterday."

"Is there a public pool?"

"Our guests have the privilege of swimming in the town pool. It's Olympic size and has eight lanes. Everything is clearly marked on the town plan." He pulled out a map of the town and pushed it across the counter.

"Thanks." She picked up the map and her key card. "By

the way, did a British journalist named Bryce Hambrick register at the hotel recently?"

He shrank away from her. "The Englishman who was murdered?"

"That's right."

"Are you a police officer?"

"I'm a reporter. For the *London Times*."

He became cagey. "You don't have an English accent."

"It's not a condition of employment." She tried a big, Pine Creek kind of smile. "Have there been any rumors about Mr. Hambrick being sighted in the Kakadu area?"

"I am no conduit of rumors, Miss…" he looked rather pointedly at her registration form, "Pelerin."

Not a conduit of charm either, thought Dinah. But maybe she'd give a little extra thought to her cover story.

She carried her suitcase and tote bag up the stairs, which were the croc's left front leg, and down the long, vertebral corridor to her room in one of the lower ribs on the second floor. The room was quite modern with a bright blue carpet and bedspread and a little balcony. The croc's middle had been bifurcated into two long spines of rooms, separated by a courtyard and a small, fern-fringed pond. Her balcony faced the balconies on the other side of the beast.

She took all of the pilfered items out of her tote except for the Glock and the flash drive and set them on the desk. Tonight she would nerve herself and read her mother's letter. What seamy revelations could it hold that would make her feel any worse?

It was already six o'clock, but a cool dip before dinner would refresh her spirits. With unaccustomed foresight, she'd packed her bathing suit. She put it on under her street clothes and looked at the town map. The Olympic pool was within easy walking distance. She grabbed a bath towel and retraced her route through the croc's anatomy and out into the tropical sunshine.

After the air-conditioned interior, the muggy heat hit her like a blast furnace. She could feel her pores begin to drip. She cut across the parking lot and started down Leichhardt Street. Out of the corner of her eye, she noticed a tan car pull out of its parking space in front of the hotel and creep to the exit. She crossed the street and, for no particular reason, glanced back over her shoulder. The driver sat at the exit, apparently waiting to enter the street, but there were no cars to wait for.

She walked on for half a block and, on the spur of the moment, turned down a side street behind a large blue house. She stopped and futzed with her map as if she were lost and waited. In a matter of seconds, the tan car turned in after her and glided past.

She recognized the driver right away. It was the American from the Leaping Flea Café in Pine Creek. The man who didn't smile.

THIRTY-EIGHT

KEEPING HER EYES peeled for the tan car, she doubled back to the hotel. She crossed the hotel parking lot on hyper alert and hurried into the Crocodile's open jaws. Who was following her? Was he a hit man for Wendell, a private eye for Cleon, a spy for Jacko? No, he wasn't one of Jacko's men. She'd heard the guy order lunch and he was definitely an American.

Safely back in her room, she fastened the door chain and placed a chair under the knob. No one from the lodge could know where she was and she hadn't noticed anyone on her tail when she left Katherine. Was she overreacting?

She mixed a gin and tonic and reconsidered her decision to play detective, acknowledging that if she gave proper thought to these crazy impulses in the first place she'd have a lot less reconsidering to do. In light of the stalker, she was feeling less sanguine about going all the way to Black Point. If Hambrick had gone there by land, he would have had to come through Jabiru. If she couldn't turn up a sharp-eyed witness who'd seen him here, she needn't press her luck any farther. Tonight, she would go around to a few local hangouts, show the photos she'd brought, and hope for the best. So long as she kept her eyes open and did her detecting in public places, she'd be fine.

The Manila envelope with her mother's letter lay on the desk, mocking her. If she had the least iota of courage, she'd open it and read it right now. It was probably the farewell letter Lucien said Swan had written to Cleon.

Her swan song to a dying man. No doubt it would be edifying. The dead had no use for postscripts.

She left the letter where it lay, lit a cigarette and went out onto the balcony. She didn't go back inside until dark.

SHE FOUND THE Jabiru Sports and Social Club behind a gas station next to the lake. The club was well lit, but the closest parking space seemed a very long, dark way from the front door. A trace of fear skittered along her nerve endings. She opened the Rav's window a crack. The shrilling of a thousand frogs pervaded the night and the acrid smell of wood smoke leached in through the vents. There was nobody in sight.

A bleary crescent moon loitered over the lake. She scanned the shoreline. A dead log floated in the shadows not four feet from her front bumper. A dead log or a croc disguised as a dead log? She shivered.

"Don't think about it," she said out loud. She closed the window, shut off the engine and scuttled toward the door.

Once inside the restaurant, her fears dissipated. There was a mixed crowd, black and white, and a general hail-fellow ambience. She took a small table close to the kitchen, quickly ordered the pork almond ding and the squid in black bean sauce, and settled down to people-watch. She had her newspaper photos of Fisher and Hambrick at the ready, but looking around at all the good cheer and normalcy, she began to get cold feet. How could she just barge up to a stranger and start quizzing him or her about a grotesque murder?

"This is your first day in Jabiru or I would have noticed you," said a sonorous male voice behind her. He was tall for an Aborigine with inky black skin, a masonry of large, square teeth, and rows of raised, bead-like scars across his forehead.

"I just arrived this afternoon," she said, feeling lucky. Was it possible that the nosiest man in town had found her first? "My name is Mallory Hayes."

"Please call me Bill. My last name is formidable, an encumbrance needed only when filling out forms." His accent wasn't Australian, but Mack had expanded her ideas of what sounded and looked Aboriginal. Maybe Bill was another member of the Lost Generation, raised in New Guinea or someplace where scars were fashionable.

"May I join you, Ms. Hayes?"

"Certainly."

He sat down, sipping some sort of liqueur.

"Do you live here in Jabiru, Bill?"

"Yes, Jabiru has been my home for the last five years. I find life here more spiritually fulfilling. In the age of electronic communication, one can arbitrage from the back of beyond."

Bill was larding it on pretty thick, making sure she understood that he was a cut above the ordinary denizens of Jabiru. He was obviously in love with the sound of his own voice, but she was willing to chum the waters for a few minutes in hopes of catching a useful lead.

She said, "How fascinating. What sorts of commodities do you deal in?"

"Wheat, ethanol, financial instruments. One must be flexible."

She said, "I was thinking exactly the same thing earlier today."

"Are you here with a tour?" he asked.

"No. I'm an investigative reporter with the *London Times*."

"I knew it! You have the perceptive eyes of a journalist. What is it that you're investigating?"

"The murder of another journalist. Bryce Hambrick."

"A terrible thing. It was in all the papers. Was he a colleague?" His voice was tumescent with concern.

"No. But my paper is giving the story a lot of coverage."

He nodded. "What do you journalists say? If it bleeds, it leads? Well-known journalist brutally murdered in an exotic location, no suspects. The public is voracious and must be fed. But what brings you to Jabiru? Mr. Hambrick was murdered on an island belonging to the Tiwi people."

She said, "The Cobourg Peninsula isn't all that far from Melville by water. I'm looking into the possibility that Mr. Hambrick passed through Arnhem Land on his way to Melville. I know you must have seen his picture on the news." She brought out the newspaper with Hambrick's picture and showed it to him. "Did you by any chance see him come through Jabiru?"

He scrutinized it for a hundred years, give or take. "No. I don't think so. I'm probably just remembering the photograph."

Her food came. She picked at it and looked around the room for another interview prospect. "Do many people go overland to Black Point?"

"Not many," said Bill. "One must have a permit, of course, to go on to Oenpelli. It's nearly three hundred kilometers from there and the track is quite arduous, often impassable."

"I assume there's no record of Hambrick applying for a permit to travel overland through Arnhem Land, but is it possible he could have been a passenger in someone else's vehicle? A local? Or somebody who did apply for a permit?"

"Of course. There is no cause to search private vehicles."

She said, "A friend of mine thinks that Hambrick may have taken a boat from Black Point."

"There are no boat rentals. He could have met someone there who had a boat."

She seemed to have garnered all the info Bill had to offer and was wondering how to politely send him on his way. There was one last question and she could think of no way to couch it that didn't risk giving offense. Substance abuse was the bête noire of every Aboriginal culture the world over, but if anybody in Jabiru could parry an embarrassing question, it was this dude.

"Bill, has there been any scuttlebutt in the community about drug smuggling?"

"Drugs?" His smile flattened.

Uh-oh. "I'm sure the people of Arnhem Land aren't involved, but I have reason to believe that Black Point is a port of call for something illegal."

"Black Point would hardly rank as a port."

"Drop site then. Maybe it's not drugs. It could be weapons or currency. Any type of contraband. It's possible that Bryce Hambrick uncovered the operation by accident while reporting another story or," she hadn't thought of this before, "he could have *been* one of the smugglers and there was a falling-out among thieves." She pulled out the obituary of Desmond Fisher and showed Bill his picture. "I think this man was one of the smugglers."

Bill's forehead corrugated in thought, making the scars bulge. "He wore a sun hat with flaps that covered the sides of his face, but yes. This man was here."

Dinah's toes twinged. "Sixtyish, salt-and-pepper hair and beard, safari jacket? He's kind of an Ernest Hemingway lookalike?"

"Yes. Desmond Fisher. He gave me his name. He talked to me about making a living will."

This was too good to be true, wasn't it? "When was this?"

"About two weeks ago. He ate here at the Social Club

with a tour guide named Zachariah. The two conducted themselves as if they were, how shall I say, up to no good." He smiled at his colloquialism.

"What did they do that struck you wrong?"

"Their slyness, their deportment."

Deportment? Dinah made a special effort not to throttle him. Was he spinning her some kind of an intrigue in order to get his name in the paper? With his jones for attention, he wasn't above spinning. She pressed him for particulars. "Did Fisher say where they were going? Did you hear anything about their plans?"

"They had bought camping supplies. Dr. Fisher said they were going to hunt pig. Zachariah owns a four-wheel-drive vehicle. They were loading it with propane tanks, ice chests, and so forth. They could have gone on to Black Point. It's about a six hour drive from the East Alligator crossing. Perhaps they had someone with a boat waiting for them there."

Dinah was used to coincidences. Coincidences rained cats and dogs in her world. Why should she shy away from this one? Jabiru was a small town, Fisher was a big gasbag, and Bill was a disinterested witness. There were probably other witnesses whom Jacko would find when he brought his investigative team to Jabiru.

Bill said, "I have a friend who works in the Visitor Center at Black Point. He has a good memory for faces. He will know if Hambrick or Fisher boarded a boat from his dock. I'll speak to him in the morning and arrange a meeting so you can show him the photos."

Her skin tickled. This was the classic had-I-but-known scenario. A guy has a vital clue and promises to reveal all, but he can't talk right now. He'll do it tomorrow. Inevitably, he's dead as a mackerel by sunrise. "Can't we talk to him tonight?"

"I can try to reach him if he is in town. Where are you staying, Mallory?"

"The Crocodile."

In her excitement, she'd forgotten to eat. She asked the waiter for a doggy bag and told Bill to call her the instant he got hold of his friend. "And tell him to be extra careful."

"No worries, Mallory." He showed her a toothy smile.

She flashed to the croc masquerading as a log and asked him to walk her to her car.

THIRTY-NINE

THE CROCODILE WAS lit up like a Star Wars set. Before getting out of the car, she looked around carefully for any sign of the tan car or the shaven-headed man. She kept a hand on the Glock inside her tote as she walked from her car into the hotel. The dazzlingly bright lobby was empty, which heightened her heebie-jeebies. She ran up the Croc's left front leg to the second floor, and down the backbone into the safety of her room.

Once inside, she locked and chained the door and buttressed the desk chair under the knob. The room was cold as Siberia. The dials on the air conditioner wouldn't budge and she left the sliding glass balcony door open to let in some warm air. The courtyard below appeared deserted. Strange ferns billowed in a dry breeze and threw eerie shadows across the pond. The rooms on the other side were dark behind their heavy drapes, but somebody had left his balcony door open and a TV gunfight resounded through the night. Across the courtyard catty-cornered from her room, a red ember caught her eye. Somebody was standing on his balcony smoking a cigarette. Smoking and watching.

She closed and locked the door and pulled the drapes. A large moth of a particularly repulsive type followed her inside and she grabbed the room service menu and went after it. She lost it under the bedside table where she discovered a hole in the drywall with a stubble of wires poking through. It was an unfinished electrical socket.

Antarctic temperatures, live wires, loathsome insects. It almost made her homesick for Crow Hill. Almost.

She lost the moth under the bed and could only hope that he fried on a hot wire or froze to death before lights out. Freezing, herself, she snatched the bedspread off the bed, wrapped it around her shoulders, and paced. The same TV shoot-'em-up was blasting through the wall from her next-door neighbor's room. Probably some international spin-off of *Law and Order*. In a fit of recidivism, she thought of Nick. If she didn't hate him so comprehensively, he'd be the perfect person to talk to right now.

There had to be something constructive she could do while waiting for Bill's Black Point friend to weigh in. She reread the *Darwin* Star's account of Hambrick's murder. The body was discovered by Tiwi fishermen who notified the territorial police. The remains had been exposed to the elements for several days and the exact time of death could not be determined. There was the requisite run-down of blood and guts; a quote from the police about the dearth of suspects; an overview of Hambrick's career; a summary of the articles he'd written while on assignment Down Under and their possible relevance to his murder; and at the very bottom of the inverted pyramid of facts, the announcement of a wake to be held by the deceased's mates at the Ducks Nuts Bar & Grill in Darwin.

Only in Oz, thought Dinah. If his wake was held at the Ducks Nuts, Hambrick was evidently a regular. Maybe he'd confided something juicy to one or more of his fellow elbow-benders. The wake was a week ago, but maybe one of them was enjoying a brew there right now. Q and A over the telephone would be a crap shoot, but nothing ventured, nothing gained.

She was on hold for a long time, during which she considered what story would get the most bang for the bull.

She could pose as a reporter from London or some faraway place, but the Ducks Nuts was probably a watering hole for reporters like Hambrick. His murder was their scoop and they'd be none too keen to share it.

She could pose as a detective. Just a few more questions if you don't mind. But even if she could pull off a credible Aussie accent, Jacko would've left his calling card and anyway, impersonating a cop was a prosecutable offense pretty much everywhere.

Hambrick wasn't married and in the photo he looked unkempt enough to chance that he wasn't gay. What about an old girlfriend come to town for a visit who's just heard the sad news?

"Nuts. You want somebody paged?" The voice was irascible.

"Yes, please. Bryce Hambrick's best friend."

There was a pause. "Who's this?"

"A friend from the U.S. He told me he hung out at the bar when he wasn't working and I…Please, I only just found out…" she embellished her ruse with a small, dry sob, "I have to talk to somebody who loved him as much as I did."

"Bloody hell." There was a thunk. Over the sounds of the crowd, she heard, "Hey, Sam! Some sheila says…"

Gay after all? Dinah wished she knew anything at all about Bryce Hambrick's life, but then that was the point of this phone call.

"Is that you, Mary Ann?" It was a woman, whiskey-voiced, brusque. "If I'd known your last name or your address, I'd have written you a letter."

Could it be she was unacquainted with Mary Ann? Dinah finessed it. "Bryce and I were supposed to meet in Darwin and take a trip into Kakadu National Park, but I arrived and, well, you know."

"I do know," said the woman. "I know that you're a liar and you've got a hell of a lot of nerve. Who are you and what do you want?"

The penny dropped. "There isn't a Mary Ann, is there?"

"I'm Mary Ann and if he had anything on the side, I'd have murdered Bryce, myself."

"You and he were more than friends, then?"

"Who wants to know and why?"

Stumped for another lie, Dinah fell back on the truth. "My name's Dinah Pelerin and I…"

"You're staying at the lodge where Desmond Fisher died."

"That's right. How'd you know that?"

"Friends where they count. Why'd you lie?"

"Because I think I know who's behind his murder, but I need some corroborating facts."

"And I'd need to know how you come into the business before I'd give you the time of day."

"I was dragged into the business because my family is under suspicion for Hambrick's murder and Fisher's, too. If you can tell me anything he may have said about the story he was working on or his itinerary or the people he talked to or planned to talk to…"

"Fisher was murdered?"

Dinah felt blindsided. First bitten by a lie, then by the truth. "Are you a reporter, Mary Ann?"

"Mary Ann Becker of the *Star*. The police aren't calling it murder. What do you know?"

"Nothing yet. But I think I'm onto something important in Jabiru and if you'll help me out, maybe I can get you an exclusive."

"You think the two murders are connected?"

"Yes."

"What is it you want and what do you have to barter?"

Omitting names and specifics that might boomerang on her in three hundred point boldface in tomorrow's headlines, Dinah bartered. "I think Bryce stumbled onto a drug smuggling operation."

"Drugs? Why haven't the police homed in on this?"

"They haven't seen what I've seen," answered Dinah.

"Okay. Here's the poop on Bryce. He was a political heretic, always looking for a pet cause to debunk or a pious halo to knock cock-a-hoop. The party line, anybody's party line, he took as a personal challenge, a balloon he just had to pop. He twice won the Pringle for excellence in journalism, but he wasn't a snob and he never was..." she broke off with a frog in her throat.

Until now, Hambrick had been for Dinah an abstraction, the faceless victim of a ghastly murder, devoid of personality. Mary Ann's little eulogy humanized him. She said, "It must be hard for you to talk about him."

"No use getting mawkish. But he would've hated to die like a character in a bloody Crocodile Dundee flick." She laughed. "Although he did wear one of those hats with croc teeth on the hatband. At five feet four, he looked as if the croc had bitten off the top half and corked the rest for later, but Bryce thought it made him look less of a Pommie."

Endearing, but not the kind of poop Dinah had hoped to get. "And Bryce never mentioned anything or anyone that he might have been investigating in Arnhem Land?"

"Not to me. He was there a couple of months ago doing a story on white poachers harvesting prime didgeridoo timber for mass production by non-Aborigines. Evidently, there's quite a burgeoning global market. He came back complaining about Nigerian hustlers harassing the tourists. He said anyone not from Australia wouldn't realize they weren't Aborigines and might be taken in."

Dinah felt ill. "How did he know the hustlers were Nigerian?"

"Oh, he'd spent a lot of time in Nigeria. He recognized the ritual scars of some tribe or other. Yoruba, I think it was."

FORTY

Had. Again. This time by a Nigerian. I must be setting some kind of a record, thought Dinah. She should've spotted Bill for a ringer. Too tall. Too gregarious. Too slick. And festooned with weird scars which should have been a dead giveaway. But no. She'd been so all-fired intent on proving her theory of the crime. All he had to do was bait the trap with an eyewitness and she walked right into it. Oh, yes, Bill. I'm staying at the Crocodile. Jerusalem, would she never learn?

Who was he and what did he want from her? Was he just an opportunistic, unaffiliated con man attracted by her please-lie-to-me pheromones? *One can arbitrage from the back of beyond.* Ugh! But what was his racket? Was he selling bogus securities? Hawking faked Aboriginal art? Or was he Wendell's henchman sent to retrieve the flash drive? And who was the man who'd followed her from Pine Creek? Were he and Bill in league?

She laid the folded-up luggage rack sideways in the track of the sliding glass door to the balcony. The rack wasn't quite long enough. She dismantled it, cutting the cloth with her nifty Swiss Army knife. The slats still weren't quite long enough, but they would prevent the door being opened more than a few inches. She double-checked the main door chain and anchored the chair under the knob a little tighter. This, she lashed herself, this is what comes of not waiting. Of not going to Jacko when she had the chance.

Should she call him right now, this instant, tell him she was scared and throw herself on his mercy? Maybe she should call the local police. Maybe she should call Wendell and tell him she'd already given the police his Flash Voyager. Once it was out of her hands, he had no reason to come after her.

The shoot-'em-up in the next-door room raged on. Each pop ricocheted through her nervous system until she felt as if she would jump out of her skin. She poured a gin and tonic, turned on her TV to drown out the sound, and surfed until she found the news. A mobile phone mogul had dropped dead on his morning walk in Melbourne. Australian Idol judge "Dicko" Dickson had made a disparaging remark to a contestant. A high-speed car chase in the Top End ended when two men hurled a stingray-barbed spear through the door of another car.

She shuddered and killed the TV. Maybe if she read for a while…She felt the presence of her mother's letter to Cleon almost like a physical ache. Why did she so dread knowing the truth? Wasn't it what she'd wanted all along? Wasn't the truth what everyone said they wanted? Yet now that it was within her grasp, Dinah wasn't so sure. If the letter confirmed that her mother had been a party to Cleon's crimes, could she still love her? Or would she feel forever estranged, the way she'd felt estranged from her father all these years?

The shootout raged on. She washed her face, brushed her teeth, changed into her boxing croc nightshirt, and crammed cotton balls into her ears. Still waffling, she drifted over to the desk and took the letter out of the Manila envelope. Just holding it made her feel icky. Like a voyeur. She stuffed it back in the envelope and, by default, picked up K.D.'s journal and turned to the section on Wendell.

Harbour Hotel, June 5th. He binges on potato chips
when he thinks no one sees him and bites his finger-
nails to the quick. He went all misty when Daddy
told us he didn't want any sanctimonious words said
over him. Later, I heard Daddy ask Mother if maybe
Wendell's having a breakdown. Mother said he's just
sad to be losing Daddy.

Dinah gave a little salute to Cleon with her gin. He
certainly knew how to tweak the lovers' noses and make
them squirm. She wondered if, in addition to cutting Wendell out of his will, he had opposed his takeover of the
drug business. If he didn't think Wen had the gumption
to pull a fire alarm without a memo, maybe control of the
operation had been supposed to pass to Fisher. But then,
he thought Fisher had lost his rudder, too. Maybe he was
bringing Seth on board to take the helm.

June 6th. Sandra Faye called Wendell in the middle
of dinner. She is a cliché, a total shrew of a wife.
Wendell stepped away from the table, but we could
all hear her bitching at him. I could see that Mother
felt sorry for him. She wears her heart on her sleeve.
I think she'll depend on Wendell to help her man-
age Thad when Daddy's gone. Wendell bribes him
with expensive toys and tries to "relate," but it only
makes Thad act all the more off the Richter to get
more out of him. I'm the only one who knows that
Thad's ADD is totally pseudo. He cons everybody,
even his shrink. My brother will make Wendell his
tool. Poor Wen. He's pathetic.

Dinah finished her gin, closed the book, and switched
off the light. She lay wide awake in the dark for a long

time. When she finally fell asleep, she dreamed she was in a jet boat bounding across a stormy sea while being shot at by pirates. The shots that woke her whacked into the headboard a scant twelve inches from her right ear.

FORTY-ONE

"SOMEBODY SHOT AT me! Call the cops!"

Quaking like a leaf, she hung up the phone, jumped into her clothes and edged around the room. The sliding glass door had been jimmied and opened about three inches. The shooter must have shinnied up one of the support posts under the balcony. The courtyard looked as eerily empty at 3:00 a.m. as it had at 10:00 p.m.

She tried to light a cigarette, but her hands trembled too uncontrollably to work the lighter. She gave it up and turned on the TV. A man was talking about sheep shearing.

Somebody banged on the door. She grabbed Seth's gun, moved the chair, cracked the door to the length of the chain and peeped out. It was the bearded man in the turban who'd checked her in. She unfastened the chain and let him in.

"What happened?"

She showed him the bullet hole in the bed.

He said, "This is unprecedented."

What the hell was she supposed to say to that? Were there hotels where getting shot at was precedented? She said, "He jimmied open the sliding door and shot at me through the gap."

"Who?" His eyes were riveted on the Glock.

She put it back in her tote. "I don't know who." It could have been Bill or Wendell or the man with the shaven head who'd tailed her from Pine Creek or the man-shaped shadow across the billabong. "Did you call the police?"

A woman with wild dark hair and a disheveled sari

appeared in the door. "What's wrong, Sandhu? What is that smell? Did someone set off a firecracker?"

"I don't know. Go unlock the lobby door for Koolatong."

He stood in the door as if to prevent Dinah from escaping and the woman broomsticked down the hall.

"I have called the police," said Mr. Sandhu. "We shall see."

Why were they sore at her? Did they think she'd asked to be shot at? Did they think she got off on bullets singeing her hair?

A burly black man in a crisply ironed uniform shouldered through the door and introduced himself as Sgt. Koolatong of the local police. His brow was scarless, she was relieved to note, but deeply lined, as though the burden of keeping the peace in Jabiru weighed heavily on him.

"What happened?" he asked.

She showed him the hole in the headboard.

He leaned over the bed and inspected it minutely.

Mr. Sandhu said, "This has never happened before. This is a first."

There were times when the screaming-meemies seemed the only logical response. With near-superhuman effort, she fought the urge. "Will you give me a light, Sergeant?"

Sandhu wagged his finger. "This is a non-smoking room. That is the rule."

This was the thanks she got for stifling a screaming fit she was perfectly entitled to have? This was what she got for being considerate of the other guests? "I thought this was a non-shooting hotel, but your rinkydink door didn't stop it from happening."

The sergeant took her lighter and lit her cigarette.

Sandhu picked up the pieces of the luggage rack she'd laid in the door track. "You are a troublesome person. I will add this damage and the hole in the bed to your room bill."

"Mr. Sandhu, you cannot fathom how troublesome I will become if you add one cent to my bill."

"We shall see," he said and marched off in a pet.

"Sue me," she fumed under her breath.

The man on TV said that shearers who shear more than 200 sheep per day are called gun shearers.

Sgt. Koolatong said, "I know who you are, Miss Pelerin. Inspector Jacko Newby asked me to assist his man to watch out for your safety."

"He…what? He has someone watching me?"

"As well as the Community Police. This shouldn't have happened. I am responsible. The Inspector will be very unhappy."

"What does the Inspector's man look like, Sergeant?"

"White, brown hair, late twenties."

"How about your man?"

"Black, sturdy build, late thirties." He slipped on latex gloves and began digging the bullet out of the headboard.

"No facial scars?"

"No, why?"

"I seem to have more tails than a trick kite." She should have known she couldn't give Jacko the slip that easily, but if the skinhead who'd been bird-dogging her wasn't his man and Bill wasn't Koolatong's man, who were they?

The opening bars of *Night Fever* detonated from the sergeant's cell phone. Disco. The incongruities in the Top End just wouldn't quit. She felt as if she'd been beamed onto another planet where the life forms and the language were vaguely reminiscent of Earth, but the total effect was insane.

"Yes, sir. Yes, she's unhurt. I realize that, sir. No. No, I won't let it happen again. Here she is." He handed his phone to Dinah. "Inspector Newby."

Jacko was going to be hacked off that she'd run away

and gotten herself shot at, not to mention costing man-power that could be used to better purpose. And when she told him about the stolen flash drive, he'd go apeshit. Well, she deserved it.

She took the phone. "Hi."

"The sergeant informs me you've had a fright."

"Yes."

"I know you're spooked, luv, but are you all right? No large-bore holes in your chassis?"

She laughed. She hadn't expected kindness. It pulled the rug out. She sat down on the bed and almost choked up. "No. I haven't looked in the mirror to see if my hair's turned white, but otherwise I'm okay except for a bad case of the shakes."

"Who wouldn't go quivery in the knees after such a close call? But I hadn't thought you'd be attacked or I'd have had you in protective custody."

"Why did you have me tailed then?"

"You're too much of a chancer, luv. I don't know what you think you're about up there, but your rellies are all of a twitter since you left. They seem a bit narked with you. What did you do to get on the outers? Didn't suss one of them for murder, did you?"

"Maybe. I took a computer memory stick out of Wen-dell's briefcase. It contains files that make it look like Wen-dell's and the doctor's fish processing business was a front for a drug-running operation. I think they're using Black Point as a drop site. Somehow Bryce Hambrick must have caught on to their scheme and they had him killed."

"So drug-trafficking was their lurk." He made it sound as if all of a sudden everything clicked. "But wasn't your Uncle Cleon the one who touched the doc to bring Wen-dell into the bizzo? Drew up the partnership agreement, as I understand it. Surprising a man as shrewd as Cleon wouldn't tumble to their criminal doings."

"Maybe. I don't know." Surprising if a man as shrewd as Cleon wasn't the mastermind and ur-trafficker. But she wasn't ready to hear it out loud. The ramifications were too painful. "I'm sorry if I've caused trouble by running off with the evidence, Jacko."

"We'll cross that bridge when we come to it. For the nonce, I've pinched Wendell for Fisher's murder."

"But why? On what evidence?"

"His fingerprints came up clear as a rubber stamp on the filleting knife. And if his take under Fisher's will weren't motive enough, six weeks ago he took out a two million dollar life insurance policy on the doctor naming himself the sole beneficiary."

Dinah rubbed her head. Something didn't square. Wendell wouldn't make that blatant a mistake, would he?

Sgt. Koolatong extracted one of the slugs from the headboard and held it up to the light in a pair of needle-nose pliers. She felt scared and vulnerable. All she wanted was to curl up in a fetal ball and hibernate.

Jacko kept his voice calm and low-key. "Anything you can tell me about the bloke who took a shot at you, luv?"

"No. But I think a man with a shaved head has been following me and a Nigerian named Bill singled me out for some kind of a scam."

"You'll be all right, Dinah. I'll hive off and be there in a couple of hours. Sgt. Koolatong will stand guard until then. Does that work for you?"

"Yes," she said. "That works for me." How could it not? She'd dodged a bullet and now the pros were taking over. Once she relinquished Wendell's memory stick, she'd be hors de combat, a civilian, no longer the bumbling amateur making believe she was V.I. Warshawski. "Jacko…?"

"Ay?"

"How are the others…the rest of the family taking Wendell's arrest?"

"It's crueled the party for one and all, luv. But we'll yack about the rellies over brekkie."

FORTY-TWO

Sgt. Koolatong bagged the bullet, dusted the glass door for prints, stationed a uniformed sentry outside her door, and went back to his office.

Dinah tried to collect herself. She brewed a pot of coffee and sat down to wait for Jacko and brekkie. The sheepathon was still going on. Who knew there was so much to know about sheep peeling? In 1892, a man named Jackie Howe had peeled 1,437 sheep in 44 hours and 30 minutes and one week later, 321 sheep in 7 hours and 40 minutes using hand-shears. His record lasted for 58 years until another man using machine-shears outgunned him.

She drank coffee and paced and tried to get some traction under her slippery thoughts. If Jacko had found her so easily, maybe Wendell had, too. Maybe before Jacko pinched him, he'd placed a call to his accomplice in Jabiru and ordered him to kill her and get back the flash drive. If the information it contained incriminated the other members of the gang, they'd want it regardless of what happened to Wendell. But why hadn't they just robbed her as she was leaving the restaurant? Trying to shoot her while she slept was sadistic. And pointless. For all their meanness, they hadn't gotten what they were after.

Job's tears! Suppose they came back and tried again before Jacko arrived? Suppose they overpowered her guard and came through the door shooting? But that made no sense. The people who wanted the flash drive wouldn't shoot her until after they found it, which meant that somebody else was gunning for her. Who? Why? Her brain felt as if it were flopping around loose inside her cranium. She rubbed her temples and ran her eyes around the room. At least she could make sure Wendell's crowd didn't find the flash drive.

She grabbed her tote and ran her hand across the bottom. The flash drive was small, but it made a conspicuous bump. She scrabbled through her cosmetic bag for tweezers and tweezered the stick through the hole in the lining. Where wouldn't they look? It would almost fit into the hole made by the bullet, but that was no good. Inside the overhead light? Inside the toilet tank? She could tape it to the underside of the desk. Too easy.

Where then? The electrical outlet with the exposed wires. She moved the bedside table and got down on her hands and knees. How to wiggle the stick through the hole without losing it in the interstices of the sheetrock and insulation, and how to do it without being electrocuted in the process?

Dinah Pelerin, wannabe interpreter of ancient cultures and conservator of Native American myths, fried by a hot wire while secreting stolen evidence.

She got up, took a roll of adhesive tape out of her bag, cut a longish strip, and went back on her knees. Keeping clear of the loose wires, she winkled the stick through the hole with her index finger and with a piece of tape stuck to her middle finger, she affixed the stick out of sight on the other side of the wall. No one would think to look there and, if they did, they wouldn't see anything but an unfinished electrical socket. Feeling pleased with herself, she got up and started to dust off her jeans.

Shit! She'd found the missing moth smushed on her right knee. There was a knock on the door. "Miss Pelerin, it's Sergeant Koolatong."

She grabbed a towel out of the bathroom and was scrubbing the pus-colored moth innards off her knee as she swung open the door. "Ser…"

A gassy rag clapped over her face. She clawed at the rock-hard hands that held her. Her lungs burned. She had no feet, no bones, and then there was nothing.

FORTY-THREE

THE NOISE WOKE her. Squawking, screeching, grunting. Her eyes slotted open. She was lying on her side on the gritty floor of a van or truck. One of the rear doors had been left open and she could see blinding-white sand and, in the distance, blue water with whitecaps. She was parked beside the ocean. Or a sea, or a wavy lake. She ruled out the possibility it was a mirage only because she didn't think optical illusions made noise, and those waves were definitely whooshing. The sound could be heard above the squawking and screeching.

Her hands and feet were tied and her throat burned from the residual effects of the gas that had been used to knock her out. How many hours and miles ago was that? She rolled onto her back, raised her head off the floor, and scoped out the front of the van. It had only a driver's seat, currently unoccupied. The rest of the space was stacked with wire crates and camping gear. She pushed herself into a sitting position and tried to recall the face she'd glimpsed in that fraction of a second before the gassy rag blinded her. She was pretty sure it belonged to Bill. She wondered if he'd killed her bodyguard. She wondered what fate he, or his higher-ups, had in mind for her.

Not death. At least, not right away. The inside of the van was too hot for comfort, but somebody had left a door open so she wouldn't be baked alive. Her hands were tied in front, the bindings snug, but not tight enough to cut off circulation or restrict movement. Did they think that anyone dumb enough to be taken in by Bill's jive would be too dumb to untie a simple overhand knot? Did they think a girl would be too dainty or sissified to gnaw rope? Or did her kidnappers intend her to escape and run off down the beach?

She scooched her bottom along the floor of the van until her back was against the wall, drew her knees up to her chest, and began to work loose the rope around her ankles with her fingers. It wasn't much of a trussing. The knots pulled apart with minimal effort. In just a few minutes, her feet were free and she used her teeth to loosen the rope around her wrists. She wriggled her hands free and looked herself over for signs of wear and tear. Other than a few minor abrasions, everything seemed to be in working order.

The cacophony outside sounded like a zoo at feeding time and she got up on her knees to look out the side window above her head. What she saw both astonished and appalled her. Rows of wire crates like the ones in the van sat under a long canvas canopy and each crate held some eye-popping bird or reptile. Nearest to her, she saw parrots with blue heads, orange breasts, and green bodies; black cockatoos with resplendent red tails; a vibrant green snake with pale blue spots and a confetti of white speckles down its back; and some kind of a wading bird with long orange legs and a ruff of iridescent black feathers. This was no private menagerie. These creatures had been poached from the surrounding forest by the owner of this van and his cohort. There were no doubt collectors who would pay dearly for some of these beauties.

Crouching low, she moved to the opposite side of the van and looked out the window. A green cabin-style tent had been erected at the edge of a clearing skirted by tall, scraggly trees. There was no one in sight. Either her captors were taking a siesta in the tent or off in the bush trapping more birds. Poachers. Bill might have nothing whatsoever to do with Wendell or drugs.

The heat inside the van was enervating and the stench from the dirty crates and animal droppings was making her nauseous.

Sweat trickled out of her hair and dripped into her eyes and her throat felt parched. She took stock of the van's contents. Gas cans, shovel, plastic tarp, boxes of canned goods, a large searchlight probably used for signaling incoming boats, and thank you, Jesus, a six-pack of bottled water. She unscrewed the cap on a bottle, took a long, luxurious drink and splashed the rest over her face and hands. She opened a second bottle and drank half of that.

Her thirst assuaged, she turned her mind to the business of escape. If her kidnappers worked for Wendell, then she was probably in the vicinity of Black Point and the water she was looking at was the Arafura Sea. If they were independent poachers with a sideline in kidnapping, she could be anywhere, but most likely somewhere in Kakadu. She could take off down the beach and hope to find a house or a settlement. But which direction and how far? Or she could follow the truck's tracks and ditto the hope part.

Was it too much to hope that somebody had left the key in the ignition? Keeping low, she went to the front. Incredibly, the key was there. What was wrong with this? She didn't like to look a gift horse in the mouth, but relying on a piece of luck too good to be true was what had landed her in this unholy mess.

She considered the situation in front of her—a sandy dead-end littered with a few logs of driftwood. The poachers had apparently pitched their tent where the dirt track they rode in on met the sea. She searched the glove box and the side pockets in hopes of finding a map marked

"You are here." No luck. Evidently, Fate wasn't going to overdo the serendipity. She'd have to wing it.

How deftly could she turn this buggy around? It would be a tight squeeze. Assuming she didn't get mired in deep sand or collide with a log or a tree, she'd still have to dodge the tent and accelerate fast enough down the track to keep someone from jumping onto the hood or grabbing a door handle and holding on. At the sound of the engine, whoever was in that tent would come running.

The back door of the van was hanging open. The birds were still making a ruckus, but the sound of a slamming door would be heard. Moving back to the rear, she grabbed the ropes she'd cast off and quickly lashed the door to its mate. She returned to the front, slipped into the driver's seat, belted herself in, and hit the electronic door lock button. She thought, this must be what the astronauts feel like before blastoff.

She took a deep breath, let off the brake, and turned the key. The engine thrummed to life. She stomped on the gas and the van lurched forward. She wrenched the wheel hard to the right, but the turning radius was too wide. She sideswiped a tree, backed up, and kept turning. As she straightened and jounced toward the track, the shaven-headed man ran out of the tent in front of her with a gun in his hand. Panicked, she veered into the tent, which collapsed like a soufflé across the windshield.

She jumped out, ready to run for her life, but her assailant was flat on his back under the crumpled canvas and the gun lay loose at her feet. Instinctively, she grabbed it and drew a two-handed bead on his head, like one of those C.S.I. chicks.

Holding his left arm and grimacing, he struggled out from under the canvas and got to his feet. "You crazy bitch, how'd you get loose?" His voice was sharp and searing, like acid. He looked older than she'd thought when she first saw him in Pine Creek. Lines fanned out from around his eyes and his mouth puckered as if he tasted acid.

"Don't move," she said, backing away.

A black man limped out of the tent, clutching his leg. He said, "You broke my leg."

"I'm glad," she said, noting that his forehead was adorned with the same bead-like scars as Bill's.

Acid took a step forward. "Put down the gun. I'll drive you back to Jabiru and we'll forget this ever happened."

She backed up against the truck. The engine was still running. Her whole body seemed to vibrate with it. At least, the hand that held the gun was vibrating. "One more step and I'll shoot. I swear I will."

"You'd better put down that gun before you hurt someone seriously."

Who? She spun in the direction of the new voice. It belonged to a big strawberry blond with a freckled face and a rifle as long as California.

"Shoot the bitch," said Acid.

Dinah's attention triangulated. She shifted her aim from man to man to man. It looked like a zero sum game. If she put down the gun, she was a goner. And if she didn't, same difference. Her head throbbed and her hand shook.

She aimed the gun at the newcomer. "I don't know if I have the nerve to pull this trigger. But you're not giving me much choice here and my fingers are starting to spasm."

He laid down his rifle.

"What the fuck are you doing, Burdett?" Acid looked at him in disbelief.

So did Dinah.

"Thank you," she said. Her heart was whanging away so loudly they all must hear it and she had no idea what to do next.

Burdett said, "Why don't you just get back in the truck and drive away. Nobody's going to stop you."

It sounded so obvious. So simple. "Where are we?"

"A couple of miles from the Black Point wharf. You'll be there in no time. Without the truck, we can't follow you."

For a kidnapper, he was a remarkably accommodating guy. Too accommodating. The rest of the gang would no doubt be lying in wait for her in Black Point. She willed her thoughts to slow down. Gradually, her heart quieted and her fear subsided enough to keep her voice from quavering. "Mr. Burdett, I want you to tie up your two friends. Use the tent's guy rope."

"Lady, you're holding a gun. Why don't you declare victory and leave?"

"Do as I say."

"Buggeration." He walked over to the tent and began to disjoin the rope from the tent and stakes.

Dinah pointed the gun at Acid. "What's your name?"

"Sykes."

"And you?" she asked the black man.

"Tommy."

"Well, sit down on the ground, both of you. Tie their arms behind their backs and their ankles tight together."

"But my leg's fractured," said Tommy.

"Then you'll have to keep very still and not let Mr. Sykes toss about and make it worse."

Burdett grabbed Tommy under the arms and forced him onto the ground.

Acid said, "Are you insane, Burdett? What gives? Did you let her out?"

"Of course, not. Get down and don't be a jackass."

Dinah eagle-eyed the operation to make sure there was no funny business.

When Sykes and Tommy were incapacitated, Burdett

threw a covering of canvas over them. He said, "It'll keep the flies off." He put his finger to his lips, jerked his head toward the water, and mimed a walk down the beach.

What fresh treachery was this? Dinah picked up a bent tent pole for a staff and with the gun, gestured him ahead of her. They walked about twenty yards, past row upon row of cages, more than she'd been able to see from inside the truck. The squawking had abated somewhat, but there were a few rowdy diehards, especially the parrots.

When they were out of earshot of Sykes and Tommy, Burdett turned around and said, "You're making a big mistake here. I'm a federal drug enforcement officer, undercover, investigating a major cartel."

"And I'm an undercover Martian. Investigating the disappearance of humanity in humans. Cops don't shoot at innocent women or gas them and truck them off to the boondocks."

"You were never in any real danger. If you were, I'd have stepped in."

"My hero." She cast a leery look over her shoulder. "Where's the other Nigerian? The one who calls himself Bill?"

"He's going to meet us later tonight. Look, I'm telling you the truth. My name's Josh Burdett, AFP, Australian Federal Police. Don't you speak English?"

"Well enough to know it's used almost exclusively for the telling of lies."

"What do I have to do to convince you?"

"Show me your ID."

"I'm undercover. I can't carry ID."

"And I can't wear green hair. Everybody would know I'm an extraterrestrial."

"Look, this is a major operation. There's a boat due in

tonight from Papua, New Guinea with four thousand kilos of heroin on board. I have to be ready to play my part."

"You see what I mean about the lying?"

"Undercovers have to lie or we'd never get any evidence."

"I'll keep that in mind. Who do Sykes and the Nigerians work for? Who wanted me shanghaied and why?"

"The big kahuna, the money man who calls the shots. He thinks you have a portable hard drive with some data that jeopardizes his operation. I'd like that, too. You can trust me to get it to the right people."

"Uh huh. And did the kahuna order me killed back in Jabiru?"

"He just wanted you out of the way for a day or two. Sykes got gun-happy."

"Did he get spear-happy, too? Is he the one who killed the journalist?"

"Probably. I wasn't there. The crew took its orders from a man named Fisher, but he's dead now. With him gone, there's a lot of suspicion. Tonight's shipment could be the last one for a long time. That's why we have to make the bust."

"The man who ordered Sykes to get me out of the way, have you ever seen him?"

"No, but his name is Wendell Dobbs."

"How do you know?"

"We've got cell phone taps on most of the crew. Hard to believe an old duffer like that's the brains of the outfit. Talks like a hayseed. Y'all bettah taste the product to make sure it ain't mixed with sugah, you heah?"

Dinah dashed away a tear. The truth ain't for sissies.

A scaly lizard with a gaudy orange neck frill gaped and hissed at them like an espresso machine and the birds amped up their screeching. She raised her voice. "What does animal poaching have to do with drugs? Do you hide the stuff inside the cages to deter custom officials from any hands-on inspection?"

"The poaching's a natural offshoot of the drug operation. Boat comes in with the drugs, goes out with the birds and snakes and what have you. Same as with truck drivers, they don't like to deadhead. This way, they've got cargo to sell at their next port of entry."

"Not this time, they don't."

"What?"

She was seized by an epiphany, maybe the spirit of some indigenous deity, or maybe just her sense of outrage and fair play. These creatures were quintessentially Australian. They belonged here, in the wild, not plucked or skinned or caged for some foreigner's amusement. "Open the cages."

"You'd blow a whole year's worth of undercover work? Just when we're about to spring the trap?" Burdett was incredulous. "Empty cages will tip the people on the boat that something's wrong."

"Something is wrong, especially from the animals' point of view. Let them go."

He shot her a corrosive look. "The goanna back there is mean. You want me to get my face chewed off?"

"Use this to shunt it aside." She dropped the tent pole on the beach and stepped out of its reach. "If the goanna turns on you, I won't let you suffer."

They were standing in front of the last row of cages. Angrily, he snatched up the pole and, working his way back down the line, he began to dislodge the latches and liberate the captives. Lizards and various small marsupials scampered out and made a beeline for the trees. The parrots and cockatoos squawked and flapped as they swooshed off into the bush. The green snake uncoiled and crisscrossed the sand with surprising swiftness. The goanna hissed and charged, switching its heavy tail from side to side, but Burdett deflected it with the pole and it scuttled away toward the safety of the woods.

When all of the cages had been emptied, Burdett stood at the opposite end of the line from Dinah, a short sprint to the truck. A shorter sprint to the rifle he'd put down. She felt a rush of panic. What if he drove off and left her stranded? What if he picked up the gun and started shooting?

His face was a study in disgust. Shaking his head in frustration, he hurled the tent pole like a javelin into the trees and slogged back across the sand toward Dinah. The nearer he came, the queasier she began to feel. Why hadn't he driven off? In hindsight, she should've given more thought to why her hands were so loosely tied, why the key was left in the ignition, and why he laid down his rifle so obligingly when asked.

He flumped down on the grassy dune where she was standing and handed her a cell phone. "You'd better dial zero-zero-zero."

"Is that…?"

"It's Oz's nine-one-one."

FORTY-FOUR

DINAH PACED UP and down in Jacko's Katherine office, scratching her mosquito bites and listening to his end of a conversation with somebody she surmised to be high up in the Australian Federal Police.

"You should've notified local law enforcement about your bloody federal lurk if you didn't want a balls-up. And that drongo Burdett who let my witness be gassed and kidnapped couldn't organize a piss-up in a brewery, much less a major bloody drug bust."

Dinah felt bad for Burdett. She hoped he didn't suffer any career repercussions as a result of her recklessness, but she didn't have time to sit around and postmortem the government's mistakes. This was D-Day, the end of denial, and she had places to go and things to do.

"Stop your whinging, Danneman." Jacko hunched over his desk and stabbed a pen up and down on a notepad with measured ferocity. "It wasn't my lot that put the mockers on the operation and reaming me out gets you sod-all. It's down the gurgler and you may as well admit you bollixed it up when you tried to do an end run around us yobs here in the Territory."

Dinah got the sense that a turf war between Jacko and the feds was the only reason she wasn't scratching her mosquito bites inside a jail cell. Not that Burdett or anyone else could blame her for what happened. She hadn't gone to Black Point of her own free will or torpedoed their drug bust on purpose. They should be thankful she hadn't killed

anybody. Not yet, at least. Of course, the day was young.
If Jacko didn't cut her loose soon, she would strangle him
with her bare hands.

She'd been forced to spend last night in Jabiru where
she was debriefed by what seemed like a whole battalion
of policemen. The hours had oozed by like molasses in
January and by the time she arrived back in Katherine
this morning, she was mad to be on her way to Crow Hill.
Jacko had promised not to keep her long, but the phone
call from Danneman had lasted approximately a millen-
nium and still no wave of dismissal.

She tuned out his voice, pulled her mother's letter out
of her tote, and read it again. *Remember Campiglio.* That
was it. Two slapdash words scrawled on a piece of scented
blue stationery were the sum total of her mother's contri-
bution to knowledge. The freaking mystique never ended.

"Bloody hell, Danneman, are you going to rabbit on
about it all day or am I...you what?"

Dinah could stand it no longer. She picked up her tote
and walked out. If Jacko had anything more to say to her,
he could bloody well chase her down. She ran out into the
street and jumped into the Rav. It's go time, she thought,
and drove to the Katherine Lodge where she made a call
from the public telephone.

SETH LOAFED OUTSIDE the lodge bouncing a tennis ball off
the side of the house. There were only two cars out front,
Seth's and Cleon's. She parked behind Cleon's Mercedes.
Her thoughts were yeasty, foaming with anger and disil-
lusionment and a host of disorderly feelings she couldn't
sort. She tried to marshal them, line them up to march
into battle. Get him talking, lull him into a relaxed state
of mind, be oblique, go with the yin. Or was it the yang?

She got out of the car and started toward the door.

Jiggling the ball in one hand, Seth walked around and joined her. "I was hoping I'd see you again before I left."

"Where is everyone?"

"Your friend, the inspector, carted Wendell off to the clink day before yesterday. Margaret's in town doing the mother hen thing and trying to round up an attorney for him. Tanya quit and Neesha and the kids had an emergency. She's taken Thad to the hospital."

"Oh, my God! Drugs? What happened?"

"Seems Thad wouldn't give K.D. her journal back and she rubbed some of those poisonous Gympie-Gympie leaves on the inside of his jeans. The kid left here wearing nothing but his briefs and screaming in agony. I think K.D. got more payback for her prank than she counted on."

Neesha certainly got more payback than she'd counted on when she mated with Cleon Dobbs and bore his devilish progeny, thought Dinah. She felt a pang of guilt that Thad had taken the rap, and suffered K.D.'s over-the-top revenge, for her meddling. But sometimes people were punished for things they didn't do, which was what had brought her here this afternoon. "Where are Mack and Lucien and Eddie?"

"Mack came back this morning, all was forgiven, and the three of them motored off in pursuit of art. Cleon and I are the only ones holding down the fort."

She knew that Cleon was here. She'd telephoned and warned him to expect her. "I need to speak with you, Seth."

"Let's go inside. There may still be some coffee." He salaamed. "After you."

The kitchen was dark and cool with a greasy smell of fried mutton. The late morning sun filtered through the dirty window above the sink, but it seemed only to accentuate the gloom. The room had the feel of a grotto. Poor little Cantoo, abandoned and despondent, rested her head on her paws in front of the pantry and paid them no heed.

Seth poured leftover coffee into one mug, filled another with water and set them in the microwave. The seconds ticked by. Neither spoke. When the beeper beeped, she flinched.

He handed her the mug of coffee, dropped a tea bag into the hot water and dunked it up and down. "Shall we sit?"

"No."

"You sound kind of uptight. What's on your mind?"

"How did Cleon take Wendell's arrest?"

"Howled like a hyena. He and Margaret can't believe he's guilty."

"He's not. Not of murder anyway."

Seth shrugged.

She said, "Cleon must be pleased. In spite of sticky-fingered Thad and meddlesome me, his plan worked like a dream. I expect you'll be rewarded for your stellar performance."

"What plan are we talking about?"

"Payback. Vengeance. A final settling of accounts."

"Against Wendell, you mean?"

"Wendell, Lucien, Neesha. And you were instrumental, weren't you?"

"I just know that if I stand here long enough you're going to say something I can follow."

"You're not Cleon's son. That was a pretext, a way for him to introduce you into the household and jerk everybody's chain."

"Why would he want me around if I'm not his son?"

"To help him punish Lucien and Wendell. They'd each betrayed him. He hatched a plan to out-Judas the two of them before he died."

"And how is it you think I furthered this fiendish plan?"

"That first night, you phoned the lodge to let Cleon know you were on your way. You identified yourself to Mack as Kellerman, Cleon's P.I. But you couldn't keep the name straight. You told me that Kelliston was the P.I. For a pro, you're not a very adept liar, Mr. Farraday."

"I misspoke. We'd had a fair amount of wine as I recall."

"The night Fisher died, you didn't go into Wendell's and Lucien's rooms to search. Your job was to plant. The memory stick you slipped into Wendell's briefcase lays out the details of a huge drug operation. Cleon's operation, not Wendell's. Wendell may be a cad, but I'm guessing he's clueless about his father's avocation as a money man for the sale and distribution of illegal drugs."

"Why would I help the old man frame Wendell?"

"Somehow you got wind of poachers in Kakadu and connected the operation to Fisher. That shouldn't have been hard to do. Fisher did a lot of reckless talking. You traced him to Sydney and found him keeping company with Cleon. I don't know how you and Cleon fell into your conspiracy. You wanted to spy on the doctor, maybe kill him. But Cleon made you a separate proposition, didn't he?"

"You're strung too tight, Dinah." He smiled his Mona Lisa smile and bunched into a t'ai chi stance, moving his arms in slo-mo as if floating under water. "The dark and downward-seeking force is the yin. The t'ai chi master learns to yield so that the negative is overbalanced by the opposing force of the yang."

"Cleon probably brought the knife with Wendell's prints on it with him from Sydney. But tell me this, did you poison Fisher or did he?"

He rotated his torso, pivoting on the ball of his left foot while his right hand rose in a balletic arc. "You know, t'ai chi would mellow you out. It cleanses the mind, lets the negative energy flow past."

"The negative flow from you would shame Niagara."

He reached out a hand and caressed her hair. "Come on. Let's go upstairs and relax."

"Don't!" She jumped away and slapped him across the jaw.

He grabbed her arm. "Hit me again and I'll deck you. You know I didn't kill Fisher or you wouldn't be fronting me off like this without a gun in your hand. Where is my gun, by the way?"

She twisted free and regarded him with loathing. "Jacko impounded it."

"You've got me all wrong, Dinah. I'm on the side of the angels. Fisher was a poacher. All I wanted was to watch him and figure out when and where I could catch him in the act with my camera."

With an effort, she dialed back her anger and softened her tone. "Did Cleon know you were an avenging angel for Earth's Turn?"

"What do you think?" Seth tasted his tea and put it back in the microwave. "Cleon knew who I was from the get-go. The poaching operation might never have shown up on our radar if he hadn't put out the word and invited me to come and see for myself. He said if I pretended to be his son, I'd have access to Fisher. I didn't know he planned to murder him."

"Then you must have been fit to be tied when you arrived to find Fisher dead and Cleon about to instigate a full-scale murder investigation. You had to know that Earth's Turn was already under suspicion for the murder of Bryce Hambrick."

"That was something of a facer. But now you know it wasn't us that killed Hambrick. I spoke with your friend

Inspector Newby on the phone this morning. He says that Hambrick's killers are the same men who abducted you and carried you off to Black Point. He's already got a confession out of one of them."

Dinah believed Seth when he said he hadn't killed Fisher. It was all Cleon from the start. He had planned to poison Fisher from the time he left Sydney, and he'd built too many redundancies into his frame-up of Wendell for Jacko to do anything about it.

The microwave beeped. She waited until Seth's tongue touched the superhot tea and asked, "Where's the money Thad found, Seth?"

"Like the Buddha says, the world's an illusion. Love is an illusion. Happiness is an illusion. That sack of money is an illusion. You haven't heard Cleon report it stolen, have you?"

"No, but I believe it exists, one more clincher in the case against Wendell. Cleon probably dusted it with coke or heroin."

"If Wendell's innocent, then you should be glad I'm weakening the case against him by taking the money. And it'll go to a good cause. Some of it already has. You wouldn't believe the way Tanya's crabby old face lit up when I tipped her ten grand for her trouble."

Against her will, Dinah liked him for that. She'd told Jacko about the money and it wasn't her job to get it back. If some of it went astray and made Tanya happy, then she hoped Jacko never found it. And she didn't really care if Seth profited from Cleon's crimes. Up to a point. "I want the paintings back, Seth."

"Now that's out of left field."

"Not really. You made another slip."

"What's that?"

"I watched Lucien mat and frame them. The little

Maltese crosses you saw are watermarks, a design impressed into the paper when it was manufactured. They were in the margin of the painting, under the mat. You couldn't have known they were there unless you'd taken off the mats and held the paper up to the light."

"You're really taking me to school, aren't you? All the same, I think I'll hang onto them. Cleon will leave you a nice cushion and the money those babies will fetch can do more good for the environmental movement."

"They'll get you busted. They're fakes."

"Lucien?" He started to laugh. "So forgery's Saint Lucien's secret vice."

"Where are they, Seth?"

"My room. Behind that 'Welcome to the Trough' drawing of the pig Lucien so graciously penned for me. Take them. Consider it my parting gift to the family. I wouldn't want you to think money is all I'm about."

She said, "I'm revising my assumptions about everyone. Doesn't the Buddha say to forget your old assumptions and begin anew if you want to shed your illusions?"

"It's called satori." He finished his tea. "I'm going upstairs to pack and then hit the trail. If you're ever in Phuket..."

"Good-bye, Seth. Convey my deepest sympathy to Mrs. Farraday."

FORTY-FIVE

THE GREAT ROOM was cloaked in shadow. Cleon lolled in a club chair in his dressing gown, listening to Willie Nelson and waving an empty martini glass in time with the music. He seemed to be staring up at the boars who stared back with their usual ennui.

"Hello, Uncle Cleon."

"It ain't polite to keep an old man waiting, especially one who's a short-timer on this earth." He pushed himself out of the chair and ambled over to the bar. The butt of a gun peeked out of the pocket of his dressing gown.

His face was grim. No more the avuncular old charmer, he'd crossed some internal boundary. The rawness of his voice gave her goose flesh. Belatedly, she wished she'd brought Seth along for the reading of the indictment.

He said, "Come have a drink with me."

"Why would I want to drink with someone who tried to have me killed?"

"I told those bozos to handle you with kid gloves. But you can't hardly find reliable help nowadays."

As if performing a sacrament, he spritzed a mist of vermouth into two chilled glasses, tonged a few cubes of ice into the old silver cocktail shaker, sloshed in a pint of gin and shook twice. "We've all had ourselves quite a time these last few days." He poured the martinis and sank the olives. "Don't just stand there. You called this meetin'. Are you comin' in or not?"

She lifted her shoulders and stepped through the door, crossing an internal boundary of her own.

He handed her a glass and touched his to hers. "To the love that lies in a woman's eyes…and lies and lies and lies." He chuckled.

She said, "It's you who've told the lion's share of the lies."

"I may have fudged the truth once or twice. It ain't a capital offense."

"Murder is."

"The inspector tells us now that Wendell did the dirty. Couldn't wait to inherit poor Dez's money, I reckon."

"Oh, stop it. Save the innocent act for somebody who'll buy it."

He sipped his martini and regarded her with glacial detachment. "I can see you ain't satisfied with my story line. But that's all right. What you believe is immaterial. It's what the police believe that matters."

"How many false clues did you plant, Uncle Cleon?"

"What with you and Thad unplantin' 'em, I had my work cut out for me."

"Wendell didn't know anything about the flash drive. What did he think I had?"

"Aw, Neesha got all worked up and wrote him a mash note."

"Which you took." She shook her head in disgust. "Why didn't you just tell them you knew? Throw down the gauntlet and have it out? All this playacting garbage is sick. I would have thought it beneath you. Beneath the man I thought you were."

"You're a smart girl, Dinah. Not wise like your mama, but smart. Swan, now, she knows what to bear down on and what to leave alone."

"Like your involvement in the drug trade? She let that alone."

His face was a wall. She could picture him sitting at the defense table staring down the prosecution's witnesses with just that face.

He said, "Go on and drink your martini. It'll help you to refine your argument."

She took a galvanizing sip of the gin. "You've been dabbling with drugs for decades. In the beginning, when you were young and broke, you were probably just a courier. You were good at it, the way you've always been good at whatever you turned your hand to, and you were ambitious. Even after you became a successful attorney, after you were making legal money hand over fist, you couldn't retire from drugs. You no longer had any physical contact with the product, of course. You just put up the money and hired Desmond Fisher as your go-between with the smugglers and retailers."

"Objection." He fished the olive out of his martini, popped it into his mouth and rolled it around. "Supposition."

"Overruled," she said. "And don't BS me."

"Both prosecutor and judge? Well, I reckon I'm in the right place to be tried by a kangaroo court." A suggestion of the old wit tugged at the corner of his mouth, but she was no longer susceptible to his subversive charm.

"Was it just for the purpose of framing Wendell that you killed Fisher or had he become too much of a loose cannon?"

"Half and half, I'd say. Dez couldn't lay off the bottle or politics, kept gettin' hisself written up in the papers. He had a hankerin' for publicity. He was feedin' that unfortunate journalist, Mr. Hambrick, his usual crap about death with dignity, but Hambrick had his own pet peeve about Nigerians insinuatin' themselves into the Aboriginal community. When he spotted Fisher with some of our Nigerian friends, well. One thing led to another. Can you believe not one of 'em had sense enough to make it look like an accident or weight down the body and throw it in the ocean?" He was as blasé as if he were talking about a blown play in a football game.

"Your associates killed a man and that's all you can say about it?"

"It was a foul-up and I was riled, but it didn't affect Dez's life expectancy. I decided to kill him months ago."

Who was this monster? Dinah tried to throw a mental grappling hook back to the past, to catch onto some constant, some irreducible kernel of truth. But her memories were liars. The past had changed. "You must have gone to a lot of trouble tracking down Lucien's forgeries. Why?"

"The fool was turnin' out copies like a damn rollin' mill. Somebody had to clean up after him. I couldn't have Swan see him end up in the pen."

"How'd the paintings end up in Fisher's estate?"

"Dez didn't know they were fakes. I told him I'd laundered a few million in the art market and asked him to take title for me so Neesha wouldn't get 'em. I humbled myself and told him she was whorin' with a new man."

"You didn't tell him it was Wendell?"

"That didn't fit my plan." He finished his martini and poured himself another.

"So Dez made his will in favor of Lucien and Wendell just out of the goodness of his heart?"

"Drug smugglers ain't much diff'rent from the folks down the road when it comes to parcelin' out their holdings when they die. As you know, Dez was a bearcat about matters relatin' to death. He had a medical directive and burial instructions more detailed than a pharaoh, but no up-to-date will. I was changin' mine and advised him to do the same or his money would wind up in the government's coffers fundin' socialized medicine. He always had a soft spot for Maggie. I figured he'd make her and Wendell his beneficiaries and, since the art was mine, I told him to leave 'em to Lucien."

She said, "The copies started out as a joke. Lucien didn't intend to sell them."

"People don't fabricate affidavits and certificates of authenticity for what they don't mean to sell, or put a million dollar price tag on their jokes."

"Lucien faked the documentation?"

"Somebody did. Lucien claims it was his friend. He wasn't supposed to sell 'em. Lucien went back to New York City and got into it with the fella. But it's all water over the dam. I've pulled his chestnuts out of the fire."

She wondered if Cleon had bought back Lucien's forgeries or stolen them. She thought about what Margaret said about Swan's cygnets. "So Lucien gets a pass for his sins, but not Wendell?"

"There's sins and there's sins. Bein' cuckolded by my own spawn is where I draw the line."

"If you hated Wendell so much, why didn't you kill him, too?"

He emptied the last of the gin into his glass and stepped behind the bar to mix another pitcher. "I thought about killin' him. But a bullet's too quick and easy. Durin' my first round of chemo, I commenced to reflect on a more judicial revenge. Bein' deprived of his freedom and his family for all time, that'll be Wendell's punishment." The ice clattering in the shaker sounded like Chinese New Year. "You better finish that drink, sugah. You're gonna need it."

"What do you mean?"

He topped up her glass with his right hand and with

his left, pulled the gun out of his pocket. Its short barrel stuck out from between his knobby fingers like an animal's snout.

Her body tautened. "What are you...?"

"Carry on with your prosecution. I'm interested to hear your summin' up."

She tried to pick up her thread of thought, but she couldn't tear her eyes off the gun. "You set Wendell up as a fall guy long before there was any adultery by persuading Fisher to give him an interest in the fish processing plant. I guess the connection to a pillar of the community lent a semblance of legitimacy to the business if it should ever come under scrutiny."

"At the time, there wasn't much risk."

"You turned it into one. His partnership with Fisher, the will, the flash drive, the prints on the knife. What other clues did you rig to incriminate Wendell? I assume there's a dusting of drugs in that sack of money you and Fisher brought home from Katherine."

He belted his martini and poured another without taking his hand off the gun. A lesser man would be bombed by now, but the gin seemed to have no effect on Cleon except to make his eyes more glacial. "Are you restin' your case?"

The thought of what might happen after the prosecution rested unnerved her. She strained her ears. Maybe Seth hadn't left the house yet. Maybe if she screamed...

"What's th' matter? Cat got your tongue?"

"Apart from sending her lover to prison, what revenge have you cooked up for Neesha?"

"A right good one. I've spent all my assets and then some. All of the clean money, and I've borrowed heavily against the farm and other properties. I've emptied my retirement and partnership accounts and short-changed the I.R.S. by several hundred thousand. I'm leavin' the whole shebang to my darlin' wife and if she can hang onto that diamond ring after my creditors are done pickin' over the bones, she'll be lucky." He looked at his watch. "Well, there's your Perry Mason confession. I won't be repeatin' it on the stand."

"I can," said Dinah. "I can testify that you confessed to everything."

"Anything you repeat of our conversation would be hearsay. You're not wearin' a wire, are you, sugah?"

I am an idiot, she thought. If she'd asked Jacko to fit her up with a wire, her problems would be over now. Not to mention Wendell's problems. "I'm not wearing a wire."

"I believe you." He dispatched the last of his martini, picked up the gun, and motioned her toward the door. "Let's move out onto the veranda."

"Uncle Cleon, no. Let's call Inspector Newby. You don't want to do this to Wendell."

"Time's past for an appeal." He took her elbow in a vise-like grip and strong-armed her out the door.

"Let go of me. You're despicable. Consumed with revenge."

"Lay out your facts and save the rhetoric for closin'."

He released her arm and pointed the gun at her. The man who'd taken her to Disneyland for her tenth birthday was pointing a gun at her. Fear flooded her thoughts, fear not just that he would kill himself but that he would kill her. If Cleon had ever loved her, it made no difference now. He was unhinged.

"*Actus non facit reum nisi sit rea.* In the eyes of the law, it ain't always what we do that makes us guilty, it's what we're thinkin' when we do it."

"Did you have a guilty mind when you watched Dez Fisher die?"

"I thought I was doin' the world a service."

"What *do* you feel guilty about, Uncle Cleon? The drugs you've sold must have destroyed countless lives over the years."

"Doin' drugs ain't compulsory. It's one of a million ways people can waste their lives if they've a mind to. I did what I did and in the end, the only judgment that matters is my own."

She played the daughter card. "You care what my mother thinks."

"That's as may be." He frowned and looked at his watch. "My extracurricular money is in a numbered account in Panama, Banco Dorado de Colon. The account number's on a slip of paper in my right-hand pocket along with some travelin' money. I want you to take charge of it, dole it out to the twins on an as-needed basis as you see fit."

Fear changed to disbelief. "What in the name of God are you talking about?"

He said, "Don't spoil 'em with a lot of expensive falderal. Make it go as far as you can. Thad'll have to give up whinin' to that pushover psychologist of his. But he'll prob'ly be in the reformatory before too much longer and have a court-appointed shrink. Give 'em college if they want it and the balance when they turn thirty."

Disbelief ratcheted toward fury. "They're children. Your children. My God, how can you make them dependent on dirty drug money?"

"What they don't know can't hurt 'em. It didn't hurt you."

She hated him. "What makes you think I won't keep the money for myself?"

"You won't. And if you don't take charge of it, the kids get nada from me. I've left instructions. It's you or nobody. The feds will probably freeze Fisher's assets, so I reckon th' young'uns will turn out paupers without your good offices."

His callousness made her blood boil. "Lucien was right about you. You never loved any of your children."

"I love you. I love Lucien."

"No, you don't. You didn't buy Lucien's forgeries back for him because you love *him* and you didn't establish a trust fund for me because you love *me*. You did it for my mother. Everything you've done since the moment you met her has been for Swan." Suddenly, the years of ambiguous undertones and subliminal impressions coalesced into a lurid vision. A body was flying through the windshield of a truck. "You were there the night my father died!"

He didn't blink. "You'll prob'ly hear a lot of guff from Neesha 'til she lands herself a new sugardaddy. Don't give in to her cryin' or let her soft-soap you for more money than's needed. And pay yourself a fat commission. I want you to. It's your inheritance, as well as the twins'."

"Damn your money." Her throat felt too tight for the words. "Did you kill him?"

"You don't want to rehash your daddy's death. It's ancient history."

"Answer the question. You thought you could get my mother back if he was dead, didn't you? What did you do, tell him how he could make a fast buck moving a truckload of marijuana for you and then cut the brake lines?"

His eyes shuttered, as if he were casting into the dark sea of memory for some elusive detail. "My truck was broke down and he'd loaned me his. I picked up a shipment in Florida and was on my way back to Brunswick when a storm blew up. I stopped off at y'all's place for a cup of coffee. You and your mama were out. Your daddy had business in Brunswick the next mornin'. He said he'd drive on up there with me that night and stay over. I told him I was haulin' hay."

"You tricked him?"

"I'll take a plea. Guilty as charged."

"Liar. He wasn't such a rube he couldn't tell hemp from hay."

"The weather was bad. He didn't stick his nose under the tarp. It was his truck so I handed over the keys and took the passenger seat. The road was wet, slick in spots. A bolt of lightnin' flushed a fox and it ran across the road in front of us. Hart braked, the truck flipped into the ditch. I climbed out without a scratch. He wasn't so lucky."

"Was he killed instantly?"

"I don't know."

"You don't know?" Her chest was so tight she could scarcely breathe.

"He was pinned. I couldn't save him."

"Couldn't or wouldn't? Tell me the truth for once, damn you. He was alive and you left him to suffocate under a bale of wet weed."

His eyes were unrepentant as stones. "There was nothin' I coulda done."

"I hate you."

"Then I reckon you can stop hatin' your daddy."

No! Was she being had again? Had he exonerated her father just to make her feel better? To make himself feel human? Or was this just another ploy to make her more pliable and willing to do his bidding? "Does Mom…does Swan know?"

"Swan never knew any of it, Dinah. She ain't like you. She don't go lookin' under rocks. She trusts what folks tell her."

Trust. It seemed to Dinah as quaint a concept as corsets and crinolines. "I don't know whether to believe you or not."

"I've allocuted. Restored your daddy's good name, vindicated his honor. You can believe me or not. It's your choice. By and by, we all gotta choose what to believe."

"What happened in Campiglio?"

His grip on the gun tightened and his eyes welled. "Swan, you remember."

Sweet Jerusalem! What madness had she sparked? He was projecting her mother onto her. He'd lost it, forgotten who she was, forgotten the twins and the account in Panama, forgotten everything but Swan Fately, the woman he idolized, the woman who'd rejected him, the woman Dinah looked just like. He was going to take her out with him, to possess in death what he couldn't possess in life.

She looked around wildly. What could she do? Lunge for the gun? Dive for the bushes?

He raised the gun to his head.

"Please, please, please no." She squeezed her eyes shut.

The report erupted in her ears like Krakatoa. She felt sick. The air smelled burnt and bitter. She drew a ragged breath and forced herself to open her eyes.

Cleon was still standing. The gun dangled limply from his hand. He looked more surprised than she was. "I couldn't do it."

She felt a surge of relief. And to her astonishment, compassion. "I can't hate you, Uncle Cleon."

"Thank you, darlin'." A sheepish smile creased his face. He seemed focused on some ineluctable irony on the horizon just behind her. She glanced over her shoulder as Margaret pumped two rounds into his chest.

FORTY-SIX

PETUNIA BUCKED AND bounced across the rough grass, gathered speed and lifted off at a cookie-pitching angle, her right wing clearing the red and yellow banded trees at the back of the lodge by inches. The lodge receded to postcard size. A miniscule Norton helped a miniscule Margaret into the Land Rover. Margaret shaded her eyes and looked up. Dinah looked away into a garish red and purple sunset. Like a hemorrhage, she thought.

When the police arrived, Margaret had stood ramrod straight, her head held high—not so much defiant as disinterested. She offered no denials. She'd been hovering outside the great room when Cleon admitted what he'd done to Wendell and to Dez. She'd been hovering just inside the door to the veranda when he described the night Hart Pelerin died. But Dinah didn't think any of those sins were the reason she shot him.

"What will happen to her?" she asked Jacko.

He was somber. There'd been none of his usual banter this afternoon, no flippant Strine, no flak. He'd seemed genuinely moved by the tragedy. She loved him for that.

"Juries always have more sense than the government," he said. "They'll let her off light."

"She'll have to stand trial?"

"No such thing as justifiable homicide in Oz, luv. Not legally."

"But she saved my life." Dinah had rehearsed Margaret very carefully on the saved-my-life story. One or two more lies wouldn't amount to a hill of beans next to the mountain of treacheries in this sorry tale and anyway, Margaret had only done what Cleon couldn't do himself. Dinah wondered if his last thank-you was for her or for Margaret.

Jacko's long nose twitched as if her perjurious thoughts gave off a sulfur smell. "With any luck, you won't have to testify under oath."

"But I want to if it will help Margaret."

"Of course, you do. And your statement's a perfect pearl. Mr. Cleon Dobbs confessed to the murder of Dr. Fisher and the framing of Mr. Wendell Dobbs and summarily aimed a gun at your heart. He threatened explicitly to kill you. Mrs. Margaret Dobbs, having returned unexpectedly from Katherine, showed up with a loaded pistol and Bob's your uncle." He slewed his eyes at her and added, "I wasn't trying to make a funny."

"I know." But his doubting tone irked her. "You don't buy my story?"

"It's a notch to the pat side, luv. You'll want to throw in an earnest stammer now and again, and maybe a skerrick of doubt. Juries like probability, but not perfection. A dead cert cheats them out of the chance to be Sherlocks for a day."

Was he suborning perjury or just letting her know he was onto her? Of course, he wasn't onto all of her crimes. The piece of paper with the number of Cleon's secret bank account in Panama nestled at the bottom of her purse like a live scorpion. She didn't want to think about the jillion unpleasant ways it could bite her. Fishing it out of Cleon's pocket while the blood pooled and spread would be a recurring nightmare. Margaret had stood stoically by while Dinah frisked the corpse. She didn't offer to share the responsibility for dealing with the spoils of the drug trade, or the dangers. Maybe after the shock wore off, she'd have something to say about Cleon's spiteful devices and devisals. But for now, Margaret seemed to have lost her stomach for anything to do with the man.

Jacko said, "We'll need you to keep in touch in case there are more questions."

"You have my mother's address. I can be reached through her if anybody wants to subpoena me, or whatever you call it in Strine."

"A subpoena, we call a bluey, after the blue paper it's printed on. The truth, we call the truth, although it doesn't always serve justice. I'm assuming your zeal for justice is why you're covering for the first Mrs. Dobbs, but perjury's a crime in Oz. You could go to prison for giving false evidence."

"I'll take that into account."

"Right. Well, there may be some latitude in the system. I'll have a chinwag with the prosecutor, see if he'll reduce the charges against the lady to possession of an unlicensed firearm and manslaughter in defense of another person."

He checked the altimeter and pointed Petunia's nose north toward Darwin. Below them, the Stuart Highway snaked across the land, a rainbow serpent of commerce connecting the Southern Ocean to the Indian Ocean, the spatial footprint of the continent's modern-day movers and shakers. She was beginning to cotton onto this song lines business—shape-shifting ancestral spirits unbound by time, trampling through your life with their outsized egos and festering passions, leaving behind an emotional geography you can't escape and indelible tracks on your heart.

With Cleon's confession, her father's song line had veered into new territory, changing the landscape of the past. He was absolved, rehabilitated, an upstanding citizen who'd been rooked into doing something illegal. And her mother was innocent of any unsavory knowledge hidden under the rocks. If Cleon had told the truth. She wouldn't decide until she heard what her mother had to say for herself. But no matter what she said, Dinah's perspective on the history and inhabitants of her world had altered. Was altering still. As Mack said, the Dreaming is an ongoing process.

Lucien was certainly a case in point. She wasn't sure who he was anymore or how he came to have such versatile ethics. She loved him, but it just wasn't the same. She couldn't trust him, and while trust wasn't an essential component of love, it was kind of a big deal. To her, anyway. Still and all, it was oddly liberating not to feel like the mistake-prone kid sister forever kneeling at the altar of his greater experience and wiser judgment. They were on an equal footing now, all of their feet made of clay.

They'd said good-bye at the lodge. Lucien had catapulted through the door on his crutches just in time to see Cleon's body loaded into the ambulance and driven away to the morgue. As promised, he hadn't wept. And she hadn't told him that his father killed hers. The secret was hers now, her legacy from Cleon. Telling Lucien would only complicate their relationship the more. She hoped Eduardo would win the battle for Lucien's soul. But if Mack induced him into another round of forgeries, there was nothing she could do about it.

If it was true that Swan didn't know about Cleon's drug business, Dinah wouldn't tell her the extent of his evil. Perhaps, she already suspected. But telling her for fact that her first husband had murdered her second because of her would be gratuitously cruel. Dinah was glad she'd found out the truth. But pop psychology to the contrary, the truth hadn't set her free. It most definitely hadn't set Margaret free. Confession, as it turned out, was more freeing for the confessor than the confessee.

When she got back from Panama, she would write to
Neesha and ask what she and the twins needed during
their transition period. She hoped Thad wouldn't need a
lot of medical care from his brush with the stinging tree.
Maybe a few weeks of chastening pain would transform
him into a decent young man. Or if that failed, there was
always military school, something to cut his Dobbsian ego
down to a safe size.

K.D. was an even thornier problem. Dinah had left her
a note of condolence about Cleon and an apology for swip-
ing her journal, but somehow that felt like a cop-out. K.D.
was going to need somebody more down-to-earth than her
mother, and somebody with more clout than her English
teacher to help her through the throes of adolescence. She
was an intelligent girl. Like Dinah, she might someday
want to know the truth about *her* father. But she wouldn't
hear it from Dinah.

It was scary to be suddenly burdened with responsibility for a pair of spoiled, angry teenagers whose father had
just been murdered and whose mother was embroiled in
an affair with their incarcerated half-brother. She had left
Cleon's original will on the dresser in Neesha's room next
to her jewelry case. It would take the widow some time
to digest the fact that Cleon had annihilated his wealth
and bequeathed her a big fat goose egg. Dinah didn't look
forward to telling her that she controlled the purse strings
now. But since she did, she was determined to contribute
significantly to Wendell's defense fund. If Cleon rolled
over in his cryogenic crypt in Houston, so much the better.

"Isn't there something you can do to spring Wendell,
Jacko?"

"Maybe somewhere down the line. Right now, Wendell's deep in the poo."

"But when the prosecutor reads my account of his

father's dying declaration, the charges against Wendell will be dismissed, right?"

"Maybe the murder charge. As for the drug charges, it depends where he's tried and whether the feds want to clear cases and beef up their conviction stats or do the right thing. From what I hear, Wendell's lawyer will try to have him extradited to the States."

"Cleon knew it would be like this. He knew that even if Wendell eventually walks, he'll be caught up in a legal morass for years."

"Junior's copped the rough end of the pineapple, no question. The best thing he's got going for him is your blooper."

"Mine?"

"Scarpering with that memory stick, luv. The evidence wasn't properly obtained and it was out of your possession while you were off consorting with your mates, the parrots and the snakes. It can probably be used against the rest of the gang. But a good mouthpiece will argue that some-body found it in your motel room, input false data to make Wendell the bunny, and put it back before you returned."

"Bunny meaning the fall guy."

"Strike a light! You're becoming bilingual." He reached under his seat and pulled out a Foster's. "I don't suppose you'd care for a coldie?"

"I don't mind if I do."

"There's a girl!" He popped the tab and passed it over. "Apart from that line of legal brilliance and his big sad eyes, Wendell's a no-hoper. The fella whose leg you broke has already cut a deal with the feds to testify against him in exchange for a lesser sentence."

"But those lowlifes never even saw Wendell."

"They never saw your uncle either, but he used Wendell's name when he communicated with them."

She rolled the frigid beer can across her forehead and took a deep draft. She'd like to get juiced tonight, enter one of those dissociative fugue states, forget everyone and everything. It occurred to her that Nick hadn't crossed her mind in days, an excellent start on forgetting.

She said, "I still don't understand how a gang of Nigerian poachers and smugglers could infiltrate the Aboriginal community."

"They passed themselves off as tourists, probably bought off some malcontented locals to help them trap the animals. The big note with the frilly words who called himself Bill simply permitted you to assume he was an Aborigine."

"Like you permitted me to assume you were just a nice guy with a thing for unsolved crimes, like Cleon permitted me to assume he was our family angel, like Seth permitted me to...never mind." She thought about his melting kisses and wondered if he'd make it out of the country with his sack full of cash.

Jacko turned his inquisitive eyes on her. "You were attracted to young Seth, weren't you?"

"Not really. I have a glitch in my hypothalmus. And maybe bad karma."

He laughed. "You'll board the right tram next time, Dinah."

He put on his earphones and turned his attention to flying. Dusk was settling over Darwin as they descended. The lights were beginning to wink on, but sailboats were still visible on Fannie Bay. This was where the Land of Oz ended, where her erroneous assumptions ended and the past and the future converged. She felt a terrible homesickness for her family, both living and dead, blood and non. She'd had a lot more she needed to say to Cleon and there was a lot more she'd needed to hear him say. But if she'd

learned anything in this weird place, it was that your ancestors don't shut up just because they're dead. Cleon might
not speak to her out of the trees or boulders, but he would
speak to her again out of a safe deposit box in Panama.

Parallel rows of lights illuminated their glidepath. If
only life were so straight and narrow and well lit. She felt
the landing wheels drop and Petunia hit the runway like
a kangaroo, hopping and boinking a few times before she
decelerated to a glide. They taxied for a few minutes and
came to rest some distance from the main terminal in front
of a darkened hangar.

"Well, this is where we say oo-roo," said Jacko. "You've
been a pain in the arse, luv, but I admit I've grown fond
of you. If you don't come back, I'll have you extradited."

"I'll be back. I'm going to stand by Wendell and Margaret, vouch for their innocence, do whatever I can to thwart
the prosecution."

He helped her climb down and set her suitcase on the
tarmac. "You're a pip, luv. If I were thirty years younger,
I'd have a go at changing your mind about policemen."

"You already have." She stood on her toes, kissed him
on the cheek and walked off toward the main terminal to
begin the first leg of her odyssey across the International
Date Line and another fusion of Time.

* * * * *

REQUEST YOUR FREE BOOKS!

2 FREE NOVELS
PLUS 2 FREE GIFTS!

WORLDWIDE LIBRARY®
Your Partner in Crime

YES! Please send me 2 FREE novels from the Worldwide Library® series and my 2 FREE gifts (gifts are worth about $10). After receiving them, if I don't wish to receive any more books, I can return the shipping statement marked "cancel." If I don't cancel, I will receive 4 brand-new novels every month and be billed just $5.49 per book in the U.S. or $6.24 per book in Canada. That's a savings of at least 31% off the cover price. It's quite a bargain! Shipping and handling is just 50¢ per book in the U.S. and 75¢ per book in Canada.* I understand that accepting the 2 free books and gifts places me under no obligation to buy anything. I can always return a shipment and cancel at any time. Even if I never buy another book, the two free books and gifts are mine to keep forever.

414/424 WDN F4WY

Name _____ (PLEASE PRINT) _____

Address _____ Apt. # _____

City _____ State/Prov. _____ Zip/Postal Code _____

Signature (if under 18, a parent or guardian must sign)

Mail to the Harlequin® Reader Service:
IN U.S.A.: P.O. Box 1867, Buffalo, NY 14240-1867
IN CANADA: P.O. Box 609, Fort Erie, Ontario L2A 5X3

Want to try two free books from another line?
Call 1-800-873-8635 or visit www.ReaderService.com.

* Terms and prices subject to change without notice. Prices do not include applicable taxes. Sales tax applicable in N.Y. Canadian residents will be charged applicable taxes. Offer not valid in Quebec. This offer is limited to one order per household. Not valid for current subscribers to the Worldwide Library series. All orders subject to credit approval. Credit or debit balances in a customer's account(s) may be offset by any other outstanding balance owed by or to the customer. Please allow 4 to 6 weeks for delivery. Offer available while quantities last.

Your Privacy—The Harlequin® Reader Service is committed to protecting your privacy. Our Privacy Policy is available online at www.ReaderService.com or upon request from the Harlequin Reader Service.

We make a portion of our mailing list available to reputable third parties that offer products we believe may interest you. If you prefer that we not exchange your name with third parties, or if you wish to clarify or modify your communication preferences, please visit us at www.ReaderService.com/consumerchoice or write to us at Harlequin Reader Service Preference Service, P.O. Box 9062, Buffalo, NY 14269. Include your complete name and address.

WWL13R